ABOUT THE AUTHOR

Mick Farren was born in Cheltenham, raised in Worthing, educated in London and lives in New York. In his youth, he had multiple adventures in both rock & roll and the underground press. In addition to compulsively producing science fiction and fantasy, he also writes music and television criticism. In his spare time, he still sings with bands, drinks too much, collects toy robots and dotes on a large black pedigree Persian cat. It would make him very happy if you bought this book..

By Mick Farren and published by New English Library

THE SONG OF PHAID THE GAMBLER
PROTECTORATE

PROTECTORATE

Mick Farren

NEW ENGLISH LIBRARY

A New English Library Original Publication, 1984

First NEL Paperback Edition September 1984

NEL Books are published by
New English Library,
Mill Road, Dunton Green,
Sevenoaks, Kent.
Editorial office: 47 Bedford Square, London WC1B 3DP.

Printed in Great Britain by Cox & Wyman, Reading.

British Library Cataloguing in Publication Data
Farren, Mick
    Protectorate.
    I. Title
    823'.914[F]   PR6056.A753

    ISBN 0 450 05708 9

One

THE GUARD pulled the collar of his tunic close around his throat and hunched his shoulders against an involuntary shudder. There was a damp chill coming off the Blackwater and from the Great River beyond. It was the kind of drifting chill that flowed over rooftops and curled between buildings; it penetrated clothing and seeped through to one's very bones. With the chill and the damp came the smell of brackish, dark-green decay, the smell of water that has lain too long and has had too much drowned in it. The smell drifted in from the long-dead waterfront with its rotting piers and its ancient hulks sunk in the shallows. It was the smell of a city that had been neglected almost to the point of death.

The guard turned and walked with a measured stride. One pace, two pace, three pace, four, turn again and start back across the platform in front of the huge, ornate bronze doors. Once across, once back, thinking all the time of the party going on behind those doors, inside the main hall. The hall was not for him, though. He wished he was down in the big kitchen, basking in the cosy orange glow, boots off, warming his feet in front of the bread oven. He'd be drinking hot broth with maybe a shot of something strong in it and flirting with the cooks and the serving girls. Guard to the household of Proprietor N'Ssad was hardly an arduous or dangerous post now that the Proprietors were prevented from warring. He knew that he would be the envy of many who scratched for a living on the lower levels, but that knowledge didn't ease the ache in his feet, keep out the damp or make the watch pass any faster.

On a warm, clear night, the city could be beautiful in its decline. Its shimmer and glow spread all the way to the horizon and far beyond. It was not without cause that they called it The City That Went On Forever. On a warm night he could stand for hours, following the pinpoint riding-lights of drifting carriages, imagining the games of the wealthy behind the gem windows of the tallest towers. To

1

the west was the pale, cold radiation that leaked from the forbidden areas where the Wasps had their compounds. The guard avoided looking to the west for long; the Wasps were too much of a fear and a puzzlement. On a night like this, when the air was opaque with mist, the only view was down, down to the dull, red glow of the man-made canyons, to the poverty and squalor of the lower levels. The guard also avoided looking down. He didn't like to be reminded that but for a small accident of fate he too would be down there.

The guard eased the strap of the pulser that hung from his shoulder. The weapon was starting to grow heavy. There was still a third of the watch to go. His old leg-wound was starting to nag and he wanted nothing but to be relieved right there and then. Better than the big kitchen, he wanted his own warm bed in the soldiers' quarters. The new woman would be there waiting for him. At least, she had better be there waiting for him if she knew what was good for her. Many of the soldiers' women were dull, sullen trollops, going with soldiers but believing they deserved much better, seeing themselves as fallen on hard times. This one was different. She was a vigorous little strumpet, eager and perverted, always willing for games. Oh yes, she'd better be waiting for him when he came off watch.

The small postern set beside the huge bronze gates opened, letting a narrow band of light fall across the platform. There was the distant sound of music and chatter. They were enjoying themselves inside the hall. A figure stepped out through the postern, black and unidentifiable against the light. The guard's hand went down to the pulser and moved it to the ready position. The gesture was one of habit and routine rather than necessity. The Proprietor N'Ssad lived a quiet life and there was rarely a problem that required weaponry.

'Halt and make yourself known.'

A weary voice answered, 'I'm the poet who's been entertaining your master.'

The guard nodded. He had been told when he came on watch that there was a visiting poet in the hall. Proprietor N'Ssad favoured the occasional poet. For his part, the guard couldn't see the attraction. He'd far rather listen to a raucous balladeer with a suitably dirty mind.

'They didn't ask you to stay the night, then?'

The Poet shook his head a little ruefully. 'No such luck. I must have been off form tonight.'

2

The guard could see him a little better now. He was slim and reasonably tall. His black curly hair hung down to his shoulders and a gold hoop earring dangled from one ear. The lines on his face had been formed by worry and calculation, punctuated by bouts of laughter. There were the clear signs of prolonged dissolution around his eyes. He was dressed in a black tunic with flowing sleeves. His high top-boots had seen better days. A black cloak was folded over his arm. He shivered in the night air and threw the cloak around his shoulders. 'It's turned chill.'

The guard nodded. 'That it has.'

The Poet seemed uncertain what to do. 'Did anyone say anything about a carriage?'

'Carriage?'

'To get me out of here.'

The guard shook his head. 'Nobody's said anything to me all watch.'

'Could you go inside and ask?'

'I can't leave my post.'

'Then let me go back inside and make some arrangement.'

'You can't go back now that you've left the hall.'

The Poet was starting to grow angry. 'How in hell's name am I supposed to get down from here?'

'To the lowers, you mean?'

The contempt in the guard's voice slowed the Poet's temper. 'Aye, to the lowers.'

'And you've got no belt?'

'You can see I've got no belt.'

'If you've got no belt and nobody has bothered to arrange a carriage, you've no choice but to climb down the steps. It's a long way down to the lowers by the steps.'

The words *a long way down* were the understatement of someone who lived his life safe in a tower. As the Poet started to descend the steps he chanced to glance over the edge and down. The drop to the lower levels of the city looked as though it were infinite, as though a man could fall through eternity before he smashed into the ground. In that instant the Poet felt sick and dizzy with vertigo, and all but plunged forward to test the illusion. For some minutes he leaned back against the wall with his eyes shut, letting the damp wind from the Blackwater whip past him. Finally his heart calmed and the strength came back to his legs. With great caution he started down, cursing the long-dead architect who, believing that all men would be permanently

3

equipped with flying-belts, had designed such narrow, delicate steps so high in the air with only the skimpiest of safety rails.

Since the coming of the alien invaders almost all humanity's dreams and aspirations had either been adapted or cancelled. The flying-belts were a perfect example. No new ones had been manufactured in two hundred years. When they broke or burned out, they weren't replaced. Those that remained were for the privileged, tower-dwelling few, the wealthy, the powerful and the military. Technology was something the Wasps doled out grudgingly. They tolerated the minimum that would sustain a semblance of civilisation, and no more.

Although the Poet had no way of telling, the descent, with its constant twists, spirals and right-angle turns, took over an hour, including the three times that he stopped to rest. Even when he reached the bottom he still had a long way to go to the tavern in the artists' quarter that he thought of as home. Walking through the lowers could be a hazardous business. In its days of glory, the city had reared so high that it lost touch with its roots and its foundations. Great tracts had fallen into ruin and disuse; mazes of basements, cellars and narrow alleys had been left to the spiders, the rats, the blind slitherers and the armoured cockarows.

In among the feet of the great towers the going was fairly simple. The worst the Poet had to fear was his own imagination and the temptation to make monsters out of the rustlings, the scramblings, and the invisible dartings that preceded his footsteps. In the outlying areas there were worse and more nameless dangers. There were the huge pits, excavated in the constant search for ancient artefacts from the city's golden age. There were whole neighbourhoods abandoned to the flooding of the Blackwater. According to legend these areas of swamp and ruin were the hiding place of ghoul and wampyr, but the Poet didn't dwell on these stories. A man walking on his own in the empty lowers did well to ignore legend and concentrate as completely as he could on the matter in hand.

The Poet stuck close to ways that were lit by the low-key orange glow of everburn. Almost all the dark ways of the lower city had once been illuminated by the iridescent material. It was coated on the walls of streets and alleyways and on the roofs of the miles of tunnels that honeycombed

4

the deeps of the city. Two hundred years in the past, the light had been a bright yellow-white. Now it was faded and drab like a fire that had burned down. In some places it had failed completely. It could not be replaced. Everburn was one of the hundreds of secrets that had been lost since the coming of the aliens.

The Poet was confronted by a choice. He could take a well-lit, three-block detour around a massive and quietly throbbing power conduit, or he could go under it, through a short but badly lit underpass. The Poet was getting to be past caring. It seemed as though he'd been walking for ever, and he chose the underpass. He started down the worn steps into the shadows. It was a neighbourhood that had been virtually abandoned by humans. It was an unlikely place either for thieves or the kind that liked to kill and mutilate for fun. If they lurked there, they faced a long lurk between victims.

Slightly more than halfway through the underpass he encountered the first living creature he'd seen since he'd taken his leave of Proprietor N'Ssad's guard. A cockarow, over a yard long, stood in the middle of the tunnel facing him. The Poet flapped his cloak at it but the big insect stood its ground. The Poet took a couple of steps forward, hoping that it would turn and run. All it did was to wave its feelers at him. The Poet stopped. He had never had an unpleasant experience with a cockarow, but there were stories. A friend of a friend lost a hand or had a baby carried away by a horde of cockarows. The Poet waved his arms and yelled. 'Piss off!'

The feelers waved back. He tried again. 'Piss off, you!'

One feeler went down. The other came up until it was almost vertical. The Poet started to feel distinctly foolish. He stooped down and picked a half brick from the garbage and rubble and threw it as hard as he could at the insect. It missed the cockarow's head and bounced off the middle of its back. The feelers stiffened. The gesture was uncannily similar to a man narrowing his eyes. The Poet blinked and waited to see what would happen next. For three or four seconds the creature didn't move, then it scuttled quickly backwards, turned and ran off. The Poet let out his breath. 'Who's the dominant species, then?'

He emerged from the tunnel feeling more than a little pleased with himself. Sadly, the feeling was shortlived; within five minutes someone had thrown a half brick at him.

He had just passed a sign on a boarded-up basement that announced in crude letters: THIS IS WHERE KRANT LIVES – BREAK IN AND HE'LL KILL YOU. It told him that he was back in the habitation of humans. This was something of a mixed blessing. He no longer had to worry about the shuddering possibility of ghosts, but on the other hand his fellow humans were an infinitely mixed bunch and among them were those who, if they had the inclination, would do him more serious harm than any cold, wandering spirit. The lowers had more than their fair share of the crazy, the vicious and the homicidal.

The half brick missed the Poet's head by scarcely a hand's-breadth. He spun around. 'What the hell's the deal?'

'Wampyr!'

Another brick spun towards him. The Poet danced back, his cloak flapping. Four small pale faces peered over a section of broken wall.

'Wampyr!'

'Get outa here, dirty wampyr. We ain't afraid of you!'

The Poet was outraged. He was being attacked by urchins. 'What do you kids think you're doing? I'm not a wampyr!'

There was a pause, but there were also no more bricks. One of the urchins stepped around the section of wall. He was maybe nine years old with a dirty face and hair the colour of damp straw. He was dressed in a torn tunic and thonged leggings. In one hand he held a rock and in the other a curved knife. 'If you ain't a wampyr, how come you wearing a cloak?'

This was ridiculous. 'I'm wearing a cloak because it's cold.'

A second urchin had climbed up and was sitting on the fallen wall. 'Wampyrs wear cloaks.'

'Plenty of people wear cloaks.'

A third urchin bobbed up. 'My brother saw a wampyr over by the Blackwater. It was wearing a cloak. He told me.'

'I'm not a goddamn wampyr.'

The Poet was unwilling to be stoned to death because a bunch of kids had mistaken him for a legend. The first urchin abruptly changed the tack. 'You got any money?'

'No, of course not, I'm a Poet.'

The urchin with the rock and the knife nodded. 'You better get out of here, Poet. If Krant tries to rob you and finds you don't have nothing, he's liable to kill you, just out of spite.'

The second urchin jumped down from his perch on the wall. 'Make him stay and tell us a story.'

The Poet shook his head. 'I've got to be going.'

The second urchin pulled a knife from under his tunic. 'I want to hear a story. What else has a Poet got to do 'cept tell stories?'

The first urchin waved the second one back. 'Leave him be, there's no time for stories. Krant'll be back soon. We don't need that sort of trouble.' He faced the Poet. 'On your way.'

Being ordered along by a child caused a twinge to the Poet's pride but he didn't stop to argue. He was too tired and he didn't like the look of the urchins' knives. Another twenty minutes would see him in a brighter, more populated section of the lowers. His route led him through the quarter called Oldmarket. This was the centre of the artefact trade. All over the city, men and women who had nothing better to do with their lives dug and delved into the buried foundations, searching for remains and relics of the old times. Most of what came out of the pits, quarries and excavations was junk; rusted pieces of metal, shards of pottery and glass, strangely shaped plastics with no recognisable value. The burrowers were always hoping for the big score, a cache of jewellery, a sealed vault with undisturbed books and papers that wouldn't turn to dust when the air touched them, or the biggest score of all, a machine that still functioned.

Only a fraction of one per cent of burrowers ever hit even a small score, maybe just enough to create the rumours that kept the others digging. Even without a score, though, it was possible to scratch a bare living in the excavations. The people of the city attached an unreasonable importance to anything that was old. They looked on even the most humble, misshapened and corroded artefact as being to some degree magical. They were links to what was thought of as a golden age, the time before the Wasps arrived. The Poet wasn't a particularly strong believer; he saw himself as a pragmatist and prided himself on a healthy cynicism, but even he carried a small steel disc, that might once have been a coin or maybe a tiny part of a machine, sewn into the sleeve of his tunic. Where luck and magic were concerned, the Poet again saw no reason to take chances.

Even though it was well after midnight, the Oldmarket was still wide awake. The wheeling and the dealing, the seduction and the crime never seemed to stop. Burrowers haggled with merchants, pitchmen harangued the passing crowds with offers of priceless treasures at give-away prices. It all mingled with the whine of beggars and the shrieks and laughter of drunks and bawds. A whore stood in a lighted doorway, a hip-tilted silhouette against a garish glow of scarlet. She was naked from the waist down. Even from a distance it was clear that she was no longer young. Her white, sunless flesh was doughy and pitted from too much bread, too much wine, too much waiting, and a lack of hope and protein. She noticed the Poet's cursory inspection and smiled at him. The Poet smiled back, but shook his head and extended his hands in the age-old gesture of the penniless. The smile went out.

The most prosperous and successful of the merchants had whole shops to hold their wares, the lesser contented themselves with booths and stalls down to a tray hung around the neck, a blanket on the ground or the lone object clutched in an out-stretched hand. One such thrust itself in front of the Poet; it was a brown claw belonging to a wild-eyed crone, trying to catch his interest with a fragment of broken mirror still in a plastic frame. The Poet side-stepped with the skill of one who has spent a lifetime on the streets of the lowers.

The Poet was in no mood to be jostled, hustled or solicited. He looked for a way out of the noisy, slow-moving crowd. Almost immediately he saw an escape. He ducked around the colourful canvas banner that was part of the display in front of one of the biggest artefact houses. He was making for the black entrance of a dark alleyway. For the second time that night he was taking a route that was dark, potentially dangerous but short, as opposed to the longer and safer. He had developed the unshakeable courage of the footsore and exhausted.

The Poet was more than halfway through the system of alleys, passages and tunnels that was his shortcut to the artists' quarter. All had gone without incident. The worst thing he'd come across was a large, overfed rat that looked at him insolently and waddled away. He was approaching a point where the alley intersected with a strip of usually deserted street. Without warning a swath of bright white light cut through the tired yellow of everburn. The Poet halted and ducked back into the shadows. A white light in the lowers usually signified the presence of some kind of official from the upper levels. The Poet did his best to avoid all contact with officialdom.

They came past the end of the alley almost like a procession. In front were three of the Protector's Killers. They moved with the ponderous stride that seemed to come with the black and silver uniforms and the burnished helmets with their sinister, masklike faceplates. The Killers were the strong right arm of the Protector, the final enforcement of his will and, indirectly, the will of the Wasps. Each Killer cradled a lethal-weight pulser. They were the only men and women in the whole of the city, the whole of the Protectorate, who were legally entitled to bear weapons that killed from a distance. The pulsers employed by the guards of the Proprietors and merchants' minders could only stun or inflict pain.

Behind the Killers walked a pair of petty Endents. They had none of the Killers' assurance and looked around anxiously as if quite distressed that they had been forced to come to this ill-favoured part of the city. This was already a sizeable entourage for anyone's stroll through the lowers. The Poet wondered what would come next. A picture formed in his mind of some arrogant, self-important mandarin from the Halls of the Protector. No sooner had the picture formed, however, than it was proved to be completely in error. To his shock and surprise, a Wasp walked into his field of vision.

The Poet could count the number of times that he had seen a Wasp on the fingers of only one hand. Even though the alien creatures had now ruled humanity for over two hundred years, they kept themselves very much to themselves. They stuck close to their compounds in the areas that were forbidden to humans. According to rumour, only the utmost necessity drew them out into the habitations of men. The Poet observed the Wasp with curiosity and a good deal of fear. Rumour further claimed that the Wasps had the power not only to detect hostile thoughts in the humans around them but also to destroy those who harboured those thoughts. They did this by literally frying their nervous systems.

The Wasps were hardly well-named. Their bipedal form made them appear less like any insect and more like a tall and angular caricature of a man. Legend wasn't clear about who had first dubbed them Wasps. Somehow, without benefit of logic, the name had stuck. The most insect-like parts of them were their elongated, ovoid heads that seemed too large for their spindly bodies. At the pointed end of the head there were two dull patches on the otherwise gleaming, patent-leather black of the rest of their skin. These patches were generally assumed to be some kind of eyes. The Wasps' bodies were laced with an interlocking network of flexible tubes: large major tubes with complicated ribbing that followed the structure of the limbs and the torso, and fed into or were fed by clusters of smaller, smooth, subsidiary tubes. One theory was that the Wasps' circulatory system was on the outside of their bodies. An opposing theory suggested that maybe the black-patent skin and the tubes were some sort of suit that helped them survive in the native atmosphere. Neither theory had gone any way beyond speculation. The Wasps volunteered absolutely no information about themselves.

The Wasp was directly opposite where the Poet was standing, very still, in the shadows. It was framed exactly in the middle of the rectangle of light created by the end of the alley. Abruptly, the Wasp's head swivelled. It didn't miss a stride. The head just swung around until the pointed end was directed straight at the Poet. The Poet froze. He prayed that fear would make his mind go blank. The head continued to point in his direction for two, maybe three, seconds, then it swung back again and the Wasp was gone. The Poet remained perfectly still, doing his best to think about nothing. It wasn't easy; his heart pounded and he could feel cold sweat running down from his armpits. He didn't step out of the shadows until the white light had completely faded. When he did move, despite all previous weariness he set off at a very brisk pace that didn't slacken until he was safe inside the long bar of Denhagel's Tavern.

As the tavern door closed behind the Poet he was suddenly in a new world. With its warm lights, its crackling fire and brewery smell it was a safe haven. It felt as though not even the Wasps could get him in here. Denhagel's wife was serving behind the bar. In her youth, Denhagel's wife had been a celebrated beauty on the upper levels until the scented and slightly unreal night when she had fallen for Denhagel's solid affability and joined him in a life of hosting the most accommodating tavern in the whole of the artists' quarter. Despite the thickening of age, there were still suggestions of her past glory in the way she moved, in the way she carried herself and in her violet eyes which widened considerably when the Poet stumbled through the door.

'Jeen Vayim the Poet, what's with you? You look like you've seen a ghoul.'

The Poet leaned heavily on the bar. 'I saw a Wasp.'

Denhagel's wife raised an eyebrow. 'Not something I'd wish to encounter on a dark night.'

'It looked right at me.'

Denhagel's wife shook her head. 'That must have been unpleasant.'

'You know what they say the Wasps can do if they think you're . . .'

'I've heard the stories.'

The Poet mopped his brow as if the memory still made him sweat. 'There were a couple of moments back there when I thought I was going to get my brain fried. You can't help it when a Wasp looks at you.'

'What did you do?'

'Damn all nothing. I just stood there trying to keep the palpitations down.'

Denhagel's wife nodded.

'We had a fellow in here once who claimed he'd been there when this woman tried to take out a Wasp. She was trying to get near it with a homemade bapgun but the Wasp somehow sensed her and did it to her. He said how her eyes . . . I can't repeat it . . . it was really disgusting.' She pushed a tot of brandy towards the Poet. 'You'd better have this, you look like you could use it.'

Vayim the Poet raised it gratefully to his lips. 'Damn right I could.'

Denhagel's wife leaned on the bar. 'What did the Wasp look like? I've never seen one.'

The Poet spread his hands. 'It was black.'

'A poet lost for words?'

'You start to think about them in terms of people, in human terms, even animals or insects, but then you realise that none of it works, you just can't think that way. It's the black glittering skin and those slithering . . . I don't know . . . they kind of pulse, all those tubes. The way the head swivels.' Vayim swallowed the rest of his brandy. 'They don't belong on this world.'

'They run this world, Jeen Vayim.'

Vayim the Poet pushed his glass towards Denhagel's wife who refilled it. He quickly drained half of it. Denhagel's wife smiled at him. 'You feel better now, Jeen Vayim the Poet?'

The Poet grinned. 'You're calling me Jeen Vayim tonight. Usually it's just Poet.'

It was something of a ritual. Denhagel's wife tossed her black curls. 'Think nothing of it, Poet, think nothing of it.'

She moved away to serve a customer at the other end of the bar and the Poet turned to see who else was in the place. With a brandy inside him, the fright was starting to fade. He was relieved to see that the usual pretentious riffraff were fairly thin on the ground. The night was late and most of the drunks had hauled themselves away, leaving pools of ale on the uneven flagstones, and on the tables a litter of mugs, bottles and assorted debris, which was being slowly removed by the ancient, arthritic potman. A young man came through the door, unpeeling a flying-belt from around his waist. He didn't look the kind who belonged in the lowers. His red leather tunic with its silver studs and buckles was a prize to tempt any one of a hundred street and alley thieves. The Poet hoped that the young man could protect himself. Already a previously sleeping deadbeat, who called himself a musician but who had long since left his instrument in pledge to an Oldmarket moneylender, was weighing up the situation, wondering if he could pull himself together sufficiently to follow the young man when he left the tavern, and take him in the darkness. Finally, he decided the project was beyond him and his head flopped back onto the table.

The Poet's attention moved on. There was another set of strangers in the far corner. They also looked as though they didn't belong in the lowers. It was hard to tell exactly where they did belong or even to guess from where they came. The group was composed of a young, bearded man and five women. The women were all young and all very attractive, if a little grubby in a way that indicated a recent history of travelling. They were not the usual kind of group that came wandering through the lowers. The Poet couldn't tell much about the young man since he had his back to him. All that was apparent was that his blond hair hung well past his broad shoulders. The women on the other hand were quite visible and they were strange enough. Apart from being young and comely, there was an odd uniformity about them. Each had a half-smiling expression of unnaturally complete contentment. The Poet wondered idly what this

12

young man could be doing to make all five of them look that way.

The Poet signalled to Denhagel's wife for a mug of ale. When it came, he picked it up and moved nearer to take a better look at the unusual group. They were dressed in coarsely woven homespun the colour of oatmeal, the women in long plain dresses and the man in a tunic and thonged leggings. The Poet could only imagine that they must come from one of those wild areas about which equally wild stories were told; areas far from the central towers, where the plantlife had started to reclaim the ruined buildings and broken streets. All manner of strange people with all manner of strange customs and attitudes were supposed to live in those parts.

Vayim the Poet sat down at a table from where he could see the young man's face. The Poet was discreet in his observations. Even though the young man clearly didn't belong in the lowers, the Poet saw no reason why he shouldn't be extended the normal courtesies. For a while Vayim studied his ale and then he looked up. The young man was regarding him with an expression of amusement. For the second time that night he was meeting a stare that did nothing for his peace of mind. The young man was unnaturally good looking. His features were so regular that there was something close to unreal about them. It was almost as though he were the idealised creation of an artist rather than a real person who had lived through the knocks and growing pains of a normal childhood and adolescence. His eyes were large, deep, near-black and totally compelling. The Poet saw how this boy could travel with five apparently devoted women.

The young man's stare was not only disturbing, it was also extremely impolite by the standards of the taverns. When some time had passed and he still hadn't looked away, the Poet knew that he had to make either a joke or an issue out of it. Somehow it was hard to get mad at the young man, so he opted for the joke. 'You like the look of me, boy?'

The young man nodded. 'I like the look of everyone.'

The young man's voice was a soft monotone, almost, but not quite, a purr. The Poet sighed. 'Is that a fact?'

'Oh, yes.'

The Poet wondered if, with all the good looks, the young man was also pig-stupid. There would have been a certain

13

justice to that. While he was sipping his ale, one of the women smiled at him. The women may have been comely but they were nowhere in the same class as the boy. The Poet put down his ale and smiled back. 'Have you come far?'

The young man answered. 'What is far to the wanderer?'

Another woman smiled. She waved a slow hand that took in the whole of the room. 'This is just the illusion that hides the reality of dreams.'

The Poet didn't like this at all. It smacked of the mystic, and mystics were all too frequently the cause of endless trouble. It thus came as something of a surprise to him when he found that he was still smiling, picking up his ale and accepting an invitation to join them at their table.

Two

THE CARRIAGE lurched slightly in a swell of choppy air. Legate Horfon grabbed for a handgrip as the horizon abruptly tilted. Immediately he was embarrassed. The crag-faced steersman glanced at him contemptuously. The Protector didn't even bother to look up from the sheaf of papers that he was studying. Legate Horfon could feel a warm flush creeping up the back of his neck. Why was he making it so obvious that it was his first day as Private Legate to the Protector? The carriage lurched again. This time Legate Horfon rolled with it in his seat and controlled the urge to reach for a handhold. The air was always rough in among the high towers. The buildings formed strange spirals and eddies. Legate Horfon had only been this high in a flying-belt, never in a carriage. In the flying-belt, it was exhilarating. You spun and bobbed like a cork in a whirl-pool, safe as long as you avoided being blown into a tower. A carriage was a different matter. In the stiff formality of a carriage, a ride among the high towers could be tiresome, uncomfortable, maybe sickening, even dangerous. It could even prove an embarrassment for an untried and totally inexperienced Legate. Horfon could scarcely believe that the Protector willingly made this high air-trip between the residence and the Halls at least twice each day.

The high collar of the Legate's dress grey cut into the soft flesh just below his jaw. The fabric was stiff and prickly in its newness. The carriage ran smoothly for a while. He was able to forget a little of his nervous awkwardness and look beyond the immediate intimidations. The sky was blue, fading through to pink and only turning to dark red-brown at the very horizon. It was a beautiful day on the outside. The whole city was spread out below him. It didn't matter how many times he saw it, he couldn't help but be impressed. There was a sense of awe at the sheer size of it that could never be diminished. That humanity could create something that stretched from horizon to horizon, that it could con-struct things as massive and complex as the high towers but still be deprived of it all in a single encounter, was beyond the Legate. Such power and pride and then such a fall was too terrible to completely accept.

The Legate abandoned concepts and just looked. Through the middle of it all, the Great River snaked like a giant, brooding reptile. The sun and the morning breeze had blown away the mists of the night. The only place that it lingered in was down in the lowers where the dawn light had yet to penetrate. In those trenches and hollows it was tinged dull red by the depressing glow of everburn. The Legate looked up from the lowers. It didn't do to think about what went on down in those depths. He stared out, between and beyond the towers. The Blackwater shone like polished glass. It was a wonder that something so corrupt could, at times, look so splendid.

'We'll be throwing you in off the deep end, boy.'

Legate Horfon snapped back to the carriage. 'I beg your pardon, my lord?'

Again he felt foolish. Fortunately, the Protector wasn't looking at him. He continued to study the papers in his hands. The corners fluttered in the carriage's slipstream.

'I said we'll be throwing you in off the deep end, my boy.' The Protector looked up from his papers. His eyes were small and rather too close together. He ran a hand over his dark, close-cropped hair. 'Today we have an audience with the Wasps.'

The Legate could think of nothing to say. He was becoming convinced that tomorrow would see him returned to the outer tiers in disgrace; a promising career ruined before it had even started. His position was precarious enough to begin with. He couldn't deceive himself that it was either talent or personality that had caused him to be sitting uneasily in the Protector's own carriage. As in so many other matters, it was influence that counted. Although his father was only a minor Proprietor and he hadn't even been raised in the high towers, the complex sprawl of his extended family was well represented in the corridors of power. His great-aunt Sybelle, the acknowledged matriarch, had not only the ear but even the total confidence of the Protector's sister, the Lady Mariko. Thus, when the young Horfon had expressed a desire to enlist in the Legates, it had been only natural that the family should automatically start pulling strings and manoeuvre him into a largely undeserved junior position on the Protector's personal staff.

16

Awkward and profoundly unhappy, he finally managed a stammer.

'Wasps, my lord?'

'Aye, boy, Wasps. Do you feel ready to meet our rulers face to face?'

'I would hope I'd be ready for anything I might encounter in the line of duty, my lord.'

Horfon hoped that was a more acceptable answer, but was quickly deflated.

'If you think you're ready for the Wasps, you're a fool, boy. Nobody is ever ready for the Wasps.'

There was something direct and absolute about the Protector. His words were to the point, his clothes were modest and functional, his whole attitude was one of impatience with all that was unnecessary and extraneous. It was a complete contrast to the Legate's superiors in the tiers. Those men and women used up nine-tenths of their energy in flattery, intrigue and conspiracy. Later, on reflection, Horfon would realise that the contrast wasn't so surprising. The officials in the tiers had nobody to deal with except each other. The small, hardfaced man sitting among the cushions and rugs in the sternseat of the carriage was not only the ruler of humanity but also its representative. He dealt with the Wasps.

'The temptation is to think of the Wasps as though they're human. That's where we have always gone wrong. We've used human psychology on them and we have expected them to react with human emotions. They are not human. They are more alien than you can understand, boy.' The Protector scrutinised the young Legate. '*Do* you understand me, boy?'

'I think so, my lord.'

'I very much doubt that. It's best not to even try to understand the Wasps. It is much simpler to be constantly on your guard.'

'Will I be expected to communicate with the Wasps, my lord?'

'Communicate with them?' The Protector smiled as though he was amused at the very thought. 'The most you'll be is in the same room with them. I'm only telling you all this because, with the Wasps, it's as well to expect the unexpected. It's hardly an original thought, but it's apt.'

'What do I do if the unexpected happens, my lord?'

'If the unexpected happens, boy, do what I do. Just

17

watch me and copy me the best you can.' The Protector laughed grimly. 'That's one of the strangest things about power. Those around you and those below you provide you with a distorting mirror. It may be the principle thing that drives tyrants insane. Do you regard me as a tyrant, boy?'

Legate Horfon twitched. 'No, my lord, not in the least.'

The Protector's smile faded and his voice turned bitter.

'No, my lord, not in the least. Protector Trenhyass is no tyrant. He can blame all that is bad on the Wasps. An occupying conqueror provides the perfect excuse for any inept but power-hungry ruler.'

The remark clearly terminated the conversation. There had been a hundred occasions when Horfon had tried to imagine the first time that he'd speak with the Protector. Not one of them had come close to the reality. He had expected the Protector would be aloof and distant – somehow splendid, different from other mortals. Horfon had even expected to be totally ignored. Nothing in his fantasy had prepared him for this terse, maybe bitter man in his drab black uniform that lacked even the silver trim sported by the Killers. At first glance nobody would have taken him for the most powerful man in the world, and yet there was an air about him, an aura that he was both confident and comfortable with power. It was a sense that he needed no badges or spangles to display his rank. He was absolutely certain about exactly who he was and what he was able to do.

The carriage was now nearing the Halls. The steersman delicately adjusted the controls, and directed the long, pointed and decoratively carved prow in the direction of the central mooring spire. A squad of Killers in flying-belts moved up to meet them, a swarm of black dots flying in loose formation. The carriage passed the first of the outlying spires, and Horfon was given a chance for a close look at the stone dragons and marble gargoyles, the steel eagles and bronze heroes with which the old-time tower builders had felt compelled to festoon the tops of their creations. The Killers drew level with the Protector's carriage. They formed into a flying guard-of-honour and the pomp that Horfon had so far missed started in earnest. As the carriage bumped softly against the landing platform, uniformed attendants rushed forward with mooring lines. A crowd of Aides, Endents and Legates, all wearing insignia that clearly displayed their seniority and their closeness to the Protector, jostled for position. The landing stage looked like an uncontrolled scrimmage of plumes, epaulets, cloaks, sashes and decorations. For a moment the jostling became so forceful that Horfon expected to see at least one of the colourful flunkies topple over the parapet and take the long plunge to the depths below. In the end, they managed to organise themselves into two ragged receiving lines without sustaining casualties.

Concealed soundports began to throb with grim, almost funereal music. The Protector pushed aside the rugs and cushions and stood up. This seemed to be some sort of signal. The Killers formed themselves in a hemispheric defensive pattern as though expecting an attack on the Protector. Horfon scanned the sky but Trenhyass shook his head.

'Don't fret, boy. It's just part of the daily ceremony. Think of it as an attempt to convince ourselves that we still have half a hand in our own destinies. The truth is that we don't, but it doesn't hurt them to pretend now and again.' He stepped out of the carriage. 'Stick with me, boy.'

Without any hesitation he plunged straight into the flamboyant press. It closed on him like a herd of predators, all moving at once, smiles beaming, lips demanding, hands gesticulating, each one trying to grab the exclusive attention of the Protector and direct it to his or her own petition, problem or request. The Protector ignored them all and strode through the crowd as though it had nothing to do with him. Horfon was hard pressed to keep up. There seemed to be a rule that no one might touch the Protector or physically impede his progress. No such rule applied to a very junior Legate. He was pushed, pulled, elbowed, and one of the other young Legates even tried to trip him. He remotely managed to comply with the Protector's order to keep up, only because the Killers started landing on the platform; they fell in behind Trenhyass, pushing everyone else in front of them.

Inside the Halls, things calmed down a little. More Killers on the inside had the situation under control. Without any reference to lists, they separated those who might be of use to the Protector from those who were simply pursuing their own ends. As the party around the Protector was progressively whittled down, Horfon found it easier to keep up with his impatient stride. Even speeding down the corridors and up the flights of steps, Horfon couldn't help but be impressed. In this most select and inner part of the Halls of the Protector everything seemed built on a scale too large for mere humans. Those who came and went were dwarfed by the rearing pillars and hulking statues; they were made insignificant by the monumental sweep of the architecture. As they approached the Grand Audience Chamber, the Protector turned with an amused expression to the four Legates who were all that remained of the entourage now it had been thoroughly screened by the Killers.

'You can get bored with anything if you see it enough times.'

Legate Horfon couldn't imagine how anyone could grow bored with the Halls. They seemed to be much more than just a complex of big buildings. Walking through them was like being inside some vast, living organism. When he entered the Grand Audience Chamber he realised that, if such were the case, the Chamber was the heart of the beast. It was too much to have been built simply for a man. It was a decorative container for an illusion of power. The black marble walls with their gold moulding and filigree soared and arched like towering waves until they reached the ceiling with its clouds and painted stars. The pink marble floor seemed to go on for ever. The footfalls of the Protector and his party echoed back from a hundred surfaces.

The Chamber was dominated by a desk as big as an altar. It was for the individual who ruled through that illusion of power, the man or woman who claimed to control the beast. Only he or she could sit behind it in the highbacked throne under the gold eagle. If the effect hadn't been so awesome, it would have been absurd. Horfon caught himself gawping like a fool from the lowers. He quickly straightened his face as he noticed a tall, bearded figure standing beside the desk. The figure wore a full-length grey robe, much in the style of the scholar or historian. Its beard and thinning hair were the purest white. Even in his state of mild confusion, Horfon recognised it immediately. Dole Euphest was Trenhyass's most consulted adviser, his closest friend and possibly the only being that the Protector trusted.

The two men greeted each other warmly while the Legates came to stiff attention. Trenhyass motioned for the Legates to stand at ease, then he moved to the desk and flipped through the papers that had been arranged there, waiting for his arrival. When he finished he glanced up at Euphest.

'I presume you've heard that the Wasps are coming for an audience.'

Dole Euphest nodded. 'I was informed.'

'Do you have any thoughts about it?'

'I was wondering what we might have done to give them cause for complaint.'

'You think that they only come here to complain?'

'I've had the feeling at times, but it's so nearly impossible to tell with Wasps. Are you worried?'

The Protector raised a hand and then let it drop back to the desk. 'I don't know. I've also been trying to guess what we might have done.'

Trenhyass was silent for a few moments, then he shook his head as though putting aside the problem. 'I need some time to myself. Will you instruct the Legates?'

Dole Euphest nodded. 'Of course.'

Trenhyass stepped back from the desk. A small concealed door opened in the wall behind him. He stepped through and the door closed. Horfon wondered what kind of private bolthole was behind the door. He didn't, however, have much time to ponder the matter. Dole Euphest was scrutinising the four Legates. 'You Legates seem to get younger year by year.'

He appeared to require no answer to this. He paced once around the young men. 'Have any of you been present at an audience with the Wasps before?'

One Legate raised his hand. Euphest pursed his lips. 'So I suppose you think that you know it all?'

'No, my lord, I wouldn't presume.'

Euphest positioned himself in front of the Legate. 'I'm Dole Euphest, boy. I'm nobody's lord and you don't have to address me that way. Save it for the Protector.'

The Legate jerked to full attention. 'Permission to speak?'

'Speak away, boy.'

'How do we address you?'

'You can address me as you like. Just make sure that you know I'm coming before I even know it myself. Now pay attention, all of you, because I'm only going to go through this once.'

He paused for effect and then started into what was clearly a lecture that had been delivered many times before. 'The first thing you have to remember is that any meeting with the Wasps is potentially dangerous. You've heard all the horror stories about what they can do to people who have bad thoughts about them, how they can boil your nervous system. Roughly speaking, the horror stories are true. We don't know what constitutes a bad thought and we don't know how the Wasps detect them or how they do the killing. All we know for sure is that any kind of physical attack on them is quick but painful suicide. To our knowledge, nobody has so much as laid a hand on them. From time to time, though, there is also the occasional innocent bystander whose brain implodes as a Wasp passes by. Nobody can quite believe that the Wasps simply kill at random and that's how the idea of their punishing bad thoughts got started.' Euphest paused again. 'It is just an idea, nothing more. It's an assumption and, in all your dealings with the Wasps, you should *never make assumptions*!' He let this sink in for a while.

'The second thing that you have to remember is that the Wasps don't care. All our observations indicate that they are not particularly interested in us. They would appear to be here for their own purposes. At best, we are an inconvenience. If we prove to be too much of a nuisance, there's no reason to assume that they wouldn't turn around and wipe us all out. We have no ideas of their morality or their attitudes to death or the possible destruction of another species. We have no idea what they think of us.' Euphest looked directly at Horfon. 'Am I scaring you, boy?'

'No, sir.'

'You're a damned liar, boy. At least, I hope you're a damned liar because if you're not you're too stupid to be a Legate to the Protector.'

'Sir?'

'You're supposed to be scared, boy. I want you to be scared shitless. The Wasps are terrifying. They have taken our world and there's not a damn thing that we can do against them. We still don't know our eventual fate and we'd be idiots if we weren't afraid.'

Horfon wished that he could simply sink into the ground. Euphest turned away. 'The only thing that we can do around the Wasps is to be on our best behaviour and pray, only I wouldn't advise praying in the same room as them. There's always the chance that they might not like it.'

The eldest of the Legates came to attention. 'Sir?'

'Legate?'

'When do the Wasps actually arrive?'

'We don't know. They don't use the same time-scale as we do. They've never bothered to explain theirs to us.'

Horfon attempted to redeem himself. He too came to attention. 'Sir?'

'What?'

'What are our duties when the Wasps do arrive?'

'Good question, boy. You do absolutely nothing. You stand in a neat line against that wall over there. You'll be at attention, looking as smart as you can manage and, if you know what's good for you, thinking about nothing at all, particularly not about the Wasps themselves. You have one slight consolation: the Wasps have never killed anyone inside the Halls.'

They waited a full four hours before the Wasps arrived. When they finally came, it was another circus. Their flat, black, elliptical aircraft came slowly and silently. It was trailed, at a long distance, by a curious but apprehensive crowd of humans in flying-belts and carriages. When it docked at the same central spire that was used by the Protector's carriage, it was immediately surrounded by over a hundred Killers. The Wasps hadn't ever requested protection but it didn't seem to displease them, so Trenhyass had gone on with the courtesy. The Wasps almost certainly didn't need the guard-of-honour but it did help deter would-be heroes among the human spectators. Inside the Halls all activity came to a dead stop. Three Wasps had emerged from the aircraft and, as they moved through the corridors with a further escort of Killers, all but the guards froze in their tracks. Conversation faltered and died as everyone tried to think about nothing. All along the route to the Protector's office people were transfixed by the thought of the Wasps' power.

Despite all that he had been told, Legate Horfon watched out of the corner of his eye as the Wasps entered the chamber. There was an instant of first impression that they looked almost human, but then, as he saw them move, the impression was shattered. Nothing that he had ever seen moved like that. Nothing that originated on this world moved like that. They walked forward with their angular, inhuman stride until they were roughly in the centre of the expanse of pink marble. They halted and their heads swivelled almost, but not quite, in unison, taking in the whole of the room. Horfon felt himself growing angry and resentful.

Their behaviour seemed a supreme piece of arrogance. He had almost forgotten Dole Euphest's lecture but then the three alien heads swung in his direction. It seemed as though the dull patches were looking straight at him. Despite all the control that he could muster, he felt his breathing quicken. Was he doing something wrong? Would the aliens take offence? Would the unthinkable happen? The heads swivelled away and Horfon could hardly restrain himself from letting out a sigh of relief.

One of the Wasps was carrying a small, asymmetrical, dark-red box. It set the box on the floor. Horfon had been told about this device, the Wasp translator through which they communicated with their human subjects. The centre Wasp of the three pointed its head down at the translator. Horfon thought that he heard a swift wash of high-pitched sound but he wasn't sure if it was his imagination. There was also a smell in the air of something akin to ammonia. Then the voice came from the translator. It was the most inhuman thing of all.

'We . . . require . . . with hope . . . that all still remains.' Horfon had also heard how the translators were less than precise. 'Protector.'

The Protector had been standing behind the desk when the Wasps first entered. Now he walked forward to meet them. For one flesh-crawling moment Horfon thought that he was going to shake hands with or in some way actually touch the aliens. Instead he halted a few paces from the creatures. The aliens seemed to tower over him. They were almost half as tall again as the average man, and the Protector was shorter than average. He didn't seem daunted by the Wasps. He stood his ground and looked up at the one in the centre. 'Everything remains according to your previous directives.'

'That . . . is practical.'

'What is the purpose of this audience?'

Again Horfon thought he heard a ripple of high-pitched sound.

'An inconvenience.'

'We have discussed before how we are an inconvenience to you. It is hardly our fault that we are on this planet. We evolved here and your species destroyed our space-travel capabilities when you first arrived here.'

The Protector was polite but firm. He wasn't rude but he clearly refused to grovel. He maintained a tone of mild dislike, although whether Wasps had a concept of anything like mild dislike was a debatable point.

'Or are you here to complain about a new inconvenience?'

'An ideal totalling comes . . . to function integrate . . . alack the facility . . . are not . . .'

The Protector nodded. 'This you have also mentioned previously. I think I am profoundly grateful that the facility are not.'

There were times when the boredom of subservience spurred the Protector to take risks in his audiences with the Wasps. Trenhyass was something of a fatalist. He was sure that the time would come when the Wasps would reveal what they had in store for him.

'Compromise solution as . . . in . . . currrent continuation . . . schraahk monif . . . accorting . . . sot . . . to the directives.'

'We accept that. Not willingly, but we accept it.'

'Observations among your species indicate an unfolding.'

This came out of the translator without any of the hesitations, pauses and odd alien noises. It sounded almost as though it had been rehearsed. The Protector raised his hand and shook his head. 'I'm sorry. I didn't understand that.'

'Observations among your species indicate an unfolding.'

'An unfolding? What is an unfolding?'

'A stretch . . . demographic grabbernash . . . an unfolding commencement of change . . . not provide or negate the linear directive.'

'And will you issue a new directive to provide or negate?'

'Granish.'

'I beg your pardon?'

'Await . . . the fullness.'

'Of the unfolding?'

'Nard ulcer await.'

The Protector smiled. 'I often await ulcers.'

'Nard ulcer await unfolding full to count inconvenient and implement . . . directive . . . hoc . . .'

'So we wait.'

'Await.'

'I might be able to minimise the inconvenience if I had some idea of the nature of this unfolding.'

'Observe your own species.'

Trenhyass, despite all that he had been taught and all that he had observed for himself over the years he'd been dealing with the Wasps, could have sworn that the last remark was delivered with almost human impatience. It also proved to be the final remark of the audience. Without goodbye or ceremony, the translator was picked up. The Wasps turned on their approximation of heels and jerked towards the door. There was a scarcely-controlled pandemonium among the humans in the corridor as the aliens made their exit. The curious fled in front of them, pushed by the squad of Killers jockeying for position in the protective escort. Once the double doors had closed behind them, the Protector moved his shoulders as though trying to shrug off a mass of tension pains. He slowly walked back to the desk and flopped into the decorated throne. Dole Euphest looked at him questioningly. 'Did you make anything out of all that?'

The Protector sighed and swung his feet up onto the desk. He leaned forward and opened a drawer. There was something incongruous about the fact that this desk should have regular, human-sized drawers when it seemed to have been built for a giant. He took a vodka bottle and two glasses from the drawer. He carefully filled both glasses and motioned to Euphest to take one. 'This was bottled before the Wasps came; the real thing.'

The Legates remained at attention, apparently forgotten. Dole Euphest sat down on the edge of the desk and sipped the clear spirit. 'This is the good stuff, right enough.' He paused thoughtfully, as though reflecting on the liquor. 'Can't you imagine what it was like back then? No Wasps, our own world, our own civilisation.'

Trenhyass shook his head. 'I try not to. It depresses me.'

'So do you have an idea of what they wanted?'

'I'm not sure. There were the usual threats: obey all the directives or we get function-integrated. I've never discovered what function-integrated means exactly, but I've never liked the sound of it.'

'What about this unfolding business?'

The Protector frowned. 'That was odd. They seemed to have the idea that something's going on or, at least, something's about to go on.'

'They usually just issue a directive.'

'That's what's odd about it. I know it's dangerous to make assumptions where the Wasps are concerned, but it seemed to me that they were really unsure about whatever was bothering them.'

26

'You still think they understand us better than we understand them when they use that translator?'

'I don't see how they could be satisfied with the system if they didn't.' He looked up and noticed the uncomfortable Legates. 'Oh yes, I'd forgotten about you. Cut along and report to Hall Captain Drygall. You'll hear about it if I want you.'

The Legates hurried away. Euphest shook his head. 'You still inflict Drygall on the Legates.'

'It gives him something to do. When he has something to do, he doesn't plot against me.'

Euphest raised an eyebrow and sipped his vodka. 'And how does this new communication from our alien masters fit in with your theory?'

Trenhyass smiled. 'What little I gleaned fits perfectly.'

'You always say that.'

'That's because my theory has held up so far.'

'And you still maintain that our Wasps are simply a military garrison – an outpost?'

'That's right.'

The conversation was moving on the well-oiled rails of familiarity. Trenhyass opened another drawer. He produced a pipe and a leather pouch and started to stuff the pipe.

'It's the only scenario that makes sense. The Wasps have gone to a great deal of trouble to come here but they show little or no interest in exploring or exploiting either the planet or its inhabitants. They only act as conquerors or colonists in the most limited sense. They take little interest in us even though the universe is hardly crowded out with technically advanced species. What does that sound like to you?'

Euphest smiled and poured himself another drink. 'You want me to say "the military mind".'

'Would it hurt you? You have a better theory?'

'No, but I don't always want to be the straight man for yours. Also, I've never quite been sold on the explanation of why the Wasps should need to put their very own Fort Apache right here.'

The Protector finally had his pipe going.

'That's what's always puzzled me. Who the hell knows what goes on in a whole damn galaxy? We can't even guess at it. Maybe there's some huge interstellar war that's been going on for centuries; the occupation of our world could be some minor, routine manoeuvre.'

For a while both men sat in silence. Trenhyass puffed on his pipe. Euphest sipped his drink. Suddenly Euphest chuckled. The Protector glanced at him.

'What's so funny?'

'Think about it. If the Wasps are one side in some terrible galactic war, do you care to think what the enemy might be like?'

Three

JEEN VAYIM knew that there was going to be trouble from the moment they walked into the place. The Poet had an instinct for when trouble was looking for somewhere to happen. It had been his salvation on countless occasions. Right at that moment, instinct was telling him to get the hell out before the row started. Curiosity, on the other hand, kept him sitting tight in an unobtrusive corner seat. In this instance it wasn't too hard to smell trouble brewing. It didn't take any great gift of clairvoyance to tell him that a trio of drunken Killers, slumming on an all-night pass from the upper levels, would end up being a source of grief for those around them. They had clearly been roaring for some time. They were red in the face and their black and silver tunics were unbuttoned. Mercifully, their sinister helmets and lethal pulsers had been taken from them before they had been allowed loose in the taverns and bordellos of the lowers, but their apparent leader, a burly woman with tiny eyes and a shaved head, was hurrahing them on to greater measures of raucous excess.

It wasn't simply a matter of the Killers. On the other side of Denhagel's Tavern, Gywann and his growing entourage of young women were resting after a day of doing whatever it was that they did. Through the two weeks that the young man and his female companions had been residents at the tavern, Gywann had started to make a positive, if somewhat ambiguous, mark on the artists' quarter. It went beyond his good looks, even though it wasn't quite clear precisely what he intended to be or what his aims were. Some called him a prophet, others called him preacher or teacher. The more cynical suspected that he was really only out to collect a harem. There were a few who claimed that he was a poet, but Vayim had hotly objected to this. The too-blond, too-handsome Gywann had none of the traditional attributes of a poem-teller.

Each morning, he and the women left the tavern and found themselves a pitch on one of the busier corners or flights of steps in the quarter. Their routine was infinitely variable. Some days, events would start with the women roundsinging or playing soft, hypnotic percussion rhythms on wrist drums and tarbons. On other days they would just sit and stare blankly with a unique inward expression. Whatever they did, a crowd quickly formed. The artists' quarter always had a surplus of idlers up for a free show, but there was something quite unusual in the speed at which crowds would gather around Gywann. There was a definite and seemingly abnormal magnetism about him. He could not only draw a crowd but he could hold them, apparently by doing very little at all. People seemed happy to just stand and stare and listen to him. This power of Gywann's caused a good deal of chagrin among many of the other inhabitants of Denhagel's who made their living off the street. Cooze dancers, saraff players and even the crouching obsessives who did the sand painting on squares of sidewalk and loudly demanded alms, regarded him with the special hostility reserved for over-bold, too-clever, smiling interlopers.

In some moods, the Poet might have joined them in their muttering and complaints, but he found himself taking a fairly benign interest in Gywann, his troupe and his act. It wasn't just curiosity; there was also the matter of Messila. Messila was the tallest, blondest and most wide eyed of Gywann's original quintet of disciples, and the Poet had been working hard to bed her ever since they had first arrived. She had been responsive to his best poetic charm and there seemed to be no hindrance to the idea of casual sex in Gywann's somewhat impenetrable philosophy. The only problem had been that she insisted the Poet become, at a very minimum, a temporary fringe disciple. He had resisted for three days but in the end he'd given in.

Since then he had spent his nights rolling and bouncing with Messila and his days squatting on the roadside listening to Gywann talk. He had learned little from the experience. It wasn't that Gywann didn't have impact. Indeed, there had been moments when the Poet had been charmed, elated, pushed towards tears, but he had learned nothing about why Gywann was there or what he wanted. Essentially, Gywann said nothing. It intrigued Vayim. Gywann's voice rose and fell in melodic cadences, the words formed attractive, even seductive pictures; vignettes and anecdotes tumbled but it amounted to nothing that made sense. It imparted nothing. It was pure massage. Vayim had spent a lifetime growing in the art of poem-telling. He knew tricks when he saw them. He could spot the tiny charms of the voice that had the power to slither into minds or imagination. Gywann had plenty of tricks, but they were of a kind that the Poet had never seen before. They either came from a discipline that was totally unknown to him or it was some unique invention of Gywann himself.

About the only thing that Vayim knew for sure was that Gywann was not the kind who should sit, flanked by adoring women, in a tavern where a trio of nasty-drunk Killers are roistering. He was quite surprised that it took the Killers as long as it did to spot him. Twice he warned Gywann that it might be a good idea to go somewhere else for a few hours, but Gywann had simply smiled, shaken his head, and made no move to leave. There were some things that the Poet saw as fundamental street wisdom which Gywann dismissed as an endearing lack of faith.

Initially, Gywann was staying away from the Killers' notice and out of trouble because Raif the Fire-eater, Dirty Sulanda, the Perforated Woman, and the three Zilla Brothers were crammed into a booth right next to their table. This sextet was more than sufficient to hold the attention of even the most bellicose drunk. The largest of the Zilla Brothers had rolled his eyes back into his head and was doing the special trick with the green jelly thing. This wasn't the regular trick that he did on the street for diems, pieces and the amazement of passers-by; this was the really disgusting version that he saved for those who were as misshapen as himself. It rocked the Killers in their seats. The woman with the shaved head laughed so hard that she began to look as though she were going to have a stroke.

Eventually, though, even the Killers started to get bored and looked around the room for some other diversion. It was the burly woman who first spotted Gywann and his people. Her little pig-eyes narrowed and she ran a hand across her sweating scalp. 'Now what kind of shit is that?'

She climbed to her feet and stood swaying. She swallowed a large shot of gin and coughed. She undid another fastening on her black tunic. One large breast threatened to spill out. She waved a hand towards Gywann. 'Isn't he just too good to be true? What the fuck is he?'

Out of the corner of his eye, Jeen Vayim saw Denhagel slowly stiffen. He carefully set down the glass that he was polishing. The burly woman stumbled forwards as if she were going to take a closer look at Gywann. She stopped in front of him and leaned heavily on the back of a chair. 'So what the fuck are you, gorgeous?'

Gywann had his hands folded on the table in front of him. He was staring down at them, refusing to acknowledge the Killer. The Poet tried to slide away without being too obvious. The Killer scowled. 'I'm talking to you, boy.'

Denhagel's voice cut through the mounting tension. 'I want no trouble in this place.'

One of the other Killers was instantly on his feet. He was a tall, thin male with cropped hair and a mean-spirited pencil moustache. 'You keep your mouth shut, tavern-keeper.'

He spoke with the authority of a man who is used to people being afraid of him. Customers were starting to edge towards the door. Vayim knew that the tavern was sliding, uncontrolled, to the point where things turn ugly. The woman's jaw jutted. She thrust her face towards Gywann. 'I asked you a question and I want an answer!'

This time Gywann looked up. He smiled. 'What was your question?'

'I asked you what the fuck you were supposed to be.'

Gywann smiled again. 'I'm none of your concern.'

The Poet closed his eyes. It was time for the eruption. The woman's mouth fell open and shocked words tumbled out.

'You insolent little shit.' She stretched out a meaty hand for Gywann's windpipe, but she never touched it. A strange glazed look came over her face. Her hand faltered and shook. Her mouth twisted in pain and her eyes changed colour. She seemed to be trying to say something. The Killer with the moustache stepped forward. The woman made a strangling noise and her head began to change shape. It was as though her skull had turned to jelly and her whole head was being sucked down through her neck by something inside her body. Folds and wrinkles appeared across the previously smooth surface of her shaved head. Her eyes bugged above sunken cheeks, her lips drew back from her teeth. Thick, pinkish-grey fluid welled from her right ear. Then there was a hideous, moist, slurping sound. The head was reduced to half its original size. More of the grey-pink substance sprayed from the eyes, nose and ears. It was the most disgusting thing that the Poet had ever seen

32

but he couldn't look away. An awestruck whisper came from behind him.

'She imploded!'

'She headsucked!'

The Killer with the moustache stood stunned. Some of the mess had splashed on his tunic. The headless body's knees buckled and it crashed to the floor. The tavern was silent, then there was the noise of someone throwing up. A woman started screaming. It was cracked and hysterical but nobody paid it any mind. The two remaining Killers snapped together as training and discipline reasserted themselves. They grasped for the weapons they didn't have.

'Nobody move! Nobody leave here!' The Killer with the moustache rounded on Gywann. 'Did you do that?'

Gywann shook his head. Of everyone in the tavern, he seemed the least touched by the horror of what had just happened. 'How could I do a thing like that?'

His face was blank. It wasn't the blank expression of someone in shock, it was the blank expression of complete unconcern. The Killer with the moustache seemed about to explode in violence. Vayim attempted a cautious rescue. 'You were there. You saw. He didn't move a muscle.'

The middle Zilla Brother was looking down at the corpse. 'Reckon you should be looking for a Wasp.'

The Killers both turned. 'What?'

'The way she died, that's the way the Wasps do it.'

'How do you know this?'

'I seen it done. It was years ago, when I was a kid. This lunatic tried to get a Wasp with a meat cleaver. His head went just like hers did. You don't ever forget a thing like that.'

The Killers seemed at something of a loss. Denhagel came out from behind the bar. 'So what are you going to do about all this?'

The Killers looked at him. 'You own this place?'

'That's right.'

'This is a bad business.'

'You can't blame it on the place.'

The Killer with the moustache looked hard at Denhagel. His eyes were like flint. 'One of our own is dead. We're going to blame it on someone.'

Jeen Vayim thanked providence that these Killers were unarmed. Revenge was one of the service's most strongly promoted traditions. Nobody killed a Killer and got away with it. Nobody killed a Killer and lived. A decade earlier, a terror group called the League of Nine had blown up four off-duty Killers riding in a carriage; in response to the outrage the Protector had given the whole force free rein to rampage through the city for a full week. Over a hundred people had died, either 'resisting arrest' or 'in the course of interrogation', After something like this gruesome death, they would quite likely feel within their rights to slaughter everyone in the tavern.

Someone placed a coat over the shattered head. It seemed to defuse the tension slightly. The Killers got down to business. One guarded the door of the tavern making sure that no one could leave. The other used Denhagel's talkie to call up reinforcements. Within fifteen minutes, there were twenty Killers in and around the tavern, with weapons in their hands and helmets masking their faces. The helmets were what really gave the Killers their aura of deadly uniformity. The Poet suspected that whoever had originally designed them had deliberately sought to echo the faces of the Wasps. For a few moments after this second squad of Killers had arrived, it had again seemed as though there might be an eruption of indiscriminate violence. Fortunately, they were under the command of an experienced old Wingleader who was able to temper anger with common sense. He was well aware that to massacre everyone in the tavern might be satisfying, but it would hardly be practical. This was no ordinary murder. As far as anyone knew, it was beyond human capability to kill in such a way. It was a matter that demanded careful investigation rather than random vengeance.

After three hours, the process of investigation was starting to wear on the tavern's customers. Fear was giving way to boredom. They sat and waited. They had been questioned and re-questioned. There had been oblique offers of rewards and direct threats of torture. More Killers arrived, including a grim, self-important group of high-ranking officers and their aides. They had stood for a long time around the body, conducting an urgent but inaudible conversation; then they had ordered the body removed and turned their attention to Gywann. He was the closest the Killers had to a suspect even though the whole tavern full of people was prepared to swear he hadn't made a move. He was the one to whom the victim had been talking the instant she died, and it could be said that her death had saved Gywann from whatever she had in mind to do to him. The thread was tenuous but Gywann was still taken into one of Denhagel's back rooms and kept there for over two hours while a stream of higher and higher ranked interrogators passed through. When he finally emerged he was supported by a Killer on either side, his right eye was closing, there was a swelling bruise under his left, but his expression was still one of serenity and calm. One of his woman followers shrieked and hurled herself at the nearest Killer.

'How could you do it? How could you hurt him? How could you do *that* to *him*?'

She tried to pull his arm away but was hurled aside like a helpless doll. Her hair and robe flying, she fell into a table, upsetting it with a crash of glasses. She finished up on her knees inspecting a cut on her hand. Gywann was unceremoniously dumped in a chair. The other women quickly surrounded him, kneeling beside him, cooing, comforting and treating the Killers to looks of baleful reproach. The most senior of the Killers returned these with contempt and then shifted his attention to the other occupants of the tavern.

'A Killer is dead. Murdered.' He clearly took a sombre delight in his power. His helmet was gold, with a sunburst crest. He strutted up and down inspecting each of Denhagel's customers individually. 'The murder of a Killer is a crime that strikes to the root of our society. The murder of a Killer has to be paid for. You have all been recorded. If any of you flee we will find you. We will find you and we will assume that your flight means you are an accomplice in this crime. Do you understand me?'

A few heads nodded sullenly. This wasn't good enough for the senior Killer. He took a pace forward. His voice turned icy.

'Do you *all* understand?'

More heads nodded. The senior Killer's voice turned harsh.

'A Killer is dead. You should make no mistake, we will leave now but this is not the end. There is one fact you can count on. We will find the perpetrators of this crime and they will die. A second fact is that we don't care who else might die in the process. We will not be obstructed.' He glanced briefly at Gywann and his attendant women. 'You will not talk about what happened today. None of you. I want no rumours spreading and growing. I know what can happen with rumours. I shall treat the spreading of tales as a deliberate obstruction. Remember that I can come back at any time, come back and raze this tavern to the ground.'

When the last Killer had kicked off into the air, carried by his flying-belt back to the towers where everyone felt that he belonged, Denhagel walked wearily back behind the bar. 'After all that, the drinks are on the house.'

'Some weird fucking thing went on down here today.'

Denhagel nodded. 'You don't have to say that twice.'

'If that had been any regular killing, if one of us had slipped a knife into that drunken pig, they'd have burned this place and us in it. No questions asked.'

Dirty Sulanda swallowed her shot in one gulp and coughed.

'They didn't burn the place because what happened here's got them baffled. Only the Wasps can kill like that and there wasn't a Wasp anywhere near.' She slowly turned, looked at Gywann and his entourage of women. 'What about you, beauty? What about you, boy prophet? What do you know about all this?'

Gywann looked up. 'I know nothing more than I told the Killers.'

'Which was what?'

'That I knew nothing.'

One of the Zilla Brothers leaned into the conversation. 'You didn't look too surprised when that Killer bitch imploded right in front of you.'

Gywann stood up. He swayed slightly. Messila quickly took his arm and steadied him. He straightened his back and looked at Denhagel. 'Perhaps we should leave.'

Denhagel nodded. 'That might be the best thing all round.'

The Perforated Woman's lip curled. 'Don't go too far, we don't want the Killers tearing the place apart looking for you.'

As Gywann and his women were leaving the tavern, Dirty Sulanda nudged Jeen Vayim. 'Aren't you going with them? You've been so tight with that bunch lately.'

Messila caught the remark and also looked at the Poet. Vayim shook his head. 'I think I'll stay here for the moment.'

The Perforated Woman laughed. 'So, Poet, it was all enough to scare you away from that little honey, was it? Or have you just tired of bedding her?'

Messila coloured, then she turned on her heel and followed the others, banging the door closed behind her. Vayim didn't say a word until Denhagel had refilled his glass.

'Okay. I admit it. What happened here scared me. What do you think I am? Some kind of hero? Right now, I don't want to be anywhere near Gywann or his troop of women. Like you said, something weird went on down here and I think he had something to do with it.'

'What, though? He didn't actually do anything,'

'How the hell should I know? The Killers don't know. I just have a feeling.'

The larger of the Zilla Brothers shrugged and turned to the bar. 'What the hell. He's gone now and good riddance. Him and all those dopey bimbos gave me the creeps. Maybe things'll settle down now. Business as usual.'

Vayim thoughtfully bit his lower lip. He shook his head. 'I don't think so. I don't think we've seen the last of our boy prophet.'

Four

'FROM THE very start, let us entertain no illusions. The time before the Wasps came was no golden age. It wasn't a time of freedom and enlightenment. Any historian who tells you so is a liar and a charlatan. His words should be given no more credence than the fanciful ramblings of the poets. It may be good for the common people to blame all their troubles on our alien conquerors but we have to know better than that. Those of you who come through this year of instruction will be in the direct service of the Protector. You will be the buffer between humanity and the Wasps. You can afford to deal with nothing but the absolute, objective truth.'

The Hall Captain paused, as if to allow these facts to be absorbed by the class of silent Legates. When he decided the process had been given enough time, he continued. 'One of the most essential truths is that even before the Wasps came human civilisation was tired, we were lazy and without ambition or discipline. We had moved onto the thresholds of space, we had colonised the nearest planets, but after that we had come to realise just how big space really was, and how small we were in comparison. We became scared and turned in on ourselves.'

Legate Androx raised a tentative hand. It took a certain amount of courage to interrupt Hall Captain Drygall. Courage, however, was something that this particular Legate seemed to possess in abundance. Legate Androx had most things in abundance. She was a statuesque blonde with the authority and the unshakeable sense of rightness that is exclusive to the truly highborn, those who have been reared at the very top of the highest towers. Drygall raised a thin eyebrow.

'Androx? You have something to contribute to our discussion?'

It was inevitable that the two of them should clash. They were total opposites. She was a young thoroughbred, energetic and arrogant, while he was old and withered, an embittered husk whose humanity had been leeched away by a life of institutional service.

'I have a question, Hall Captain.'

Legate Horfon shot Androx a sidelong glance. He envied the girl her ability to resist the dehumanising process that seemed so much a part of preliminary training. Her absolute certainty of her position enabled her to rise naturally above all attempts to grind her to uniformity. Although he hated to admit it, Horfon was in awe of Androx. Part of this awe came from the fact that her rebellion wasn't without a price, a price that she paid without complaint. Only three days earlier, she had been beaten by Drygall after a large quantity of toadfold had been discovered in her locker during a snap inspection. Toadfold was the fungus that grew on decaying patches of everburn. When eaten it produced interesting shifts of mood. The drug was widely used on all levels of the city but was perversely forbidden to Legates in training. The theory was that deprivation moulded character. Androx didn't agree with the theory and thus she refused to obey the rule. As a result of this refusal, stripped of her dignity and her breeches, she had been thrashed in front of the assembled class. Drygall used a flexible, clear plastic rod that hurt like hell. After every punishment, he assured the class that pain was the fastest route to correct thinking. Horfon wondered if Androx was going to be beaten for a second time in the same week. Drygall was regarding her with an icy stare.

'What is it, Androx?'

'I was wondering, Hall Captain: if our civilisation had been healthier, more vigorous, might we have been able to resist the Wasps? If we'd been more ambitious, and more disciplined, could we have driven them back into space . . . Hall Captain?'

Androx was a master of subtle insolence. Drygall slowly nodded.

'Years of training Legates have made me a careful man, Androx. I suspect all motives. I shall, however, take your question at face value. The answer is no. Even if we'd been totally prepared for an invader from deep space, there would have been nothing we could have done. The technology of the Wasps is thousands, maybe even millions of years in advance of ours. Once again we can only measure them against our own ignorance. We don't know enough even to gauge our own inferiority but, unfortunately, we are smart enough to know that we're inferior. It's a degrading experience for any species.'

Hall Captain Drygall seemed to take the Wasp occupation as a personal injury. He was approaching old age, dried out by the habit of suppressed anger. He was like a dead brown leaf that continued to fight the wind because it was simply too mean to drop from the branch. Had he lived in some violent era of war, adventure and instant valour, he might have been a leader, even a hero. In the Wasp-enforced peace, there was nothing but the knowledge of defeat; his only comfort was the spite of a bleak sadism. Over the years, even his body had shrivelled to his angular frame until he looked like a pale-faced carrion bird, a cross between a vulture and a corpse. His honorary Killer's uniform hung on him like the folds of a shroud.

'They came on our fathers before they knew it. The colonies on Mars and Venus went out first. A few hours later they were followed by the city on the Moon, the satellite stations and the ring bases. As the first waves of their probes hit our atmosphere they emped out most of our data banks and nearly all of our communications. What weapons we used against them were turned back on us. Within seventy hours our humiliation was complete. A few pockets of military were making futile last stands in remote areas of mountain or jungle, the big cities across the world were deprived of most of their essential services and the civilian population was in a state of complete panic. It was only then that they brought down the big ships. The final irony was that it had taken only their advance guard to vanquish our species and conquer our planet. They had hardly had to flex their muscles.'

There were times when Drygall talked about the Wasp conquests, that he spoke as though he'd actually been there. In fact they'd taken place over a century before his birth.

'Humanity was dazed. There were confused attempts at hit-and-run resistance but these all ended in the deaths of everyone concerned. There were equally confused attempts at collaboration, but the Wasps tended to misunderstand them. They seemed unable to tell an attack from an overture and these too finished up killing all those involved. You have to remember that immediately before the Wasps came, the conflict between the Proprietors, the so-called Undeclared War, had reached its peak. Mankind was so divided that it was impossible to co-ordinate any response to the Wasps. It didn't really matter, though. The confusion was shortlived. Before we could adjust to the conquerors, the plague struck. Eighty per cent of the human race died in the space of two months.'

Drygall allowed himself a second dramatic pause.

'We have never been sure whether the plague was deliberately created by the Wasps or whether it was simply some alien bacterial matter that came with them and proved fatal to human beings. It's not unusual for conquerors to bring a deadly disease with them. There are numerous examples in our own history.'

Legate Horfon shifted on the hard wooden classroom seat. Drygall pinned him with a look. 'I trust I'm not boring you, Legate Horfon. You've scarcely been with us long enough to have heard it all before, unless, of course, you've had prior tutoring. I understand you rode in here with Protector Trenhyass himself. Am I correct, Legate Horfon?'

Horfon's voice seemed to knot in his throat, as if it wanted to choke him. 'Y-yes, Hall Captain.'

Drygall tended to become extremely negative when any of the Legates under his charge had contact with the Protector. There were those who claimed that Drygall had once wanted to try for Protector himself, but fear of the selection process had held him back.

'Maybe the Protector himself has told you all this already.'

'No, Hall Captain.'

Horfon was the newest arrival to Drygall's instruction. The rest of his intake had laughingly sympathised with him, so far as privileged adolescents are capable of sympathy, when it was learned that he had pulled Drygall as a Hall Captain.

'Perhaps you'd tell the class why you came to be riding with the Protector, Legate Horfon.'

'I . . .'

'Please stand, Legate. I'm sure the whole class would like to hear about their exalted new colleague and his direct links to power.'

Horfon came out of his chair and snapped to attention. He could feel a blush creeping up from under his collar.

'I was rated top of my intake, Hall Captain. I . . . can only imagine that I was selected for the honour on that basis.'

Drygall laid a hand on the wooden lectern from which he normally taught. His fingertips were just a fraction of a centimetre from the transparent rod. Drygall always kept the rod both to hand and highly visible.

'Are you sure it had nothing to do with your family, boy? It can hardly be a hindrance to have a relative who is an intimate of the Protector's sister.'

'Hall Captain, I . . .'

Horfon's voice faltered. Drygall was also notorious for his hatred of the offspring of powerful, patrician families.

'We shall have to keep an eye on you, Legate. I always pay special attention to anyone who's top of his intake and a friend of the Protector to boot. We must ensure that the thinking of anyone so well connected remains absolutely correct.'

'I . . .'

'What, Legate?'

Horfon had been about to blurt out that he certainly wouldn't presume to call himself a friend of the Protector but, in the nick of time, the meaning of the gesture towards the rod and the reference to correct thinking sank in.

'Nothing, Hall Captain.'

'Sit down, Legate.'

Horfon sat. Drygall looked slowly around the bare stone walls of the classroom. Drygall didn't believe in decoration or even visual aids. It was a small, strange room, an ideal place for a man to wither in. The ceiling was unnaturally high and there were five walls, one of which curved inwards. It was an irregularly shaped nook that had been superfluous to some complicated grand design. Drygall's classroom was an architectural left-over. He brought his attention back to the class and became brisk.

'For the rest of the morning we will examine the organisation that took place after the plague. We will consider how our own technology was destroyed and restricted until it posed not even a minimal threat to the Wasps and how, indeed, they even introduced facets of their own science, particularly the centralised power source, that we could operate but hardly understand. We will assess our almost total dependency and, if there is time, we will consider the establishment of the Protectorate and the process of selection for the Lords Protector. I trust this will keep you all amused.'

Another hand was raised. It belonged to Legate Rodin. Rodin was another class troublemaker. Rodin, like Androx, seemed to take a delight in seeing how close to the edge he could sail. He and Androx seemed to compete with each other to see how far each of them could push Drygall. Also like Androx, Rodin had been beaten on a number of occasions.

'You have something on your mind, Legate Rodin?'

'I would like your opinion, Hall Captain.'

Drygall gently touched the rod with his fingertips. 'On what matter, Legate Rodin?'

'There are people who believe that we brought the Wasps on ourselves, that it was our own deep-space probes that told them of our existence and brought them to our planet.'

Drygall shook his head impatiently. 'I don't subscribe to that theory. Space travel was never wholly popular. Three centuries ago, when we sent out the big starships, there were many who prophesied doom. Even more thought them a one-way ticket, an expensive gamble, and we'd never know if we'd won or if their cargoes of colonists arrived or even survived. The starships were unpopular but space is an infinitely large place and it's infinitely unlikely that any of them encountered the Wasps. Does that answer your question, Rodin? I do not think we brought the Wasps upon ourselves; they are a part of much larger events.'

'What is your theory, Hall Captain?'

Drygall treated Rodin to a penetrating look.

'The most popular theory is that normally attributed to Protector Trenhyass himself . . .' Before he could elaborate, there was a loud rapping on the classroom door. Drygall turned with an expression of annoyance.

'Enter.'

A Major Legate came through the door. He saluted Drygall.

'Greetings, Hall Captain, I'm sorry to interrupt your class.'

'What is it?'

'There is a message to go to the Protector. Two Junior Legates are required at dispatch.'

Drygall waved a curt hand at the class.

'There are none here who can afford to miss class. They are a uniformly ignorant collection.'

'None the less, two are required.'

Drygall addressed himself. 'Yes, yes, but which two? I suppose the Protector's little friend for one. Up, Horfon.'

Horfon came to his feet and to attention.

'Now, who to send with him? You, Androx. Up, Legate.

43

You can afford to miss a class. You believe you know it all already.'

Once outside the door the Major Legate gave them directions how to get to the dispatch office, but he did not accompany them. Instead, he went about his own business and left them to get there as best they could. Horfon was all for making the maximum possible haste. Androx looked at him in amazement.

'Are you nuts? This detail's a gift. We can make this last all day.' She unhooked the stiff collar of her tunic. 'That's better.' She noticed that Horfon was still staring at her with his mouth open. 'What's the matter with you?'

'Won't they miss us? Won't we be punished if we don't show up right away?'

'You're a stuffy, kiss-ass little prick, aren't you?'

Horfon had never been spoken to like that. Particularly by a young woman of roughly his own age.

'I . . .'

'Every time anyone speaks to you, you make a face like a choking fish. It figures that you came top of your intake.'

'You shouldn't talk to me like that. It can't be correct.'

'Correct? You don't want to believe all that garbage. It's strictly for us junior Legates, to keep us confused so we buy all the bullshit about bowing down to the Wasps.'

Horfon involuntarily looked around as though he feared someone had overheard her.

'You mustn't speak that way. You've been beaten once this week.'

'Did you get your jollies watching that?'

Horfon's jaw dropped. He avoided looking her directly in the eye. Androx laughed.

'There you go again, choking fish. Why don't you unsnap your damned collar and relax. We're on a goof. Enjoy it.'

'But what if we *are* missed?'

'Nobody cares about us. Junior Legates are the lowest of the low. As long as you walk around looking vaguely like you know what you're supposed to be doing, nobody's going to bother you. That's the Legates' first lesson. Anything that gets you away from Drygall has to be good.'

Horfon put a tentative hand on his collar but then took it away again. Androx looked at him as though he'd just crawled out from under a rock. 'Undo the damn thing, you idiot.'

Horfon reluctantly tugged his collar open. He was totally at a loss. He didn't know which was the worse prospect, Androx's contempt or the consequences of being caught in an unauthorised absence. Androx seemed to be winning, possibly because she was right there and official retribution was further off in some possible future.

'Doesn't that feel better?'

They walked slowly down the passage that led away from the classroom. 'Maybe we could find ourselves a drink somewhere before we report to dispatch. There are shebeens all over the Halls.'

Horfon didn't like to admit that he didn't drink and that he wasn't even exactly clear what a shebeen was, except that it had something to do with the selling of illicit liquor.

'I think we ought to go straight to dispatch. It might be something important.'

'I bet you don't drink.'

'As a matter of fact . . .'

'I bet you're still a virgin, too.'

'I don't think you should ask a question like that, not until we know each other better.'

'I lost my virginity when I was ten. To my uncle, the Proprietor, as a matter of fact. We develop early in the high towers.' She raised an eyebrow. 'You don't sound as though you were raised in the towers, though.'

'I wasn't.'

'I thought you had this almighty, heavy-duty family.'

'I do, but my father's only a minor part of it. He's a small-time Proprietor out in the Ranges.'

'You have a lot to learn.'

The passage had opened into a spacious but disused hall. It might once have been a ballroom, but a long time had passed since anyone had danced there. An elaborate chandelier had shed its crystals like an ice cascade that's started to thaw. The drapes that covered the walls had decayed to tatters and part of the ceiling had fallen in, damaged by a major leak of water somewhere above. No one had ever attempted to repair it. Horfon reflected that it was the kind of derelict place ideal for boojies. He really disliked meeting boojies. Boojies were the other parasite that had arrived in the Wasp ships and now ran loose all over the city. The boojies were quite harmless and about the same size as a large dog. The problem with them was that they were so extremely alien that people had difficulty in looking at them without an unreasoning sense of panic and revulsion.

'I'd never realised that there were so much of the inner Halls that's never used.'

Androx glanced around the ballroom. She had seen it all before. 'Like I said, you've got a lot to learn. You have to realise that behind the facade and all the top dressings of power, there's nearly complete chaos. Most of the Aides and the Administrators are incompetent and absolutely corrupt. That's why no one's going to miss us. The only people who do their job are the Killers, and you want to keep away from them as much as you can.'

The floor of the ballroom was thick with dust. Their boots kicked up miniature clouds with each step. Androx kicked a broken chairleg and the noise reverberated round the high ceiling.

'There's probably more of the Halls unused than used. There simply aren't enough people to fill this pile. Enough of the right people, anyway.'

The drapes on the opposite wall suddenly moved. For an instant, Horfon thought that it might be a boojie but then they were pulled back. Dust billowed outward. The drapes had been covering a concealed alcove. A figure in uniform breeches and an undershirt stepped out. There were two more figures behind him, squatting in the alcove.

'Either of you got any toadfold?'

''Fraid not.'

'We've got a tenhigh game going in here. You want to join in?'

'We've got to go to dispatch.'

'Suit yourself.'

The figure ducked back into the alcove and the drapes fell into place. Horfon was bemused. 'What was that all about?'

''Round here, goofing off has turned into an artform.'

'Does anyone do what they're supposed to do?'

'The Protector, maybe.'

'You don't object to the Protector, then?'

Horfon's tone had a trace of mockery. It was his first tentative shot at asserting himself with the outspoken, domineering girl. Androx looked down her nose.

'I object to what he's doing, not the way he does it. I don't see why we have to spend all our time kowtowing to those damned aliens.'

'What else can we do?'

'I don't know, but one day it'll be our turn. Then things will be different, you can bet on that.'

Horfon laughed out loud. 'You seriously think that you'll be Protector one day?'

'Maybe not Protector, but our turn will come. The Wasps are not invincible. Everything has a weak spot.'

Horfon no longer laughed. He wasn't even smiling. There was something chilling about the girl's certainty. He suspected that by the time she had grown into womanhood she'd make a dangerous adversary. For a while they walked on in silence, out of the ballroom, up two flights of stairs and along another passage. They were moving into a more occupied area of the Halls. At first the people came singly, a page wheeling a heavy bundle in a pushcart, a cleaner, a woman with a veil and a furtive walk. Then a group of functionaries huddled outside a closed door, conspiring in low voices. Clerks hurried from one place to another, Courtiers swept past, perfumed and oblivious, followed by their trotting retinues, Killers swaggered and made a lot of noise with their boots. At one intersection, they passed a pair of very young boys. They wore sarongs and their faces were painted like a couple of whores from the lowers. Androx grinned at Horfon's expression of gauche surprise.

'Are you heterosexual, Legate Horfon?' Before he could say anything, she answered her own question. 'I was silly to ask. You probably don't even know yet.'

The dispatch office confirmed the picture of chaos and bureaucratic confusion that Androx had been painting. It was a long narrow hall with a counter running all the way down its longest side. It smelled of too much humanity and was chipped and scuffed from over-use. Long lines of Aides and Legates waited for the graceless attention of a group of slowmoving and surly clerks who seemed to have given up all hope a long time in the past. From the way they behaved, it appeared that almost every message was either lost, delayed, misfiled or forwarded to the wrong department. There was litter under foot, anger and impatience in the air. Tempers were frayed and there were occasional outbreaks of hysteria. A pair of Killers patrolled the area to ensure that the hostility never escalated from verbal to physical; for centuries, humanity had relied on logical electronics to organise their lives. When the Wasps, as one of their first acts, wiped out the computers, mankind never quite regained the knack of simple efficiency. Horfon and Androx waited almost an hour before they got to a clerk. When they told him the details of their task, he immediately asked what had kept them.

Even though the name of the Protector did slightly stir the sluggish motion of the clerks, it was still a further fifteen minutes before the red leather pouch with the black official seal that could only be broken by Trenhyass himself was located and handed over.

Despite all of her previous bravado, Androx seemed to be touched by a certain degree of awe that she was actually taking a package to the Protector. Even awe, however, came with a measure of rebellion. Directly they were away from the restive crowds in the disptach area, she thrust the package at him.

'Here, teacher's pet, you can carry this. It'll give you a kick.'

Horfon shook his head. 'You're going to get into a lot of trouble one day.'

'What's life without a little trouble?'

The Grand Audience Chamber of the Protector was somewhat different from the previous time that Horfon had seen it. There were between sixty and seventy people in the large room, what was generally considered to be the cream of Protectorate society. There were Proprietors and their relatives, there were the mandarins who ran the Protector's civil service, high-ranking military competed in gold braid and decorations, a sprinkling of the most courted courtesans moved through the press like silk on the breeze. The order was lavish, satins and brocades, elaborate coiffures and burnished leather; drifting perfume mingled and clashed. There was a sense of luxury, opulence that was completely at odds with the reality of a conquered and debilitated planet. Some of the wealthy and powerful formed themselves into the kind of tight, low-voiced huddles that tended to indicate the conversation was urgent and of great import. Others were less serious; they nodded, smiled and waved and, above all, they circulated. Among them, the chatter was bright, brittle and of no import at all. Some were followed around by their personal servants. One particularly effete young man was accompanied by a painted funchild attached to him by a silver collar and a fine silver chain.

'This is the real decadence. This lot go as far as it goes.'

Even though Androx hissed the words defiantly out of the corner of her mouth, her tough facade had wilted a little in the face of such ostentation and display. The Protector himself sat behind his enormous desk. He hardly seemed a part of the freeform but highly ritualised dance of manners. He was still dressed in the plain black uniform without insignia or decorations, and he seemed somehow distanced from what was going on around him. He reclined in his chair, resting on his left arm. His face had the blank expression of the politely, if disdainfully, bored. The only person talking to him was his sister, the Lady Mariko, and he appeared absolutely uninterested in whatever she might be saying.

Once past the Killers who guarded the doors to the Audience Chamber, Androx and Horfon stiffened their spines and marched in perfect step through the crowd, doing their best to make it look like something that they did every day. They halted in front of the Protector's desk and saluted with a well-drilled flourish. The Protector held out his hand for the message pouch. The Lady Mariko, who had been half sitting on the corner of the desk, showing off her legs, pushed herself upright and slowly walked around the two Legates as though conducting an inspection. A little absentmindedly, she toyed with a large ruby that hung from a gold chain.

'What's your name?'

'Legate Horfon, my lady.'

'Yes, of course. Horfon. Your great-aunt Sybelle seemed particularly anxious that you did better in life than your father. I hope you don't disappoint her.'

'I'll try not to, my lady.'

'Good.' She turned her attention to Androx. 'You're very handsome, Legate. You suit a uniform.'

Androx snapped off a salute. 'Thank you for the compliment, my lady.'

'You don't have a prestigious aunt as well, do you?'

'I'm afraid not, my lady.'

'Never mind. Perhaps I should have you transferred to my personal staff anyway. You'd make a decorative addition.'

The Protector glanced up from the papers he'd taken from the pouch. 'Stop trying to be sleazy, Mariko.'

The Lady Mariko was as flamboyant as her brother was reserved. She was one of the city's great uninhibited beauties, with a reputation for wildness that had spread all the way to the taverns of the lowers, where even the poorest of the poor would titillate himself with tales of her adventures. Particular favourites were a number that involved dwarves and large domestic animals. When Trenhyass had first been selected as Protector, there had been some who had believed that his sister would prove to be a liability to him, a potential point of weakness. From the start, however, he had quite successfully divorced himself from her peccadillos. If anything, the fact of the Lady Mariko and her notoriety proved to be something of a humanising factor in his otherwise coldly austere image.

On this particular day, the Lady was rather less outrageous than usual. Her dress was a comparatively simple construction of stark black and white silk that fitted closely across her hips, accentuating the lines of her body, and then flared out into a pair of wide, exaggerated shoulders and a high stand-up collar that served as a frame for her face. Currently, her hair was white with a mass of tiny seed pearls threaded into it, but it tended to change week by week. As far as Legate Horfon was concerned, she was the most exotic creature he had ever seen. His sheltered upbringing hadn't prepared him in any degree for a sight like that. He didn't, though, have very long to be dazzled. The Protector threw the papers down on the desk.

'You, Legate, go over and tell Dole Euphest to come here.'

Euphest was over on the other side of the chamber. He was dressed in his usual shapeless grey robe and talking to a very fat man in a black tunic and plumed hat. Horfon hurried over.

'The Protector wishes to speak to you, my lord.'

'How many times do I have to tell you Legates that I'm nobody's lord and you don't have to address me as such.'

'I'm sorry.'

Horfon followed Euphest back to the Protector's desk. He once again felt sheepish and stupid even though nobody seemed to notice him. Both Euphest and the Protector had much more important things on their minds than the shortcomings of a very junior Legate. He was completely ignored as Trenhyass came straight to the point.

'I have the fully detailed report here of that incident in the lowers.'

Euphest nodded. 'I heard the investigation had hit a blank wall.'

'So what do you make of it?'

Euphest shrugged. 'It beats me. On the surface, it would seem like this kid who's trying to set himself up as some kind of freelance religious leader has somehow acquired the power to make people implode.'

Lady Mariko looked around, suddenly interested. 'Isn't that impossible? Surely only the Wasps can do that.'

Trenhyass picked up the report and then let it drop again. 'That's what I would have thought, but it happened and one of my Killers is dead.'

'Is it possible that there was a Wasp somewhere in the vicinity and it's all just a coincidence?'

'Anything's possible but if there was a Wasp about nobody saw it. We weren't informed of any Wasp excursions and they do usually notify us before they go walking around in the lowers without an escort.'

The Lady Mariko saw no real problem. 'Why don't you simply have him killed? That surely would put a stop to it all.'

The Protector shook his head. 'That would be too easy. If this man has actually assumed a power that was previously exclusive to the Wasps, I want to know why and how and what it means.'

'We could bring him in and sweat him.'

'Not yet. It's possible that he may not even know what he's doing. For now, I just want him watched. I have agents all over the lowers. It's time for them to earn their keep.'

Dole Euphest rubbed his nose. 'You want me to deal with this?'

'I'd be obliged.'

The two Legates were still standing at attention. They had apparently been forgotten. When no one was looking, Horfon leaned towards Androx and whispered, 'Do we just stand here all day or what?'

Androx hissed back, 'Shut up. This is interesting.'

The Protector was up on his feet. He came around the desk and stood beside Dole Euphest. 'I want you to take personal charge of this matter.'

'You think it's that important?' Euphest wasn't burdened with any false modesty.

The Protector nodded. 'It worries me. I can't stop this feeling that the Wasps are somehow behind all this. I can't for the life of me imagine why they should want to give this power to a human, but I also can't imagine any other way by which he might have got it.'

'And, for the moment, I just watch?'

'You just watch. I want to hear every detail. We don't know what other surprises he may be capable of.'

'I'll get right to it.'

'There's one other thing. I want all this kept damped down. This man . . . what's his name?' He consulted the report. 'This man Gywann seems to fancy himself as some sort of prophet. If it gets out that he can work miracles, it could easily trigger some kind of religious crowd madness. God knows, the people are more than ready for something of the sort.'

'And you want it stopped.'

'Absolutely. It's the very last thing we need right now.'

Dole Euphest was thoughtful. 'Are you thinking that maybe this is part of the unfolding that the Wasps talked about?'

'I'm not ruling it out.'

One of the dozen or so talkies on the desk lit up signalling an incoming call. A flunkey picked it up. The Lady Mariko took it from him. She listened for a moment and then she looked at Trenhyass.

'It's the captain of the lower gate. It would appear that Kraymon has returned from the outlands.'

The Protector's eyebrows lifted. 'Kraymon?'

'Kraymon.'

'I want him here, right now. I don't want any of his excuses. I want him here immediately.' He glanced at the two Legates. 'Just stand where you are. In a few minutes you will have a chance to see the legendary Kraymon, right here in the flesh.'

Five

'AT DAWN she rose and left the judge's bed.

'She left the silks and furs and the satin pillows and the old man sleeping.

'She left the crystals and the hangings and the lines of leather law books, the wine spilled on the carpet and the gross act of his sleeping.

'She left the cloy of incense and the stench of his old, eager sweat.

'A servant let her out from the back of the house, through a small iron-studded door so low she had to stoop. It was a door all too perfect for shame.

'Into a morning that was both cold and clean and where a single bird sang mournfully for a new-dead mate, she stepped into a future that the past just made unthinkable.

'Into a morning with no comment on the long night's desperation, she stepped from dark of sacrifice to daylight condemnation.'

The Poet was rolling. If he could keep this up, there wouldn't be a dry eye in the house. There wouldn't be a dry eye or a closed purse.

'Blinking at the pale sun, she pulled her shawl close around her shoulders. She stooped under the weight of the thing that she'd done.

'Blinking at the pale sun, she stumbled, with eyes that had gone to that place of blankness somewhere on the other side of hate.

'Blinking, she refused to weep.

'She looked back once at the judge's house. One single look before she squared her shoulders and stiffened her spine. She had made her choice and she had done what had been needed. She couldn't bear the past; she could only trust the future.

'At a fork in the road she came upon a small crowd of people, silent and sombre faced, walking back in the direction of the town.

'She called out to one of them and caught him by the sleeve. "Please tell me, sir, what are so many of you doing walking here so early?"

'The man turned and looked her in the eye. "There was a hanging. A man was hanged before the dawn and we all came to witness!"

'"How could a man die before the dawn? It's contrary to custom."

'"The judge so ordered," the man replied.

'One hand of fear gripped her throat, the other sank cold fingers deep into her belly. She asked the question that she scarcely dared to ask.

'"Who was this man so cruelly hanged before the sunrise? What was his crime that he should be denied one final dawn?"

'"His name was Veris Di' and he died for the crime of sedition, although some of us see it as little more than speaking out."

'The judge had lied.

'The judge had cheated and deceived more cruelly than could be imagined.

'The judge had taken all she had to give with no intent to honour their bargain.

'The judge had taken all she had to give and hanged her lover, Veris Di'.'

All the Poet had to do was to roar to the end. Conversation had stopped. Even the drunks were watching him. 'Veris Di' and the Sacrifice of the Lady Emdial' always went down a storm. Vayim could practically feel the money in his pouch.

'The earth shook and the sky became like scorching flame. She thought of Veris Di' and his laughing eyes, his fireworks and the finality of his poetry. She thought of her lover Veris Di' and then she thought on the judge who'd slain him even as she lay with him, surrendering to his lying bargain.

'Liar Judge.

'Lecher Judge.

'Hanging Judge.

'Judge devoid of honour.

'She tore her gown, she tore her hair, she called aloud for all to hear.

'"Oh curse you, Judge, may you never again do what this night you did to me."

'"Seven times cursed, crawling, blind, cancers eating at your bones."

'"Seven times cursed, bleeding, burned, rotting flesh seared by

54

hot irons. Penniless and brought so low, scourged and chained in filth, rats eating at your bones, denied all justice, helpless, alone, voice cracked and pleading to be allowed to die."

'And as she cursed the judge he stirred, mouthing meaningless sounds from the depths of sleep. A cold had come into his house, a cold that swore never to leave, a cold cursed cold that haunts that room, and waits beside that bed that saw the deed.'

A swarthy, overdressed individual with gold hanging from his ears and a ruby set in his front tooth broke the momentary hush that hung in the air at the end of the poem and is always a sign that the poet had done well. A twenty-diem bounced ringingly on the flagstones. It was a flashy start to the poet's usual tribute. The swarthy, over-dressed individual could well afford the twenty, he owned one of the most notorious funhouses in all of the lowers. His entertainers were famed for their hardness of eye and swiftness of duplicity. It was unlikely that his generosity was rooted in his love of poetry. He had only been listening for the final third of the poem. The Poet was well aware that he'd probably only pushed to the front of the small crowd in order to flaunt his contribution, There was a certain kind of man who became a funhouse boss. They liked nothing more than showing off how much money they made. Vayim didn't mind. There was room in the Theatre for everyone. Particularly anyone who kicked off a poet's tribute with a fat twenty. There were nights when a poet didn't even make twenty. Vayim could tolerate being upstaged when it was done with money. He raised his eyebrows, grinned and nodded.

The twenty was followed by a handful of fives thrown by some not-so-high rollers whose pride it had touched, and a bunch of small change and applause that came from the poor folk. The Poet leaned forward and scooped up all the money. He always did well in the Theatre. It was, after all, the hub of the artists' quarter, the hub of all culture in the lowers. Even to merit a pitch in the Theatre a poet, musician, juggler or whatever, had to have already earned a certain reputation in the streets and the taverns. Another twenty dropped from above, hitting the flagstones with some force. Twenty feet in the air, a pair of fops, probably from the towers, hung in their flying-belts. Although they were applauding the Poet quite vigorously, there was something mocking in their attitude. They had the look of those who believed they were slumming. Jeen Vayim stopped and retrieved the coin with a flourish. What did he care? If they hung around too long and kept up that kind of behaviour, the more aggressive of the youth would undoubtedly pelt them with rocks and garbage. If nothing else, the lowers took care of themselves.

The Poet stepped down from the slightly tilted slab of rock that had served him as an impromptu stage. When you worked in the Theatre, you selected your spot with some care. The tilted slab had a shattered pillar behind it that not only gave great dramatic effect but also did a lot to reflect the voice. A slope of tower root reflected a blue light that added a certain level of intimate detachment to that particular nook. It was ideal for really working on a small, well-heeled crowd; in fact, it was the Poet's favourite kind of place. You could do the great classics with a soft, understated delivery that could bring the audience to both tears and generosity, particularly if you were on enough of a roll to hold the spot until the drinkers with money had become maudlin. In his final hour he had given them 'The Doom of Galifrey', 'The Vision of Ro-Aun' and of course, as a finale, 'Veris Di' and the Sacrifice of the Lady Emdial'. All three were violent tales of lust and betrayal in the grand manner. It continued to be the most favoured and lucrative mode. As a little light relief he had also included his own work, 'The Sorcerer's Clothes', a brief piece about an acolyte who borrows his master's clothes to wear to the tavern and impress a serving woman, and then discovers that the more he poses and postures, the more the clothes start to strangle him.

Off the rock, with the crowd melting away, Jeen Vayim stretched and took a deep satisfying breath. He was off, he had more money in his pouch than he expected and the rest of the night was his. If anyone had suggested that there was magic in the Theatre that night, he wouldn't have disagreed with them. He looked out across the great bowl with its crowds and moving lights. It was the place that he thought of as home. The actual structure of the Theatre was something of a mystery. There were those who maintained that it had once been a huge stadium with pillars supporting a massive roof. Others claimed that it was some long-abandoned industrial structure that had been destroyed by the Wasps just as they had destroyed most of human science, and what looked like pillars had some totally different function. The reality behind the theories was a wide shallow bowl with what indeed looked like shattered pillars jutting up at regular intervals. Between some of the pillars there was a complex of giant, irregular blocks of tumbled masonry. They formed a random jumble of tunnels, alleys, arches and areas of open space. Over the years that the city had had to do without sophisticated electronic media, the Theatre had become the traditional place where the street entertainers of the lowers could perform to a strolling, parading crowd.

A certain amount of everburn still clung to the ruins and it provided a soft basic glow. It was augmented by bonfires, and torches burning in cressets and even carried by revellers, and a number of continuously flaring gas burners. Their origin was also lost in antiquity and theory. Every so often, a firework maker would stage a demonstration of his wares. It all added a primitive excitement to the proceedings. It increased the illusion that it was a place of wizards and angels. On a more practical level the flames also helped to break up the fogs that tended to coil, snakelike, through the lowers when the nights were damp.

In among the crowd were a full complement of those who always arrive where large numbers of people are bent on enjoyment. While the entertainers maintained their own loose set of standards, there was no one to either deter or regulate the hundreds of pedlars, pitchmen, cutpurses, prostitutes, beggars, bellowing fanatics and the just plain insane. The Poet beat his way through the sometimes monstrously assorted press of humanity that trailed up and down the well-trodden paths and ruined stairs. The Poet had been working high up, near the rim of the great shattered bowl, and it was a considerable descent to the pitch of his favourite wineseller. He skirted the very edge of the moving crowd, risking fissures and jumbles of rubble that could trap the unwary into a broken bone or worse. It was the Poet's way of demonstrating that he was someone who knew the Theatre like the back of his hand, and how he was infinitely superior to a mere rubbernecking visitor.

He took three mugs, one straight after the other. Now his act was done, he needed to be one of the crowd again. He had to drink himself down from the tense elevation that poem-telling always gave him. When he was up there he twitched too much, he couldn't handle the faces in the crowd. There were too many of them, the guarded, the hostile, the vulnerable, the vacant and the searching; some lips laughed and others concealed sharp white teeth, some eyes flirted while others sought the danger that they were certain was concealed in this permanent carnival. If he didn't get himself down, he was liable to see too many predators and too many victims.

By the end of the second drink he was no longer intimidated by the painted eyes and the painted mouths and he no longer bled for the sob stories of beggars. After he'd swallowed the third he had his defences back, he'd achieved that pleasant blindness that made it all so much more sympathetic.

'You look like you're over the water.'

The eyes that were looking at him and the mouth that was talking to him were both painted to beat the band but at least they were familiar.

'Sulanda, my own precious love.'

'You are such a degenerate, Jeen Poet.'

'That's not bad coming from a woman whom half the world calls Dirty Sulanda.'

'You're a degenerate because you swallow a handful of toadfold and slide out those damn classics as smooth as silk, then you pick up twenty-diem pieces off sleazebag funbosses and yahoos from the towers, and run off and get drunk because it's all too much for you.'

There had once been a time when Jeen Vayim and Dirty Sulanda had been fairly constant lovers. Somehow it had slipped away without either of them really knowing why. Magic had given way to a derogatory warmth that led them to insulting each other with the accuracy that only comes from affection.

'What else would you expect me to do?'

'You know as well as I do that the stuff that you're writing is as good as the stuff that's being done by anyone who calls himself a Prismist or a Progressive.'

'That's because the Prismists and the Progressives are writing garbage.'

'That's what I mean. That bit you did about how the kid steals the sorcerer's clothes and then nearly gets strangled by his own vanity, you just tossed it away like it was a joke. That was a great telling. Why didn't you make something of it?'

The Poet could handle this kind of criticism that obliquely told him how good he was. He shrugged. 'I made out of it what it was. If it was as good as "The Doom of Galifrey", or it brought in the twenty-bits as good as "Effrael", then I'd make more of it, but it ain't "The Doom of Galifrey" and it don't make the money like "Effrael" and that's it. Hell, you know me. I don't want to try and ease my way into the towers with some kind of art shit.'

'So you stay in the lowers?'

'So I stay in the lowers. You're not dumb, Sulanda. You know what every performer thinks about. We've never really been troubled by Wasps down here but it's always in the back of everyone's mind. If you really start to rant, if you start to shout it all out, are you going to get your head sucked? That's why we have to put up with something like the fucking Prismists. It's a way by which they think they'll get round that fear. I say stick with the classics, we're a conquered species.'

'You don't really believe that.'

'Of course I do. It happens to be true.' A teasing glint came into his eye. 'Your trouble is you're a whore with a heart of gold. It blinds you to reality.'

It was Sulanda's turn to shrug. 'There's one who's not afraid to rant.'

The Poet pursed his lips and nodded. 'Oh yes, our golden-boy prophet. From what I hear, he's not afraid of anything.'

'He's playing in one of the lower basins tonight.'

'Playing?'

'What else is it?'

'I haven't seen him lately.'

'You still grieving for that holy bimbo?'

'Nobody seems to believe me that it's nothing to do with Messila. I don't like Gywann or any of his gang.'

'It's growing, too.'

'That's what I mean. It wasn't only what happened at Denhagel's. Even when I was bedding Messila, there was always something that didn't seem quite right.'

'But she helped distract you?'

'There you go again. All you women instinctively distrust him, too. Only he's so cute you have to put it on the women. You never even trusted the original bunch. You all acted as jealous as hell. Normally you wouldn't have cared but subconsciously you knew something was wrong and it came out in jealousy and snide remarks.'

'We didn't sense any damn thing. They were just such bimbos.'

They stopped at another wineseller's cart. Sulanda swallowed nearly half a mug in one gulp. She looked at Jeen Vayim with sadness in her eyes. 'What the hell went wrong with us, Poet?'

Vayim couldn't for the life of him think of an answer. For a while they strolled in silence, letting the Theatre swirl around them. They paused to watch a sprightly, four-piece reed band that was filling the air around it with a jigtime sense of wellbeing. When their charm started to fade Vayim and Sulanda moved on. The Poet could take only so much high-pitched jollity. Sulanda was walking slightly in front of Vayim. She was dressed in tight black breeches of some shiny, black, stretch material, high boots and a loose black tunic. The Poet caught himself watching the sway of her hips. The motion started a train of thought which clearly indicated that the embers of what had once been between them weren't completely cold. He quickened his pace, caught up with her and grinned. She looked at him quizzically. 'What are you smiling at?'

'I was just thinking.'

'Thinking what?'

The knowing look in her eyes hinted that she didn't really have to ask. Vayim winked. 'Just thinking.'

They started across a flat, fallen span that served to bridge a rocky fissure. Without accurate history, it was again only possible to guess at the awesome forces that had once torn at the roots of the city. Halfway across the less-than-secure bridge, a troupe of bodydancers with luridly painted faces pranced and contorted past them. The antics of one particularly exuberant dancer almost spilled the Poet onto the rocks below. The fall would not only undoubtedly have killed him but also quite possibly have injured one of the many couples who had taken candles and blankets and created snug lovenests for themselves in among the broken slabs of masonry. Vayim cursed after the painted fool. He had always had a very low opinion of bodydancers both as a breed and an artform.

Vayim cursed again when they reached the other end of the bridge. A number of women in long white dresses and with garlands in their hair were moving through the crowd, handing flowers to passers-by. When anyone accepted the offered flower they let themselves in for a low-voiced, smiling sales pitch. The Poet had no doubt at all that they were followers of Gywann. The number of the boy prophet's disciples had doubled and redoubled since the Poet had divorced himself from the cult. As religions went, Gywann was very successful. Where once the followers had been a mere half-dozen, some estimates now ran as high as two hundred. Gywann was starting to make his mark in the lowers. Even the normally aloof funbosses had taken to eyeing his tribe of adoring women and speculating out loud about exactly what his secret was. One of the faithful appeared to have selected Vayim and Sulanda as possible targets and was homing in on them. The Poet put a hand on Sulanda's elbow. 'Let's avoid this, shall we?'

'We might as well hear what she's got to sell.'

'It's only Gywann's bunch.'

'What harm can it do?'

The Poet wasn't exactly happy, but he didn't want to make an issue out of it. He felt too good about the prospect of spending the rest of the night with Sulanda.

'Okay, suit yourself.'

The woman in the white robe positioned herself in front of them. Her expression was one of beaming meekness, but she was quite effectively blocking their path. She handed a small white flower to the Poet.

'Please say you'll come and hear our master speak. He's holding a meeting in the lower basin tonight.'

Vayim tried to hand back the flower. 'I don't think so.'

The woman deftly avoided taking it. 'Many people find great comfort in our master's words.'

'I do okay on my own.'

'If you just heard him one time . . .'

'I did.' His expression took on a hint of devilment. 'I was once a friend of Messila. You know Messila?'

The woman looked a little awed. 'Messila is one of the original circle. I don't understand . . .'

Sulanda took the flower from Vayim's hand. 'Don't worry about him, honey. He's a hopeless case. We'll come and see your boy do his stuff.'

'I would be so . . .'

'You just run along and try to find yourself some other converts.'

With a start of relief, Gywann's follower almost leaped away from Sulanda and the Poet. She looked around wildly and immediately buttonholed another pair, a blowsy, middle-aged woman and a particularly epicene young man. Jeen Vayim sniffed the flower and shook his head. 'He really has them working their buns off for him. You think he beats them if they don't come home with enough converts? It's no wonder the funbosses are looking at him with such fish eyes. I'm wondering how long it's going to be before a few of them start joining up.'

Sulanda seemed a little awed herself. 'Can you imagine how much money he must be pulling in? I mean, look at the people heading down for the lower basin. Those girls have really done a job.'

She pointed to the stairs that led to the lower basins. A steady flow of people was moving out of the Theatre and down. 'Are we going to see what he's getting up to? It's got to be spectacular to get these results.'

'Do we have to?'

'You're really not interested? Not even on a professional level? Maybe it's not just the funbosses who're getting fish eyed.'

The Poet got impatient. 'When is anybody going to listen to me? There's something wrong about Gywann and his whole setup.'

'But you won't tell anyone what.'

'I don't know what.'

'So come and see him. Maybe it will come to you.'

Vayim made a helpless gesture. 'I'd really rather stay up here and get drunk.'

'I'll make it worth your while.'

Vayim raised his arms in submission, wrists together as if he was ready to be handcuffed and led away. 'If you're that determined.'

The lower basins were shallow oval bowls, directly below the main bowl of the Theatre. They radiated outwards like the petals of a great stone flower. Each of them could hold some eight hundred or so people although many, like parts of the Theatre itself, were damaged to the point where they were of no use except as a natural maze for those who wanted a secluded place to make love. The basin that Gywann had chosen, however, was almost perfectly preserved. It was marred only by one, long, diagonal fissure and a network of smaller cracks. It was ideal for conversion to a simple, makeshift theatre. There was nothing makeshift, though, about what Gywann's people had done. A large stage had been erected at the far end of the basin. It was complete with a bank of overhead sun-guns and acoustic pressure horns. On the stage, a twenty-piece female choir in the uniform white robes was warming the growing crowd with a lilting, wordless chant. They flanked a raised podium from which Gywann himself would presumably address the assembly. His operation had grown almost beyond recognition since the Poet had seen it last. As he looked around at the setup, he shook his head in disbelief.

'Who the hell is bankrolling all this?'

Sulanda also seemed surprised at how elaborate it had all become but she had a ready answer to the money question. 'If all those vacant bimbos bring in the cash as hard and as fast as they bring in the recruits, he doesn't need bank-rolling.'

The Poet was bemused. He hadn't expected anything so outrageous.

'I don't believe it. He's built himself a perfect, self-sustaining machine. He can't be stopped like this.'

'Are you jealous?'

'Of course I'm jealous. Who wouldn't want this? If it's not the most ambitious piece of theft that I've ever seen, it's something so totally weird that I don't really want to think about it.'

Vayim and Sulanda climbed up the inclined edge of the basin for a better view. The area directly in front of the stage was packed with the truly faithful who stood transfixed and waiting. Many of them were dressed in white and were holding torches, adding a seasoning of anticipation and expectancy to the singing. There was also a new variety of the truly faithful, one that the Poet hadn't seen before. Young men in a rough uniform of black leather sleeveless vests, matching wristbands and black breeches clustered in gangs at strategic points on both sides of the stage.

'He's even got his own goon squad.'

'There goes my idea.'

The Poet looked at Sulanda. 'What idea?'

She laughed. 'I was wondering if we could steal the night's take.'

They reached a spot where it was possible to sit on the rim of the basin and see the stage over the heads of the crowd. Vayim leaned back on his elbows.

'They usually like to keep you waiting at things like this. I wish we'd brought some wine.'

In fact, the Poet was wrong. Quite suddenly the sun-guns flared and the horns began to thrum and woof. The crowd fell silent. The singing swelled and rose in pitch. It picked up a tempo that wasn't too far removed from sexual excitement. Then, suddenly, it all stopped. The sun-guns became white hot. There was a gasp, a kind of mass sigh from the faithful. As if from nowhere, Gywann appeared on the podium. He, too, was wearing a white robe but he also had a gold collar of some sort hung around his neck, though it was too far away for the Poet to see exactly what it was. All he knew was that it flashed in the light. Gywann slowly raised his arms above his head. An intense hush fell over the crowd. He remained motionless for four long beats, then his voice rolled out from the horns with a powerful resonance.

'The palace had become a place of sorrow. The windows and doors that the Kings and Queens had closed against the Black Strangers had also shut out the sun and the wind. The children were born pale with wide, staring eyes. Their skin was translucent and lined with a tracery of blue. Their blood was as thin as their tears. They looked neither up nor down.' His voice had become very quiet. It was as though Gywann was whispering softly in the Poet's ear. Vayim knew that it must be a trick of the amplification, but he still found it disturbing. *'They neither saw the sun nor felt the wind. They had never known the look of a flower or the feel of the rain in their hair. They were the White Children and they couldn't comprehend the meaning of freedom.'*

He allowed the crowd a long pause. Almost visible devotion flowed toward the stage. Abruptly, his voice boomed from the horns. *'The White Children!'*

There was a murmur in the crowd. Vayim leaned toward Sulanda. 'This is very different from what he used to do on the street.'

'The White Children.' Gywann's voice fell away into a strong but tuneless crooning. *'The poor White Children.'*

'The poor White Children.

'Crouched in the darkness.

'Always in darkness.'

The choir came in behind him with well-rehearsed harmonics.

'*Always in darkness.*
'*Always in darkness.*'

Despite himself, the Poet found that he was nodding in time. A wave of synthetic sadness was creeping over him. It forced an admission from him. 'It's very slick. It's very slick indeed.'

Sulanda was cradling her head in her hands. Her voice was sleepily wistful. 'I think it's beautiful. It makes me want to cry. And I don't want you to laugh at me if I do cry and I don't want you to call me a whore with a heart of gold. It's not funny any more. I don't want to be called a whore.'

For some reason, Jeen Vayim felt terrible, rejected and alone. He looked back at the stage. Gywann seemed to be beckoning to him and offering comfort. Half the crowd had joined in a gentle, swaying dance. The Poet felt himself jostled from behind. A squat, matronly woman was pushing forwards, moving to the unstated rhythm. Her eyes were fixed upon the figure on the stage. She was sweating but she scarcely seemed to notice. There was a desperation about her need to get nearer to Gywann. She breathlessly mouthed the words of the chant.

'*Lonely White Children.*
'*Frightened White Children.*
'*Lonely White Children.*
'*Frightened White Children.*'

Gywann was speaking again. '*A Friend arrived at the Palace. He had come down the road that wound its way from out of the mountains. The Black Strangers who stood at the door of the Palace didn't notice the coming of the Friend. The Friend was unafraid of the Black Strangers and they couldn't perceive him. The Black Strangers could only see fear.*'

The voices of the choir rose in pitch. '*The Black Strangers can only see fear.*'

'*Fear!*'
'*The Black Strangers can only see fear.*'
'*Fear!*'

Something seemed to be loose among the crowd. They no longer swayed in time. Now they nodded and stamped their feet. Whatever Gywann was creating in the basin had taken on a serious urgency. Jeen Vayim felt something wet running down his leg. The shock jerked him loose from Gywann's almost hypnotic hold. He glanced down in confusion. It was a stream of red wine that came from the leather flask of a stout, red-faced wineseller. He was grinning like a maniac and bouncing up and down on the balls of his feet. As he bounced, he uttered short, involuntary grunts. In his absorption he had let the nozzle of the wineskin drop below the level of the bag and the liquid was running out onto the ground and onto the Poet.

'You're pissing away your night's profit there, friend.'

The man was deaf to his warning. What the hell was going on here? Had everyone gone crazy?

'Fear!'

'Fear!'

Jeen Vayim had lifted the nozzle of the wineskin and, after taking a surreptitious drink, tried to press it back into the man's hand. He still didn't respond. Then something dark and oppressive seemed to descend on the bowl.

'Fear!'

'Fear!'

Jeen Vayim couldn't pretend that he didn't feel it. It was dark, cold and dangerous and pressed down, trying to surround and engulf the crowd. The hairs on the back of his neck stood on end and cold chills chased each other up and down his spine.

'Fear!'

'Fear!'

And then, miraculously, the dark danger began to lift, as though forced back by the chanting.

'Don't fear the Stranger and the Stranger won't see you.'

'Don't fear the Stranger and the Stranger can't harm you.'

'Fear! Fear!'

Vayim whispered to Sulanda, 'This isn't just craziness, it's getting damn close to sedition.'

'I think he's magnificent.'

Sulanda's voice was breathy, almost hoarse. Vayim couldn't believe that she was being taken in by all this. She wasn't some half-starved dullard who'd follow any persuasive rogue who offered a promise of salvation and better times. Sulanda was tough, cynical and smart as a whip. If she hadn't been, she'd never have survived the process of growing up on her own in the lowers. It was as though Gywann was able to hook directly into her mind. She seemed unable to take her eyes off the stage. Her expression was a combination of heavy-eyed lust and religious adoration, like an angel hot for her god. Her index finger unconsciously traced a pattern up and down her thigh. On the stage, the chant went on and on, picking up speed and rising in volume.

'*Fear! Fear!*'

'*Waah!*'

'*Fear! Fear!*'

'*Waaah!*'

The crowd was trying to bellow away its own ills and the ills of the world. The Poet could feel what was going on, but there was no way that he could become a part of it, even though there was something inside him that ached to submerge itself in whatever was happening. Something else inside him backed away, suspecting that if he didn't he might never surface again.

'*Fear! Fear! Fear! Fear!*'

The wineseller was making strange signs with his fingers. Over on the other side of the crowd a small knot of people had surged forward, threatening to crush those in front of them. There were some noises of panic, but once again no one took any notice. The piece of Jeen Vayim that refused to become transfixed tried to work out what Gywann was doing. It was certainly much more than a mere trick. Originally, he had thought that the influence Gywann seemed able to exert worked more strongly on women. It was an idea that didn't hold too much water. The wineseller appeared to have lost not only his mind but his reason, and the young men in black vests were dancing as hard as any of the women in white.

'*Fear! Fear! Fear! Fear!*'

If Gywann's handmaidens had been passing something around, some sort of ceremonial food or drink, water, wine or what-have-you, Vayim would have been certain that Gywann was doing it all with a chemical mood-modifier. There was nothing, however, that the Poet knew about that could change the mood of a crowd of this size from a distance.

'It's just knee jerk nonsense, you realise this?'

Sulanda ignored him. Jeen Vayim wasn't even sure if she'd heard him. Abruptly, on some cue that Vayim was quite unable to detect, the chant stopped. There was a loaded silence. Then Gywann's voice came like a roar. The sun-guns swung upwards, sending probing fingers of light up towards the towers.

'We have nothing to fear!'

The crowd reacted to the words as though they were a physical shock. Sulanda jerked. Her finger dug into her leg.

'There is no need to be afraid. There is no need to be frightened or alone. We are all one in the warmth of our freedom. No one need be cold and lonely any more.'

A large tear was rolling down Sulanda's cheek. She made no attempt to wipe it away.

'We will drive out our fears. We will drive out our loneliness. We will drive out the cold.'

The choir came in behind him.

'We will drive out the Black Strangers. We will drive out the cold. We will throw open the doors and the windows and let in the sun. We will welcome our friends with love.'

Both the crowd and the choir echoed the last word, lingering over it as though they relished its very taste.

'Loooove.'

The Poet muttered under his breath. 'This is ridiculous.'

Gywann hadn't quite finished. *'We will replace fear with love and we will welcome our friends. We will come in from out of the cold and let in the sun. We will welcome all of our friends. Our love will be the great unfolding.'*

Another shudder seemed to run through the crowd. It was like a long, lingering sigh. The sun-guns swivelled back to the horizontal. Gywann again raised his arms. The choir hit a long high note. The lights slowly dimmed. The choir went down with them. Voices in the crowd could be heard, begging and pleading for Gywann to tell them more, for him to stay with them, not to leave them, but Gywann was already gone, away in the darkness with the young men in the black vests ranked around him. Jeen Vayim stood up, stretching his cramped stiffening legs. He offered a hand to Sulanda and helped her to her feet. She seemed dazed, tears streaming uncontrollably down her face.

'Are you aware you're crying?'

Sulanda blinked. 'Huh?'

'What's happened to you?'

Sulanda stumbled slightly, she hung on to Vayim's arm for support. 'I . . . I don't know. It was all so beautiful.'

'Are you okay?'

Sulanda straightened up. She pulled a handkerchief from her sleeve, wiped her eyes and blew her nose. Her strength seemed to be coming back.

'Yeah . . . I think so. Wasn't that the most wonderful thing you ever saw? It was so sad when he finished. I wanted it to go on all night.'

'You wanted *what* to go on all night? What exactly did he do?'

'Didn't you feel it?'

'I felt something, but I'm not sure what.' The Poet looked round at the crowd. It seemed unwilling to disperse. At least two-thirds of those in the bowl were as stunned as Sulanda, waiting around as though hoping for more. Some were shaking, others weeping beyond control. 'I certainly didn't feel it like you and the rest of these people. What was happening to you just now?'

Sulanda shook her head. She was clearly confused. 'I don't know . . . I can't put it into words. All I know is that he touched me, deep inside somewhere. I've never been touched like that before. He made me feel new and clean and alive. He made me feel . . . powerful.'

'But that's ridiculous. He really didn't say anything. He's got something but I swear it isn't real. It's all flash and gimmick and mob hysteria. He can whip it up, but what's he whipping it up for? What does he *want*? All I know is that I don't trust him.'

Sulanda was outraged. 'How the hell could you say a thing like that? Haven't you any soul?'

'About the only thing he said was that we ought to get rid of the Wasps. Even oblique as it was, it's a dumb thing to do.'

Sulanda's eyes went cold, moving towards angry.

'You're so fucking jealous, Jeen Vayim. You can't see any good in anything!'

Her anger took the Poet by complete surprise. It was as unnatural as her previous ecstasy.

'Wait a minute . . .'

Sulanda had turned and was starting to walk away. Jeen Vayim stepped quickly after her. He caught hold of her elbow. 'Will you just wait a minute? I don't understand what's going on here.'

Sulanda shook herself free. Now she was furious. 'Will you take your fucking hands off me!'

'What is going on?'

They walked angrily side by side. The crowd, realising that Gywann wasn't going to return to the stage, was starting to drift away. Women disciples with begging bowls had moved to cover every possible way out. Each one was backed up by one of the young men, presumably to deter anyone from the idea of redistributing the offering, or taking rather than giving. They had clubs and cudgels stuck ostentatiously in their belts. The Poet found this a little over-threatening for a religion. As they started up the steps that led back to the Theatre, one of the faithful moved in on them.

'Alms, please. Alms to continue our master's . . . Jeen Vayim!'

'Messila.'

The Poet had been hoping that this wouldn't happen. She threw her arms around his neck.

'You came back to listen to the master again. Oh, Jeen Vayim, you don't know how happy this makes me.'

Sulanda glared at the Poet. 'I wouldn't celebrate too soon, honey. He didn't like it too much.'

Messila stepped back as if she'd been stung. 'You didn't like it?'

Messila's escort, the young man in the black vest, was starting to look unhappy. He was nervously running a length of chain through his hands. His movements were not unlike those of an agitated guard dog that isn't quite sure if it's time to snarl yet.

'What's going on here?'

Sulanda smiled sourly. 'Just a little reunion.'

Messila was still shocked. 'You saw it and you didn't like it?'

The young man was now looking hard at the Poet. At least he knew in which direction to snarl. Vayim didn't like the look of the length of chain. It was too easy to imagine it biting into his scalp. Sulanda continued to scowl at him. 'He doesn't like anything these days. He claims he has these feelings.'

Messila looked increasingly desolate. Sulanda took pity on her. 'If it's any consolation I thought it was really beautiful.'

Messila's face lit up. 'You did?'

Sulanda began to thaw. 'It was one of the most beautiful things I've ever seen.'

'You mean that?'

'I was crying and I didn't even know it.'

'I'm so glad for you. You will come and see the master again, won't you?'

'Of course I will.'

Jeen Vayim was starting to think that everyone had forgotten about him, except of course the young man with the chain, when Messila suddenly took hold of both his and Sulanda's arms.

'I have a marvellous idea. Why don't you come with me now and meet the master. I'm sure he wouldn't mind. He'd be pleased to see you again, Jeen Vayim; he has a special love for those who were there at the start.'

'I . . .'

Before he could form an answer, Sulanda was almost pleading. 'Could we really meet him?'

Vayim couldn't believe this. What had Gywann done to the woman? 'You met him before. He used to practically live at Denhagel's.'

'It was different then.'

'How?'

'I don't want to talk to you.'

'You will come and meet the master, won't you?'

The Poet shook his head. 'I don't think so. I don't think I could deal with any more tonight.'

Sulanda had no such doubts. 'I want to meet him.'

'I thought you and me were . . .'

'I'm going with Messila, Vayim. I'm sure you can manage on your own.'

Arm in arm, Messila and Sulanda started to walk away. They were quite a contrast, Messila in flowing white and Sulanda in tight black. The young man prowled after them. The Poet was left on his own. The crowd had gone; only a couple of drunks were left and a handful of dopey-looking kids who seemed not to want to leave. A crew of young men in black were breaking down the sun-guns and the pressure horns. The basin had that desolate look of any auditorium when the show's over. An eddying breeze swirled paper and other debris in circular patterns. The Poet suddenly felt cold. He kicked a bottle. It spun and clattered across the stones.

'Damn!'

One of the young men looked around but seemed to assume the Poet was just a left-over drunk. Vayim looked around for something else to kick.

'Goddamn it!'

He had started out looking forward to a wild night of reunion with Sulanda and he'd finished up being dumped in favour of a phoney religion. To add injury to insult, it was a long climb to his next mug of wine. He blamed Gywann for everything. He was starting to hate the so-called prophet. He looked around for something else to kick.

'Goddamn it to hell!'

Six

SHAFIK KRAYMON smelled bad. Fastidiousness was something a man tended to forget during six months in the outlands. He was also in a foul temper. There were a lot of things he wanted far more from civilisation at that moment than an audience with Protector Trenhyass. He wanted a hot meal, a hot bath, a willing woman and a few days lolling around in a friendly tavern in the lowers. He wanted out of the greasy buckskins that he'd lived in for half a year and he wanted a barber to take off his full growth of beard and the hair that was now halfway to his waist and providing a home to God knew what. He had little time for the rich and powerful. In fact, he had little time for humanity in general. That was one of the reasons that he had chosen his largely solitary way of life. Unfortunately, the rich and the powerful always had time for him. They also had their armed lackeys to make sure that he satisfied their needs before he satisfied his own.

Kraymon was so much in demand because Kraymon was unique. Where all but a scattered few of the human race were penned up in the three giant cities that constituted the Protectorate, Kraymon wandered at will across the outlands. There were other wanderers in the outlands, but they weren't able to get into the cities. Kraymon and only Kraymon was able to penetrate the sanitary cordon with which the Wasps had surrounded the cities after the plague and the relocation. There were many who viewed his ability to move from city to open plain, apparently undetected by the Wasps, with a good deal of suspicion. Some even voiced the idea that he might be some kind of Wasp agent. He was, however, such an invaluable source of information about what went on beyond the cordon that he was always in urgent demand at the highest levels and kept safe from all threats. The way that the Protector and the Proprietors watched over Kraymon while he was in the city was largely unnecessary. He cared little for the opinion of his fellow-men and it would take a brave person indeed to threaten him physically. He was close to being a giant.

Shafik Kraymon was a subject of legend on all levels of the city but even the most fanciful versions were hardly any preparation for the awesome, larger-than-life reality. He was a huge bear of a man who stood a full head taller than the tallest in the room. He had broad, powerful shoulders and the kind of hands that could break furniture without effort. On one hip a large, leaf-bladed knife hung in a fringed sheath. On the other, in a well-worn holster, was an enormous, four-barrelled cap-and-ball gun. Everything about Kraymon was truly formidable.

He stalked into the Audience Chamber two paces in front of an escort of Killers who almost had to run to keep up with him. The assembled dignitaries had been watching the door expectantly after word had gone round that Kraymon was coming. When the doors had flown open, they'd instinctively moved forward to greet and to look, but with the first sight of the man from the outlands many recoiled; some quickly stepped back and one particularly vocal wife of a Proprietor stifled a small scream with a silk handkerchief. It was as though a wild animal had prowled, snarling, into the chamber.

His anger carried him all the way to the Protector's desk. Trenhyass came to his feet and extended a hand in greeting.

'So, Shafik Kraymon, you have returned from the outlands. With news, I hope.'

Kraymon ignored the hand. 'Nothing so important that I needed to be dragged here before I've had time to either eat, sleep or collect myself.'

'Still hostile as ever, Kraymon?'

'I don't like cities, Trenhyass. I particularly don't like the time I spend in them being wasted like this.'

The Protector smiled. He wasn't used to being called 'Trenhyass' to his face. 'You'd rather be drinking and whoring?'

'That I would.' Kraymon turned and surveyed the gathered notables. 'You weren't surrounding yourself with this gang of thieves, fops and overpriced strumpets the last time I was here. Are you going soft as you get older?'

Every eye in the chamber was on him. There was some shocked muttering that this wildman should talk to the Protector in such a way. The Protector himself, however, didn't seem in the least perturbed.

'Even I have to observe certain amenities.'

'Not with me you don't.'

The Protector laughed. 'You're probably right.' He signalled to the Killers of his personal guard. 'Clear the room.'

The Lady Mariko was outraged. 'What do you mean, clear the room? It took me weeks to put this audience together.'

'At the moment, Kraymon here is the most important person in the city and I want to talk to him alone.'

'And what do I tell our guests?'

'I'm sure you'll think of something.'

'You're impossible.'

'I'm allowed to be, I run the world.' He turned his attention to Dole Euphest. 'I want you to stay.'

'Whatever you say.'

Once the protesting dignitaries had been ushered out with a limited courtesy that was the best the Killers could muster, Trenhyass addressed himself to Kraymon.

'Are there any changes in the outlands?'

Kraymon's eyes narrowed. 'There's some. Have there been changes in the city, then?'

The Protector ignored the question. 'What kind of changes?'

Kraymon raised a large gnarled hand. Its skin was the colour of old mahogany. 'You're too fast and too anxious for me, Trenhyass. You're talking to a man who's been spending his times with rocks and clouds. The mannerly thing would be to sit me down and give me a drink and let me tell it in my own time. I know you keep the best booze in the city in your own private stock.'

Trenhyass shook his head as though he was surprised at his own behaviour. 'I'm sorry.'

'Are you succumbing to the stress, Trenhyass?'

'Maybe. Maybe I just have things my own way too much of the time.'

Dole Euphest watched the exchange impassively. The Protector touched the hidden control set in the desk. The door slid open in the wall behind it. Trenhyass motioned for Euphest and Kraymon to follow him into his concealed sanctuary. It was a sparse, almost spartan room, little more than a cell. The walls were without windows or decoration. The only concessions to comfort were the lingering smell of pipesmoke and three very old and worn leather chairs.

Beyond these, there was nothing but a practical work table, with orderly piles of paper and a single talkie, and a large bookcase that covered most of one wall.

Trenhyass unfastened his collar and motioned at two of the chairs. Clearly, all formality had been put aside. He produced a bottle of pre-invasion schnapps and three glasses. He filled them, then he settled himself and began the ritual of filling and lighting his pipe. Kraymon picked up his glass and swallowed the spirit in one gulp. He threw his head back and closed his eyes. Then he coughed. 'That's the one thing you really miss in the outlands.' He unhitched the wide belt that carried his two weapons and hung it over the back of one of the chairs, then he sat down. Dole Euphest seated himself in the third chair. Trenhyass refilled the wildman's glass, sat back and waited. Kraymon also downed this in one. His eyes stayed closed for a full minute, then his face cracked and he grinned at the Protector.

'So, you want to know about the outlands bad enough that you'll keep me from my bath and a soft bed.'

'I think you've made your point.'

'And you want me to get on with it.'

'Indeed I do.'

Kraymon glanced sideways at the Protector. 'Does the usual financial arrangement stand?'

Trenhyass began to lose patience. 'Damn it, man, you know it does.'

Kraymon poured himself a third drink. 'Well, I doubt you want to hear how the game and the wildlife have come back now we're no longer there. You probably also aren't busting a gut to hear that the boojies are also spreading and that they've taken to digging burrows in the dirt. I've thought about that but it doesn't tell me a damn thing about their home planet. There's also some new alien thing running around. It's like a lump of bright green garbage about the size of a dinner plate that kind of squirts itself along the ground. I've thought about it, there's always the chance that they're boojies in another stage of development. The animals and the birds give them both a wide berth.'

'I want to hear about the Wasps.'

Kraymon nodded. 'Right. What else?'

'So?'

'Well, Mr Protector, sir. You know as well as I do that without exception it's damn near impossible to be sure what the Wasps are up to, but as far as I can tell they seem to be closing ranks.'

The Protector raised an eyebrow. 'Closing ranks?'

'Let me give you an example. You remember I told you about those people that the Wasps turned loose in this canyon without clothes or tools or anything, and how these two Wasps were living nearby in one of those white domes, seemingly monitoring them?'

Trenhyass nodded. 'I remember.'

'I was thinking that it might be some kind of study, an anthropological experiment or such like.'

'I do recall.'

'Well, the Wasps have gone. They packed up their dome and they moved on.'

'What about the people?'

'They're still there. At least, some of them are. A lot of them died during the winter, but the survivors are living in a cave.'

'Have you talked to them?'

Kraymon shook his head. 'Hell no! I can't get near them. I've tried, but when they see me coming they take off like rabbits. If they don't want to socialise, I'm not going to make an issue of it.'

'What other examples have you seen of this closing of ranks?'

'It's happening all over. There was a time when bunches of Wasps were everywhere, going about their inexplicable business. Now they've gone. They left the outlands to me and frezets and the coyotes.'

'Where have they gone?'

Kraymon drained his glass. 'I couldn't say for sure. My guess is that they've withdrawn to that colony around the big ship, way out on the high plains. A second ship came down there.'

'Another big ship?'

'Pretty much the same as the first one, only it hasn't off-loaded or anything. It just seems to be sitting there.'

The Protector was thoughtful. 'You have a theory about this?'

Kraymon shrugged. 'Maybe. The best interpretation that I can put on it is that they've pulled in the civilians.'

Kraymon again reached for the bottle. 'Look at it this way. If we go along with your theory that what we have is some sort of garrison, an outpost in some huge galactic war, then it's possible to suppose that the Wasps who were running around the outlands were scientists of some kind. They'd ride along with the military but their real job is to study occupied planets.'

Trenhyass didn't look convinced. 'That's making one hell of a parallel to human behaviour.'

'It's possible, though. They must have specialists that are broadly similar to human scientists. Or what used to be scientists.'

'And you think that these studies have been terminated.'

'Or suspended.'

'Why would they do that?'

'It'd be nice to believe it was because they were about to move out but somehow I don't think so. I'm sorry to tell you this, but I think they're expecting trouble.'

'You don't seriously imagine that they're expecting trouble from us, do you?'

Kraymon laughed. 'Hell no. I don't think they hardly notice us.'

'But they're still expecting trouble?'

'All I'm telling you is that it looks like they're pulling the wagons into a circle.'

'But why?'

'Perhaps they've heard the enemy is nearby.'

Trenhyass and Euphest both looked at him hard.

'Enemy?'

'The enemy in the supposed galactic war.'

There was a long silence. Trenhyass looked acutely unhappy. 'I feel my theory coming back on me.'

Kraymon was stonefaced. 'You have to admit that it all hangs together. It's all too plausible.'

'If you're right, it could easily be the end of us all, the whole human race.'

Kraymon chuckled. He didn't seem particularly concerned. 'One thing you learn in the outlands is not to worry about things you can't do anything about.'

The Protector stood up and walked to the desk. 'I need to think about this.'

Kraymon and Euphest also got to their feet. Euphest regarded the wildman. 'I've got one question before you go.'

'And what might that be?'

'What about you, Shafik Kraymon? Where do you fit into all this? How is it that you alone can come and go at will? How do you manage to get close enough to spy on their installations? Most everyone else who tried it, imploded.'

Kraymon stroked his beard. His expression wasn't pleasant. 'That sounds like four questions to me.'

'One answer will do.'

Kraymon sighed. 'It also sounds like the old story about me being a Wasp spy. You know that's a load of shit better than anyone. How the hell could anyone spy for the Wasps? You're the only people on the planet who even attempt to work for them. I don't know why they leave me alone. Maybe I'm a freak, maybe there's something about me that blocks their perception. Maybe it's just that I smell so bad. The only sure thing is that they leave me alone and I thank whatever gods there might be left for that alone.'

'Is that the best you can do? You must have thought about it at some length.'

A vein in Kraymon's forehead started to throb. 'Sure I've thought about it. What the fuck do you think I think about, damn it? I particularly think about how one day it may stop or run out or whatever and I'll find I've got jelly for a head. The best I can come up with is that maybe I don't think human, maybe I think more like an animal. They don't bother the animals, either. That's another reason why I don't like hanging around with you people. You might humanise me.'

There was a long pause, then Dole Euphest spoke as though the outburst had never happened. 'You do believe they read our thoughts, though.'

Kraymon gritted his teeth, visibly bringing himself under control. When he spoke, his voice was calm and measured. 'I've always reckoned something of the sort. Maybe not our actual thoughts, but I figure they can scan our moods. How else would they know when they're being threatened?'

Trenhyass sighed. 'The more you learn about them, the less you understand.'

Kraymon scratched himself. 'Are you both done with me? Can I finally take a bath?'

As he spoke, the talkie on the desk lit up. Euphest glanced at the Protector. 'Should I answer that?'

'Please.'

He picked it up, listened for a few seconds and then put it down again. 'Talet Heizen is on his way here and he seems to be quite agitated about something.'

'Talet Heizen is always agitated about something.'

Kraymon raised an eyebrow. 'You still distrust your chief of Killers?'

The Protector made a dismissive gesture. 'Who should I distrust more? After me, he's the most powerful man in the Protectorate.'

'Does this mean that my bath is going to have to wait?'

'I'm sure when Heizen sees you, he'll have something to say to you.'

Kraymon grunted. 'He's another one who thinks I'm a Wasp agent.'

They waited for the Marshal of Killers in the main Audience Chamber. Trenhyass saw no reason to let the man who was overtly after his position into his private sanctuary. Heizen made his entrance through the wide, ceremonial double doors. He had six of his private Killer guard at his back, the elite Iron Fist unit. The gesture was a subtly threatening signal. Trenhyass knew that if it ever came to an open rift between himself and the leader of the Killers, the Iron Fists would undoubtedly side with their Marshal. On the odd occasions that Heizen needed a favour from the Protector, he invariably came on his own.

Talet Heizen, the Marshal of Killers, was a man who was devoid of all warmth; he had none of the fallibility that makes someone human. His expression was so uniformly bleak that it was almost no expression at all. His hair was white, and his eyes were a deep, penetrating blue. They had the same implacable quality as the eyes of a reptile. He was only the minimum regulation height for a Killer, but his rigid will maintained his body in perfect condition even though it was starting to ease into middle age.

He came across the pink marble floor with the urgent walk of a man who is approaching the end of his patience.

'You would be well advised to think in terms of permanent solution to this business in the lowers, Protector Trenhyass.'

Trenhyass faced him calmly. 'What particular business would this be, Marshal Heizen?'

The Iron Fists formed a black-clad line behind their leader.

'The matter of the man Gywann.'

'I didn't know you were responsible for the surveillance of the man Gywann and his followers. I seem to recall that I put Euphest here in charge of the problem.'

Heizen permitted himself a thin, humourless smile. 'Then

he will doubtless have told you how the man is now exhorting the rabble down there to open rebellion against the Wasps.'

Trenhyass looked sharply at Euphest. 'When did this happen?'

'I've no report of anything of the kind.''

'Perhaps that's because my agents are considerably faster and more efficient than your pack of hired informers.'

The Protector's expression was hard. 'I'm not happy about this, Dole Euphest.'

Euphest didn't seem too happy either. 'I know it.'

Trenhyass turned his attention to Heizen. 'What have you heard?'

The Marshal looked coldly at Kraymon. 'I'm certainly not going to repeat anything in front of anyone of such doubtful loyalty.'

Kraymon stared down at the smaller man with almost open contempt. Then he shrugged.

'What the hell? I'd rather be out of here anyway. If you want me, Trenhyass, I expect I won't be too hard to find.'

The Protector nodded and Kraymon started toward the doors. Heizen raised a hand as if to halt him. 'One moment, Kraymon.'

The wildman halted, paused for a few seconds and then slowly turned. 'You want something with me?'

'Are you still slinking around the outlands like an animal?'

'There's a lot of things in the cities that make the outlands very appealing.'

'Are you still working for the Wasps?'

Kraymon's contempt was now not masked at all. He repeated what he had said to Euphest with even more scorn. Heizen took a couple of steps towards the giant. His entourage was watching the man from the outlands intently.

'That weapon on your hip, are you aware it's illegal?'

'Every punk in the lowers is walking round with a home-made bapgun under his coat.'

'And they would be arrested for it just as you should be.'

Trenhyass quickly stepped in. 'This man is under my protection. He can carry anything he likes.'

'Are you saying that this animal is above the law?'

'I'm saying that he works for me and I don't want him interfered with.' He looked at Kraymon. 'Go along. I'll talk with you later.'

Kraymon turned to go. He looked back at Heizen and

grinned. 'Is it true what they say about your private life, Marshal Heizen?'

The Protector's voice snapped out curtly. He was starting to get angry. 'Get out of here, Shafik Kraymon.'

Heizen watched Kraymon go, then he looked at the Protector. 'Does that man never bathe?'

Dole Euphest coughed. 'In fact, he was quite anxious to.'

Trenhyass had had enough of this byplay. 'I want to know what your agents have told you, Marshal Heizen.'

Heizen locked eyes with the Protector for a full count of five. Then, with an infinitesimal gesture of resignation, he started to outline the report of his agents.

'Just two hours ago, the man Gywann held a meeting, a ritual or performance, call it what you will, in the ruins of the ancient impulse plant. He had some two hundred followers with him and it was attended by a crowd of nearly a thousand. It is my opinion that this in itself, coupled with the fact that the man is at the head of a religious revival that is spreading like a plague through the most volatile sections of the lowers, is quite enough reason to place him under interdiction and round up the whole pack of them.'

'Please continue with the facts. I've yet to hear anything I don't know. Gywann has been holding increasingly large and better organised meetings for some weeks now. If his so-called religion starts to look like a threat to stability, he will be dealt with. There is always the possibility that an outbreak of religion could have the reverse effect. It could keep them quiet.'

'Not when he's preaching overthrow of the Wasps.'

'Are you certain about this?'

'The man Gywann addressed the crowd. It could be described as a dramatic monologue accompanied by a choir of women. I have a copy of the text. He constantly refers to something he calls "The Black Strangers".' Heizen snapped his fingers. One of his escort handed him a slim sheaf of papers. He flipped through the pages. 'Here: "the Friend was unafraid of the Black Strangers and they couldn't perceive him. The Black Strangers could only see fear", and later, "don't fear the Stranger and the Stranger won't see you. Don't fear the Stranger and the Stranger can't harm you!"'

The Protector didn't look particularly impressed.

'It could be construed as an allegory. If he means the Wasps he could be in trouble, but it's hardly overt sedition.

The main point in Gywann's favour is that he's still alive. The Wasps can't see him as a threat or they would have imploded him.'

'He's under suspicion of doing some imploding himself.'

'As far as our present knowledge goes, that's not possible. I think you're getting excited about very little, Marshal Heizen.'

'There are these lines further on: "We will drive out the Black Strangers. We will drive out the cold. We will throw open the doors and the windows and let in the sun". . .'

'Closer to sedition, but still nothing to get worked up about.'

Heizen ignored Trenhyass. 'It goes on: "We will come in from out of the cold and we will welcome all of our friends. Our love will be the great unfolding".'

The Protector's eyes narrowed. 'Did you say "unfolding"?'

'"Unfolding." That's right. I thought it might pique your interest.'

The Protector appeared to be controlling his temper with difficulty. 'I wasn't aware that you were present at the last audience with the Wasps.'

'I wasn't.'

'I also wasn't aware that I'd authorised you to receive a transcript of the exchange.'

'My Killers routinely report to me.'

Trenhyass bristled. 'Whose Killers?'

Heizen made a small mocking bow. 'I'm sorry, my lord, I didn't presume. It was just my *esprit de corps* getting out of hand.'

Trenhyass turned on his heel and walked slowly back to his desk. He didn't want Heizen to see his face. He stood for a moment fighting down his fury at the man's calm insolence. He composed his face and turned round.

'So, Marshal Heizen, having come this far, I suppose I should listen to your proposals for dealing with all this.'

'I think it's high time that there was a general cleansing of the lowers.'

'Do you have any idea what we might be dealing with?'

For the first time Heizen hesitated. 'Frankly, I don't. I simply feel that something strange and potentially dangerous is going on in the lowers and rather than waiting to find out what it might be, we should put a stop to it before it grows any bigger or any stronger. The lowers require a short but harsh shock to correct their thinking.'

'Slaughter?'

'A short harsh shock.'

'Do you have any other answers but mass murder?'

'We can't limit ourselves when we fight a war for our very survival.'

Trenhyass sat down. He looked very weary. 'Why don't you stop scoring points off me and attempt to co-operate.' He turned to Dole Euphest. 'What do we have if all the stories about Gywann are true?'

Euphest scowled at Heizen. He was still irked that the Killers had beaten out his own agents. 'We have a seditionist mystic who can implode people.'

Heizen affected something close to boredom. 'Something that should definitely be liquidated.'

Euphest looked down his nose at the Marshal of Killers. 'It might well be something that we should handle with extreme care.'

The Protector held up his hand. 'I've made up my mind.'

It was only a small gesture but somehow it seemed to restore order to the situation. He was the Protector. There would be no more argument. Both Euphest and Heizen fell silent. It seemed enough to remind Heizen that no matter what his ambitions he was still a subordinate and subject to discipline. Trenhyass stood up. His was the final authority under the Wasps.

'I am not yet ready to let your Killers go on the rampage through the lowers, Marshal Heizen. I want you to understand me very well on this. You will hold your men strictly in check.'

Heizen stiffened and nodded. 'Yes, my lord.'

'I don't, however, want this Gywann to run on unchecked. You will have him brought in for questioning.'

'Yes, my lord.'

'But you will use tact rather than brute force. If there's any resistance, I want it dealt with with minimum violence. I do not want a riot in the lowers. I do not want a lot of casualties.'

'Yes, my lord.'

'I also do not want the man Gywann tortured. I will supervise his interrogation myself. Do you hear me, Marshal Heizen?'

'I do, my lord. The man will be ready for you in a couple of hours.'

'Gently, Heizen.'

'Gently, Protector Trenhyass.'

'You're dismissed, Marshal.'

Again the Marshal offered a half-mocking bow. Heizen hadn't completely finished with the game. 'I thank you, my lord.'

Once the Marshal and his guard had left, Euphest slumped a little. 'One day soon you're going to have to do something about that man.'

'I will, directly I've found a way to neutralise his Iron Fists. More to the point though, Dole Euphest, I shall have to do something about you. I particularly wanted Heizen kept out of this Gywann matter. Thanks to you, I find his informants are ahead of mine. How is it that you didn't hear about this address of Gywann's before he did?'

Dole Euphest was starting to look discreetly resentful. 'You had me at that damned reception and then Kraymon arrived.'

The Protector lay back in his chair. 'I expect you to remind me of my priorities.'

'I'm sorry. I seem to have failed in this matter.'

Trenhyass closed his eyes. 'We'll shelve the discussion of it until we've had a closer look at this Gywann.'

Seven

IT WAS a cold, pink-and-blue dawn at the top of the high towers. Light slid over the roof gardens and terraces and made coloured beams through jewelled windows. Down in the lowers, however, red night still prowled even though the excitement had worn off and it was starting to grow weary. The Poet had finally given up. Even though he had spent most of his money, he hadn't been able either to cap the elation of poem-telling or wipe out his resentment at being dumped by Sulanda. He sat huddled in a corner by the fire wondering if he should pay Denhagel what he owed him, leave himself broke but get his room and his things back, or whether he should simply nod out where he sat. Denhagel probably wouldn't care either way. He was full of brandy and his wife had gone to bed. Along with Fok the Turrier, he was listening to Kraymon the wandering man-mountain tell his increasingly slurred tales of the mysterious outlands.

Earlier, before the Poet had returned from the Theatre and his subsequent drunk, Kraymon had been the hit of the evening at Denhagel's. Bathed and barbered and dressed up in a yellow plaid suit that he'd bought in the Oldmarket and that was a number of sizes too small for him, he seemed intent to have a six-month of city life all in one evening. His first stop had been at Celastrine's Idea of Heaven and there the story was being told and retold how he had hired nearly half of the complement of women in the big cavelike bordello, plus a brace of small boys for good measure, and how everyone in the place had assumed they'd seen the last of him for the night. Inside an hour, though, he'd been up and roaring once again. He had by all accounts stopped at four more funhouses, growing worse at each until, by the fourth, he was making both the performers and the other customers visibly nervous. It wasn't only his size. His four-barrelled pistol was scarcely concealed at all by his skimpy yellow fopcoat.

In the end, the funboss of the final place had decided that

despite the way that Kraymon was spending the Protector's credit he was becoming bad for business. Summoning his courage and a trio of his minders, he had approached the big man and politely suggested that maybe it was time to slow down and it might be easier to do this in some other establishment that didn't have quite such a variety of temptation. At this point Kraymon, who always retained a core of innate good sense no matter how drunk he might be, homed on Denhagel's. He was well aware that Denhagel was one of the few tavernkeepers in the artists' quarter who'd never lost his respect for the truly excessive. At Denhagel's he was under no constraints as he drank more and more and bellowed out his tall tales of the strange and frightening lands that lay beyond the end of the city.

For people who talked about 'the city that went on forever' and at times had trouble conceiving that there was anything at all beyond the buildings and stone streets, his stories were the stuff of magic. They hung on his every word as he bragged of living rocks, rivers of blood, encounters with Wasps on ice mountains taller than the towers, and of strange hermits who lived in caves and believed that they came from a totally different era. When he recounted how he had once made love to a she-bear, they still laughed and applauded, even though not a single one of them had anything but the most hazy idea of what a she-bear might be.

Bottle by bottle the booze had done its work, things had slowed, even Kraymon couldn't hold an audience for ever. As his tongue thickened and his words came more and more slowly, the listeners either drifted away or passed out in their chairs. By the time the dawn was tipping the towers he was down to two listeners and having trouble maintaining a thread from one sentence to the next. The Poet had given up trying to follow these ramblings. His eyelids had started to weigh heavy, and instinctively he settled his head more securely so it wouldn't fall forward and wake him with a jerk. Kraymon's stories worked their way into his disoriented, half-sleeping dreams. He stood on a high black mountain looking over a vast, dark, flamelit plain. The flames came from a black volcano that belched fire and smoke. There was a woman who seemed to want to push him into its molten heart.

Someone threw a fresh bundle on the fire and the Poet woke with a start.

'Wha . . . wassamatta!?'

In his turn, he attracted the attention of Kraymon, Denhagel and Fok. Kraymon grinned.

'Wha's your trouble, my frien'? Having a bad dream?'

Vayim blearily shook his head. It was too hard to form words. 'She . . . ee . . . it.' He felt dreadful. He closed his eyes and tried to find his way back into sleep. The second interruption came from outside the tavern. It was the sound of a commotion maybe two or three streets away.

There seemed to be screams and a hubbub of shouting. Night noise was common enough in the lowers to go largely unnoticed. At that hour, however, night noise usually came from small groups of stumbling drunks and there were more than three or four people involved in whatever this was; a whole crowd was making this noise. The Poet sat up. Nobody else in the tavern seemed to be taking any notice. Then there was the dull, almost subsonic boom of a pulser. Now everybody who wasn't sleeping looked around. From the sound, it was one of the lethal kind used by the Killers. Kraymon raised a bushy eyebrow. 'There's trouble abroad tonight?'

Denhagel shook his head. 'There hasn't been trouble down here in quite a while, but you never can tell.'

Vayim stood up. He was still sufficiently drunk to be foolhardy. 'I'm going out to see what's happened.'

There was another pulser boom. Everyone in the tavern was either awake or stirring. Denhagel straightened up.

'That's a damn fool idea, Poet. If the Killers are out, the safest thing to do is to stay right here.'

Kraymon pushed himself away from the bar. 'I'm curious myself. I'll come with you, Poet.'

Fok laughed. 'I'll go too.'

Denhagel cursed their foolishness but he stood up just the same and followed the three towards the door. Weaving more than a little, they emerged into the alley that ran past the front of the inn. They followed the sound out of the alley onto the cobbled open space that was the top end of the complex maze of winding, criss-crossing steps and tunnels known as Pynchon's Stairs. The noise, the shouting and yelling, still seemed to be coming from somewhere below them. Pynchon's Stairs, if you followed them down for long enough, eventually led out onto an even larger open space called the Stoneplane, a traditional haunt of thieves, moneylenders and political agitators. The quartet of drunken adventurers decided that this was the most likely site for any sort of trouble.

Pynchon's Stairs was a dark, shadowy and confusing place at the best of times. Much of its everburn had been worn away and its layout was so haphazard that it was hard to know which alley or which flight of steps led where. The four got lost a number of times, but by the simple process of continuing to go down, they kept getting nearer to the noise. The uproar grew louder and louder. It started to sound like a full-blown riot and Denhagel, at least, began to wonder if the whole idea of seeing for themselves had been extremely ill-advised.

They were standing at the head of a particularly twisting section of steps discussing which way to go next, when two figures came round the turn below them. They were just silhouettes against the dim everburn but clearly they were running as though their lives depended on it. The four drunkards moved back to give them room, Kraymon and Fok shouting encouragement. As the two figures pounded past, white faced and fighting for breath but not slackening their pace in the slightest, they got a closer look at them. They were two young men, not much more than boys. They were dressed in almost identical clothes, black sleeveless vests and black breeches. Jeen Vayim recognised them straight away.

'They're Gywann's boys.'

Denhagel glanced at Fok. 'Didn't his people get themselves a place somewhere down by the Stoneplane?'

Before Fok could answer, three more figures came around the curve. These weren't running. Using flying-belts, they were coming up the steps at high speed just an inch or so above the ground. It was a dangerous trick in such an irregular and enclosed place. The three performing it were instantly recognisable as Killers. One of them took the turn a little too wide and crashed into the wall but the other two kept on coming. At the top end of the next flight of steps, one of the boys stopped and turned. In a gesture of desperation, he pulled a homemade bapgun from inside his vest. He let go a charge at the nearest Killer. He missed and the Killer's pulser came up. The funnel-shaped emitter glowed, the subsonic boom and the slight shift in spectrum came together. The boy jerked, convulsed, and crumpled to the ground. He rolled down five steps and then lay still, blood running from his ears.

From that point on it all became extremely confused. The Poet had been too close to the pulser blast. His head was vibrating and he was temporarily deaf. There was an imminent possibility that he might vomit. The other three appeared to be in a similar condition. The Killers swept past. One slowed and turned, coming back towards them. At the same time more people came streaming up from below. A panicky, frightened mob was being herded up the steps by more Killers wielding shock rods. There seemed to be a number of Gywann's female followers in the crowd. The Killer who had turned back from the chase was hanging in the air in front of Vayim and Kraymon. He was waving his pulser and clearly shouting something. The Poet couldn't make out a word. He was still as deaf as a stone. The Killer was either overexcited, extremely stupid, or carried away by the extra height afforded him by the flying-belt and the power of the pulser in his hand. He did something very foolish. He pushed Kraymon. The big man was also still groggy from the pulser blast. He took one pace back down the steps. He stood swaying with a look of dazed surprise on his face. The Killer made to push him again. Surprise turned to outrage. Kraymon's hand moved like a striking snake. He grabbed the Killer by the wrist. The man's expression was concealed by the faceplate of his helmet but his body told it all. The pulser swung up.

For Vayim, the world had become totally unreal. His inability to hear gave him a strange detachment from the violence that was about to break out all around him. It was like being a fish in a glass bowl. He could see what was going on but it wasn't really anything to do with him. Quickly as the Killer brought up his weapon, Kraymon was even faster. He jerked the Killer's arm as if he was cracking a whip. The artificial weightlessness provided by the man's flying-belt worked against him and he spun in the air. He tried to save himself by cutting in the belt's forward drive, but misjudged his position and powered straight down the steps. He finished up hopelessly entangled with the first of the oncoming mob. The chaos was multiplied. The Killer's partner, who had witnessed the incident, started back, making for Kraymon with a drawn pulser. He was hampered by the first wave of the crowd as they milled past and around Kraymon and Vayim. More Killers were in and among them, swinging out left and right with their shock rods. Denhagel and Fok were lost to sight, carried on up the steps by the violent confusion. A woman in white, clearly a follower of Gywann, lost her footing and slammed into Vayim, pushing him back against the wall. To save herself from falling and being trampled in the panic, she grabbed for his shirt. Her fingernails raked his chest. There was blood on her robe. For a moment her face was right up close to Vayim's. Her eyes had the desperate vacancy of the terrified. She seemed to be trying to say something. A Killer lashed at her with a shock rod. As her face twisted in agony, the pain was transmitted through her body and into Vayim's. The next moment she was gone. Another woman was hurled out of the way as the Killer with the pulser fought to get at Kraymon against the flow of the crowd.

Kraymon wasn't going to be caught off balance a second time. Both the knife and the pistol were out as he waited for his man. Two other Killers had noticed the commotion and were also fighting their way through the crowd towards him. Just as it looked as though it would all end in homicide, an officer in a flying-belt dropped from above, kicking himself a space in front of Kraymon with his steelshod boots. At the same time, Vayim's bubble of silence broke and noise crashed into him like a second vicious shock. All around him people were shouting and screaming. There was the particular, sharp, popping sounds of shock rods when they made contact with human beings. Above it all, there was the officer yelling at the top of his lungs.

'Leave him be! Leave him! Anyone who kills him dies straight after!'

For a moment it looked as though discipline might not hold as the angry Killers converged on Kraymon, but a Killer without discipline is nothing. It is the central core of their long and brutal training. They halted in a small angry knot. The officer was positioned to shield the wildman. The crowd had now almost passed. A few of the Killers bringing up the rear stopped to see what was going on.

'Who is that big motherfucker?'

'Who is that bastard? Is it true that he attacked one of our boys? How come he ain't on the ground bleeding and twitching?'

'Cover it, you scum!' The officer was at the end of his patience. 'When I want your comments, I'll ask for them. For your information, his name is Kraymon and he's a special pet of the Protector. The Marshal himself has ordered that he must not be harmed under any circumstances.'

One Killer was still holding a belligerent posture. The officer advanced on him. 'You hear me, Stencraw? I said the Marshal himself.'

Another Killer pointed to Vayim.

'What about him? It seemed to me that the two of them were together.'

Kraymon still had the pistol in his hand. The seams of the yellow plaid suit had long since given up the uneven fight and it hung in tatters. He looked like a wild animal brought to bay.

'You touch him at your peril.'

Vayim, still sick, half doubled over from the combined effects of the shocks and the pulser, flashed him a grateful look. Unfortunately, it started to seem that the gesture might precipitate more trouble. The Killers stiffened. The officer regarded Kraymon through the eyeslit of his helmet. He seemed to be weighing the prospect of disobeying a direct order from the Marshal against the satisfaction he might get from blasting Kraymon where he stood. Before he'd made up his mind, a single Killer came running up the steps. She shouted to the officer.

'They're bringing him up. Get your men ready.'

The officer came down on the side of duty. He started yelling at his men.

'Up! Up! Clear the steps!' He looked at Kraymon and made a dismissive gesture. 'You get out of here, too. Get up those damn steps and out of my sight.'

Back at the top of Pynchon's Stairs, Killers were clearing the centre of the cobbled area. Many of them kept looking up as though they were expecting a carriage or some other flying craft to descend from the towers. The now quieter, but still surly crowd was being held back behind a circle of black uniforms. Kraymon and Vayim were pushed in among them. They spotted Denhagel just behind the lines of Killers and elbowed their way towards him. There was no sign of Fok, however. As they moved up beside Denhagel, he glanced over his shoulder and grimaced.

'You two look a mess. Have you any idea what's going on?'

'They're bringing someone up Pynchon's Stairs, probably from the Stoneplane.'

Denhagel stood on tiptoe, craning for a better view.

'I don't think we're going to have to wait too much longer to find out. There's a whole crew of Killers coming up the steps. There's definitely someone in the middle of them.' He paused, still looking. 'I think it's . . . yeah, hell, I should have known.' He relaxed and looked at the other two. 'Well, they did it. They've picked up Gywann. God help the poor bastard, I doubt if anyone else can.'

Denhagel wasn't the only one who had seen that Gywann was the prisoner of the Killers. The crowd was no longer silent. There were shouts and catcalls; some of the women in white started a high keening wail. Vayim wondered if they were the choir from the lower basin. Some pushing and struggling started, cutting short the idle thought. Some of the more vocal of the mob seemed to be trying to reach Gywann. The shock rods came out again. The popping sound started. Vayim took a number of steps back, easing through the crowd away from the Killers; he didn't want to be hit a second time. He'd been lucky in choosing his position, however; most of the trouble was over on the other side of the cleared space.

There were lights high up beside the nearest tower, two probing spots and a set of red and yellow riding-lights; these were the identity code of a Killer aircar. It was coming down quickly. As more of the crowd noticed the dropping lights the violence slackened off. Soon everyone was looking up. The Killers pressed their advantage, they pushed forward, enlarging their circle. Someone just behind the Poet ventured a theory.

'Maybe it's the Protector coming down.'

Someone else picked up the idea. 'The Protector's coming.'

There's a mass gullibility in any crowd and this one was no exception. The rumour rippled outwards, gaining strength as it went.

'The Protector himself is coming.'

'The Protector is going to meet with Gywann.'

'The Protector's coming.'

Kraymon turned and, with a look of disgust, roared over the mass of heads. 'The Protector's not coming. They're just sending transport to take away your prophet.'

Nobody seemed to be very interested in what Kraymon had to say and almost immediately he was drowned out by a much louder roar from above.

'MOVE BACK!'

A hugely amplified voice was booming from the Killer aircraft.

'MOVE BACK! CLEAR THE AREA! WE ARE COMING DOWN. IF YOU DO NOT CLEAR THE AREA, WE USE PULSER FIRE TO CLEAR IT BY FORCE.'

Denhagel muttered to Kraymon, 'By the standards of the Killers, this is delicacy and tact.'

'They want this boy alive.'

Two powerful sun-guns flared into life on the underside of the craft, making the area as bright as day.

'MOVE BACK! MOVE BACK OR WE OPEN FIRE.'

Instinctively the crowd did as they were ordered. Many were blinking and rubbing their eyes. Those who spent all their time in the lowers were unused to bright lights. Even at high noon there was still artificial dusk in these man-made canyons. The aircar came down slowly until it was hovering less than a metre above the ground. Up close, the sun-guns reflected off the cobblestones were close to blinding. The Killers on the ground took the chance to push the crowd back even further. The Killer aircar was the same elongated gondola shape as a civilian carriage, although it had none of its baroque decoration and elaborate carving. Both its hull and its superstructure were heavily armoured, and pulsers were mounted at no less than six points along its length. The most extreme modification was at the rear of the craft. The entire stern was a spherical, openwork steel cage, just large enough to house a precariously standing man or woman. It was towards this that Gywann was being led by his escort. There was now no room for doubt, even in the mind of the most fanatically optimistic of his followers, that Gywann was being arrested and taken to the Halls. It was common knowledge in the lowers that few who went to the Halls ever came back. All at once the noise and shouting started up again. Kraymon grabbed Vayim and Denhagel by the arms. 'I'm getting out of here. This isn't my fight.'

They both nodded. 'It ain't our fight either.'

As the three of them struggled to push their way out of the crowd, Gywann was dragged at a dead run towards the cage. He and his escort cast long sinister shadows as they ran into the light of the sun-guns. Some of the crowd, led by a gang of Gywann's young male followers, burst through the line of Killers. There was the snap of bapguns followed by the thud of pulsers. The cage door was slammed on

94

Gywann and the aircar lifted clear. One of the young followers managed to get his arms round the bars. He was jerked upwards, clinging to the cage's underside and waving his legs in empty air. Kraymon, Vayim and Denhagel turned to watch. Gywann appeared to be standing up in the cage, holding on to the bars to steady himself. He was looking down at the kid but he made no attempt to help him. The young man seemed unwilling to let go. He rode up some forty or fifty metres, then his strength gave out and he plummeted down again.

Once the aircar was gone, the other Killers prepared to withdraw. With the precision of a thousand drills they fell back into a tight, orderly square. While the outer ranks held back the crowd with pulsers, those in the centre activated their flying-belts and slipped into the air. Immediately the last of the Killers were away, the crowd began hurling rocks and garbage at their departing figures. This was an extremely stupid idea. The area at the top of Pynchon's Stairs was hit by a hail of debris as the missiles fell back to earth. Kraymon, Vayim and Denhagel ducked into the nearest cover.

'These people are crazy. Why does religion turn them into morons?'

The Poet was examining himself for major injuries. 'Maybe that's what it's for.'

Denhagel peered out. The crowd was breaking up in angry, muttering groups. 'We should go back to the bar.'

Vayim nodded. 'We should never have left it in the first place. Does anyone know what happened to Fok?'

Eight

HORFON WAS shaken awake by a heavy hand. He blinked at the light that was shining in his face. For a few moments he had trouble knowing where he was. Part of his mind was still in an anxious and frustrating dream. He had been in a bordello in the lowers. At least, he had been in what he imagined a bordello to be like. He had never actually visited such a place nor, for that matter, had he ever set foot in the lowers. It was hazy with smoke and full of exotic women who somehow lacked faces, and huge men in dirty buckskins. He had been trying to talk to the only woman who had a face. She'd worn a red dress and feathers in her hair and looked uncommonly like Legate Androx. Each time he found the words to say to her, someone or something would interrupt him or distract her attention. The final interruption was the light, the loud hectoring voice and the rough hands.

'On your feet, worm! Move! Move! Wake up, worm! The Protector wants a brace of Legates.'

Junior as he might have been, Horfon's training went deeper than his dreams. He was out of his bunk and onto the floor before he even knew what was going on. Even then, though, the voice wouldn't let up.

'Stop stumbling about in your skivvies, worm! Move! Move, you worthless piece of shit!'

Horfon instinctively reached for his breeches and shirt. He was starting to locate himself. The narrow bunk in which he'd been dreaming was in the Legates' duty room. He was part of the reserve watch, the group of Legates who were on instant call to run errands and carry messages according to the needs and whims of the Protector. The room, with its stone walls, narrow metal cots and smell of sleeping bodies, became drearily familiar. What wasn't familiar was the face that was pushing into his, mouthing abuse and spitting slightly with each syllable. It was pink, sweating and remorselessly clean-shaven, with small eyes and pale, almost white eyelashes. The uniform was familiar enough, however; the black meant Killer and the symbol on the chest meant Iron Fist. As Horfon struggled into his own uniform, he wondered what might be going on that merited a Killer of the Iron Fists being dispatched to rouse Legates. The Killer treated him to one last burst of obscenity and then transferred his assault to one of the other cots.

'And you, up, up, maggot! Move! Move! Get your scabby body out of the pit!' The Killer suddenly burst out laughing and took a step back as Androx stumbled out of her bunk in dishevelled underwear, blinking and pushing her hair out of her eyes. 'Well, well, well, look what we've got here. How are you doing, Legate Androx? You been dancing on any tables lately? We've missed you down in the Iron Fists' mess and that's a fact.'

Horfon paused in fastening his tunic. He could scarcely believe what he was hearing. Androx simply scowled.

'Dream on, cessmouth. I've never danced on your table and I never will.'

The Killer's voice quickly switched back to the official shriek. 'Did I just hear you volunteer a comment to a superior officer, Legate?'

Androx came back with equal volume. 'No sir! You heard nothing, sir! It must have been a cough, sir!'

'That's good, Legate! I'd hate to see you beaten for insolence.'

The Killer continued in this vein while Androx and Horfon readied themselves for duty. Finally he paraded them and insisted on conducting a full inspection. When he was quite satisfied that they were fit to be seen by the Protector, he nodded. 'Get your flying-belts.'

Horfon couldn't keep a flicker of surprise out of his face. The Killer clearly counted it as a minor victory.

'That's got your attention, hasn't it Legate? Wondering what they might want of you that involves a flying-belt, I dare say. Well, Legate, it's not my place to tell you. No doubt you'll find out when you need to, and not before. You just make your way to Landing Stage 3020. Those are the only orders I've got for you.' He turned his head and winked at Androx. 'You know where Landing Stage 3020 is, don't you, Blondie? It's down in Killer country. In fact, Landing Stage 3020 is the entrance to the Gallery of Questions.'

Horfon felt his stomach turn over. The Gallery of Questions was a name fenced around by notoriety and horror. It was where the Killers conducted their formal interrogations. The common people called it 'the place where men have their minds changed'. He couldn't imagine why he should be summoned there. Was it something that one of his relatives might have done? When a wealthy or powerful man was suspected of major crimes against the Protectorate, it was a common practice to round up his immediate family also. Such had been the case of his childhood playmate, Darfarc, who had vanished with his father and three sisters when his mother, a salon pamphleteer of some note, had been accused of sedition and chaosism. And yet, as far as Horfon knew, the Killer hadn't come for him specifically. All he wanted was two Legates. This wasn't an arrest, it was simply a summons to duty. He kept telling himself this while he wound his flying-belt around his waist. The Gallery of Questions had this effect on people.

It was fortunate that the Legates' duty room was comparatively near to the outside of its particular tower. When a flying-belt wasn't activated it weighed heavy on the wearer, and to activate a flying-belt inside the Halls of the Protector was another convenience that was forbidden to Legates.

Their home landing stage opened out from the hundred-and-tenth floor of the tower. Once they were out there, the two Legates walked straight towards the edge while the Killer watched. It was like being a belt-happy kid again. The cool thing was to step off high places without a flicker, as if you were part of your belt and the belt was part of you, like being a bird. You were supposed to look as though you were immune to that twinge of irrational doubt that came when you walked out into thin air and trusted that your belt would hold you up. Of course nobody was. Although it tried its hardest, humanity couldn't really treat flying as something to which it was born. It couldn't totally lose its monkey-fear of high places. Stepping off a tower was the worst. The distances were so great and the ground was so very, very far away that monkey-fear clutched at the throat, certain it would fall for ever.

And then the belt cut in and Horfon started to rise. With skill that can only come from a lifetime of practice, he inclined and arched his body, riding out through the mantle of currents and eddies that cloaked the tower. He found a strong updraught and soared. He was master of the air. The city spread out beneath him, all the way to the horizon with the morning sun slanting through it. The air was sweet and clean. He suspected that it must have rained in the last few hours and washed away a lot of the city filth. He luxuriated in feeling free as a bird. All monkey-fear had been left behind on the landing stage. Androx rose beside him. Her technique was equally immaculate.

'You fly pretty good.'

'Thank you, you look pretty good yourself.'

He executed a slow roll, showing off a little. He had a lot more confidence in the air than he had in conversation with this wildly precocious young woman. They were hit by a particularly fierce area of turbulence. They rode in unison, ducking and rising like fish in water. When they were through, Androx brought them back to matters in hand.

'This is a lot of fun, but if we don't get down to 3020, I figure they'll have our hides.'

'You've changed your tune. I thought you were queen goof-off.'

'I don't take any chances when it's the Gallery of Questions.'

She didn't wait for a response; she dropped away, falling fast. Horfon plunged down after her. Even from a distance it was clear that something was happening on and around Landing Stage 3020. A squad of Killers was standing on the actual platform as though guarding it from attack. A little way off, a formation of Legates hung motionless in the air, riding their belts and apparently waiting for something. Androx slowed her descent. Horfon followed suit.

'What do you think we should do?'

'I think we should report to the senior Legate in that formation. I don't like the look of those Killers.'

'We were ordered here by a Killer.'

Androx nodded. 'I've been wondering about that, but I still think we ought to stick with our own kind.'

The senior Legate in the formation was a Quartercaptain called Steige with a face like leather-covered granite. Only his voice betrayed that he was at the end of his patience.

'What we have here is something of a show of force.' He nodded in the direction of the Killers waiting on the landing stage. 'Unfortunately we don't have too much force to show, seeing as how they have all the lethals.'

Horfon glanced around at the other Legates. Most were unarmed, three had lightweight pulsers that would do little more than briefly stun.

'It was a Killer who ordered us here.'

Steige nodded. 'More than likely you were supposed to bring a message but he neglected to give it to you. There's been a lot of that sort of thing in the last few hours.'

Androx, who'd been sinking slightly, adjusted her position and asked, 'What's going on?'

Steige regarded her coldly. 'You're Androx, aren't you?'

'That's right, Quartercaptain.'

He slowly looked her up and down. 'Well, Androx, for your information, I'm not in the habit of having junior Legates ask me what's going on. When they do, I'm even less in the habit of telling them.'

'I'm sorry, Quartercaptain.'

'In this instance, I'll make an exception. If there's any hope of you behaving intelligently, it's best you know what the situation is.' He glanced around as though he was faintly hoping to see something but expecting nothing. 'Just before dawn a detachment of Killers, led by the Iron Fists, picked up a man called Gywann in the lowers and brought him to the Gallery of Questions for interrogation. He's some kind of religious troublemaker. When word of this reached the Protector, he ordered us down here to make sure nothing happened to the man before he had a chance to question him in person. I don't have to tell you about the Killers' interrogation techniques, do I?'

Both Androx and Horfon shook their heads.

'Anyway, we turn up here just after dawn and we find this bunch waiting for us. They say they have no orders to admit us and we're not coming in. I get on the talkie to the Main Hall but they say that the Killers' central command refuses to answer. They claim they're running a simulated combat drill and there's a communication blackout until it's over. We're told to wait here until the Protector himself can get here and that's exactly what we're doing.'

Horfon stiffened to attention. 'What does all this mean, Quartercaptain?'

'That's a good question. It probably means that Marshal Heizen's taking the chance to flex his muscles. It's not secret that he wants to replace the Lord Trenhyass as Protector. Just how far he wants to press his luck remains to be seen. We could be looking at a simple gesture or we could be looking at the start of a coup.'

Horfon and Androx fell back into the formation. At first there was a sense of tension and excitement. For the very first time in his life, Horfon felt he was playing a part in events of high importance. Tension is a hard thing to maintain, however, and as the hours passed and the sun climbed to noon and beyond, boredom and discomfort began to take over. On two occasions Horfon, who had only been asleep for a short while before being awakened by the Killer, found himself dozing off in his flying-belt and drifting out of formation. The second time, it had taken a sharp kick from Androx to snap him back. The Killers also stood their ground, each group staring at the other across a space of empty air. Only the possibility of what might happen next stopped the confrontation turning into a farce.

In fact, what happened next was that the Protector arrived. His carriage came in fast and without the usual ceremonial manoeuvring. Horfon noticed that there was no sign of the usual Killer escort. As the carriage slowed almost to a halt beside the formation of Legates, it was pointedly evident that the only other passengers were the steersman and three more Legates. The Legates, however, carried lethal pulsers at an ostentatious high port. For Legates to be so armed was not only unheard of but, as far as Horfon was aware, a direct contravention of Wasp law. As the carriage moved slowly past them, the Legates braced themselves and followed in neat line abreast. It was an obvious show for the Killers, even though the Corps of Legates had never had the same reputaton for precision drill as their rivals.

The Protector's carriage came alongside 3020. Trenhyass stepped onto the landing stage. His three Legates followed him. None of the Killers moved, either to repel or to greet him. At a signal from Steige the rest of the Legates halted, still hanging in the air, just two paces out from the platform. Trenhyass clapped his hands in a gesture of patently phoney joviality. 'So is this the way you greet your Protector?'

The senior Killer, a female Wingleader, snapped to attention. 'No, my lord, we simply had no orders indicating that you were arriving.'

'I have to announce myself before I come to Killer country?'

The Protector had dropped the mask of fake good humour. The Wingleader, on the other hand, kept hers in place. She was so impassive that it verged on insult.

'It's an exceptional circumstance, my lord.'

'What circumstance?'

'The whole of the in-tower regiment is conducting a combat simulation. The tower is sealed and communications are black, my lord. We have orders to admit no one.'

'And this is why you refuse to admit Legates carrying out my direct orders?'

'My orders were also direct, my lord, and very specific.'

'But you'll admit me, Wingleader?'

'Of course, my lord. You're my Commander in Chief.'

'I'm glad to hear it.'

At a barked order from the Wingleader, the Killers fell back into a double ranked guard of honour. The Protector walked between them with only the barest acknowledgement, heading directly for the shallow arch of the almost cavelike entrance to the tower. The three Legates fell in behind him. The Killers stiffened. Trenhyass glanced back. 'Are you going to refuse to admit my personal entourage?'

'No, my lord, not if you so order.'

'I do so order.'

The three Legates walked forwards. At a sign from Steige, the others followed. The Protector walked out of the sunlight and into the darkness of the entrance, but within just twenty paces he ran into the next obstacle. As obstacles went, the spiked iron portcullis was quite formidable. Although it had almost certainly been built for dramatic effect rather than actual defence, when it was in the down position, it still presented an impenetrable barrier to anyone who didn't happen to be carrying a cutting torch. Trenhyass angrily ordered the nearest Legate to fetch the Wingleader.

'Open this!'

'I cannot, my lord.'

'Damn your insolence, woman. Open this fool thing or I'll have one of my men shoot you on the spot.'

The Wingleader was meticulously polite.

'You can shoot me, my lord, but I shall not be able to raise the portcullis. It can only be opened from the inside. In the combat simulation we are a suicide squad. If we are attacked by superior forces, we cannot retreat inside.'

'So how do I get inside?'

'I don't know, my lord. We have no contact with the tower until the simulation ends at sunset. Beyond suggesting that you come back then, my lord, I . . .'

'I don't believe this.'

There was a series of metallic clanks and the portcullis began to rise. The timing seemed a piece of deliberate humiliation. It was as though someone inside had grown tired of the game.

'My dear Protector, I'm so sorry that you've been subjected to all this inconvenience. We are conducting a drill. Directly I heard you were here, I came myself.'

Marshal Heizen stood just inside the portcullis at the head of a large squad of Iron Fists. He executed a formal bow.

The Protector stared at Heizen for a full five seconds; his face was like stone. Then without warning he marched quickly forwards. The Legates instantly bunched around him, leaving the Killers to join the procession as best they could.

'I've come to question Gywann.'

Heizen had to break into a run to stay beside him. 'Of course, my lord.'

'You have Gywann?'

'Of course.'

'Have your butchers started on him?'

'He hasn't been touched. I wouldn't ignore your orders.'

'You killed twenty-seven in the course of picking him up.'

'As you requested, the operation was conducted with a minimum of force.'

'You call twenty-seven a minimum of force?'

'We could have killed a lot more, I assure you.'

They marched in silence for a while. Trenhyass maintained the same swift, angry pace. 'There is one other purpose to my visit.'

'There is?'

'I have to inform you that I have officially designated a number of my Legates who will be permitted to carry lethal weapons. I have done it in such a way that I believe it conforms to Wasp law as we interpret it.'

'It won't make them Killers.'

'It wasn't my intention to make them Killers.'

Like most other towers, that of the Killers allowed itself the indulgence of thousands of miles of corridor and passage. The ones that led to the Gallery of Questions had been designed for maximum effect. They would cancel all hope and instil a desperate fear and dread in the minds of the wretched unfortunates who were led along them on their way to interrogation. The predominant colours were black and red, angry red lighting that was the colour of burning pain and black stone that was permanent and relentless. The keyword of the architecture was elaboration. Even in the corridors, ornate pillars supported vaulting arches. Heroic bronzes of ancient fighting men and monstrous mythical animals postured and snarled in side alcoves. At a number of points they passed displays of mouldering battleflags, remnants of almost forgotten campaigns of the Undeclared War and all the other conflicts of ages before the Wasps had arrived as conquerors.

In their own domain, even the Killers seemed different. Their faces could be seen. Inside the tower they discarded the masked helmets and settled for brief black forage caps. Some of the officers affected red or purple capes. On their own ground they seemed, if it were possible, even more arrogantly sure of themselves than they did in the outside world. There were even children, grimfaced tots who looked as though they rarely, if ever, laughed or played but instead went about their infant duties with the same seriousness as their elders.

Horfon noticed that the Killers' tower was also an extremely noisy place. Even above the considerable crash of the Protector's party's boots on the basalt flags, there was a constant rumble, more boots, shrieked orders, the throb of heavy, unspecified machinery. Androx used the din as a cover under which to whisper to Horfon, 'I sure hope we don't stay here for long. This place gives me the creeps.'

'I'm glad I didn't enlist in the Killers. There was some talk about it at home for a while.'

'When you get down to it, they all want to be Wasps.'

Horfon was confused. 'What are you talking about?'

Androx glanced around at the Killers. 'Think about it.'

'You're just looking at the helmets and the uniforms. It's simply a coincidence.'

'You think so? What about this place? The way they keep themselves to themselves and the way they love their monopoly on lethal weapons. I'd like to know what Heizen was thinking when the Protector told him that he was giving lethals to some of our people.'

'I still don't believe they want to be Wasps.'

'Prisoners often fall in love with their jailers.'

The outer corridors might have given Androx the creeps but when they reached the Gallery of Questions itself, the creeps gave way to the more solid grip of revulsion. The pillars and statues were replaced by lines of openwork holding cages. Of almost a hundred or so, ninety had a human occupant, although some were scarcely recognisable as human. Horfon had never imagined that people could look the way that these did. A number had clearly been beaten, bruises were visible and faces were caked with dried blood. Others, shrouded in bandages, seemed actually to have been mutilated. Horfon tried not to look too closely. Among the worst were the ones who showed no sign of physical hurt save for their eyes. These stared so blankly that it could only be assumed that the extremes of horror that they'd seen and suffered had caused their reason to flee. Many cringed away at the sight of such a mob of Killers, but one or two crawled forwards holding out begging, beseeching hands. The very air was full of the stink of pain and fear. Some of the cages were decorated with rows of death masks made out of an opalescent plastic. Horfon didn't want to think about what they might represent. It was taking every last measure of his self-control to stop his mind racing loose in this awful place. Every so often they would pass a half-open door with light shining out. As Horfon hurried past, it was just possible to catch fleeting glimpses of grim figures going about their work, interrogators bending over their victims. As they passed one door, there was a burst of hideous, uncontrolled screaming. The door was quickly slammed shut. Horfon couldn't remember when he'd been so frightened. His stomach had turned to frozen water and even refused to promise that it would stay in place.

'You think these prisoners love their jailers?'

Gywann was being held in one of the larger of the question chambers. For one dreadful moment, Horfon imagined that the whole troop of Legates was going to be marched inside to witness the proceedings: then, to his relief, he saw that the Protector and Heizen had elected to go inside with just one guard apiece. The door to the chamber closed behind them and Horfon and his comrades turned to the comparatively easy task of matching the hostile stares of the massed Killers.

At least there was white light in the interrogation chamber. Trenhyass had grave doubts about the Killers' preoccupation with the colours black and red. They seemed too intent on turning their stronghold into a cheap, over-decorated imitation of hell. Gywann was seated in the middle of the room in a solid wooden chair that was bolted to the floor. A small sun-gun just above his head bathed him in white light. His wrists and ankles were secured to the chair with wide leather straps. His body sagged forwards. His chin was on his chest. Beneath the chair was a pan-shaped depression. A series of runnels connected it with an open drain that ran down one side of the chamber. The Protector realised distastefully that the purpose of this system was the easy removal of blood and urine. There was no pretence that the chamber had been constructed for any other purpose but for torture. The walls and floor were of white, easily swabbed ceramic tiles. A number of hooks and pulleys were set in a beam in the ceiling. Along the wall opposite the drain were a set of racks and a glass-fronted cabinet. The racks held the larger, more mundane instruments: whips, clamps, iron pincers, electrical contacts and lengths of chain. In the glass cabinet there were devices that not even Trenhyass recognised. A figure in a leaf-green robe was standing in the shadows behind Gywann's chair. This was not what the Protector had expected.

'What are you doing here?'

It was Heizen who answered. 'Orfall here is a Six Elder of the College of Healers.'

'I know what Orfall is. What I want to know is why he is here. This is hardly a place of healing.'

'I summoned Elder Orfall. It occurred to me that a simple and obvious, but possibly crucial examination would be to determine at the start if the man was actually human.'

The Protector's face was blank. He looked directly at Elder Orfall. 'And is he?'

'Just about.'

Trenhyass was now keeping his temper in check only with the greatest of difficulty. 'What the hell is that supposed to mean?'

'If I had more sophisticated equipment . . . the Wasps killed so much of our technology.'

'I don't want to hear about what happened two centuries ago. What do you mean by "just about human"?'

'I mean that I've scanned him as best I can and he's perfectly normal except in one respect. There's this abnormality at the base of his brain, a mass of tissue that shouldn't be there. I'd say it was a tumour, but with a tumour that size he should have been dead years ago.'

'But he's alive and healthy.'

'He's in perfect health.'

'So what is this thing in his brain? This growth?'

Elder Orfall looked uncomfortable. 'I don't know.'

There was a long silence. Trenhyass paced the length of the room, then he turned to Heizen. 'Has he said anything?'

'He talked a bit about a vision he had.'

'You have a record of this?'

'Indeed.' Heizen held out a hand to his guard. 'Notes.'

The Killer pulled a number of papers from his tunic. Heizen shuffled through them. He read aloud: '"I was nothing and I was lost. I had come to a dark place far beyond the Blackwater and then I saw the sun".'

'Son?'

'We took it to mean sun, as in sky, if you see what I mean.'

Heizen went on reading. '"I was alone and I was afraid. I had lost my home and the dark strangers were abroad in the land. I walked beside the waters and I heard the mournful wind moving through the reeds." There's a lot more of the same kind of thing. He seems incapable of talking normally.'

Elder Orfall chimed in, anxious to vindicate himself. 'It could be a result of the growth on his brain.'

Unnoticed by anyone, Gywann's eyes had opened. Trenhyass was looking hard at Orfall. 'The growth that should have killed him?'

'Yes.'

'I'm not impressed.'

Heizen came partway to Orfall's rescue. He cast a significant look in the direction of the racks and the cabinet and sniffed. 'You might have been more impressed if you'd allowed my people to stress him a little.'

Gywann's head was slowly lifting. He was turning his face up towards the light. His lips were starting to twitch. Still no one noticed him. They all had their backs to him, absorbed by their argument.

'You know my feeling about unnecessary torture.'

Heizen's mouth twisted into a sneer. 'I know your feeling about torture and I also know how you've frequently benefited from information obtained that way.'

'The words I used were unnecessary torture. You hear me? Unnecessary.'

Heizen glared at Trenhyass. 'Are you prepared to lay down a rule as to what pain is necessary and what isn't?'

'If one is needed.'

Heizen shrugged, as though giving up hope of any understanding with the Protector. 'You want me to go on reading this stuff?'

'Please do.'

Heizen started again. '"I was far beyond the Blackwater. I was deep in the swamps, where only the bad things can survive."'

Gywann was now staring directly into the light. His mouth opened.

'I was far beyond the Blackwater. I was deep in the swamps where only the bad things can survive.'

He was echoing Heizen exactly. His voice was hoarse and cracked. It rasped painfully and was so lacking in intonation that it sounded as though he were in a trance. Trenhyass and Heizen spun around. Gywann's right hand jerked against the strap.

'I was far beyond the Blackwater and the sun came down to me. The sun came down in the night. Its light shone all around and I was afraid. The water was so bright that I feared I might go blind but the sun embraced me in my fear and took me up. The sun took me into itself and carried me away to where I was safe and warm. I slept inside the sun for the longest time and I knew nothing until the black demons came with the pain. I knew nothing until the black demons attacked me. I fought them back but they were too strong. Even in my sleep, I felt the pains in my head. The blue friends came to me. They wanted to ease my pain but they couldn't. The blue friends couldn't understand. They didn't know about the pain and what the black demons could do.'

The Protector looked from Heizen to Orfall. 'Has he been drugged?'

'No.'

The Protector didn't seem convinced. Orfall was becoming increasingly anxious. 'I didn't use any drugs, I swear.'

Gywann went right on talking. 'But then the demons left me and the pain was gone almost as though it hadn't been. Again I slept for a long time and the tiny dancers came to me and surrounded me. The tiny dancers led me back to the sun and again I was blinded and again I was taken up by the light. Only this time it let me fall. I fell and I fell and I believed that I would surely die.'

Gywann's expression changed. His head fell forwards. He was blinking. His eyes were bloodshot and watery. He looked at the people standing around him. 'But I didn't die.'

Heizen muttered under his breath, 'You might yet.'

'I didn't die. I woke by the roadside. I was naked and the sun had gone. The tiny dancers were no more and the blue friends were nowhere to help me. I was hurt but it was a plain human hurt and I knew that my vision was over. That was the way the first woman found me. She fed me and she clothed me and she dressed my wound and, with her, I discovered that the blue friends had left me with a little of their power.'

The Protector leaned over Gywann. 'What was this power you discovered?'

Gywann's face changed again. His eyes focused and the twitching stopped. His expression was open and calm. His voice ceased to rasp. 'I could create comfort. I could bring people to me and make them forget their pain. I brought joy to the first women and they followed me. I brought comfort and joy to those who found me along the way. I could make them warm the way that the blue friends made me warm.'

'Who are the blue friends.'

'I don't know.'

'You don't know?'

'The sun took me to them. That's all I know. It was my vision.'

Heizen shook his head. 'I don't understand why you waste time with this doubletalk.'

'All I can do now is to tell my vision to all who will listen. All I can do is to release the love and spread the warmth that the blue friends gave me.'

Orfall was watching Gywann with widening eyes. A look of sorrow was spreading over his face. Trenhyass noticed what was happening to the Elder but he didn't say anything. Heizen's voice, on the other hand, took on the hardness of the interrogator. 'And as you go around spreading love, how is it that the Wasps don't bother you?'

'I don't know. I just feel that I don't have to be afraid of the Black Strangers. If I'm not afraid of the Black Strangers, the Black Strangers can't see me. I've made no secret of that.'

'So you admit that when you preach about these Black Strangers, you're talking about the Wasps.'

'Things have many names.'

Heizen looked triumphantly at Trenhyass. 'That's sedition.'

'We're looking for facts, not charges.'

Heizen showed signs of exasperation. 'Then torture him.'

'Not yet.'

Heizen turned back to Gywann. 'Perhaps you'd like to tell me how you managed to implode one of my Killers?'

'I don't know. It just happened. I have told this story many times before. She meant me harm and it happened. Perhaps her own evil came back on her.'

Heizen rounded on the Protector. 'Let me put him to torture, damn it. I'll quickly stop this nonsense.'

Trenhyass drew Heizen to the corner of the chamber. He hoped that they'd be out of earshot of Orfall, Gywann and the two guards.

'Did it ever occur to you that he may not be talking nonsense? He may be describing as best he can something that happened to him.'

'What? That's absurd.'

'Imagine this scenario. This man is nothing. He's lost somewhere beyond the Blackwater. He sees something like the sun. An alien craft perhaps. He's taken into it. The craft takes him somewhere. It's completely alien. There is nothing familiar, nothing he can grasp. He sleeps a lot, but he also suffers pain, particularly in his head. He is tended by beings that he calls his blue friends. There are also other beings that he calls the tiny dancers. In the end, he's returned to the sun craft. He experiences a sensation of falling and then wakes up on earth. Does it say anything to you?'

'It tries my patience.'

The Protector's patience was also being tried. 'Think, man, think for once instead of just reacting. It's garbled, I admit, but the man could be describing how he was picked up by some nonhuman craft and taken to a place where he suffered pain; where he possibly underwent some kind of surgery. We already know that there's something abnormal about his brain. Finally, when the surgery or whatever is over, he's dumped back here in the city where he finds that he has a number of unexplained powers.'

Heizen's face was contemptuous. 'Are you saying that he's the product of some Wasp experiment?'

'That's one possibility.'

'What are the others?'

'I don't know.'

'I seem to be hearing that a lot today.'

Trenhyass swung round and faced Gywann. 'What is the unfolding?'

Heizen shook his head. 'I think you're losing your grip.'

The Protector raised his voice slightly. 'What is the unfolding?'

'The nature of the unfolding will only be clear when its course has run.'

Heizen advanced angrily on the Protector. 'Just give me two hours to work on him. I'll have anything you want unfolded.'

Gywann's face abruptly changed for a second time. His jaw slackened, his eyes became furtive and cunning. Suddenly he could have been any hustler, pimp or petty thief. His hands tugged at his bonds. An ingratiating smile flickered across his face, his voice came out as a wheedling whine.

'Please don't torture me, my good lords, I'm really not worth it. It's the women. They just like to listen to me speak. You must know how it is, my lords. There must be many women around powerful men like you. I daresay you can handle it, but I'm just weak, I can't resist them. I was just trying to make a diem, my lords, and it got out of hand. Please don't torture me. I'm nobody. I'm nothing at all. You lords don't want to bother with no one like me.'

'What is all this?'

Orfall leaned forward and put a hand on Gywann's forehead. Gywann flinched and tried to twist away.

'Don't hurt me, lord, I beg you.'

Orfall lifted one of his eyelids. 'He seems to have undergone a complete personality change.'

Heizen glared at the Protector. 'Do you still refuse to let my men probe him? We're getting nowhere here.'

Gywann looked to the Protector with hurt animal eyes. 'Don't let him have me, Lord Protector. Protect me. That's what your name says, isn't it? It was the women who did it. They were the ones who caused all the trouble. Don't let him . . .' Gywann suddenly stiffened as though he were suffering some sort of seizure. His face spasmed and then faded to a blank. His head lifted and tilted back until he was once more staring into the light. Orfall was watching in fascination.

'It's as though there were a number of people inside him fighting for control.'

Heizen continued to face Trenhyass. 'What do you intend to do?'

'Are you demanding an answer from *me*?'

'I am.'

The Protector very deliberately turned to the two guards, Heizen's Killer and his own Legate.

'Leave us.'

The Legate made for the door; the Killer hesitated, looking to the Marshal for instructions. Heizen nodded. The Killer also left.

'You too, Orfall.'

When they were alone with only the silent and transfixed Gywann, Trenhyass straightened his back and with the careful deliberation of a duellist faced his opponent.

'So, Marshal Heizen, perhaps you'll now explain to me exactly what you want. Do you want the man Gywann or is he just a pretext?'

Heizen glanced at Gywann. He was still staring blindly. Trenhyass shook his head. 'I don't think he's paying us any attention. Why don't you just do whatever you have in mind.'

Heizen allowed himself a cold smile. 'There's very little that I couldn't do right at this moment.'

'You feel you have me in your power, Marshal?'

'You are in my power, Lord Protector. There's a full regiment of Killers on combat alert in this tower and I'm confident that in any conflict at least two-thirds of them would remain loyal to me.'

'And now you'll kill me?'

Heizen slowly drew a pulser from his belt. 'That entirely depends on you, my lord. You could abdicate, step down in my favour, or I can kill you. It can be announced that you suffered a stroke. No one will doubt it. You came here of your own free will.'

'And you think the people will simply accept you as Protector?'

'Who has to accept me? A handful of Proprietors, the civil service mandarins? Who will challenge me with the Iron Fists at my back?'

Gywann's voice suddenly rasped out. 'The unfolding continues.'

Heizen jumped as though the voice startled him. His head whipped around. 'What?'

Gywann didn't reply. He was exactly as he had been. In

112

contrast to the Marshal, Trenhyass seemed hardly concerned. 'You've omitted one factor from your calculations, Marshal Heizen.'

A faint sneer tugged gently at the right side of the Marshal's upper lip. 'I have? I can't think what.'

'Will the Wasps accept you as Protector?'

The sneer vanished. Although Heizen did his best to appear unconcerned, a flicker of the eyes betrayed him.

'Do you really think they care?'

'I never attempt to predict what the Wasps will do. I've stayed alive and it's quite possible that the human race has stayed alive because I and the Protectors before me were very careful never to predict what the Wasps might do. You only think in terms of power, Heizen. You never consider the idea of responsibility. You can only be a tyrant if you rule your own kingdom completely. Here you don't. Do I have to remind you that we're a subject people?'

'You're just talking, Trenhyass. You're playing for time.'

'Did you ever think what this occupation has done to us?'

'I don't need to think about anything right now. I've done my thinking. This is the result. It's time to make your choice, Trenhyass. Are you going to live or die?'

There was a pounding on the door of the chamber. A muffled voice came from beyond.

'My lords, my lords! Word has come from the landing stage. The Wasps are here!'

Trenhyass looked down at Heizen's pulser. 'Perhaps it's you who should be doing the choosing?'

'You think your friends have arrived to save you in the nick of time?'

It was a bold front, but Heizen's confidence was starting to fail and Trenhyass knew it.

'They're not my friends, Marshal. They're my masters. What you've failed to understand about the title of Protector is that it means exactly what it says. The Protector stands between humanity and its Wasp conquerors. I quite literally protect one from the other.'

Paying no more attention to either Heizen or the weapon in his hand, the Protector marched to the door and pulled it open. Outside, tension had been mounting rapidly between the opposing groups of Killers and Legates. When the two personal guards and the Healer had emerged from the torture chamber, leaving Heizen and the Protector alone with the prisoner, Horfon had felt his heart sink. The words of Quartercaptain Steige had come back to him: *We could be looking at a simple gesture or we could be looking at the start of a coup.* If the Killers and their Marshal had plans to assassinate, imprison or otherwise harm the Protector, the Legates would fight regardless of the fact that they were overwhelmingly outnumbered, hopelessly outgunned and deep in the very heart of the Killers' own territory. When he'd been inducted into the Corps, Horfon had sworn that he would die for the Protector should the need arise. He had every intention of honouring that most solemn of oaths; he had simply not expected that the need would arise quite so early in his career.

It came as a considerable relief when the door to the torture chamber opened and the Protector emerged, apparently well and prepared to make ready for the Wasps. He waved urgently at the woman Wingleader who had originally obstructed their way at the landing stage.

'Move your damned Killers out of here immediately! No, don't look for instructions from the Marshal, just do exactly what I order and do it now! I won't risk a crowd around Wasps. The rest of you move back. I want you still and silent. You come near Wasps at your own peril.'

Horfon backed up with the rest as word came down the corridor that the Wasps were getting close. As they came into view, they proved to be a little different from the ones that he'd seen that first day in the Grand Audience Chamber. Again there were three of them but instead of walking they rode on a flat, ovoid platform that seemed to be made from a polished grey rock and floated about half a metre above the ground. Each one was crouched in a strange, multi-jointed squat, arms folded in front of it. In some ways they seemed much like a trio of praying mantises but in many other ways they didn't resemble anything. As they passed the long line of cages, their flat, pointed heads swivelled slowly from side to side. It was as if some alien curiosity had been piqued by the unpleasantness that the human species could inflict one on another. A silence fell over the gathered Legates and Killers. Even the incarcerates in the cages were silent. Then one suddenly leaped forwards screaming inarticulately and straining against the bars as though trying to reach out to the Wasps. Everyone held their breath. Would the Wasps retaliate? Would they implode the torture-crazy prisoner? It was conceivable that they would implode everyone in range. Abruptly, the prisoner flopped back, not imploded or even visibly harmed, just suddenly passive. All the other humans shared a single sigh of relief.

The Wasps seemed strangely suited to the Hall of Killers. The red lights were reflected in the surface of their black shiny skins. Their icy, inhuman menace was exactly complemented by the more familiar menace of the Killers. Even their unearthly, angular forms somehow seemed to match the grimly busy, gothic interior. As the Wasps came closer, Trenhyass stood his ground, just in front of the door to the torture chamber. The platform came to a halt a few yards short of the Protector. It lowered itself until it was just centimetres above the ground. As one, the Wasps unfolded to their full height. They stepped off the platform. Horfon felt the hairs on his body start to rise as if there were a static charge in the room. The Wasps advanced on the Protector. There was something about their strange, jerky gait that caused Horfon to repress a shudder. He was sure, no matter how many times he encountered the creatures, that he would never get used to them.

'Na man sept abnorll . . .sect . . . na compreten.'

The Wasps towered over the Protector. The rearmost of them held the dark red box that everyone assumed was their less-than-explicit translation device. The Protector looked the nearest Wasp in the closest thing it had to an eye. 'I'm sorry. I do not comprehend you.'

'Sghtt . . . compren. Ecch hay man seitch most . . . abnorlll.'

One of the Wasps swivelled its head so it was looking at Gywann through the chamber door. The Protector noted the direction of the Wasp's head. 'That man is indeed abnormal. We are in the process of examining him.'

Horfon couldn't imagine how the Protector was able to stay so cool when confronting the aliens.

'Directives is . . . most unclusive monif schraahk. Man conform nonly.'

'We have examined the man but we do not understand him.'

'Warn . . . ni-ni-ni . . . warn of the potential . . . to function-integrate.'

'I am aware of that. That is the warning with every directive. I cannot be responsible for this man. I have had him arrested. The only other course of action is to have him killed. If that's what you require, we will comply.'

The Wasps appeared to confer with each other. In

addition to the static, Horfon now had the feeling that there were noises in the air that his ears couldn't quite hear. One of the Wasps stooped and moved through the door of the torture chamber. It first examined the rack and the cabinets. It removed a whip from a hook on the wall and flexed it between the multiple digits at the end of its arms. Then it replaced the whip and turned its attention to Gywann. As it moved around him, seemingly scrutinising him from every angle, Gywann's head slowly fell forwards. Then it lifted. 'I have no need of fear.'

The alien moved around him once more. It stood for a moment, and as if satisfied with the inspection ducked back out through the human-sized door.

'Exe . . . plan na lacking. Match not with current continuation . . . closeness to . . . inconvenience.'

'I would not wish to risk an inconvenience. I would certainly not wish to function-integrate. Perhaps the best solution would be for us simply to execute the man as soon as possible.'

'Negative.'

That at least was positive and without ambiguity. 'No?'

'Dib-dib, na-na . . . more continue await.'

'We do nothing?'

'Await.'

The Protector bowed slightly. 'Then we will await.'

The one Wasp ducked again into the torture chamber and took another look at Gywann. When it emerged, all three mounted the floating platform and once again arranged themselves into the squatting position. The platform lifted, made a 180-degree turn and drifted silently away, down past the line of cells. The prisoner who had tried to grab at the Wasps stirred and twitched; he made a slight whimpering noise. When the Wasps were out of sight, Heizen rather hesitantly approached the Protector.

'What happens now, my lord?'

Trenhyass's face was expressionless. 'Gywann will be kept here for the next seventy-two hours. If your men really feel the need they can rough him up a bit, but I don't want him seriously harmed. After that time, dump him in the lowers.'

This wasn't the answer that Heizen wanted. 'I meant what will happen to me?'

'You, Marshal Heizen? Nothing will happen to you. You will remain in command of your Killers. You are one of the

116

most ruthless men in the Protectorate. I have a feeling that very soon I shall require ruthless men.'

'You'd continue to trust me?'

'I've never trusted you, Heizen. I'm simply gambling that the last few minutes have somewhat cooled your desire to be Protector.'

Nine

THE STORM had been raging for two days and showed no signs of even slowing down. Black curtains of rain crashed between the towers, while gale-force winds shrieked and howled down the streets and alleys of the lowers and whipped into destructive spirals on open places like the Oldmarket and the Stoneplane. Storm drains and culverts backed up and overflowed. Whole areas were swallowed by rapidly widening lakes. The water in the deep cellars rose alarmingly. The inhabitants stuck close to wherever was warm and dry. It wasn't just a matter of comfort. There were some parts of the lowers where the winds were strong enough to be positively dangerous, capable of picking up a human being and hurling him or her against a wall or skidding them helplessly across the cobbles.

The Gywannish – this was the tag that the lowers were increasingly hanging on Gywann's followers – pointed to the storm as nature's own rage at the arrest and the supposed murder of their leader. There were a lot of people who, as they watched the downpour through their windows and listened to the scream of the wind, began to wonder if maybe there was some truth to the idea.

Sulanda, who had 'gone Gywannish' herself right after the second time she'd heard the master speak, was attempting to make her way down Moord Alley. She was headed for one of the cult's houses right by the Stoneplane, the very house in fact from which the Killers had dragged her prophet away to his death. Wind tore at her clothes and she was soaked to the skin. With her head down she kept close to the nearest wall, occasionally clinging to the stonework when the wind threatened to bowl her over. The middle of the street was a brown rushing torrent that boiled along a course carved out of the stone by a thousand previous downpours. It raced and zigzagged down the length of the street until it cascaded into the dark mouth of an open airshaft.

Sulanda was one of Gywann's women followers who

since his disappearance had discarded the white dress and adopted the black breeches and vest of the young men. This radical change of style was just one of the faithful's reaction to the loss of their leader. At first there had been a stunned disbelief coupled with the fear that the Killers might come back for the rest of them. When no more Killers came, disbelief changed to a deep, black grief, and fear hardened into anger. Where the Gywannish had previously embraced peace, there was now only talk about the battle that was coming, the battle between the forces of good and the forces of evil, particularly the forces of evil as personified by the Protector and his Killers. So far there was only talk, wild talk maybe, fuelled by the background noise of the storm, but talk just the same. No one had so far suggested any concrete action but the mood was ugly.

Sulanda reached the end of Moord Alley where it intersected with the wide expanse of the Latin Trench. Here the wind and rain spun in a miniature whirlwind. She knew that any minute her feet would go out from under her. She ducked into the comparative shelter of a doorway and considered her next move. To go around the Latin Trench would be safer but it would take time. She was frozen and her teeth were starting to chatter. On the other hand it seemed that the Latin Trench might well prove to be impassable. To underscore the point, a boojie came bouncing across the floor of the trench, squelching and whistling and helplessly waving its flippers. Sulanda watched with distaste as it rolled and bowled by. She hated the damn things. There were enough earthly parasites without having to bring in more from outer space. It struck her as strange that one of them should be running around in the rain. Usually they shunned water as if it caused them actual physical harm. It was common knowledge that if you wanted to scare off a boojie you only had to throw a slop pail over it.

She stood and watched the rain until she was convinced that there was no way to cross the concrete apron of the trench without seriously risking a broken arm or leg or worse. She was just turning to start painfully retracing her steps when she saw something else way down the trench. It was so obscured by the rain that she thought at first that it was her imagination, but as it moved towards her it became clearer and more defined. It was like nothing she had ever seen before. A glowing red sphere, maybe two and a half metres across, floating above the ground at twice the height of a man. The sphere seemed unaffected by either the wind or the rain. It maintained a direct course straight up the middle of the street, leaving a faint trail of vapour that was immediately snatched away by the wind. Sulanda took a step back. Some instinct made her press herself against the closed door behind her and make herself as small as possible. This was too much. First Gywann had been taken from them, then the storm, and now this. It had to be some *thing* of the Wasps', although she had never heard anyone tell of seeing one before. Maybe it was this sphere that had sent the boojie panicking through the downpour. It all served to convince her that epic events were afoot in the world, that strange changes were taking place.

The red sphere went on up the trench and vanished back into the rain. Sulanda stood quite still for a few minutes, wondering what she should do. It seemed somehow too important just to go back into the rain. The series of weird events, however, was not yet over. Something else was coming out of the rain, this time from above. First she saw two white lights descending rapidly, then there were smaller red and yellow lights beside the white ones. It was a Killer aircar coming down from the towers, fighting the wind to stop itself being blown into the side of one of the great buildings. It was one of the kind with a cage for prisoners set in the stern, the same kind that had taken Gywann. Pitching and rolling, the craft hovered just above the ground at almost the same point where the red sphere had passed. One of the crew jumped out and hurried back along the side of the aircar, clinging to every available handhold, until he reached the steel cage. A figure was lying on the bottom of the cage. Another Killer joined the first one. Together, they wrestled the body out and dumped it on the ground. With that accomplished, they quickly crawled back into the craft. It lifted away, lurching into the wind.

The figure from the cage lay out on the windswept expanse of stone, mercilessly lashed by the storm. It made a feeble effort to get to its knees, but it seemed too weak for even that. Sulanda knew that if she didn't do something it would certainly die of exposure if it didn't drown first. She took a deep breath, clenched her fists and made a wild dash into the rain. The storm hit at her like a club, almost knocking her off her feet. She had trouble going in the right direction, but in the end she reached the huddled shape. It was lying face down. It no longer had the strength even to lift itself onto its arms. Sulanda quickly rolled it over. She saw the face. Her mouth fell open. She clasped her hands and sank to her knees. Her voice was a gasp.

'Master! . . .'

For a moment Sulanda panicked. Gywann had clearly been systematically beaten. His face was a mass of bruises. His nose seemed to be broken. Her joy at the fact that her master was still alive was pushed aside by the knowledge that he was close to death. She tried dragging him, but he was too heavy. She looked around wildly. The only chance of moving him was if she could get help. She dashed back to the doorway where she'd been standing and pounded on the door.

'Help me! Help me! My master is dying out here!'

At first there was no sound from within and she was afraid that it was an empty building. Then, just as she was getting ready to go and try another door, there was the noise of a bolt being drawn back. The door opened a crack and a suspicious face peered out.

'What's all the noise? Isn't it bad enough with the storm?'

'Please help me. My master is hurt, he may be dying.'

'Master? What master?'

The face belonged to a middle-aged man. It was the kind of face that concerned itself with little except its own problems. Behind the man, Sulanda could see a warm, cosy, well-lit room; a woman came up behind him. She was about the same age as he, quite possibly his wife.

'What's going on, Drado? Who's out there?'

'Some women. I can't make out what she wants. One of them Gywannish by the look of her.'

'Please help me. My master's out here in the storm and he's badly hurt. If we could just drag him inside . . .'

Drado quickly shook his head. 'I can't be letting no strangers into my house on a night like this.'

His wife proved to be a good deal more charitable. 'Shame on you, man. Go out and help the poor child.'

Drado put up a final show of resistance. 'I don't like these people. I don't see why I should take myself out in this weather on their account.'

'You just get out and do it, Drado Jenkyl, and stop your complaining.'

Wrapping a cloak around his shoulders and grumbling all the way, Drado followed Sulanda out into the storm. Between the two of them, they managed to half drag and half carry the now unconscious Gywann into the cosy little room. Immediately they had him inside, Drado's wife bustled round with blankets and towels. She was surprised when Sulanda, standing in the doorway and looking as if she was about to leave, thanked her once more.

'And where do you think you're going, my girl? You can't go out into that again.'

'I have to. I have to tell the others that the master lives.' With that, she was through the door and gone.

Ten

IT WAS as though the whole of the lowers had come pouring from the inns and the cellars, the sublevel apartments and the lean-tos and even the caves and the hovels. The rain had stopped and Gywann had come back from the dead and the streets were dancing. It wasn't that everyone cared so much about the well-being of the boy prophet, even though more and more went Gywannish every day. In the lowers, even the thinnest excuse was grasped when there was the chance of a spontaneous carnival and the ability to forget, even temporarily, the details of real life. Disapproval of Gywann and his flourishing religion certainly didn't stop Jeen Vayim from leaving the bar-room and joining the parade to see what came his way while the euphoria was running. At that particular moment his reward was a comfortable quantity of wine in a leather cup and a young woman whose name he didn't know but who was wearing an exceedingly thin silk dress and seemed delighted with the idea of pressing herself against him and insinuating her tongue into his ear. The Poet suspected that she was possibly drunk enough not to know her name either, but that hardly seemd reason to disengage himself.

They weren't the only couple in the crowded streets who were entwined and stumbling. One at a time, in pairs, in threes and fours and whole gangs, everyone in the lowers milled and sang and shouted. Bedding and drapes were hung from open windows. It was a practical airing-out after the storm but it also created the illusion that the lanes and alleys were decked with flags. The beggars had taken the day off. The whores and the hostesses, the funboys and the bosses and the dancers from the joints were out in their plumes and spangles, strutting and posturing; lips were red, eyes were painted and hair was piled in festive confections. The performers of the quarter also strutted, displaying their tricks for the crowds. Pipes trilled and drums pounded; doves were conjured from out of thin air and snakes slithered from the insides of wide, mysterious sleeves. In front of the eating house known as the Final Opportunity a well-built, scantily dressed woman posed against a painted board while the knives thrown by her equally under-dressed partner flashed and thudded all around her. Proofrules danced on their hind legs and chickens pretended they could tell the future. The Poet spotted the Zilla Brothers doing the trick with the eggs, the pole and the steel slocci balls. Jeen Vayim almost waved, but decided it would be inadvisable. To distract even one of the brothers just for an instant could transform the trick into a messy disaster.

The young woman seemed to be trying to wrap her right leg three times around his. A Gywannish couple strolled by them with stupid grins on their faces. Their grins broadened as they caught sight of Jeen Vayim and his companion. Since Gywann had returned from the dead, his followers had become nearly insufferable in their smug, indulgent, goodwill to all.

'All the blessings on you, friend, Don't fear the strangers.'

The Poet wagged his finger and nodded. 'Um . . . yeah. Likewise.

A few of the Gywannish women had gone back to the pristine white robes but most retained the black breeches and vest. Since their saviour had come back to them, their whole image seemed to be undergoing yet another transformation. The previously sombre black was breaking out in elaborate, decorative beadwork. Some of the more adventurous were wearing feathers and beads in their hair. They were starting to take on the look of a wild and primitive tribe. They were developing an air of defiance. The phrase 'don't fear the strangers' was used constantly in their conversation. It was spoken like a challenge, both to the Wasps and the Protector. They were starting to give the impression that they believed Gywann had somehow developed supernatural powers while he'd been in the hands of the Killers. It seemed they no longer viewed the episode as a simple arrest and interrogation but as a symbolic death and rebirth. It was said that this new fad for beading their clothes was accompanied by ritual and chanting behind closed doors. It wasn't just an exercise in decoration, they also believed that they were making themselves invulnerable. It was something that would normally have filled Vayim with deep misgivings. People who think they're invulnerable usually finish up as victims. Success, or even survival, required a minimum of practical humility. Right at that moment, though, the Poet was beyond caring about humility, success or even survival except in its most basic and automatic form. The young woman was attempting to breathe something into his ear.

'. . . I nearly went insane during the storm, I was all by myself and . . .'

They were both sent staggering by a fat man with a load on, a big doughy karfol in one hand and a jug of beer in the other. By the time the Poet had thought up suitable abuse, the fat man had waddled on his way and was out of earshot. The street seemed to be even busier, if that was actually possible. Somewhere nearby Gywann was being hauled around by the faithful in triumphant procession. The step-up in the level of commotion seemed to indicate that this circus was coming their way.

The first movement was the bow wave of people who precede any parade, the ones who are not actually a part of it but are just driven along by its momentum. In among them, drunks who wanted to believe that they were a part of something staggered and capered, shouted and sang. The procession proper began with a line of girls and young women who trilled a happy if wordless song and strewed the cobbles and flagstones of the roadway with tiny paper flowers. These symbolic maidens were followed by what could only be described as a gang of proud savages. These were the elite of Gywannish who had gone the furthest into the chants of the beads and the feathers. Gywann seemed to be very quickly creating a warrior caste to defend his faith. There were both men and women. Some carried heavy staves or knives, some had shaved heads while others sported elaborate braids. Some had even painted their faces. They stalked and they swaggered as though ultra-conscious of some new inner power that had been given them. The Poet wasn't surprised to see Sulanda right in the middle. Since Gywann's return from the towers she had become an integral part of the legend. She was The Most Worshipped Sulanda who had brought their prophet from out of the storm to shelter and safety. She had also seen the vision of the red sphere, although no one had yet voiced an acceptable explanation for that part. From the way she held herself and the pleasure she seemed to take in basking in the admiration of those around her, it was clear that Sulanda greatly enjoyed the role of The Most Worshipped. Nobody would ever call her Dirty Sulanda again.

For Gywann himself, the faithful had built an enormous ceremonial cart on which to ride in splendour. The project had been accomplished with a good deal more enthusiasm than skill, but the crudeness of the construction was adequately disguised by thick garlands of more paper flowers. The cart was hauled by twenty or so sweating, singing young men who seemed delighted to be relegated to the level of draught animals in the service of their prophet. They were stripped to the waist, hauling on ropes that were also liberally decked with flowers. Gywann sat in state at the very top of the ramshackle structure, cross-legged and doing his very best to stay erect and serene. This was only accomplished with extreme difficulty for the cart bumped, swayed and lurched unmercifully as its solid wooden wheels crashed and rumbled across the worn, uneven surfaces of the streets of the lowers.

The cart was dutifully followed by what had to be all the rest of the faithful. As they streamed past the Poet, it seemed as though their numbers could run into tens of thousands. Gywann must be close to taking over the whole of the area. These people weren't just the young and the fanatic. These were the ordinary people of the lowers. These were the grandmothers and the noisy children, stooped old men who kept up with the parade even though every step was an effort; whole families treated the event as though it was the chance for a holiday outing. Some carried hastily daubed religious pictures, primitively romantic versions of Gywann in what the artists assumed to be divine attitudes. Others carried flags and banners, streamers and yet more paper garlands. Up in a high window overlooking the parade, a man played the control lines of a dragon kite that dipped and soared in an updraught. The more confused of the faithful carried on display the kind of ancient relics that were bought and sold on the Oldmarket. Somehow the Gywannish had managed to infiltrate and at least partially co-opt the much more vulnerable but less clearly defined worship of the past.

Drunk as he was, Jeen Vayim couldn't fail to feel a basic magic in this procession and he allowed himself to be carried along by it. It wasn't too much of an effort. Most of the winesellers were moving in the same direction. The young woman without a name had momentarily detached herself from her position on his body and was blearily casting around to find her next drink. Her attention was caught by a burly individual in the plastic suit of a router. He had a quart jar of zuiffe under each arm. The Poet was suddenly on his own again. It didn't bother him too much. He was still sober enough to know that it would have been only a matter of time before she either passed out or threw up on him. He twitched at the smell of a hot-pie vendor's wares and decided it was high time to eat himself at least partway back to reality.

For a while he munched and drank contentedly, following the parade but not quite keeping pace with it and allowing himself to fall further and further behind Gywann and his ceremonial cart. With the focus of the singing and shouting far enough ahead to be simply a pleasant buzz in the distance, it was possible to enjoy the affair as just a stroll on a warm day after the rain. Now and again he saw the big router. He was hard to miss in the bright plastic suit. He was now carrying the young woman in the thin silk dress. She was quite unconscious. The router didn't seem particularly disturbed by the burden and he went right on drinking from one of his jars and following the procession. Routers were a strange breed with decidedly odd attitudes. The Poet allowed himself a satisfied smile. It was always good to have one's instincts confirmed.

Jeen Vayim was having such a good time that it was quite some time before he noticed that, slowly but surely, the parade appeared to be leaving the lowers. They were emerging from the Passmore Tunnel and starting up the Tryonramp. This was traditionally the great divide where one world ended and another began. Once on the Tryonramp, there was only one place to go. That was straight onto the wide, windswept, open expanse of the Curvebridge. The Curvebridge was definitely no part of the lowers. Its broad but soaring span was the path to the middle levels and, eventually, the high towers themselves. The procession was going the way of madness. Vayim tried to imagine what was going on in Gywann's mind. Had the Killers beaten him insane? Did he truly believe that he and his people were invulnerable and that he could invade the rest of the city with a misfit rabble carrying paper flowers?

Vayim instinctively looked up. It took him a few moments to find them. The squad of Killers, maybe a dozen strong, was some ten storeys above him, hanging in their flying-belts.

They were tucked in close to the side of a building so they wouldn't be conspicuous. The Poet wondered how long they'd stay that way. What Gywann was doing must constitute a direct challenge to their power and authority. He suddenly wanted to be somewhere, anywhere, else. He was rapidly becoming convinced that this parade was going to end in disaster. He looked behind him. For as far back as he could see there were people, all coming on, all oblivious to the potential for danger.

The singing had stopped. Vayim assumed that at the front of the procession they were fanning out across the Curvebridge. Rank after rank they came over the top of the Tryonramp and moved out onto the awesome span of stone bridge. In a city of wonders, the Curvebridge was one of the most breathtaking pieces of construction. It arched across a thousand metres of empty air, rising in a wide, easy spiral until it finally ended in the hanging Windplaza that was itself suspended between two towers. As the Poet came over the top of the ramp and was able for the first time to see the thousands of people streaming up the impossible span of stone, he simply had to stop. He shook his head and took a drink. The world was truly crazy. He had often tried to imagine the people who would have erected such a structure but he had never managed a satisfactory image. He knew that they must have been men like himself but he had difficulty accepting that. The thing was just too big, too hugely grandiose, too monstrously out of proportion. Forty storeys below were the shadowy canyons of the lowers. The Poet was struck by how much more sky there was once you started to ascend the towers. Although he spent by no means all his time in the lowers, it was something that always filled him with a cold resentment. He saw no reason why he and so many more should spend so much of their time confined in the dark roots of the city, as good as underground. Every man had a right to his own piece of sky.

This particular sky was becoming more than a little crowded. More squads of Killers were moving in on the marchers. The only consolation was that for the present they seemed to be maintaining a discreet distance. In addition to this official interest, word had spread through the towers and residences that this strange mob of singing and dancing Gywannish had appeared from out of the lowers. Untidy knots of curious civilians in flying-belts straggled between the buildings, contrasting sharply with the tight formations of the Killers. Twenty or more carriages cruised slowly above the parade. Some of the hard-core Gywannish shouted and waved to them.

'Come down and join us!'

'Don't fear the strangers!'

'Join us! Join us!'

Gywann's flower-decked car reached the centre of the bridge. It executed a slow turn and came to a stop. This manoeuvre must have been prearranged. Bit by bit, the procession also halted. The Gywannish elite ranged themselves around the cart. A team of young men seemed to be tearing down the lower part of the vehicle, removing heavy pieces of equipment from previously concealed recesses. It dawned on the Poet that Gywann's intention was to hold his biggest meeting ever, right there in the middle of Curvebridge. Vayim had to give him full points for audacity, but it remained to be seen whether the Killers would allow it to happen. The Gywannish went on with their preparations. A bank of pressure horns floated upwards, supported by a number of tethered skyhooks. An outer ring of the young elite in their beads and feathers pushed back the front rows of the faithful, clearing a space around the giant cart. An expectant hush spread outwards from this focal point. People at the back began to press forward for a better view. The young men and women in black had trouble controlling the crowd. The Killers eased closer. Tension was building and Gywann had yet to say a word. He sat still and calm on top of the cart.

When he appeared satisfied that everyone was ready for him, Gywann came slowly to his feet. He was wearing the familiar white robes and the gold device around his neck. It didn't stop with him standing; as he straightened his body he floated up and away from the cart until he was hanging in the air above the crowd. Even though it was obvious to everyone that he was wearing a flying-belt under his robe, the trick was still impressive. Parts of the crowd began to cheer and shout. Gywann drifted sideways above their heads. He passed over the parapet of the bridge and moved out until he was literally standing in mid-air. It was only then that he started speaking.

'Don't fear the strangers.'

The faithful roared back, 'We don't fear the strangers.'

Jeen Vayim shook his head. This kind of drama would

get the boy killed one of these days. He just hoped that this day wouldn't be the one.

'No one should fear the strangers.'

'We don't fear the strangers.'

The call and response went on for some time. The faithful seemed to set great store by the chance to roar out an echo to their prophet's words. Now the following had become so large it was the only taste of direct communication with their prophet that was offered to most of them.

'The great unfolding continues.'

This time there was silence. This wasn't a statement that called for a response. This was the start of his address. The crowd settled down to listen.

'Oh, my pale children, we grow in strength and we grow in numbers. The blessings are all round us and our hope protects us. We have stood firm against the wind and we have come through the storm. We have faced the wrath of our captors and the hatred of our enemies and we have prevailed.'

The Poet muttered under his breath, 'Just keep prevailing long enough for us all to get out of here.'

'But, oh my pale children, my faithful children, my fearless children, our greatest trials still await us. Our time of ordeal has yet to come. We have battled the wind and rain but there can be no rest. Our race is not yet run. Our ship has yet to reach a safe haven. We have come from the rain and the lightning but there can be no rest. Our trials have strengthened us but our ordeal will make us free. The lightning has transformed my children into men and women. It has prepared us all to face the fire. It has prepared us to walk into the flames. We will emerge as gods.'

Vayim didn't like the sound of this. Gywann seemed to be implying either that he planned even crazier and more extreme stunts or that, worse still, he was virtually inviting an attack from the Killers.

'Oh, my poor children.' His words were soft and drawn out. 'Oh, my poor children. There are battles ahead. We will struggle and we will suffer but we will not accept their fear, we will be used cruelly and reviled but we will not let them thrust their fear on us. We will walk in blindness and in pain and times will come when we are tempted to despair of an ending, but we will not be a part of their fear.'

Gywann's voice was starting to rise. It might have been an acoustic trick or just a freak of the wind patterns but each time he spoke the word 'fear', the air seemed to throb and reverberate. There was no doubt that the tricks and the rhetoric were working on the crowd. Many of them were completely transfixed. A woman, way over on Vayim's right, fell to her knees and began to shriek and bellow in a language that only she understood. Her torso twitched and jerked and her arms waved frantically in the air. Some of those around her also knelt. Her movements became so violent that she pitched forwards on her face. She beat the ground with her fists and she tore at her hair and clothes without for a minute letting up her unintelligible shouting. No one attempted to help her. Two of the hard core in black and beadwork were actually egging her on to greater levels of frenzy. From somewhere further away there was the sound of someone else doing the same thing. The noise of their raving provided a bizarre counterpoint to Gywann's voice.

'Though we stand at the edge of the world and stare into the abyss, we will not let their fear lay hand upon us.' He was fully into his stride. 'Though their shadow covers us and our enemies surround us, even then we will not let their fear near us. If we don't fear the strangers, they cannot harm us.'

The crowd roared back, 'DON'T FEAR THE STRANGERS!'

'Don't fear the strangers and they cannot move us.'

This was pure demagoguery. The Poet was close to deciding that Gywann really was mad. Again the crowd roared.

'DON'T FEAR THE STRANGERS!'

'Without fear we cannot be stopped and we cannot be destroyed.'

The choir was singing. The crowd was cheering. Everything was mounting to some kind of climax. The Killers were moving nervously, the flying thrill-seekers were drawing closer as if sensing something was about to happen. Gywann's voice had risen to an angry, fist-shaking shout.

'Without fear, we are invincible!'

The crowd exploded. It was believing every word. It roared out its strength. A captive and defeated people was being offered dignity and a wild hope. And then the cheering faltered, the applause failed and faded. The Gywannish fell silent and even the choir stumbled and stopped. A black, ovoid Wasp aircraft had emerged from between two towers and was moving slowly towards the Curvebridge. A number of the civilian carriages erupted in a sudden panicky motion, sliding away from the Wasp craft like smaller fish fleeing before the approach of a shark. The Killers held their ground but their formations lacked the usual confidence.

The Wasp aircraft seemed to be made of some dull black metal that had the capacity to absorb light. There were no breaks in its apparently seamless surface, no windows, no ports, no kind of exhaust, not even a visible door. There was no indication of what propelled it or what kept it in the air. Gywann was among the last to see it. The Wasp machine was coming from directly behind him. At first he seemed puzzled at why the crowd had suddenly fallen silent. It was something beyond his experience. He seemed unable to accept that they were no longer responding to him.

'We have no need to fear.'

It was the first time that the Poet had heard him sound uncertain. Unseen by Gywann, the Wasp aircraft loomed over his left shoulder. Suddenly he turned. Vayim would have given anything right then to see the expression on Gywann's face. For a few moments he was completely motionless. The Wasp craft advanced slowly towards the bridge. The air was filled with a high, barely audible sound, at the upper limit of human hearing but still extremely irritating. The Poet's hair was trying to rise up on his head. His skin prickled and spasmed. Gywann slowly started to sink, as though the Wasp craft was forcing him down. His body twisted and he slipped sideways so he was at least once again over the bridge. He continued to sink. Down and down, his feet touched the ground. He seemed to stand stunned, then slowly he raised his arms as though throwing off the weight that had been placed upon him. His voice was clear.

'We do not fear you.'

Jeen Vayim couldn't help but be impressed. He would never in a million years have talked back to the large alien ovoid that was now almost above them, casting its shadow on the crowd.

'We do not fear you.'

The Wasp aircraft slowed. It came to a stop exactly over the crowd. Everyone stared up. They stood motionless, open-mouthed. The world was holding its breath. Gywann spoke again.

'If we don't fear you, you cannot harm us.'

132

The Poet winced. He felt sick; this last taunt seemed a piece of monumental rashness but the Wasp craft did nothing. Gywann seemed to take it as a signal.

'You can do us no harm. We don't fear you, strangers.'

It ran like a sigh through the crowd.

'Don't fear the strangers.'

Still nothing happened. The noise of the crowd rose to a sullen mumble.

'Don't fear the strangers.'

No terrible death lashed down from above. The crowd grew bold.

'Don't fear the strangers!'

And even bolder.

'*Don't fear the strangers!*'

The anger that came from years of frustration took hold of them. Faces grew twisted with rage.

'DON'T FEAR THE STRANGERS!'
'DON'T FEAR THE STRANGERS!'
'DON'T FEAR THE STRANGERS!'
'DON'T FEAR THE STRANGERS!'

The Wasp aircraft moved. There was a mass intake of breath and a hush. The craft continued to move, it was no longer over the bridge. It was moving away. Vayim couldn't believe his eyes. The Wasps were moving on. They'd been challenged and they'd done nothing.

'We beat them.'

There was a buzz of surprise all through the crowd. Gywann's voice rode over it.

'We beat them.'

'We beat them!'

The cheering surpassed anything that had gone before. People grabbed hold of each other. There was embracing, kissing, dancing. Vayim looked down and saw that he still had a half-finished cup of wine in his hand. He drained it in one gulp. He could hear himself laughing with relief along with everyone else.

Eleven

'IS IT true that you have an officer specially delegated to beat your children, Marshal Heizen?'

'The story is a fabrication, madame. I have no children and if I had, I very much doubt that they'd require beating. Could we please get back to the matter in hand?'

The Lady Mariko gently patted the orchid in her hair and treated Heizen to a look of diamond-hard dislike.

'You're just itching to put the lowers to fire and sword, aren't you, Marshal? It's even making you forget your manners.'

'I have no desire to give offence, madame, but after the events of today I see no other course except to teach these people a lasting lesson in the meaning of obedience to discipline.'

The Lady Mariko delicately placed a sliver of candied fuissalki into her mouth.

'Is that strictly necessary? I mean, what harm was done? A Wasp airship was shouted at, so what? We don't even know that there were Wasps inside the craft. If there were, they didn't do anything. When we get down to it, Marshal, you seem to be the only one who's getting upset.'

Heizen gestured to a servant to refill his glass. A sinuous brown youth clad only in a loincloth poured wine from a copper ewer.

'This is not only an act of defiance against the Wasps, it's a gesture against us. A mob came out of the lowers and demonstrated right there on Curvebridge. Nothing like it has happened in living memory. It's a major step towards anarchy. We have to suppress this movement – this religion – with all possible harshness before it takes any further steps. The Wasps tolerate us because we maintain a stable social order. If that order goes, what will become of us all?'

The Lady Mariko continued to scowl at Heizen.

'I went to a lot of trouble to organise this dinner, Marshal, and you are quite spoiling it. Have you any idea how long it took my chefs to prepare a baffern stuffed with dwarf quails? The dessert alone required three of them to work on it for a full day. And the wine: it took my butler months to find just a single cask of what you're so carelessly drinking.'

Heizen bowed his head in a less-than-sincere apology. 'I'm sorry, my lady. The meal was exquisite. I had no intention of spoiling any part of it. Believe me, I'm fully aware of the trouble to which you must have gone.'

Mariko Trenhyass raised herself on one elbow. She had staged the dinner-party in the classic manner with reclining couches and long low tables. It was the first time that the Silver Dining Room had been used in possibly five years and it had required a good deal of refurbishing. Her plan had been to create an atmosphere that would combine the formally lavish with a chance for a degree of hedonistic relaxation. She wanted to offer a change, to put aside, at least temporarily, thoughts of the seemingly daily crises, the constant plotting and tensions and, above all, the Wasps. The silver leaf that covered the walls and ceiling of the room had been cleaned and restored, the white marble of the floor had been scrubbed until it shone like a mirror. The fountain had been returned to working order. The Lady Mariko considered that too much of the Halls had been allowed by her brother to fall into disuse and disrepair. Whenever she had the chance to reclaim a room, she took it.

She had personally supervised the final details. She had watched while the outraged peacock was manhandled into its silver cage to provide a corner conversation-piece. She had taken time to listen to a sample of the warblings of the quintet of castrati who were installed in the musicians' gallery. Finally she had checked the place settings and flowers, both on the high table that was for her real guests and on the lower tables where the lesser mortals would sit, the ones who'd spend a lifetime talking about the night they'd dined in the presence of the Protector. As a final nervous afterthought, she had once again inspected the team of pretty, scantily-clad young men whom she'd hand-picked to serve the food and the wine.

With this uncharacteristic effort behind her, it was little surprise that her fury mounted as Heizen continued systematically to ruin the conversation. The man was a one-track obsessive. When her brother had insisted that the Marshal be invited as a supposed act of fence-mending, she had had misgivings. They were now being confirmed manyfold. Heizen had succeeded in isolating and silencing the other guests at the high table. Her friend Varice Leass, Proprietor Naish and his mistress, Tomse Laffin and Conductor Fore Dortle toyed with their food and waited for the moment when they might be able to leave. Even at the low tables, the petty officials, the junior officers and the few pretty sluts who'd been invited to make the evening more pleasant watched covertly, sensing that trouble was brewing.

'Do you never relax, Marshal? Do you never drag your mind away from your work? You sound as though you live and breathe plots and politics. Don't you know any gossip?'

'I don't have time for gossip, madame. Our situation is far too serious.'

When Heizen first arrived, Mariko had entertained a slight hope that the evening might not turn out to be a total loss. The Marshal had dressed himself in a white silk uniform heavy on insignia and decorations, and for a few moments Mariko had wondered if the leader of the Killers might have a human side after all. She had even considered attempting to pair him with Varice Leass; unless of course like so many of his men Heizen was homosexual, in which case Dortle might have been more apt. Within minutes she knew that any such social efforts would be a waste of time. Heizen's clothes were his only compromise with any concept of ease or grace. Like a dog worrying a rat, he kept dragging the conversation back to the situation in the lowers and stubbornly repeating his appeals to the Protector to authorise a purge of the whole area.

'You're a bore, Marshal Heizen.'

'That may be true, madame. I have never concerned myself with how entertaining I appear to others. I see my life as a single, continuous duty.'

Varice Leass glanced up from the dessert that had previously been absorbing all her concentration. 'Duty to what, Marshal? Who or what is the object of this grim and unswerving devotion?'

The acid in her voice was measured out with exquisite delicacy. Varice Leass disliked and distrusted Heizen as much as the Lady Mariko did, but she knew enough to be on guard. The Marshal became stiff and formal.

'My duty is to my planet, to the survival of my species and . . .' He glanced at Trenhyass who was reclining, silently watching the interplay between Heizen and the two women, '. . . and to my Protector.'

The Protector nodded. He seemed more amused than anything else. 'I'm relieved to hear that.'

Trenhyass had surprised his sister by arriving in a loose black kaftan of very fine silk instead of the usual rather drab uniform. It was the ideal garment for a meal taken on reclining couches. All through their lives, her brother had made these small, unpredictable gestures. She expected that he did it to annoy her. At that instant, she was quite sufficiently annoyed by Marshal Heizen.

'That's hypocritical nonsense and you know it. Your only devotion is to the extension of your own personal power and your capacity to shed blood. You're a megalomaniac and a butcher, Marshal, and we really have no need to pretend otherwise. We all knew that when we sat down with you, so I suppose the only thing it proves is that none of us cares very much about whom we eat with.'

'If you were a man, madame . . .'

Mariko raised an eyebrow. 'You'd do what? If I were anybody else but the Protector's sister you'd have me dragged off to those torture chambers of yours long ago. What were the accusations against Lacy Levane after she laughed at you? Sedition and public lewdness? If you arrested everyone who'd ever been guilty of public lewdness to the same extent as Lacy, the towers would have been decimated and your butcher's shop would be backed up for a month or more.'

The Protector raised a hand. 'I think this has gone far enough. You're now merely abusing the Marshal. It doesn't become you.'

Mariko was no longer able to control her temper. She sat up. 'It doesn't become me? What about this thing he wants to set off in the lowers? Several hundred people will certainly be killed without any solid reason other than that Marshal Heizen has spent a lifetime turning his men into a herd of savage animals and he needs a chance to let them loose every now and again.'

Trenhyass leaned forwards. 'In this instance, I agree with him. The lowers do need a sharp, violent shock.'

Mariko was stunned. 'You can't be serious.'

'Indeed I am.'

Marshal Heizen seemed equally surprised. 'Do I have your leave to set the operation in motion?'

137

Trenhyass shook his head. 'No, you don't. We will attempt to salvage what we can of the Lady Mariko's dinner-party. I'll give the formal order in the morning and your men can move on the lowers tomorrow night.'

Mariko was shaking her head. 'You can't be doing this.'

'Indeed I am. The Marshal is quite right. This Gywannish business has gone altogether too far. These people must be rigorously discouraged.'

'But do people have to be killed because of this?'

'If that's the only way they'll learn.'

The Lady Mariko slowly drained her wine glass. 'What has happened to us? Have we abandoned all morality? Are we turning into savages?'

It was Marshal Heizen who answered. 'Morality is a luxury when you're a conquered people.'

Mariko looked to her brother for some kind of support but found none.

'I have to be a realist, my dear.'

'A realist? A descent to immorality, to savagery, is that what you call realism?'

'Questions of morality, civilisation, goodness, call it what you will, would be simply answered if it was just a matter of men against men. It isn't men against men, though. We are the subjects of the Wasps. In everything we do, we have to consider their reaction. They intrude into all aspects of our lives. They are our masters in the most literal sense.'

Mariko seemed scarcely convinced. 'How can we even know what their reactions are. We're hardly able to communicate with them.'

'That's even more reason why in a case like this we have to act swiftly, even brutally. It's my responsibility to demonstrate clearly to the Wasps that I can control our people. That I can put a stop to any kind of revolt, anything that might be an inconvenience to them. About the only thing we do understand about our alien rulers is that they won't hesitate to destroy us if we make a nuisance of ourselves.'

'So you're prepared to do their killing for them?'

'You're still failing to understand the problem.' He gestured to a servant to remove his plate. The youth hurried away with it as though there were actual danger at the high table. 'A man's death, a women's death is always regrettable, but they are nothing compared to the destruction of the entire species.'

138

For the first time in her life, Mariko saw something akin to a holy light in her brother's eyes. It made her acutely uncomfortable, particularly as it seemed to grow as he continued to talk.

'When a man dies there is always another man to grieve for him and then take his place. If the whole species dies there is nothing. We might as well have never been, never existed.'

Heizen was staring at Trenhyass with a look of near devotion, hanging on each word.

'If all mankind dies, the whole sum of human history dies with it. All the centuries, all the good and all the evil, wink out as though they'd never been. We have reached a crossroads, we shall either survive or we shall be destroyed. It is our first contact with an alien species and we are no match for them. They've all but destroyed our culture and our science. We have lost most of our history, our collective memory. We depend upon them for the technology that sustains our civilisation. In fact, we are already becoming pathetically vague as to what we invented ourselves and what the Wasps gave to us. All we have to our credit is that we've survived. I intend that we shall continue to survive. Individual lives do not matter. Millions have died already and millions more will be slaughtered before this episode is over. I hope it doesn't shock you, my sister, but I no longer care how many die. All that matters is that some of our species are still alive when the Wasps finally depart.'

Mariko raised her glass halfway to her lips but then put it down again, untasted.

'I've never realised you thought this way. I've never really seen this side of you. You were always so much in control.'

'I am in control. I want you to understand me, my sister. All that matters is that humanity survives this encounter with aliens. The order of nature is against us. The stronger species destroys the weaker. This has been our history and, in that, we are going against our own odds. If there's killing to be done, it's better that we do it ourselves rather than risk the Wasps being directly involved. The Wasps are quite likely to kill all of us. There are times when nothing else counts.'

Mariko was aghast. 'But you don't like killing and brutality. Up until yesterday you were arguing to keep Gywann alive.'

139

'Today he went too far. If I don't crush this demonstration with the utmost severity, I risk giving the Wasps the impression that I am losing control. It could edge them towards the decision simply to erase us.'

Mariko shook her head. She seemed to be fighting tears. 'You're insane. You're both insane.'

The Protector smiled sadly and shook his head.

'My dear sister, we are the custodians of humanity.'

Twelve

AT THE prearranged signal, the drums of the Killers thundered out. The sound rolled and echoed through the roots of the towers, it crashed and rang from the walls of buildings and throbbed through tunnels and conduits. There was no mistaking the drums of the Killers. These were not the ordinary drums that beat out the rhythm for dancers or that played before a performance by actors or jugglers. These drums were brutal and violent. Their purpose was to spread a primitive terror, to drive all before their relentless pounding. The Killers had brought their drums to strike fear deep into the soul of all that heard them. The Killers' drums were heralds of a terrible slaughter.

The Killers had dropped into the lowers in the quiet hours before dawn. The lowers were as close to silent as they ever were, sleeping off the drinking and dancing that had gone on twenty-four hours earlier. All through the previous night and well into the morning, the whole area had celebrated what was being hailed as a Gywannish victory over the Wasps. When the Killers arrived there were few still out and about to see them. The Killers came quietly but they came in force. They drifted down between the towers like formations of bats or black night-birds. The few drunks and street wanderers who spotted them fled in terror. There was no general alarm or warning. The Killers massed their forces at four central assembly points. Once they were in position and there had been no incident, they waited for the signal. Each assembly point had its own massive two-man war drum. The huge drums, nearly two metres across, hung in ornate frames that were decorated with centuries-old trophies and battle honours. There were those who said that the drum heads were made from human skin. Each individual drum was the symbol and sacred object of one of the four divisions of Killers. They were only brought out on solemn or serious occasions. Presumably someone had considered the purging of the lowers to be one of these. The Killers seemed to be treating their mission as some great cleansing of all that was corrupt about their species.

As well as the big war drums, each squad of Killers had a dozen or more drummer boys who would march in front of them. The Killers' preoccupation with the ceremony of drums was viewed by outsiders as less than healthy. It was seen as an atavistic reaching back to a more savage, barbaric age. It was as if the Killers believed that the grim throbbing would put them beyond the confines of any civilised restraints on their use of power or weapons. The throbbing of the drums would make them grow to fit their name. The drums would make them Killers.

When the Killers first landed, the drums were silent. Rank upon rank of black-clad figures waited with the trained impatience of hunting dogs. Each face was hidden behind an identical blank helmet. Pulsers were clutched at the port and a ceremonial dagger hung from each belt. Officers in black capes and decorated helmets paced or conferred in tense, anxious groups. Finally the word came. A small red light winked on the talkie of each of the four division commanders. Each one spoke briefly and then turned to the two Killers manning the drum and nodded. The heavy wooden hammers were raised. They dropped. The noise split the night. The hundreds of smaller drums crashed in behind the big ones. The sticks laid into the skins with clenched-teeth aggression. With a roar, the Killers began to move. Some silently rose into the air on their flying-belts. Others crashed down sleeping streets with the massed clatter of steelshod boots.

They spread out across the Oldmarket kicking over stalls and smashing everything that got in their way. They invaded the Stoneplane, breaking windows, kicking down doors, rousting people from their beds and driving them into the streets. All through the lowers there were screams of pain and outrage and the sounds of destruction. Behind it all, the drums went on and on. Then there was the dull throb of the first pulser. It was followed by another. All over the city the pulser thuds started to come in nonstop volleys. At first it was a simple slaughter. People thought that they were being arrested. Why else would the Killers be breaking down the door and dragging them into the street in the middle of the night? People were scared out of their minds, but they were docile. Nobody suspected it was to be a massacre. When they were herded into groups in the middle of the street they thought that they were going to be taken somewhere, to some kind of camp or holding pen. Then the pulsers cut in. People started falling. Some of the Killers were among them, using their daggers. There was blood on the cobbles. Hysteria spread like wild-fire. The nature of the screaming changed.

'They're killing us! They're killing us!'

Somewhere a building was burning and smoke added to the confusion. The people of the lowers weren't docile now. Some fled in panic, others fought back. A teenager with a bapgun took out four Killers before they pulsed her. Some more kids got up on a lean-to roof and were hurling down tiles at the Killers until they too were brought down. It wasn't long before the discipline and organisation of the Killers began to disintegrate as a murderous intoxication took over. The formations blurred and broke up and the Killers rapidly became nothing more than a deadly, raging mob that howled and screamed bloody homicide through the streets as they ran down their victims. Their frenzy was so out of control that individual Killers even put themselves at risk. They'd become separated from their comrades and found themselves jumped by gangs of vengeful citizens. Bit by bit, quick-witted groups equipped themselves with stolen pulsers and determinedly fought their way out towards the Blackwater.

Swiftly, the refugees from the carnage became a human tide. Killers in flying-belts swooped down on them, picking off individuals at random. For a while it looked as though the Killers were bent on exterminating everyone in the area, but as those who fled in the direction of the Blackwater and the disused area discovered to their considerable relief, the Killers hadn't ringed the entire area. For anyone who cut and ran towards the Blackwater, the attacks stopped after a while. The refugees who went this way found themselves in the swamps and marshes and scrambling through the partially flooded ruins. It was one of the most dangerous and inhospitable parts of the city, but at least they were still alive.

Some didn't run, those whose instincts told them to go to ground, to crawl, to burrow and to lie still as death itself. Some hid in closets or beneath floorboards, others wriggled into culverts or pressed themselves flat on the bottom of drainage channels. The unlucky were discovered and summarily executed; the lucky ones heard the boots of the

Killers approach. They waited, not daring to breathe while those boots stamped around, above or beside them. There were a few who heard friends, companions or loved ones killed on the other side of a door or wallpanel, but they still kept their silence even as madness closed its grip. They went on holding their breaths until the boots moved away and were gone. Even then it was a long time before they dared to peer out or to reveal themselves even partially.

The horror was everywhere. The people of the lowers had always hated and feared the Killers but they had never thought they would be loosed on them to do their worst without warning. Few linked the attack of the Killers with the parade of the day earlier. Few, in fact, thought about reasons at all. Although many screamed 'Why?' it was a nightmare in which no rules of logic could survive. The streets and houses had become a world that was fashioned out of nothing but shock and bewilderment, a world in which there were just two kinds of people, those who fled with open mouths and contorted faces and those without faces at all, with blank metal helmets, heavy boots, relentless black uniforms and lethal weapons.

'No! Please! I don't understand. Why are you killing us? Why are you killing us?'

Some of the worst of the violence was centred around the nest of lean-tos that were home to Gywann and his close inner circle. As the Killers attempted to smash their way through doors and windows, the Gywannish fought back with an intensity that seemed proof of their belief that nothing could harm them. Tragically, it was a belief with no foundation in reality. The beaded vest stopped neither pulsers nor knives. The Gywannish hurled themselves on their attackers and were cut down almost immediately. As the Killers fought their way to the upper storeys they met much more effective resistance, and Gywannish youths with homemade bapguns had to be cleared from each and every passage, landing and stairwell. As casualties mounted, the Killers could only assume that Gywann's fanatical followers were buying time with their lives so their leader might escape. If Gywann himself got away, it would at least partly defeat the purpose of the attack. If they couldn't display a recognisable body, the prophet's followers would concoct all manner of fanciful stories. The Killers redoubled their efforts to clear the cluster of ramshackle, irregular buildings.

Thus it came as something of a surprise when the first pair of Killers kicked down the door of the very last and uppermost room to find that Gywann was still there, seated cross-legged on a rush mat in apparent meditation. Five of his followers were kneeling around him. The leading Killer laughed out loud as he raised his pulser. So many of his mates had been shot trying to get into this place and the silly bastard wasn't even bothering to escape. In the next instant his head imploded and his liquified brains splattered over the walls and ceiling and the other Killers who crowded in behind him. A second later, three of them had also imploded.

Only then did Gywann make a move. With an ease as though it had been rehearsed, two of his followers jumped up and pulled open a hidden panel in the back wall. Two more scooped up the dead Killers' fallen pulsers and opened fire on the ones coming through the door. Gywann and a single companion ducked quickly through the panel and vanished from sight. By the time the Killers had finally pulsed down the last of the faithful, Gywann had disappeared into the maze of tunnels and crawlspaces that ran along the insides of walls, between floors and ceilings and eventually led either to the sewers or to the utility ducts.

Jeen Vayim was one of the few who was mercifully unaware of the first bloody carnage of the Killer attack. When they broke down the front door of Denhagel's Tavern, he'd been sleeping in his upstairs chamber. He had been roused by the thud of pulsers, the crash of broken glass and a woman screaming. His instinct for trouble told him to go, as fast and as quietly as possible, without asking any questions and without bothering to discover the cause of the commotion. Unfortunately, his instincts were not quite quick enough. His idea was to climb the stairs and take off across the roofs. It sounded as if whatever was happening was mainly happening below him. When he ducked through the door of his chamber, however, he collided almost head-on with an armed Killer coming down the passageway. As a reflex, the Killer swung the pulser, clubbing Vayim over the head rather than firing at him in such an enclosed space. For the next twenty minutes, the Poet was dead to the world. When he returned to painful consciousness, the tavern was quiet.

The Poet lay for a while, sick from surges of pain. His head felt as though it was split in half. He pushed himself up onto his knees and put a hand to his head. His hair was sticky with rapidly clotting blood. Leaning heavily on the wall, he pulled himself to his feet. He felt faint, and stood for some moments unable to do anything but sway. He could hear the sound of pulsers over on another block. The sound provided him with a sense of urgency that could even overcome the pain. He stumbled to the end of the passage and peered down into the bar-room. It had been completely wrecked. There were three bodies on the littered floor. He recognised one as Denhagel's wife. Her clothes had been partly torn off.

The Poet started down the stairs. There was a movement down inside the bar. He froze. Something was moving in the debris. Glass crunched under foot. A figure in a Killer uniform looked up the stairs. His helmet was off and there was a half-empty bottle in his hand. The Killer blinked at the Poet.

'Wha' the fu' are you?'

The Killer didn't have a weapon and seemed to be very drunk. The nearest thing to hand was a length of broken banister rail. Jeen Vayim swung it with all the force he could. For once, the Poet was lucky. The rail caught the Killer just behind the left ear. He dropped like a stone. The Poet knelt down beside him and started stripping off his flying-belt. Jeen Vayim didn't know if the man was unconscious or dead. He rolled him over and pulled the belt free. He straightened up and wrapped it around his own waist. The Killer's helmet and pulser were over on the bar. The Poet picked his way across the room, doing his best not to look at the body of Denhagel's wife. He dropped the pulser into its sling on the belt. For a moment, he thought about the helmet. Finally he put it on and made for the door.

It was a while since Jeen Vayim had used a flying-belt and the knack of control didn't immediately come back to him. He yawed and wallowed through the air and almost ran headfirst into a wall. Bit by bit, he fell into the flow and got his motion under control. He took himself up to twentieth-storey level and looked around. A few groups of Killers were drifting through the air but most of the action was down on the streets where the main gangs were systematically going through the area, block by block, butchering everyone they found. A number of buildings were burning and the Poet used the pall of smoke from one of these to vanish quickly when four flying Killers came in his direction.

He went higher, up to fortieth-storey level. It was possible to recognise that there was indeed a pattern to the Killers' attack. The intent was to drive the survivors out into the floodplains of the Blackwater.

The Poet had to make up his mind swiftly what to do. There were sufficient numbers of Killers in the air to make him nervous. The sky was getting light, and while his helmet might fool them from a distance, one close look would be the end of him. His instinct was to go up, to get as far as he could from the carnage in the lowers. There would, however, be no refuge in the towers. He was popular in the households of a number of Proprietors but they would offer him neither hospitality nor sanctuary in the face of so much Killer activity. The Proprietors and their kind took care only of their own when it came down to it. He realised, with a good deal of discomfort, that his best chance would be to follow the same route as all the other fugitives, away from the populated areas of the city and out towards the desolation along the margins of the Blackwater. The Killers wouldn't follow them into those swamps and ruins.

The dawn was angry and red, partly obscured by the choking black smoke that billowed up from the fires that were burning unchecked. Again, Jeen Vayim used the smoke as means of concealment as he sped in and out of the buildings. The first fury of the Killer attack seemed to have spent itself. Many, with their taste for murder satisfied, had turned their attention to looting and rape. Some of the Killers staggered and yelled as though they were drunk. There were bodies everywhere. They lay sprawled in the street or huddled against walls like so many broken, discarded toys. It looked to Jeen Vayim as though some of them might have been mutilated. He didn't, however, stop to investigate. He kept his head down and sped on, keeping about four storeys off the ground. His stolen helmet seemed to fool most of the Killers that he passed. One had called out to him, but the Poet had flown straight on with his teeth clenched, expecting to be pulsed down at any moment. To his relief, nothing happened.

Before he was quite ready for it, he was out of the inhabited parts of the lowers and floating over growing tracts of abandoned ruins. The Killers had been left behind. Here and there small knots of people picked their way across the uneven ground and the rubble-strewn streets. Some appeared to be walking blindly, as if deep in shock, others clung to one another, sobbing and wailing. Jeen Vayim's flying-belt began to falter. It could no longer maintain its speed. For one heart-stopping moment it cut out altogether, but mercifully cut in again just as he started to drop. Jeen Vayim knew how to operate a flying-belt but he had only the most tenuous grasp of the principles by which they worked. He'd always assumed that the belt was a human invention, but he wouldn't have laid bets on it. He did, however, know that the energy powering all the flying machines, the belts, the sky hooks, the carriages and much more was broadcast from a central point among the towers. This was controlled by the Wasps. It was no secret. It made sense that they should set limits on how far their human subjects could travel. Jeen Vayim found that his speed was being reduced and that he was dropping nearer and nearer to the ground. In the end, he was hardly moving at all. His feet touched. His legs took his weight. The belt was dead. He peeled it off and let it fall.

He looked slowly around. He was totally alone. In every direction there was nothing but abandoned ruins. A grey morning mist swirled in hollows and depressions. He had come to rest beside a small lake of oily black water. It had probably once been an excavation, one of thousands of pits that had been dug by those who constantly searched and scavenged for artefacts of the past. Behind him were the shattered roots of what must long ago have been a large building, maybe even a small tower. Low clouds scudded across an overcast sky and there was a smell of rain in the air. The Poet felt desolation closing in on him. He was thirsty, but he wasn't quite ready to drink the black, foul-looking water. He was hungry, but as far as he could see there was no help for that at all. He bent down and retrieved the pulser. Had he escaped the Killers only to wander through this ghost region until he either starved or went mad?

There was a rumble of thunder. The rain wouldn't be too long in coming. At least it gave Jeen Vayim something to think about. He had to get under cover. The nearest possibility was the ruins behind him. He hefted the pulser and went to investigate. He climbed over a crag of shattered masonry and dropped down into what must once have been part of the interior of the building. It was a square area of paved floor that was cracked and broken and fighting a losing battle with a thicket of determinedly encroaching brambles. The Poet moved through them carefully; they sported vicious thorns. Something scuttled away from him with a flurry of rustling. Vayim jumped back and stood very still for a few seconds trying to gauge how much he was shaking. His nerves were shot and he had no reserves of either courage or stamina. He couldn't conjure up even the slightest hope. He moved gingerly forwards. In the middle of the area was the mouth of some kind of well or shaft, a circular black hole that went down to black depths that the Poet didn't want even to think about. A second clap of thunder made him jerk again, but it also reminded him that he should concentrate on finding shelter. Beyond the well, a section of fallen wall had formed what amounted to a small cave. It was hardly inviting but the first few heavy drops of rain had started to fall. On hands and knees, the Poet crawled into the cramped space, praying fervently that it had no other occupants.

The rain fell in drab grey sheets. It wasn't a storm like there'd been a few days earlier, but it was a solid, steady downpour. Jeen Vayim watched it dolefully. He couldn't remember a time when he'd felt worse. Rapidly growing rivulets were forming around his boots. A green spider scrabbled out of the dark at the back of the cave. The Poet tried to drown it with his foot but it skittered away.

The dreary morning became dreary afternoon. The Poet crouched stiff and cramped while his mind slipped in and out of a dull hallucination that it seemed to be using to protect itself from the bleak reality of his situation. His head sank to his chest. He twitched and straightened up. He splashed rainwater on his face. He was afraid of this place and he didn't want to fall asleep in it. Exhaustion vied with his fear, arguing that he would have to sleep eventually. His head dropped again, and again he did his best to wake himself. The third time, his chin sagged to his chest and he didn't move. His breathing became slow and even. Jeen Vayim was fast asleep.

When he woke it was dark and the rain had stopped. All around him were invisible movings and rustlings. He reached for the pulser but he couldn't find it. There was the sound of harsh, rasping breathing, quite close to him. At first, while he was still befuddled from sleep, he thought the breath was his own. Then he realised that it wasn't. A dark shape moved, right in front of his tiny cave. A pale, skull face was pushed into his. Jeen Vayim screamed. The face pulled back. The Poet was out of the cave and running. The brambles ripped at his clothes. He barked his shins going over the rubble but he didn't care. He could hear the creature coming after him. He skirted the lake and then hit the rubble again. There seemed to be other dark figures with pale faces converging on him from a number of different directions. He could hear himself sobbing. Wampyrs? There were really wampyrs? His lungs were on fire. He couldn't run any more. The wampyrs were closing in on him. White hands were reaching out for him. He staggered and dropped to his knees. They were all around him. He could smell their dead, mildew smell and hear them panting.

An explosion cut through the night. Something was howling in pain. The Poet pressed his face into the dirt and covered his head with his hands and wished that he was already dead.

Thirteen

FLURRIES OF rain still drove across the Stoneplane but even though it whipped at cloaks and capes, and backs were turned against the weather, the worst was over. The open space was a set for grim activity. All manner of official aircraft dropped from the lowering sky, disgorged their cargoes of uniformed figures and lifted off again. The sun had sunk below the horizon and the lowers were already dark. The big banks of sun-guns that had been set up on three sides of the area were reflected a thousand times from the puddles and the slick, wet flagstones. Each time a flying machine touched, the water on the ground around it would boil up into clouds of drifting steam.

The purpose of all this coming and going was simple. The pressure was now on to restore some form of order after a day of bloody chaos. It in no way looked as though it would be easily accomplished. The Protector himself had come to the lowers and was right there on the Stoneplane, standing in the rain, conferring tersely with his subordinates. Horfon was one of the detail of Legates who clustered around him with drawn pulsers. The Killers were far from being back under control and there was a tension and anxiety in the air. The morning of organised death had deteriorated into an afternoon of equally bloody confusion. All checks had been let go, discipline temporarily suspended, the Killers had been unleashed to run wild according to their very worst impulses. There had been widespread outbreaks of looting and burning. Some Killers had drunk themselves into insane excesses of alcoholic rage, others had unearthed caches of drugs and followed the same route. Torture and mutilation were commonplace. All through the long, wet, nightmare afternoon, the Killers seemed to compete with each other to reach new depths of savage depravity.

The rain had helped extinguish a lot of the fires but smoke still rolled through the streets, adding to the impression that the lowers had become some ante-room to hell. Killers lurched and staggered, hulking in their helmets and spattered with blood. Officers were trying to organise them into groups, get them back into the air and back to their tower. In some cases, this re-assertion of discipline was successful; the Killers were quickly brought to heel. Others, however, blundered on like slavering subthings that were mindlessly determined to continue the day of absolute brutality to its final, burnt-out conclusion.

The Protector seemed less concerned with the Killers running amok than he was with the possible fate of Gywann. All through the afternoon there had been conflicting rumours. Gywann had burned to death in a flaming building. He had been killed trying to stage a futile last stand with the final remnants of his followers. The first solid information had come when the bodies of the imploded Killers were brought out of the Gywannish houses and laid out on the Stoneplane for inspection. Horfon had taken a close look at these bodies and immediately wished that he hadn't. For almost a minute he had to stand completely still, fighting down both revulsion and the lunch that was trying to crawl up into his throat. What sort of power was required to make a human head like that? The Protector had examined the bodies and immediately sent for Marshal Heizen. Heizen arrived some five minutes later with his usual entourage of Iron Fists. The normally impassive Marshal looked pale and drawn as though the events of the day had been too much even for him. Trenhyass wasted no time on ceremony.

'He's escaped, hasn't he?'

'We can't be sure of this. There are bodies everywhere.'

'Do you have the body of Gywann?'

Heizen wearily shook his head. 'No, not as of this moment.'

'Then we have no satisfactory way of proving to the whole city that the man's dead. We cannot demonstrate that he was a mere mortal and not some kind of god that could challenge the Wasps. In fact, we have quite the reverse. We have evidence of his extrahuman powers. We have these things.' He indicated the imploded bodies. 'Everyone in the city will have heard about this by midnight and the man's legend will have grown out of all proportion.'

'He could well be dead. He escaped from the house but that is not say he wasn't killed afterwards.'

'It's not to say that he was, either, and that's the real point. I need the body of Gywann or we still have him with us. Unless we can prove beyond doubt that he's dead, the

152

city will believe that he's out there somewhere just waiting for the moment to return. Your men came down here to eliminate a troublemaker and they seem to have succeeded in creating an invisible Messiah. Do you clearly understand what I'm saying to you, Marshal Heizen?'

'There are plenty of bodies. Some of them are badly mutilated. We could put any corpse on display. Who would know?'

The Protector shook his head. 'It's too risky. If his followers did get him away, he's likely to reappear sooner or later. If that happened it could make him immortal in the eyes of the mob.'

Heizen smiled. 'Surely, my lord, we don't have to worry about the mob any more. Wasn't the purpose of this day to do away with the mob once and for all?'

The Protector looked at him with an expression of impatience. 'Don't be ridiculous. You've had a fine day's killing, Marshal Heizen, but you can't imagine this is a final solution. It'll take time but they'll drift back from hiding. The mob will always be with us.'

A palely glowing Wasp aircraft drifted slowly between the buildings above them, some fifteen storeys up. The Protector swore softly to himself.

'Is this the first time they've taken an interest?'

'No, my lord.'

'No?'

Heizen had started to look a little uncomfortable. 'They've been out in some numbers all afternoon.'

'Why wasn't I informed?'

Heizen's face was like stone. 'I was under the impression that you had been.'

Trenhyass regarded him with narrowed eyes. 'Was it craft like the one that just went over?'

'Similar. Also, there have been pairs of Wasps moving around on foot, if those things they move on are actually feet.'

'What did you do about them?'

'I surrounded each pair with a guard of my own Iron Fists, to protect and watch them. One pair actually came through here and examined these things.' He nodded at the corpses of the imploded Killers.

The Protector was very unhappy. 'Did anything else happen?'

'There was one incident.'

'What incident?'

'The facts haven't all been confirmed yet.'

'What, damn it?'

'A man. He was apparently drunk, he tried to attack one of the pair with a knife. The Wasps imploded him.'

'Was it one of your men?'

'I've received no confirmation.'

'But it most likely was.'

'It's possible. This kind of thing has happened before. There were never any major repercussions in the past.'

The Protector paced up and down. He seemed to be studying the wet flagstones. Suddenly he stopped. 'Do you have the body?'

Heizen nodded. 'I do.'

'I want it and these bodies here taken to the College of Healers. I want our so-called experts to take each one of them apart. I want to know if there's any difference between the Wasp victim and Gywann's three and, if so, what.' The Protector looked around. 'Have the civilian clean-up crews started work?'

'They're moving in right now.'

'Then you can continue to pull out your men. When that's been accomplished I want you to concentrate on Gywann. I want him. I don't care if he's dead or alive. I want him.'

'Even I don't have the manpower to make a comprehensive search between here and the Blackwater?'

'I don't care how you get him. Just get him. Run your spies out. Have them infiltrate the survivors. He won't be able to stay hidden for long. He's too well known. Also offer a large reward to any clean-up crew that comes across his body. That way we have both possibilities covered.'

Heizen bowed. 'It will be done immediately.'

The Protector nodded. 'Good. In that case, I will now tour the area and take a look at your men's handiwork for myself.'

Heizen was in the process of putting on his heavy Marshal's helmet. He stopped in mid-motion. 'You intend to personally tour the area?'

'Indeed I do.'

'Is that strictly necessary? We are already well advanced in the process of moving out.'

There was nothing pleasant about the Protector's thin smile. 'Are you afraid I'll be shocked at the zeal of your men, Marshal?'

Horfon couldn't tell what the Protector felt, but he was deeply shocked by the Killers' zeal. Following the Protector through the lowers was like entering a dreadful, blood-spattered other-world that turned everything he knew inside out. As he had dropped in his flying-belt, right beside the Protector's carriage, he had done his best to prepare himself for what was to come by trying to imagine the destruction. The smashed and burned-out buildings were much as he'd expected. The number of littered bodies was far greater and nothing in his imagination had prepared him for some of their grotesque, twisted positions. Nothing, even in the depths of his worst, most fearful fantasising, could have prepared him for the ghastly games the Killers had played with the corpses. In one lane that they passed down, a Killer or Killers had hacked off the heads of thirty or so of their victims and stacked them into an obscene pyramid. Deeply perverted words and drawings had been daubed on walls in blood. Horfon mentally cringed from minds that could think that way. There was widespread mutilation of the dead. Scalps had been taken. Ears and sexual organs also seemed to have been removed as trophies. Horfon was becoming seriously sick to his stomach. He tried to stop looking and so find his way into some kind of mechanical trance where he wouldn't be aware of his surroundings. It wasn't possible. His attention was irresistibly drawn to each next grisly atrocity.

Despite Marshal Heizen's statement that the Killers were well advanced in the process of moving out, bands of them were still roaming the streets beyond all discipline or control. Some had discarded their helmets and even lost their flying-belts. Horfon's mind executed a weird flip and started wondering what reckoning there'd be in the Killer barrackrooms over all the lost equipment. Drunk, crazy or both, they staggered through the puddles clutching their daggers and pulsers. To Horfon, they were figures out of the dreams of a madman. One particularly large group spotted the Protector and his escort and started hooting and yelling.

'How you doing, my lord?'

'You like our handiwork?'

'Good day's work down here, my lord.'

'You should have joined in the fun.'

Even though there was a veneer of respect, the underlying mockery was clear. The Legates didn't even get a veneer.

'Willya look at the little soldierboys?'

'Hey scumsucker, you sure you can handle that big bad weapon?'

The Legates bristled. Pulsers were raised. For a long slow-motion moment it seemed possible that a firefight might break out, right there on the street. Then Heizen caught up with them with a guard of Iron Fists, freshly down from the towers. There was much yelling and man-handling as they moved the Killers away from the Protector and on towards one of the debarkation points.

The inspection party continued its tour, going further into the dark places of death that the roots of the city had become. They skirted a pair of heavy-duty loaders into which clean-up crews, in plastic suits and breathing masks, were heaving the bodies. The battered, ancient machines almost certainly pre-dated the arrival of the Wasps and had probably been put to the same use during the plague that the aliens had brought with them. In front of a burning building another gang of Killers was holding a celebration around the flames. Horfon was shocked to notice that some of the lurching, bellowing shapes wore the uniforms of Legates. Some Legates had in fact come down a few hours earlier in an initial search for the body of Gywann. The Protector appeared not to notice them so nobody pointed them out. Clearly visible in the lurid glare of the fire, a Killer male and a Legate female were groping each other, fondling hands fumbled inside each other's disordered clothes, without a thought to modesty. As Horfon came level with them, the man partly disengaged and took a drink from a bottle. The woman turned her head. She was slack-faced and her eyes were closed. All the other horror of the night was swept away as he recognised Legate Androx.

He felt as though he'd been kicked. He faltered. The rest of the Protector's escort went on without him. He'd never believed all those stories about her. He'd always half hoped that somehow, somewhere, she might allow some relationship between the two of them. All day his mind had been wrenched far beyond anything he'd ever believed he'd be able to stand, but this was the worst of all. Androx had betrayed his hopes down there among the bodies and the blood. The Killer blearily intercepted his shocked stare.

'Wha' th' fu' you looking at, boy?'

It was then that Androx opened her eyes. She blinked at him as though she was not quite able to incorporate him into the scene all around her. Horfon panicked and fled. He couldn't meet those puzzled eyes. He couldn't face that she'd caught him standing there gawping like an idiot. He couldn't be a part of her shame. He didn't want to know. He almost tripped on the outflung arm of a body as he hurried after the Protector's escort. She didn't mean anything to him. He must be crazy. He told himself over and over that he was being a fool. How was it that a mere girl could have such an effect on him. He was a Legate, a part of the Protector's own escort. And yet . . . And yet it kept coming back to him. When he had seen her in the arms of that scarred, bullet-headed, filthy Killer, he'd been taken up by an emotion that swamped all the fear, disgust and revulsion of the night. On top of it all, he was ashamed of himself. If he'd really wanted Androx he would have done something about it. He would have dragged her away from that damned red-handed Killer. He had a pulser at his side. He had nothing to fear from the Killers. He was as good as any of them. And yet . . . And yet he'd fled, not from the Killer, but because Androx had looked at him.

These thoughts went round and round in his head as he trailed dismally at the rear of the Protector's escort with his heart growing heavier and heavier. The only consolation was that the pain and confusion caused by Androx did something to numb the pain caused by the continuing inspection of the lowers. Horfon had almost reached the state of trance for which, earlier, he had so fervently wished. In fact he was so wrapped in his private world of dull circular torment that he didn't notice the ragged, bloody figure moving in the shadows of a fire-damaged lean-to. He hardly noticed when it emerged into the half light and slowly raised its arm. Only in the very last split second did some deep-seated warning mechanism tell him that the raised hand was holding a bapgun and pointing it at the Protector. The figure was slightly behind the main body of the party and Horfon was the first to see it. As he swung around, its voice rasped out.

'You insane, slaughtering bastard!'

The bapgun went off. Horfon's pulser thudded a fraction of a second later. It was instantly followed by the pulsers of three other Legates. The assassin fell over, quite rigid, blood spurting from his ears. At the same time there was shouting from behind.

'The Protector!'

'Lord Trenhyass has been hit!'

'The Protector has been shot!'

Fourteen

'YOU CAN get up now, Poet Jeen Vayim. I've killed three of them and the others have run away.'

The Poet rolled slowly and fearfully over on the damp ground and found himself looking up at Shafik Kraymon. The oversized pistol was in his hand and three of its barrels were smoking. The Poet shook his head. 'I think I've gone insane.'

Kraymon extended a hand and hauled Jeen Vayim to his feet. 'There's many who do in these parts.'

The Poet peered around. Nothing seemed to be moving in the darkness. 'Were those things really wampyrs?'

'Maybe. They don't speak so nobody knows what they call themselves or want to be called.'

'Would they have eaten me?'

Kraymon shrugged. 'It's possible. I've heard that it's happened and I've even seen bones, but most likely they would have just killed you and stolen your clothes and anything you had. They're nasty but they're real cowards. If you even yell loud, they run away. The worst thing you can do is run yourself. If they think that you're afraid of them, they go crazy, snapping, vicious, feral-mean crazy. All they want to do is rip and tear. When they go, they get so frenzied it can really be disgusting.' He peered down at the nearest of the wampyr bodies. 'I've got to tell you, Poet, I hate these damn things. This one must have been wearing these rags for ten years. It's probably riddled with vermin. Why the hell do they always have to wear black?'

Jeen Vayim shivered. 'How did you get out here?'

'Much the way you did, I'd imagine.'

'I thought the Protector gave you a safe conduct.'

'Safe conduct didn't mean much by the time the dawn was up and the Killers were running loose. I couldn't see any option but to hike out here with everyone else.'

'Did you see much of the killing?'

'Enough. There are times when I'm ashamed that I'm human.' He turned over the dead wampyr so the pale skull face and glazed eyes were no longer looking up at him. 'I hate these damn things.'

He squatted down and started to carefully reload the pistol. 'Perhaps I should have kept right on going, clear to the outlands, but something in me wanted to see this through to the end. I like to know how things work out.'

Somewhere nearby, something rustled. Jeen Vayim started. 'There isn't much left to work out, is there?'

'You don't think great events are afoot?'

'I've been too busy staying alive to think about anything.'

'You have a narrow view for a poet.'

'Damn it, Kraymon, I've been scared out of my wits. I'm half starved and you want to talk philosophy.'

Kraymon shrugged again, snapped the gun shut and stood up. 'Philosophy will pass the time if you've neither beef nor beer. Do you want to come with me to where the others are? They're a sorry bunch but at least they're human and there's a fire going. The boy prophet is among them. I rather thought he'd manage to escape.'

'You mean Gywann?'

'The very same.'

'But how did you find them? There's people wandering all over in this mess.'

Kraymon started out into the darkness. The Poet followed close behind so he wouldn't lose sight of the big man. Kraymon laughed. 'You think it was difficult for me?'

'I suppose not.'

'It was easy to find Gywann and what's left of his bunch. They were a little better organised than the rest and easy to predict.'

'But why should you want to find them? I would have thought they'd be people to avoid. The Killers could easily come looking for him.'

Kraymon shook his head. 'The Killers won't come. They don't come into these places.'

'So why did you bother to look for Gywann?'

'I suppose you could say that I was wagering my time and trouble that he was the key to this whole business.'

Kraymon seemed to think that that would be enough for the Poet to chew on for a while, and for some time they tramped in silence and in single file. Kraymon and his gun eased the Poet's fears of what might be moving through the darkness, following and shadowing them. It didn't, however, make him exactly cheerful. Between the growling

160

in his stomach, a feeling of complete hopelessness, and a glum and pessimistic puzzlement about what great events Kraymon believed were in motion, he had what he considered to be more than his fair share of misery. Misery and the dirty, stinking, swamp water were the only plentiful commodities in these ruins. He lost count of how many times he stumbled or tripped on the uneven surface. Even though Kraymon steered the best course he could through the unfamiliar darkness, he wasn't infallible and he too found cause to slip and slide and curse under his breath. Jeen Vayim was starting to lose track of how long they'd been walking. His legs were threatening to give out on him.

'How much longer till we get where we're going?'

'Not much further.'

'Do they have any food?'

'There was a little when I left there but nothing like as much as you'd wish.'

'Anything would be a blessing.'

'We may have to leave the problem of food until daylight.'

Jeen Vayim wasn't sure that he'd live until daylight. He wasn't sure that he wanted to. The clouds were breaking up and the moon shone fleetingly through. They were walking along a causeway of rubble with black water on either side. Behind them the lights of the city were bright and clear, looming high into the sky. It seemed to the Poet that they were looking down on him with cold contempt. At the far end of the causeway, he thought that he could just make out some dark shapes, an irregular cluster of ruins that stood a little taller than the rest. Suddenly, in among them, was a flickering of orange light.

'See that, Poet?'

'What is it?'

'That's their fire. We'll soon be warm.'

'We'll also be among a bunch of religious fanatics who've just set off a massacre.'

'For a poet, you're not very tolerant, either.'

'Poets don't have to be tolerant, just clever.'

'Maybe I should have been a poet.'

'You're better off being what you are.'

'And what might that be, Poet?'

'You know damn well what that might be, Shafik Kraymon.'

Kraymon laughed out loud. It was a sound that didn't

belong in that place and his laugh trailed away. 'Let's get to that fire.'

At the end of the causeway, they passed under what was left of an ornately decorated arch on which stone maidens leaped from stone foliage. Once through the arch, they made a right-hand turn and started up what must once have been a broad and imposing flight of steps. The steps led to a wide flat area on which coarse grass had taken hold. It was bounded on three sides by high, black, broken walls that protected it from the worst of the weather. It was natural that the Gywannish should have chosen it for a camp-site. The blaze of briars and torn-down branches showered sparks into the sky. For an instant, it was almost cheerful.

The illusion of cheer faded as they walked up to the fire. Nobody spoke to them. The refugees sat or squatted or lay huddled on the grass and stared at the flames with wide, dead eyes. Kraymon and the Poet stood, arms stretched out, warming themselves in silence. Gywann and Sulanda were among the nearest to the fire. They sat side by side, staring like all the others. It was only when the newcomers had been standing there for a number of minutes that Gywann's eyes raised and he looked at them. He said nothing. After about thirty seconds, his eyes dropped again. It was left to Sulanda to break the silence. 'We have some clean water, would you like some?'

Kraymon nodded. 'Yes.'

On the ground beside Sulanda was a small collection of what the Gywannish had managed to grab before they fled: some trinkets, a bag of meal and a pitifully small pile of other provisions, a pulser and a number of containers of water. They had been carefully sorted and neatly arranged. Sulanda picked up the smallest jar of water and got carefully to her feet. She held the jar as though it was something precious. Every one of her movements seemed shaky and uncertain and her shoulders were hunched protectively into her muddy, tattered vest. The Poet had never seen her look so painfully thin and fragile. He noticed that most of the beads had been torn from her waistcoat. She handed the jar to Kraymon who drank sparingly and passed it on to the Poet.

'Do you have anything to eat? We are very hungry.'

She took a few moments to reply. Jeen Vayim suspected that she was in deep shock.

'We have a little lachki. You are welcome to it. I'm sorry it can't be more.'

162

Kraymon nodded. 'I understand. We will do something about the food situation in the morning.'

The Poet was staring at the fire. 'You think you can find food in this waste?'

'You can find food if you look hard enough and are prepared to eat anything.'

Sulanda broke the stick of dried, salted vegetable and handed half to Kraymon and half to the Poet. Jeen Vayim was about to bite into his share when he noticed that Sulanda was staring at him intently. 'This is not the end. You do realise that, don't you, Jeen Vayim?'

'I . . .'

'You know that we'll come back, don't you? This is not the end.'

The Poet closed his eyes and turned away. He couldn't bear to look at her face. The fire blazed up and he knew that Sulanda was far beyond shock.

'You're insane. You're quite insane.'

Sulanda's voice was urgent. Her eyes were wide and bright. 'It's not over. Gywann will come again.'

Jeen Vayim was still in some calm, still place way on the other side of anger. 'Hasn't all this taught you anything?'

'He told us on the bridge that our trials were just beginning.'

The Poet's anger finally started to burn. 'Your trials are over. You've lost everything. Come out of your trance, Sulanda. It's all gone. You challenged the order of things, and hundreds, maybe thousands, died because of it..It's a pity that you and your damned prophet weren't among the first to die.'

Kraymon moved in between the Poet and Sulanda. 'I think you're going too far, Poet.'

The Poet looked at him in complete disbelief. 'Too far? Too far, Shafik Kraymon? What does "too far" mean in the language of these people? They've already triggered a mass murder.'

'Leave it, Poet. Leave it for the morning.'

The Poet scowled. 'Sure. In the morning everything will be wonderful. The Protector himself will be here to personally serve us a hot breakfast.'

He stalked away from the fire, hating the world in general and Gywann in particular. For a few moments he was tempted to walk out alone into the swamp. He didn't want to be any part of these people. He didn't even want to be

163

near them. As he retraced his steps across the grass he thought of the comfortable times of poem-telling, snug taverns and easy, drunken living that had so suddenly been torn to pieces. He thought of all the friends and companions who now lay dead, and his fury boiled over. He turned and yelled back at the figures around the fire.

'Damn you all! Damn your madness and your stupidity!'

At the top of the steps, reality cleared its throat to remind him that to start back into the swamps in the dark, without food or water, was little short of suicide. The hard truth was that if he wanted to go on living his best chance was with Kraymon and the Gywannish. Again he looked back at the fire. He didn't want to go back among those people. On the other hand, he needed them for his survival. It was possible, in the morning, that Kraymon really would find food. Bit by bit, one hour at a time, life would continue. He sat down on the third step from the top and let his head fall into his hands. He couldn't think any more. Faces were crowding into his mind. The Zilla Brothers, Denhagel and his wife, Fok the Turrier, Raif the Fire-eater, the Perforated Woman and all the others who were gone forever. Suddenly, Jeen Vayim was sobbing helplessly.

After an hour of sitting on the cold stone steps, the chill and damp managed to insinuate its way between the Poet and his grief. If he didn't go back to the fire, he'd start to get ill. He stood up. His joints were stiff and painful. With bowed shoulders he walked back. The moon was just above one of the broken walls. The grass was damp under his feet. The fire had died down but the embers were still glowing. The Gywannish were huddled together. Kraymon, on the other hand, sat apart, legs crossed and back stiff but with his eyes closed and face relaxed. Jeen Vayim found himself a place as far from everyone else as he could get and still be warmed by the remains of the fire. He squatted down on the grass.

The orange glow of the embers turned to a dead grey. Jeen Vayim could again feel the cold creeping in around his shoulders. He knew he wasn't going to sleep so he decided he might as well do something about the fire. If he went and foraged for briars or branches, the movement might do something to drive out at least part of the chill. He got to his feet, looked around and took a few tentative steps away from the last glow and out into the darkness. The moon had dropped below the level of the wall and the Poet was unable to see a thing. He also had no idea where to go foraging for fuel. The entire exercise was starting to look like a very bad idea. He turned back, looking for the fire. He thought he could make out the embers in the dark. Then his skin began to prickle. His hair seemed to want to stand on end. Somewhere beyond the black broken walls there was an unearthly red glow. It grew brighter and brigher. Without noticing the Poet was walking backwards away from it.

'What the hell is this now? Haven't we had enough?'

A bright, red sphere rose over the black walls like a small angry sun. It was hard to tell how big it was against the dark sky, but Jeen Vayim had a feeling that it was quite small and comparatively close to the ground. Not too far away there was a sudden outburst of wild wampyr howling. It was mingled with the unearthly cries of agitated boojies. His hair was now actually standing on end. He started to tremble. The red sphere was floating, quite motionless, directly over his head. He could hear his own voice.

'If this is the end, kill me now. Don't play with me. I can't take any more.'

His head was shaking from side to side. This was finally too much. His mind couldn't absorb any more shock and horror. He didn't have the energy for any more fear. He let his arms drop and resigned himself to the end. And then it started to move again. The thing hadn't killed him. It wasn't going to do anything. It was moving away. It was just like the Wasp aircraft over the Curvebridge. It had looked but it had done nothing. Was this red sphere some sort of Wasp spy device? For the first time, Vayim shared Kraymon's feeling that there might be great events afoot. The sphere suddenly accelerated; it zigzagged at incredibly high speed and then abruptly changed direction, went straight up and vanished.

'I don't want to remember this when it's over.'

He stood stunned for a while, staring fixedly at the spot where the sphere had vanished. Finally he sighed and slowly turned.

'Oh no!'

A figure had been standing right behind him. At first he thought it was a wampyr. He wanted to run but he remembered what Kraymon had said. Then he heard the voice.

'Something is very near now.'

It was Gywann. The Poet could see his eyes gleam in the darkness.

'The unfolding is almose complete, Jeen Vayim. Something is coming to us.'

'You're sick and crazy.'

'Something is coming to us.'

Jeen Vayim wondered if he might be doing the world a favour if he strangled Gywann right there and then. Sadly, he doubted that he had the strength. In the east, a thin strip of lighter sky heralded the dawn.

Fifteen

'JUST RELAX and don't concern yourself, my lord. I will take control until you have recovered.'

'You will do no such thing.'

The Protector's voice was weak but firm. It clearly pained him to talk. He lay on his side on the Lady Mariko's spacious bed. He was naked to the waist, his tunic had been cut away but he still wore his bloodstained breeches and boots. Elder Orfall, Elder Sahjii and a number of minor Healers fussed around him. The bapgun slug had lodged in his right shoulder and the Protector had lost a lot of blood. The Elders had localed him and vibra'd out the slug. Then, when it was clear that he was going to live, they'd packed the wound with setflex and hooked him to a transfuse. The Elders had wanted to sedate him completely, but the Protector had refused. Despite the pain, he had continued to talk urgently to Marshal Heizen.

'Directly the Healers are through with me, you'll get me on my feet and to the Grand Audience Chamber. I want as many people as possible to see me up and walking. I want the whole of the city to hear that I'm alive and fully in command.'

Elder Sahjii looked up from running a scan over the injured shoulder.

'I wouldn't advise that, my lord. You are very weak and too much movement could start a haemorrhage under the laminate.'

'Hold your tongue, Sahjii, this is none of your concern. More is at stake than my health.'

Heizen pressed the point. 'Surely there is no need, my lord. Why put yourself at risk? The lowers have been subdued and there is no immediate danger.'

The Protector winced and let out a small gasp. For a few moments he waited with eyes closed for the pain to pass. Sweat stood out on his forehead and his face was deathly white.

'How many times must I tell you to stop trying to take my

place, and do what you're told? The city has to know that I'm alive and functioning, then the Wasps, however they gather their information, will know also.'

'Does it matter?'

The Protector rode out another spasm of pain. 'I am quite certain that something is going on with the Wasps. I would not like to predict what they'd do if, at the same time, they start to believe that we are leaderless and in a state of turmoil.'

Sahjii tried to bedside-manner the Protector. 'Perhaps you worry too much, my lord. You are still in shock.'

'Just do your job, Elder Sahjii, then go away and let me do mine.'

'Yes, my lord.'

Sahjii removed the scanner and Trenhyass let himself roll painfully onto his back. He sighed and closed his eyes. 'I will rest until the Healers have done with me.'

Even while the Protector lay unconscious and bleeding on the cobbles, Legates and Killers had almost clashed over what was to be done with him. Heizen had immediately started barking orders to his Iron Fists. The Protector was to be taken to the Killers' Tower. Fortunately the Protector's escort of Legates was all around him, kneeling beside him, bending over him and giving first aid. The Wingleader who commanded them flatly refused to allow his lord to be taken anywhere but the Halls. He had backed his refusal with a drawn pulser. Before Heizen could use force to get his orders obeyed, the Wingleader had six Legates pick up the Protector and beltjump straight into the air. With the initiative taken from them, Heizen and his Iron Fists had no alternative but to follow in the Legates' wake.

Horfon had also followed the six who bore up the Protector. Like the other Legates, he watched anxiously for some sign if the Protector was alive or dead. At the tenth-storey level the Wingleader had flagged down a carriage. Horfon was one of those who had managed to get a handhold on the outside of the machine before it took off at top speed. They arrived at the Halls to discover that the Lady Mariko, warned in advance of the assassination attempt, had taken charge. She waited at the landing platform with a hastily assembled team of Healers and enough armed Legates to prevent any intervention by the Killers. The news had clearly interrupted some sort of passionate interlude. She was clad in only the scantiest costume of soft red leather. Despite her revealing attire, her authority was total. She entertained neither argument nor suggestion. Her brother was to be taken straight to her own private quarters where the medical team could go to work on him.

As they brought in the Protector and laid him on the bed, the Lady Mariko's boudoir became a place of bizarre contrasts. The air was heavy with a sweet, musky perfume that clashed sharply with the crisp, hospital smell that came from the emergency surgical kits. The white satin sheets on the huge oval bed were stained red with the Protector's blood. The Healers had torn away the cascades of silk that made up the ornamental canopy to give themslves more room to work. Horfon had taken advantage of the situation and slipped in with the rest of the crowd. He stood pressed against the wall doing his best to look inconspicuous, and hoped that no one would order him out. Nobody seemed to be looking in his direction. The focus of attention in the room was the group around the bed, the glare of the Healers' work lights and the prone figure at the centre of it all.

When it had been announced that the Protector was going to live, Horfon took a chance to look around the room. He excused his curiosity to himself; he had never been in a bedroom that had its own fountain and he might never be in one again. He was overawed by the lavishness of it all. The Lady Mariko clearly spared herself absolutely nothing. Over in the far corner, an exquisitely pretty, olive-skinned young man stood draped in a sheet. He had gold bangles on his wrists and ankles and a gold collar around his neck. He had obviously been the source of the Lady's amusement before the word had come of her brother's shooting. He now looked frightened and deeply unhappy. It was plain that he had no idea at all of what he should do next. An Iron Fist standing near to the young man turned and gave him a long hard stare. The boy looked as though he were praying that the wall would open and swallow him.

'Could you imagine living in a place like this?'

It was Wingleader Dalco. Horfon had been so lost in his own thoughts that he'd failed to notice the officer come up beside him. He was sure he was going to be thrown out. He came to attention and quickly shook his head.

'No, Wingleader. I don't think I could get used to this.'

'Relax, boy; it looks like it's going to be a long night.'

Horfon unbraced his shoulders. 'Should I leave the room, Wingleader? I don't have any actual business here. I just followed the others.'

'You might as well stay around. You've as much right here as most of them.'

'With respect, Wingleader, I don't think this is the time or place to claim family connections.'

'I'm not talking about that, boy. I'm talking about you. You could well be a hero if they ever get around to thinking about it. You did kill the assassin.'

'Others pulsed him at the same time.'

'But you were the first. I'll see that a commendation goes on your record.'

'Thank you, Wingleader.'

'It's no more than you deserve.' Dalco glanced around. 'Now what?'

Three fresh Iron Fists had come through the doors and were muscling their way across the room.

'There's going to be trouble with those arrogant bastards before all this is over.'

The Iron Fists approached the bed. Heizen stepped back from the bedside and there was a muttered conversation. The Protector looked up with a grimace of pain. 'What is it, Marshal? Do your men have fresh information?'

'Shouldn't you rest, my lord?'

'Damn your insolence, Heizen. What news have these men brought?'

'There are stories that the man Gywann has been seen alive and moving out into the swamps with a small handful of his followers. The stories have yet to be confirmed, but if they are I'll mount an immediate search.'

The Protector shook his head. 'No search, not yet. He'll be busy licking his wounds for a while. We'll get him directly he reveals himself. It's easier than having hundreds of men stumbling around in the swamps. Was there anything else?'

Heizen hesitated. 'It's probably nothing, a story that another of those red spheres was sighted over the swamps. Just like the one that was supposed to have been seen the night of the storm, the night my men let Gywann loose in the lowers. An action, I might add, that I vigorously opposed.'

'All right, all right.' The Protector was thoughtful. 'I wish I knew what these red spheres were, and what they meant. The Wasps have never used them before, not that I ever heard about.'

'They incidentally seem to drive the boojies into what seems to be a screaming frenzy.'

'Do they, by god?'

Dole Euphest stepped into the circle around the Protector. Until then, he'd been standing quietly, staying out of the way of the healers. 'It could be that we're being a little hasty in assuming that the Wasps are responsible for these spheres.'

'The thought had occurred to me.'

'It all fits too well. The Wasps appear to be tightening their defences and then these strange new craft come on the scene.'

'You believe that they're from another species of alien?'

'I don't know.'

'If they are, they could be some kind of advance probe, scouts or a fifth column.'

'Let's not jump to too many conclusions at once.'

Dole Euphest was still thoughtful. 'It's also interesting that the spheres have been observed always in the rough vicinity of the man Gywann.'

Trenhyass winced as he attempted to sit up. 'We don't have the time for speculation. Right now my only concern is proving to the world that I am alive and competent. Elder Sahjii, you had better give me something that will minimise the pain and keep me on my feet at the same time.'

'I must protest, my lord . . .'

'I don't want to hear your protests, Elder Sahjii. I am not interested. I know what I have to do and I am going to do it.' Trenhyass struggled painfully to sit up. 'You Legates, come here and help me. Get me on my feet.'

By the time the Protector was standing he was sweating and green with pain.

'Throw my uniform coat over my shoulders. I can't walk through the Halls half naked.' He looked at Mariko and smiled. 'I leave that to my sister.'

'The coat is badly bloodstained, my lord. Perhaps we should send to your quarters for a clean one.'

'I'll wear that one, damn it. It's my blood.'

With agonising slowness, the Protector, supported by a Legate on each side, limped out of the boudoir of the Lady Mariko's quarters and into the main corridors of the Halls. Behind him came a straggling procession of officials,

Legates and Killers. At regular intervals they would all have to stop while Trenhyass gathered his strength. A small crowd collected around him. Clerks, Aides and minor officials lined the corridors. They applauded as the Protector passed. In his turn, he smiled and waved acknowledgement. His face, however, grew increasingly waxen. Finally he leaned towards one of the Legates who were now virtually carrying him.

'Take me to the nearest landing stage. I'll take the night air and then we'll go back. That will be quite enough for the purpose.'

The small procession fell silent as it emerged onto the landing stage. A Wasp aircraft, one of the dark ovoids with no markings, hung in the air in front and slightly above them. It was silent and motionless. Someone on another tower was directing a spotlight at it. The Protector motioned to a Legate.

'Bring up the landing lights.'

Sun-guns set around the edge of the landing stage grew brighter and brighter until the whole area was more dazzling than day. Trenhyass glared at the Wasp craft. He seemed oblivious to everyone around him. His voice, when it came, seemed to be dragged from the depths of his soul.

'Do you see me? I am here. I was hurt but I live. Apline Trenhyass is alive. I am still holding together this sorry civilisation!'

He sagged back into the arms of his Legates.

Sixteen

FOR TWENTY-THREE days Gywann kept promising that
something was coming, that something was very near. At
first, it was without much conviction. He sat cross-legged,
staring straight ahead and repeating it to himself, over and
over like a constant drone. It was as though he himself
needed convincing most of all. He had become so physically
helpless that he had to be fed by Sulanda while the faithful
knelt around them in prayer. The Poet was quite convinced
that the Gywannish had retreated *en masse* to the safety of
madness. It was a madness that continued for six days. The
faithful had built a crude shelter in which their prophet
spent all of his time, either droning or sleeping, twitching in
the grip of troubled dreams. The explanation around the
small camp was that Gywann was somehow being tested.
On the seventh day the testing was apparently finished.
Gywann stopped his chanting and emerged from the shack.
There was such a half starved, wide-eyed crazy expectation
in the camp that this move was immediately invested with
as much religious significance as it would carry.

This new Gywann was still unkempt and filthy; there
was no other way in the swamps, but he stood straight and
his eyes were clear. Somewhere he had found the gold
collar that he had worn at all the biggest of the meetings
and once again he was wearing it. He was confident,
almost optimistic. He still spent long hours in silence but
when he did speak he spoke to those around him with a
happy surety.

'It is coming. It is very near now.' He was no longer
talking to himself. 'Soon you will be able to feel it, just as
I do.'

More days passed and Gywann grew increasingly
buoyant. He kept repeating the promise, exactly the same
phrase, but with steadily growing enthusiasm. He refused
to elaborate, he would answer no questions, and he resolutely kept out of all discussion of what they should do next.
The Poet became venomous in his distrust. Again and

again he would test the patience of Shafik Kraymon. 'You realise that they're starting it up all over again.'

'Maybe you're just starting to feel it coming.'

As Jeen Vayim had often theorised, human beings could in a frighteningly short time adapt to almost any unpleasantness. The camp in the swamps never became even minimally comfortable. That would have been impossible. It did, however, develop a dreary routine that offered some grim consolation. Large parts of the day were spent foraging and scavenging. Food and firewood had to be laboriously fetched. The staple of their diet had turned out to be a leathery black polyp that grew just below the surface of some of the foulest water. Even when it was boiled for hours it still gave everyone miserable stomach cramps. About the only consolation in the non-stop foraging, as far as Jeen Vayim was concerned, was that it got him away from Gywann and Sulanda's growing fanaticism.

When Vayim foraged, he invariably stuck close to Kraymon. The big man had an unerring instinct for the best beds of polyp, and could even come up with a pair of thriggies or Blackwater cray that were a welcome addition to the brutally dull diet. Also, on the few occasions that the Poet had gone out on his own the wampyrs had followed him from a distance. Despite all Kraymon's reassurances of their extreme cowardice, he was still frightened by their white faces and staring eyes.

On the twenty-fourth morning there was a second major change. Gywann stopped making promises.

'It is here. The full unfolding may now start.'

'What?'

Kraymon and Vayim were the most vocal of the unbelievers. They looked around. It was a regular, somewhat grey morning in the swamps. The pangs of hunger were moving everyone reluctantly towards a breakfast of polyp. Nothing was out of the ordinary. 'What are you talking about? There's nothing here. Nothing has come.'

'After dark.'

'After dark? You're leaving yourself less than twelve hours before you look a damn fool.'

'You will see for yourselves. All will become clear.'

Once they were on their own, the Poet wasted no time. 'Why don't we get out of here? It's been more than three weeks. Why don't we try and slip back into the city? The Killers have probably relaxed by now.'

174

'Sometimes I wonder about you, Poet. We've stayed this long, we might as well give him what he wants and wait until dark.'

'You want to see the next phase of this nonsense? You're bent on watching him spin it out to the end? I don't think I can eat another polyp. I think I'd rather die.'

'You can wait another day.'

'I don't know. I don't want to see any more.'

'You'll go back through the swamps on your own, will you?'

The Poet ruefully shook his head. 'I didn't say that.'

Kraymon laughed. 'I tell you what I'll do. Wait and see what Gywann gets up to. If it's more foolishness, we'll start for the city in the morning.'

The Poet shrugged. He really had no other choice.

Even Jeen Vayim had to admit that there was something strange and even threatening about the sunset. The sky was red, shot with green at the horizon; towering purple clouds swirled into huge conical twisters and then fled, driven before violent winds in the upper atmosphere. Distant thunder rolled and boomed and a strange shimmer flickered along the skyline. Even when the sun had completely gone, the strange display continued. Curtains of sheet lightning flared in the sky. Green fire played around the towers of the city. The Gywannish were on their knees. They clearly assumed that their master had done it all. Jeen Vayim and Kraymon climbed up to a vantage point on one of the broken walls.

'How do you think he knew? Did he just guess or does he really know something?'

'This is more than just a coincidence. Something is definitely happening. You can't deny that, can you, Poet?'

'But how can he have predicted all this?'

'Maybe we should just wait and watch.'

The sheet lightning and the green fire went on for over an hour. Again there was the muffled drumroll of a faraway storm. Gradually the most intense static flickering seemed to be gathering over a spot on the far side of the city. There was a crackling in the air. The effect became more and more concentrated until it had merged into a single pillar of white electrical fire. The Wasp ship rose on this pillar. It wasn't one of the small ovoid aircraft that were a fairly familiar sight in among the towers of the city. This was something a hundred times bigger. One of the big space-going ships that rarely, if ever, moved from their berths in the sealed Wasp enclaves. It was an irregular, almost crystalline shape, as if some giant iceberg had taken to the air. It glowed with a pale white/blue glow that seemed to throb and pulse with a varying intensity at different points on its surface.

When it had reached the apex of the column of lightning, the column simply vanished. The big Wasp ship seemed to hang on nothing. It drifted forwards over the city, much higher than the highest tower. The low thunder went on but the ship seemed to make no noise of its own. Then, suddenly, all that changed. The Wasp ship became a ball of searing white light. Kraymon and Vayim turned away, covering their eyes. The noise that followed was indescribable. It was as though the sky and the earth were being torn one from the other. Jeen Vayim was convinced that his eardrums were going to burst, that he would never hear again. When eventually the sound and the ringing in his ears faded, the Poet found himself with his forehead pressed against the stones of the broken wall. Kraymon was getting up from a similar position, shaking his head as though to free shards of sounds still trapped inside it.

'What next?'

'Do you think that Wasp ship exploded? Did it blow up?'

Kraymon was absentmindedly biting his lip. He seemed awed. 'As far as I can tell, I think we just saw a Wasp starship move out under full power.'

There was another blaze of white light way beyond the horizon and another clap of awful sound.

'The Wasps are putting ships up into space.'

'How could Gywann know this was going to happen?'

Kraymon frowned. 'I don't know yet but somehow it all interlocks.' Something caught his attention out in the swamps. 'Now what in hell is this?'

The Poet's eyes widened. 'Red spheres.'

Two of them were moving low across the surface of the black water. Just behind them was a larger dark shape. Kraymon glanced at Vayim. 'You've seen these things before?'

'One came over the first night that we were here. Gywann and I were the only ones who saw it.'

'Why didn't you say anything?'

'I didn't want to give the Gywannish any mystic ammunition.'

The two spheres and the dark object were coming directly

towards the wall where the Poet and Kraymon crouched. Something in the way they moved seemed to suggest that they were keeping low to escape detection.

'You have any theories about what these things are?'

'Hell, they could be anything. When I saw the first one I figured it to be some kind of Wasp spy device.'

'I never saw anything like them before and I've spent a lot of time watching Wasps.'

'They're still coming this way.'

Kraymon grinned. 'They are, too.'

'Doesn't anything worry you?'

Kraymon shrugged. 'I try not to let it . . .' He broke off. 'Holy shit, they really are coming this way.'

There was no mistaking the course of the objects. It was even just possible to make out some details of the third, darker shape. An upright, not quite regular cylinder was attached by a short, squat connecting tube to a bulbous, misshapen sphere. It made no sound and showed no light of any kind.

'I've never seen anything like that, either.'

'It's an ugly contraption.'

The black shape started to slow. It was now clear that it was much, much bigger than the red spheres, maybe some three storeys from the base to the tip of the vertical cylinder. It altered course slightly and the spheres followed suit. They were now close by, out on the water, almost touching the surface. They seemed to be making for the causeway that led up to the ruins.

'This is too damned strange for me. I don't understand any of this.'

'Think of all the poetry you'll have to tell when you come out on the other side of this.'

'I'd be happy just to come out on the other side.'

Sheet lightning flashed across the sky. It seemed to be tinged with green. It was reflected in what proved to be the machine's polished black surface. It had now come to a halt exactly over the causeway. One of the spheres remained beside the bigger craft while the other peeled off and lifted up and over the broken walls until it was hovering directly above the Gywannish encampment. The Poet turned carefully, watching his footing on the crumbling masonry. 'Will you look at this bunch?'

The faithful had formed up into an orderly, double-file procession with Gywann at its head. He was leading them away from the camp, apparently heading for the steps and down onto the causeway. Kraymon started scrambling down the wall. 'I've got to see this.'

Jeen Vayim followed him a little more slowly. As he and Kraymon had guessed, the Gywannish turned down the steps, went under the arch and started to march resolutely along the causeway towards the black craft. A line of white light appeared on the underside of the machine. A rectangular door was opening, lowering itself, drawbridge style, to form a ramp that led up and into the black vessel. Kraymon and the Poet halted.

'Do they intend to go inside the damn thing?'

The Gywannish kept on going towards the ramp. They were only a matter of yards away before they halted. Gywann looked up at the silent machine and said a few words that the Poet was unable to hear. Nothing happened. For long minutes everyone and everything stood motionless. More lightning crackled across the sky. Somewhere in the distance there was the high, drawn-out wail of a wampyr. Jeen Vayim started. Something was coming down the ramp.

At first it was hard to make out what it was. A kind of cube, for all the world looking like a floating cargo pallet with some kind of rack on it, it was guided down the ramp by another object, a squat dome with what appeared as a mechanical arm sticking out of its top.

'Is that what they used to call a robot?'

'It could be, at that.'

'I thought they were just a story.'

'Stories all have to start somewhere.'

Another pallet and rack followed the first. There was a third and a fourth. As the first cube reached the bottom of the ramp, the Gywannish went into smoothly organised action. They dragged the cubes off the ramp and back along the causeway. The domed robots, if that was indeed what they were, never left the ramp. They shuttled backwards and forwards, bringing out more and more of the cubes. When twenty-one of them had come down the ramp, the process stopped. Gywann once again walked to its foot and once again spoke to the black vessel. The robots retreated and the ramp started to lift. The door closed and the machine was dark again. There was a slight disturbance on the surface of the swamp as the craft started to lift away. The red spheres took up position beside it. They departed the way that they had come, silently and flying low over the swamp. When they were almost at the horizon and the large craft was once again invisible and the spheres now just red pinpoints, they zigzagged, then went straight up and vanished in yet another sheet of static electricity.

'What the hell has just happened?'

Kraymon slowly shook his head. 'I don't know but I'm sure going to ask.'

The Gywannish were coming towards them, pushing the twenty-one cubes. The pallets on which the cubes rested did indeed float a few inches above the ground and moved with comparative ease. As Gywann, who was leading the column and also seemingly exempt from manhandling one of the cubes, approached Kraymon and Jeen Vayim, Kraymon very deliberately planted his hands on his hips. 'Would you like to explain exactly what we have just witnessed?'

Gywann halted. The line of followers halted behind him. Some of them seemed glad of the pause. Perhaps the cubes were not as easy to move as they appeared. 'Your manner is close to threatening, Shafik Kraymon.'

'I want to know what you think you're doing. What is this stuff? Did it come from the Wasps or not?'

'What I predicted has come to pass.'

'But what did you predict? All you ever said was that something was coming.'

Kraymon walked forward to the nearest cube. It was indeed a rack. It held maybe fifty identical silver tubes, slightly smaller than a man's forearm. One end of each tube was smooth, the other gnarled with grooves and indentations. Kraymon nodded at the rack. 'You know what these things are?'

Gywann nodded. 'I do.'

'You want to tell me?'

'You have a lot of questions, friend Kraymon.'

'Damn right I have.' Kraymon stretched out a hand to pick up one of the tubes. Gywann moved with extreme urgency. 'Please don't touch them.'

Kraymon looked questioning but he didn't touch the tube. Gywann seemed to realise that at least some explanation was needed.

'Let us move these things back to the shelters and I will explain what they are.'

It took a good deal of time, difficulty and effort to get the cubes up the steps and there was much huffing, blowing and a few strained backs before they were neatly lined up beside the shelters. When all was done, Kraymon faced Gywann. 'I want an explanation, Prophet.'

Almost by accident, his hand was resting lightly on his pistol.

'You have little faith, Kraymon.'

'But a lot of curiosity.'

'I will show you.'

Gywann moved quickly to one of the racks. He picked up a tube. Holding it at arm's length by the gnarled end he pointed the smooth end at the broken wall. He made a slightly awkward motion with his wrist. There was a searing flash, an explosion and a section of wall was missing. Even Kraymon was stunned.

'They are all the same?'

'All the same.'

'What do you need with weapons?'

'We will gather the scattered and we will return to the city. This time not with love but with a sword. The days of the strangers upon this earth are numbered. Our saviours have brought us the instruments of our vengeance.'

Kraymon nodded. He was looking down at the rack from which Gywann had taken the demonstration tube. 'May I try one of these?'

Gywann still held the weapon. It was resting easily against his shoulder. He smiled. There was a new, larger madness in his face. 'You are a mighty hunter, Shafik Kraymon; who better to test the tools of our revenge?'

Kraymon picked up a silver tube and hefted it. He carefully aimed at the same wall. His fingers explored the configurations on what he thought of as the butt. Nothing happened. He lowered the weapon and carefully examined the gnarled end. He studied it for almost a minute, then he looked up at Gywann and smiled. He briskly pointed it at the wall. Another flash, another explosion.

'Your saviours are remarkable beings, friend Gywann.'

'Aren't all saviours remarkable?'

Kraymon nodded and very deliberately stuck the silver tube into his belt. He walked down the row of cubes. Two of the racks weren't stacked with cylindrical weapons. Instead, they held hundreds of what looked like tiny black eggs. Kraymon picked one up. 'And what are these?'

'Throw it as hard and far as you can.'

Kraymon did. The black egg fell just short of the wall.

As it touched the ground it vanished in a flash of searing white heat.

'More tools of your vengeance?'

Kraymon picked up a handful of the black eggs and dropped them into his pocket. Gywann said nothing. He seemed to have lost interest in Kraymon. He was showing Sulanda how the weapon worked. She was a quick learner. Inside a few minutes, she was blazing away at the already abused wall. Kraymon sauntered back down the line of cubes. He picked up a second tube, compared it to the tube in his belt, felt the weight and the construction and then, still giving the impression that he had no real purpose, he strolled over to where Jeen Vayim was watching the explosions. By that time, about half of the Gywannish had armed themselves and were firing at every available target. Kraymon was still carrying both the weapons. Even though his manner was nonchalant, his voice was urgent. 'Follow me, Poet, and don't be too obvious about it.'

Jeen Vayim glanced around. The Gywannish were so totally absorbed in their new toys that nobody seemed to be paying any attention at all to him. He ambled after Kraymon who was walking towards the steps. At the bottom, the big man waited for him.

'So what do you make of all this, Poet?'

'Beats me. Why in hell should the Wasps want to give weapons to the crazies? Do they want us to decimate each other? There must be easier ways to thin out our numbers.'

'They're not Wasp weapons.'

The Poet had the look of a man who absolutely doesn't understand what he has just heard. 'What?'

Kraymon handed Vayim one of the weapons. 'Take a look at it, the grip on the end.'

'What about it?'

'You've seen a Wasp, haven't you?'

'Yes.'

'So think about those things they have at the end of their upper limbs that pass as fingers. There's no way that they could fit the configurations of this grip.'

Vayim turned the weapon over in his hands. 'It wasn't designed for humans, either.'

'That's right.'

'So what are you saying?'

'I don't know for sure, but I'm starting to think that there's a third party involved in all this.'

181

'A third party?'

'Another species.'

Jeen Vayim looked at the cylindrical weapon. 'Another species? A third species?'

'The Protector himself entertains a theory that maybe the Wasps have occupied our world as a strategic move in some huge war, way out in space; that we are probably nothing more than a small outpost in a conflict that quite possibly is bigger than our imaginations. Trenhyass has often speculated on what would happen if the other side in this conflict arrived in our solar system.'

'And you think it has?'

Kraymon pulled the second weapon from his belt. He looked at it and shook his head. 'I don't know. I can only deal with what I see. Something has been agitating the Wasps for some time. Now they're putting big ships up into space. And simultaneously, three craft come in to land that are totally unlike any Wasp machine in my experience. They unload a shipment of weapons that also appear not to have originated from the Wasps, but would certainly fuel a handy civil war among us humans.'

This was pushing Jeen Vayim to the edge of total confusion. 'I can't follow any of this; if these beings are so all-powerful, why would they bother?'

Kraymon shrugged. 'Who knows? It makes a weird kind of sense. If you're one giant colonial power locked in conflict with another, why not dump a cargo of hand weapons on the natives? If you can stir them up, it's one more tiny headache for the defenders.' He stared up at the sky. 'When you think about it, it gets awesome. Even as we stand here, there could be a vast space battle forming up beyond our atmosphere.' A thought struck him. 'It could also be that our friend Gywann is the creation of this new enemy. It's one explanation for his powers.'

The Poet shivered. 'I think I'd like to get out of here.'

Lightning crashed across the sky. Kraymon nodded. 'I'm with you there. The one thing we know for sure is that Gywann now has a load of energy weapons and heat bombs and, if he rounds up more of his followers to use those weapons, he'll have more firepower than the Killers. I'm going back to warn the Protector.'

Vayim was shocked. 'After what happened in the lowers? You're crazy.'

'Despite Heizen and his Killers and all the rest of it, I'd rather Trenhyass was running things than Gywann.'

'It's one hell of a sick choice.'

'You don't know Trenhyass. He's stood betwen humanity and the Wasps for two decades. At least we weren't wiped out.'

'It's still one hell of a sick choice.'

'So are you coming with me or not?'

The Poet hesitated. 'Yeah, I guess so. I can't see me staying with Gywann and his bunch.'

'That's a pity for both of you.'

The new voice came from the top of the steps. Sulanda and a burly young man were standing there. Each had one of the new weapons and each was pointing it in the direction of Vayim and Kraymon. It was Sulanda who was doing the talking. 'I never thought you'd be a traitor, Jeen Vayim.'

'I've never exactly been one of you, either.'

'I never took you for the kind who'd sell us to the Killers.'

Kraymon was starting to edge sideways. He was still holding the silver tube. His hands hung loose at his sides. The young man gestured with his weapon. 'Just stay right where you are.'

Kraymon took one more step and then halted. 'I never thought of anything else.'

Sulanda started down the steps. 'Don't try and charm us, Shafik Kraymon. We heard the end of your conversation about how you intend to warn the Protector.'

The young man followed her. 'You cannot be allowed to leave here.'

Kraymon took another step. 'So you're going to start by killing us?'

The burly kid snarled. 'I told you to stay still.'

Kraymon took another step. He grinned. 'You're going to kill us anyway.'

'It's a holy war.'

'It always is.'

Then Kraymon was suddenly somewhere else. The Poet didn't see him move. The most positive thing was the voice in his ear.

'Jump, Poet!'

Jeen Vayim jumped. He was suddenly in an explosion. Debris seemed to be falling all around him, but miraculously none of it hit him. He dived for the ground and instinctively rolled, keeping a tight grip on the tube weapon. There were three heat flashes in rapid succession. Again he heard Kraymon yelling. 'Fire at the base of the arch.'

It took a few seconds' fumbling with the silver tube, then it shuddered in his hand and part of the arch vanished. Kraymon took out part of the opposite side. The Poet fired again. The arch staggered. One of the supports buckled and it went down in a billow of dust and masonry.

'Run!'

They were out on the causeway. Jeen Vayim's heart was pounding and his lungs wanted to quit.

'Keep going, Poet, that rubble won't hold them for long.'

Already the flickering pinpoints of torches were moving in among the ruins. Gywann was clearly organising a pursuit. They came over the arch and started out along the causeway. Kraymon stopped and turned. 'I think it's time to delay them.'

He dropped to the ground and sighted along the silver tube. Jeen Vayim did the same. He lay gasping.

'Easy now, Poet. Wait until they're about halfway across. The idea is to blow the causeway, not start a massacre.'

The Gywannish were about a third of the way to where Kraymon and the Poet lay waiting for them. They were coming on the run with the flames of their torches streaming behind them.

'One of the problems with carrying a burning torch is that you can't see too much beyond your own little area of light.'

The Gywannish were now halfway across the causeway.

'Try for about a half-dozen paces in front of them.'

Both Kraymon and the Poet fired. Right on target, the causeway exploded. The torches wavered. The Gywannish were clearly in confusion. Kraymon was up and going again. The Poet also scrambled to his feet. 'Have we thrown them off?'

Kraymon laughed. 'Sure we've thrown them off. By the time they figure out what's happened, we'll be away in the swamps.'

'I'm not sure I want to be away in the swamps.'

'Enjoy it while you can, Poet. When we get back to the city, we'll probably have this problem all over again with the Killers.'

Seventeen

THE ROOM was sombre, almost gloomy as the sun went down between the towers. Dust motes danced in the final beams of red afternoon light that slanted through the tall, narrow, cathedral windows. The figures around the long conference table were hunched and grim. Cloaks were pulled around shoulders as though in protection against the dying day. The tone of the discussion was as sombre as the scene, muted by concern and punctuated by long, thoughtful pauses. The only voice that was consistently raised was that of Marshal Heizen. The room was a small annex to the main Audience Chamber, a private sealed place that was used for secret discussion, nose-to-nose negotiation and the delivery of shockingly bad news. Trenhyass headed the table, flanked by Dole Euphest and a senior Legate. Heizen sat halfway down the table in what could only be interpreted as an adversary position. Kraymon and Jeen Vayim were side by side at the far end, the subject of everyone's scrutiny. There were a number of empty bowls and dishes in front of them. They had been permitted to eat during the anxious interrogation. Heizen alone seemed more concerned with making political points than listening to what they had to say.

'They are a disorganised rabble while we are an experienced, highly trained force.'

Kraymon growled deep in his throat. He could only believe that the leader of the Killers was deliberately refusing to grasp the full extent of what had happened out in the wastelands. 'Nobody has experience of what we're talking about.'

'Discipline will always prevail against a mob.'

'Even when the mob has many times its firepower?'

'I find it hard to give credit to this tale of yours. Why should the Wasps give weapons to the remnants of a group that was openly threatening their rule? My personal opinion is that this whole thing is a fanciful pack of lies, concocted to avoid summary execution by my Killers. You were, after all, sneaking back into the lowers for who knows what purpose when the patrol picked you up.'

Kraymon sniffed. 'It's hard to sneak in broad daylight.'

Dole Euphest doodled with a stylus.

'Isn't it true, Marshal, that your own spies have come in with reports that Gywann is rounding up what's left of his followers and that strange lights have been observed among the ruins?'

'That's hardly the same as Wasps making deliveries of arms.'

Frustration was creating a knot in the Poet's stomach. 'We didn't say it was the Wasps.'

Heizen's lip curled. 'A second race of aliens? Was that the theory?'

Jeen Vayim looked to the Protector for some kind of support or confirmation. Hadn't he, after all, voiced a similar theory for years? Trenhyass didn't, however, respond. He sat in silence, staring down at his fingers.

Outside the window, the sky was turning dark. The Poet suppressed an involuntary shudder. He wondered about the friends who were already lost, Denhagel, the Zilla Brothers and all the rest. He wondered how long he'd live if Heizen the Killer had his way. Everything was ending, everything was changing. He was acutely aware that he had no place in these high towers. He belonged in the lowers, he'd lived his life in the lowers, but now the lowers were burned and deserted.

The Protector signalled for a servant and the lamps were turned on. Here in the inner realm they enjoyed the luxury of real incandescent globes, but even their warm glow did little to dispel the feeling that chaos and destruction were gathering with the dusk. It was the first time that the Protector had done anything in an hour or more. He had been content to let Kraymon and Heizen argue and wrangle while Dole Euphest served as a referee and peacekeeper. He had quizzed both Kraymon and the Poet when they'd first been brought to the tower. He'd let them run through the story in some detail, he'd asked a few pertinent questions and then he'd simply ordered food for them. While they ate, he lapsed into a deep, distracted silence from which he'd hardly emerged since. Clearly, he was still very weak from his wounds, but there seemed to be something beyond that. It was as though he were deliberately withdrawing into a distant, private world.

The arrival of Heizen had caused sufficient commotion to at least partially disguise the Protector's lapse. Where Trenhyass seemed not to doubt what either Vayim or Kraymon had said, Heizen saw nothing beyond the potential for human deceit. He had doubted, shouted and threatened. He refused to believe that there was any way that Gywann and his people could pose any threat to his Killers. He also appeared unable even to entertain the idea of further alien intervention. After almost two hours of argument, he had finally turned his attention away from Kraymon. Clearly his purpose in coming to the Halls had not only been to listen to Kraymon and the Poet, but also to present his most recent plans to deal with the possibility of a return to the city by the Gywannish.

He started out by demanding that Kraymon and the Poet should leave the meeting. 'They have come straight from the rebel's camp with the most implausible story.'

Trenhyass looked up and shook his head. Heizen began to protest, but the Protector waved away his objections. 'They are not about to run back into the swamp and warn Gywann of our preparations.'

Heizen had scowled but he'd started his Killer Aides unrolling maps and laying out elaborate multicoloured diagrams from the start; it was obvious that Heizen, even after having listened to Kraymon's account of the Gywannish and their new weapons, saw no reason to revise his thinking. The plan was relatively simple. If Gywann did take it into his head to come in from the swamp, there were basically only three routes by which a large body of people could make their way into the lowers and from there up into the rest of the city. Accordingly, each of the routes would be cut by a defensive line on the outer edge of what had been the inhabited areas before the purge.

Huge garbage loaders, the same ones that had been used to haul away the dead after the massacre, would be parked end-to-end, motors out and immovable, across the roads, bridges and slipways that gave direct access to the city. They'd provide a high wall of rusted steel from the top of which the Killers could handle any threat that Heizen believed Gywann could offer. When the Marshal finished his deposition, he stood back almost as though he were half expecting applause or at least vocal congratulation. He was clearly proud of his handiwork.

'The beauty of it is that, starved and demoralised as they

obviously must be, they will have to bring the fight to us. All we have to do is wait. The longer they wait, the weaker they become; even if they do move, half that rabble will lose itself in the swamps before they even get here.'

The Protector said nothing. He continued to look thoughtfully at the maps. Kraymon, however, got to his feet and walked slowly to where Heizen was standing. 'You know something? You're more of a damn fool than I'd even imagined. Didn't you hear a word that I said?'

The Aides stiffened but Heizen simply looked contemptuous. 'I didn't believe a word that you said.'

'The new weapons will go through your makeshift walls like a hot knife through butter. I should know. I've used them.'

Heizen half smiled. 'The silver tubes that we confiscated? My people are examining them.'

Trenhyass' head snapped up from the maps. 'I want to see those weapons. Why weren't they brought here?'

'I thought it would be easier to have my own specialists run tests on them. These men were, after all, in my custody to begin with.'

'I want them brought here.'

Heizen nodded. 'I will have the matter taken care of, my lord. In the meantime, the more pressing matter is whether I've your approval to institute the defence of the city in the manner I've outlined.'

'I want those weapons now, Heizen.'

Heizen snapped at one of his Aides. The Killer hurried out of the room. Heizen did little to hide his annoyance from the Protector. 'It will be a while before they get here.'

'We can wait. Perhaps we could hear Shafik Kraymon's objections to your plan.'

The Poet walked to the window. It was now quite dark and there was considerable activity in among the towers, the riding-lights of carriages and red marker-lights of flying-belts drifted backwards and forwards or danced like fireflies. Kraymon turned his back on Heizen and faced the Protector. 'There isn't much point in concocting a whole lot of fancy plans until you know what Gywann is or what he wants.'

Heizen impatiently moved around him. 'He's a trouble-maker. That's what he is. That's all we have to consider.'

'Have you considered that Gywann himself might be the most dangerous weapon of the lot?'

Trenhyass immediately focused on this. 'What do you mean, Shafik Kraymon?'

'I mean we have to start to take our friend Gywann very seriously indeed. He's got powers that no regular man ought to have.' He repeated the theory that he'd first expounded to the Poet back in the swamps. 'The only way we're going to learn anything about him is to talk to him and observe him. If I were you I'd try and open some kind of negotiation with him instead of planning to kill him. He might prove to be just too dangerous to kill.'

Heizen exploded. 'You're insane. You expect us to talk with a rebel that we've already routed?'

Kraymon looked at him, shrugged, and faced the Protector. 'That's my advice. You can use it as you will.'

Trenhyass slowly shook his head. 'No, Shafik Kraymon. It's out of the question. Heizen's right, we can't negotiate with Gywann. It would send the wrong signals to too many of our own people. It would also be a very risky signal to send to the Wasps. We will continue with the plan as outlined by the Marshal.'

Kraymon thrust his hands deep into his pockets. 'Suit yourself. You seem to be assuming that the Wasps are still our best bet. They may not be, if they really are pulling out.'

'You think the Wasps are leaving.'

'I'm damned if I know.'

The Protector stroked his chin. 'I'm damned if I know, either.'

After that, there seemed little more to say. All they could do was wait until Heizen's Aide returned with the Gywannish weapons. Outside the window, sheet lightning played along the horizon. It seemed to the Poet that the whole city was waiting, either for something to happen or for an explanation. Finally, after over an hour, the Aide returned. He had nothing with him and he couldn't hide his agitation. He attempted to whisper in private to Heizen but the Protector interrupted him.

'Speak up, man. We all want to hear what you have to say. We're all fascinated to learn why you haven't brought what you were sent for.'

'My lord, I . . .' He glanced at Heizen. The Marshal sighed and reluctantly nodded. The Killer came to attention. 'My lord, we no longer have the Gywannish weapons. The Wasps came to the tower. They took the weapons away.'

Trenhyass looked like a man who has just had many more pounds added to his burden. The Killer elaborated.

'The Wasps came to our tower. They went straight to the workshops where the weapons were being examined. One of the technicians who was working on them tried to stop the Wasps and they imploded him.'

'And the Wasps now have the weapons?'

'Yes, my lord.'

'Is that all you have to tell? Did anyone comment on how the Wasps appeared, on their attitude or their behaviour?'

'It's so hard to tell.'

'Try.'

'They seemed to some to be extremely determined. They brought no translation device, they just made directly for the workshops. Although it's impossible to know with Wasps, most of the witnesses had the impression that something was very definitely bothering them.'

The room was silent. Kraymon looked from face to face but made no comment. The Killer remained at attention. Trenhyass' right eyebrow slowly arched. 'Is there more?'

Again the Killer looked unhappily at the Marshal. Heizen scowled. 'Nothing must be concealed from your Lord Protector.'

'A patrol discovered two bodies in the lowers.'

'I imagine there must still be quite a few bodies left in the lowers.'

'These had been recently hanged. The ropes were still around their necks. It also looked as though the wampyrs had been at them. Upon inspection, they were identified as two of our agents who'd been operating against Gywann in the swamps. The only assumption was that they'd been caught by the Gywannish, executed, and then their bodies were spirited into the lowers and left where we would find them.'

Heizen took a few careful seconds to slowly roll up one of the maps. When he spoke, his voice was barely under control. 'They are taunting us.'

The Protector shifted in his chair. The movement appeared to cause him a stab of pain. 'I believe you're right.'

'We have to show them that we won't tolerate this.'

'How would you go about doing that?'

'A small, highly mobile force could be sent immediately into the swamps to thin out their numbers a little. I'd bloody that damned rebel's nose for him.'

Kraymon leaned forward in his chair. 'It might be your nose that gets the bloodying, Heizen.'

'I've heard quite enough from you, Shafik Kraymon. I don't intend to listen to any more.'

Kraymon eyed the Protector. 'Are you going to let him do this?'

'Security is the Marshal's exclusive province. He doesn't need my authority to take that kind of action.'

Kraymon was about to protest, but the Protector motioned him to silence. A strange smile hovered for a moment at the corners of his mouth. Up to that moment, Kraymon had simply assumed that the assassination attempt was the reason that Trenhyass had been so withdrawn and uncertain, a total contradiction of his previous self. Trauma can do that to some men. All at once, the possibility that the Protector was up to something tapped at the back of his mind. Was he actually that devious? To lull everyone, particularly Heizen, into believing that he was losing his grip, maybe even dying? Sure, Kraymon knew that Trenhyass was that devious. The interesting question was, what the hell was his goal? On the surface, it seemed as though he was prepared to let Heizen and Gywann go at each other unchecked. Were they intended to neutralise each other? To what purpose? To leave Trenhyass free to do what? If the Protector was indeed engaged in something of this nature, he had clearly made some very serious predictions regarding the immediate future.

'Trust is everything, is it not, Shafik Kraymon?'

Kraymon half rose, made a small bow and smiled. 'Indeed, my lord.'

Out of the corner of his eye, he noticed the Killer Aide suppressing a smirk. Smirk away, you bastard. It may not last too long.

Eighteen

FIRST TROOPER Jarle walked slowly along the makeshift catwalk that had been rigged along the line of loaders that were strung out across the wide, flat concrete ribbon of the Straightlane. He dropped the nightscope in front of the eyepiece of his helmet. Nothing seemed to be moving down the length of the disused highway but the fact did little to calm his nerves. Since the defeat in the swamps, Killer morale had ebbed lower than anyone could remember. All along the improvised walls the men were jumpy and on edge. Horror stories about the power of the Gywannish weapons ran wild through the barrackrooms, while those on the night watch searched the shadows for advancing phantoms.

The attack had started out with the promise of teaching the rebels a swift and terrible lesson. The Marshal had sent his own Iron Fists, five armoured aircars and a full company in belts. Both were the special long-range models with the signal enhancer that would allow them to operate deep into the swamps. In fact, the Marshal was so confident of success that he had allowed the lead car's talkie reports to be broadcast through all the levels of the Tower. The idea was that those off duty and even the children should share in the victory and the chastisement of the rebels as it happened.

At first, everything had gone according to plan. The small force had moved out of the city and penetrated deep into the swamps. They'd conducted two wide sweeps of the ruins without finding any sign of the Gywannish. On the third, however, they had made contact. Beltmen on the far end of the left flank had spotted a small group of rebels moving across open ground. There had been a handful of men, maybe six or seven, and a larger number of women and children. The rest of the force circled for the attack. It had looked so easy. The Gywannish hadn't even attempted to run. They'd simply huddled together, apparently waiting for the end. The Killers hadn't even felt the need to hurry the final assault. They'd moved in at an almost leisurely pace, then, as they came close to striking distance, all hell had broken loose.

The sound of the awful surprise and the murderous confusion had boomed through the Tower as the Iron Fists were literally blown apart. The noise of destruction went on and on as one aircar after another plummeted in a burst of flame. Nobody in the Tower thought to shut it off. It only stopped when the lead car was hit and its talkie went dead. One of the last screamed messages was that the rebels seemed to have only four of the terrible new weapons. The enemy couldn't have struck a worse psychological blow if they'd worked on it for a year. For the very first time the Killers faced a foe that appeared to be totally superior in armament, and they were afraid.

A green flash from behind the horizon lit up the night. First Trooper Jarle ducked, knees bent, doubled over. There were two more flashes but they seemed to be harmless and he straightened up. He pushed back the nightscope. Peering into that red ghost world made him edgy.

After the defeat, the defences in the lowers had been hastily strengthened. Minefields, reinforced with pits and thickets of razor wire, were designed to stop the Gywannish before they reached the dirty brown steel walls of loaders. On the inside of those walls, a network of trestles and scaffolding had been erected to be used as observation posts and firing galleries. Finally, large numbers of armed Legates had been drafted in to augment the companies of Killers. These improvements did little to restore confidence. The defenders were still ready to jump at their own shadows.

First Trooper Jarle moved on down the line until he reached where Yashec was crouched with a firm grip on his pulser, his nightscope down, peering tensely into the darkness. Jarle knelt down beside him. Yashec pushed back his scope and eased the knots in his shoulders. 'This is making me fucking crazy, you know that.'

'You see anything?'

'Nothing.'

'Ain't that the bitch of it? Just waiting around, waiting for them to come.'

Yashec stuck his hand inside his tunic and slid out a flatsided bottle. 'You want a shot?'

'Are you insane? You could get twenty lashes for drinking on watch. The way things are now you could even get stretched.'

'What d'you think's keeping half of us here? You want a belt or not?'

Jarle hesitated and then shrugged. 'What the fuck.' He took the bottle. As he handed it back, Yashec spotted something out in the dark. He snapped down his scope and craned forward. 'Shit! It's one of those fucking red bastards!'

Jarle's scope was down. Yashec was right, one of the red spheres was moving slowly, close to the ground among the ruins.

'I hate those damn things.'

Yashec tightened his grip on his pulser. 'You think it's dangerous?'

'I never heard of one doing anything, but these days, who can tell?'

The sphere vanished behind an almost intact building. The two Killers started to relax but almost immediately froze as a terrible clamour started up, a chorus of the most unearthly shrieks and whistles.

'What the fuck!'

Down the line, a pulser went off. Two more throbbed. Jarle and Yashec pressed themselves against the protective steel. The howling rose to a climax and pulsers were going off all down the line. Yashec cautiously raised his head. Jarle hissed at him. 'Are we under attack?'

'I don't know . . . holy shit!'

Someone had cut in the sun-guns that were mounted along the top of the wall. The road leading up to the wall was bathed in white glare. Yashec slowly stood up.

'You want to take a look at this? We're being attacked all right but not by the Gywannish.'

Jarle also came to his feet. 'Boojies. Fucking boojies.'

'That damn sphere must have stirred up a whole nest of them. They're running straight for us.'

'There must be thousands of the things. They're like a living carpet!'

As though on some unnatural cue, the sky turned bright white; a terrible sound crashed across the city. It seemed to come from everywhere at once. It was as though some huge thing had grazed the outside of the atmosphere. It rang from the towers and flash-echoed through hollows and canyons of the lowers. Everyone clapped their hands to their ears. The sound was too big, too loud, too awful and out of proportion. The boojies were temporarily forgotten. Not for very long, however.

'They're running into the minefield! The boojies, they're running into the minefield!'

The shout came up from a well of deafness, muffled by the terrible ringing aftermath of the noise. People were cautiously removing their hands from their ears. The expressions of pain had yet to leave their faces. Everyone was defensive and hunched, wondering if there were going to be a second shock.

'The boojies! Look at the boojies!'

This time it got through. The boojies were indeed moving into the minefield. The living carpet had spilled into the trenches and surged all around the other obstacles. There was no pause or hesitation in its unearthly, undulating motion. The leading edge of the tightly packed mass was flowing like a strange, viscous liquid across the flat area where the mines were buried. The carpet of boojies split apart, dividing into separate snaking lines like tendrils and rivulets. Miraculously, they seemed to be avoiding the mines. Yashec looked wide-eyed at Jarle. 'Do we fire or what?'

'Hold your fire. Wait and see what happens.'

A boojie hit the first mine. When boojie flesh was blown apart, it instantly turned a livid, grotesque pink. It was like a parody of raw meat. It seemed that the boojies' initial evasion of the mines had been some blind, alien luck. A second, third and fourth mine went off in quick succession. Three exploded all together. Fountains of pink, otherworld tissue rocketed high in the air. Mines were going off all over, each one producing its own shocking pink goop. It slowly slimed down the outside of the loaders and it dripped from the wire. Jarle wiped the worst of it from the faceplate of his helmet.

'I thought those fucking mines were too near the wall.'

As boojie flesh solidified it began to smell. The closest thing to it that Jarle had ever smelled was ammonia and that wasn't even close. It also seemed to shimmer as though there was some peculiar vestige of life left in it. Yashec was scraping it off his uniform with a knife. An officer hurried down the catwalk.

'Get cleaned up on the double.'

'What now?'

'We've just had word. The Gywannish are on the move.'

Nineteen

THEY WERE hungry and they were ragged but they were on the march. To the last one, they were emaciated from the constant diet of black polyps. Many were sick. Fever sweat beaded their bodies, they had the wide-eyed stare of madness, but they marched just the same. They had received their sign. It was a holy vengeance. They had been given the magical weapons and there was nothing that could stop them. When anyone stumbled and sank to their knees, no longer able to continue the agonising advance across the swamps, through the ruins and over the endless rubble, the weapon was quickly passed to another. In many ways, it was the weapons that were going to the city. The humans had decided that they themselves were expendable. The weapons were not. They were the skyborn silver weapons. The Instruments of Adjustment. Feet bled, bowels ached, white light sucked out their vision. It didn't matter. They carried the weapons. In the wake of the ragged army, the ones who had been unable to go further sat and simply stared in the direction that the rest had gone.

Gywann marched beside the largest banner. The ragged black flag that had been stitched together from the vests of the first followers. Sulanda marched beside him, naked to the waist and daubed with swirls of green and black swamp colour as was now the custom of the fighting Gywannish. Both their faces were immobile. They seemed set in a distant but terrible serenity. In an alarmingly short space of time the handful of followers had grown into a crowd and the crowd swelled to the army that was now on the move. From the moment the weapons had been received, people had started to appear out of the swamp. The ruins at the end of the causeway became the focus of all who had survived the massacre. Gywannish and unbelievers alike came to follow the black banner. In fact, few unbelievers remained. The signs were too plain. They had not abated when the weapons had been brought. The lightning crashed almost continuously. A constant rumble seemed to hang just over the horizon. The green flash and the unbearable noise returned and, during the night, a pale violet glow would suffuse the sky.

The first thousand who arrived were given the weapons. Those who came later armed themselves with whatever they could. Some had bapguns or stolen pulsers that they'd brought with them from the city. Others had to be satisfied with crude clubs and spears. But about one thing there was no doubt: everyone, so long as their strength held up, was going back. There was no other hope. It wasn't just revenge, it was also a matter of survival.

The refugees from the lowers weren't the only ones going back to the city. Strange gnarled swamp beings followed behind, stumbling and grunting. Wide-ranging packs of wampyrs flanked the Gywannish army on either side but kept their distance. It wasn't clear whether they were simply circling in the hope of carrion or whether they too sought a revenge in the Adjustment. It appeared that everyone and everything in the swamps was moving on the city. Everyone, that is, except the betrayers Shafik Kraymon and the Poet Jeen Vayim. Before the army had moved out from the camp beyond the causeway, both their names had been solemnly cursed. If anything, they were worse devils in the eyes of the Gywannish than even the Protector or the Marshal. They had stolen two of the sacred weapons and used them against the righteous.

The advance might have been long-awaited but it was slow. Even with trained troops and experienced officers it would have been a hard task to move a large mass of people across such broken and brutal terrain, and the Gywannish were neither trained nor experienced. As well as the ones who were left by the wayside there were those who drowned in hidden sinkholes or were sucked down into the oily ooze as they struggled through the waterlogged devastation. Things became a little easier when one of Gywann's brighter lieutenants, a young man called Niarva, noticed that some of the wampyr packs had a tendency to run on ahead and then furtively scamper back. The wampyrs naturally took the course of least resistance. It occurred to the lieutenant that the simplest solution would be to follow the path indicated by the wampyrs. So long as they kept moving in the direction of the towers it would be hard to go wrong. Accordingly, Niarva took command of the vanguard. His theory almost led to hideous disaster on three occasions but each time it was narrowly avoided; in the main, it held good and in this way the wampyrs became the strange scouts of the Gywannish.

On the fourth day of the march the second sun appeared. High, dark clouds had been shuddering across a sky that shimmered with electricity, but around noon the clouds rolled past, the static subsided and the sky turned to a natural blue tinged with brown at the horizon. The spirits of the army lifted. Even those with blistered or bleeding feet seemed to walk with a more determined stride. The original sun was a bright white disc and it almost seemed that the world had achieved some essential normality. The second sun appeared only a relatively short distance from the original. The first flash turned the sky white and left the army swimming in red retinal after-image. The sheet of white shrank and condensed into a burning disc that was maybe half as big again as the real sun. The increase in heat was immediately noticeable. The army halted. The silence of total awe fell over its disorganised and straggling ranks. *There were two suns.* The enormity of the events in which they were players caught up with them. Resolve faltered. What did revenge matter when new suns appeared in the sky?

Gywann stood beside Sulanda, slightly in front of the standard-bearers. The people around him were dropping to their knees. Weapons were put down. There was a new sun. Gywann appeared to have lost control. His face unfroze. He looked around. He was no longer the centre of attention. The devotion had faded. Sulanda's head also slowly turned and she looked at Gywann. His head dropped. For long moments he stared at the ground, then his back straightened. He began to walk forwards. There was a moment while nobody seemed to notice him. He was the only one moving. His followers were motionless, stunned. There were two suns. Sulanda walked forwards, following her master. The standard-bearers fell into step behind her. The heart of the army was moving again. People began to get to their feet. Those around Gywann began to walk. The ripple spread. It was a sign. The buzz spread through the mass of people. There were two suns. It was the final sign. There was no need to fear. Even the heavens were with them. The army was up and moving forwards again. The new sun was nothing to fear. It was just another confirmation of their power and the rightness of their cause. They would take the city. This was their part in the mighty events that were coming to pass.

The second sun, however, was only a temporary visitor. For maybe two hours it remained, keeping pace with the original as it tracked across the heavens, and then it began to fade. Again there was a degree of consternation in the ranks. Having so readily adopted the second sun as their own, the Gywannish were uneasy to see it go. This time, however, they didn't falter. A comforting rumour spread. Suns might come or go, but they were going to the city. By nightfall, the second sun had gone altogether. Only one sank behind the western horizon.

When the sun rose again, it was clear to those in the front ranks that something had changed. The wampyrs had started to fall back. The packs no longer dashed ahead pointing out the paths. The creatures seemed jumpy and uncertain. The army was moving out of the swamps. The overspill of the Blackwater was now behind them. They had moved into the dry ruins. It was the final strip of uninhabited waste before the lowers really started. In this region, routes and highways almost functioned. There were discernible paths by which a mass of people might approach the city.

Niarva halted the leading column. Under his command it had become something of an elite. He had attempted, with some success, to guide the army through the swamps. It had only been the trick of watching the wampyrs but it had been enough to invest him with a practical authority. He had already earned himself a place in Gywann's inner circle having been one of those delegated to hold the final line against the Killers. He had fired a bapgun in the upper room and then fled behind Gywann into the passage. He had risen to that first occasion and from then on he had remained a pillar of strength. The young men flocked around him. Grim beyond their years, they had led the advance. They would take the first taste of vengeance, but when they faced the Killers they wanted any advantage they could get. Of all who marched with Gywann, they had the firmest grasp on reality.

All around them, the army ground to a halt. Gywann had retreated into some spiritual absolute. Practical leadership was coming from the hard, half-naked young men in their black and green warpaint who led the way. They made the decisions and dictated the routes that the army would take. Now they were out of the swamp, there was only the final approach in front of them. Choosing their way into the city was something that couldn't simply be left to Niarva's instincts. Accordingly, the five most influential of the young men gathered at the head of the waiting army for an urgent conference.

'This has to be done right. We can't just throw ourselves at the Killers. Even with these weapons, it will not be an easy fight. We have to plan our approach.'

'Have you lost your courage, Bobvo?'

The young man who had spoken scowled and shook his head. 'I haven't lost my courage. I am Gywannish. I am prepared to die. I just don't want to die unnecessarily because we didn't think about what we're doing in front.'

Niarva stated the options. 'The shortest route into the lowers would be straight through the Poldar Tunnel. It'd be quick and it would bring us out at the very edge of the lowers. The drawback is that we'd be strung out in one long line. All down the ramp, and even in the tunnel itself, we'd be terribly vulnerable to attack.'

'There's precious little everburn in the Poldar. I know that tunnel. I used to go that way foraging. There's water in it, too, some stretches are waist deep.'

'If the Killers got in among us in the tunnel, we wouldn't have a chance. In a confined space like that, our weapons would kill more of our own people.'

'Our only real alternative is to circle round until we cross the Straightlane. We follow it down all the way to the Lassus Fields and go into the lowers across the open. There's plenty of cover until that last open space. When we get there we'd have to take our chances.'

'It's better than the tunnel.'

'It'd take almost an extra day to get around to the Straightlane.'

'It's still better than the tunnel.'

There seemed to be nothing left to say. Bobvo glanced at Niarva. 'So, do we start them moving again?'

Niarva shook his head. 'No, this is too important for us. I must take this to Gywann. He must approve this final stage.'

There was a stiffening in the group, a sudden surge of tension. Nobody said anything. Nobody wanted to be the first to speak against Gywann. Nobody wanted to risk the disgrace of a betrayer. Gywann was their prophet and their master, there was no doubt about that, but now he seemed

200

to be in an almost perpetual trance; they all had their serious, private doubts about his capabilities as a military commander. He still had their devotion, but he was losing their confidence. It required more than devotion to go up against the Killers. It required at least a minimal strategy. Niarva was to the strongest degree aware of their reservations. Indeed, he shared most of them himself, but he could see no other way. He voiced it out loud for a second time. 'I have to take this to Gywann.'

The others reluctantly nodded. Niarva was right. There was no other way. They were Gywannish, they had to maintain the faith. Niarva walked slowly back through the army. The sky was again slowly being suffused with an angry blood-red glow even though there were hours to go before sunset. An unnaturally warm wind had sprung up. It had a strange metallic smell to it. A silence had fallen over the army. Every eye was on Niarva as he walked to where Gywann stood beneath the black banner. People were starting to grow afraid of the signs. There were too many of them and they all seemed portents of doom and destruction. Vengeance might be at hand, but so was death. It hovered somewhere in the red sky. The fear had not spread so far that Gywann could not have calmed it with a few words. Gywann, however, was absolutely silent. His eyes were dead. As Niarva halted in front of him, there was no flicker of enquiry, not even recognition. Niarva experienced a moment of panic. It was like facing a statue or a body in which the mind had died.

'Master!'

There was still no response. Sulanda was exactly the same.

'Master, for some time now I have been guiding the path of the army. We are very close to the city and it is crucial that we plan our approach. Very soon we shall encounter the enemy and we have to be ready.'

Gywann's eyes continued to look right through him. Niarva did his best to hide the desperation that was creeping into his voice. He had been willing to guide the army while it was still in the swamps. That had been his duty. He could not see that it was his duty to actually lead the attack. Nothing had prepared him for that.

'Master, a decision has to be made.'

Those nearby were starting to gather round and watch the one-sided confrontation. Niarva could feel the start of

201

dismay and concern moving through them like a physical force.

'Master, our basic choice is between two routes into the inhabited parts of the city. The fastest and most direct route is through the Poldar Tunnel but if we go that way, we expose ourselves to attack. There would be little we could do to resist while we were actually in the tunnel.'

Gywann continued to look as though he were carved out of stone. Niarva pressed on. 'The second option would take longer but we would be in far less danger of attack. That would involve going around the city and . . .'

'We will go through the Poldar Tunnel. The Killers will not attack us there.'

It was as though Gywann had been switched on and then off again. He had made his decision and he was gone. Niarva was sideswiped by conflicting emotions. First there was the relief that his prophet had spoken, but then the sinking feeling that his prophet might be wrong.

'Master, we could be wiped out in the tunnel . . .'

This time Sulanda came in. 'You have heard the words of our Master, Niarva. Do you lose your faith?'

'No, I . . .'

'Then start the army moving. Our revenge is close at hand.'

Niarva said nothing. He didn't even think. He turned on his heels and marched quickly back through the ranks, back to where the others were waiting. He delivered Gywann's answer in a curt, neutral tone.

'The Master wishes that we take the tunnel.'

The expression on his face told them that he would tolerate no argument.

Once again the army moved forwards. The sky had darkened to a deep magenta. The sun was partially obscured and the ruins were places of shadow. The wampyrs had moved in closer to the humans as though for protection against this strange redness. At regular intervals there were pulses of light, as if new suns were trying to be born but only had the power to linger for a split second. As the army penetrated deeper into the dry ruins a watchful unease spread through it. Even the wampyrs noticed and made low keening noises. The wampyrs might have been uneasy but they hadn't turned back. They and the other swamp things, against all their natural instincts to stay in the wet places, went on following the army. It wasn't something that particularly cheered the Gywannish. The aberrant behaviour of the swamp creatures was another disturbing thing that wasn't as it should be. Wasp aircraft now constantly flew over either singly or in formation. Each time they passed overhead, everyone hit cover but the Wasps didn't seem particularly interested in this mass of humans. They always flew straight out across the Blackwater.

The ramp that led down into the Poldar Tunnel was like a black open maw, the mouth of some dark unknown. It was flanked by broken and unrecognisable statues. Even Niarva and his determined cohorts experienced a momentary falter. Only the wampyrs seemed pleased. With loud, yipping cries they raced ahead and down into the darkness. Screams and shouts came from inside the tunnel. The pace of the front ranks noticeably slowed. There was something evil and threatening about it. Niarva moved quickly ahead. He turned and, walking backwards, waved the front ranks to him.

'Come along, my friends, we don't have to be afraid of the darkness in the tunnel. It is our Master's will. The tunnel takes us directly to our revenge and our victory. Hold on to your faith, friends, it's the Master's will. What do you say, friends? It's the last mile, are you still with me? Are you still with the Master?'

There were no shouts and no cheers. They were too hungry and footsore to get excited. What kept the Gywannish on the move was a grim, ground-to-the-bone fanaticism. It stiffened their weary spines and gave them the dull resolve to go down into the black tunnel. They knew they had no alternative. The front ranks came doggedly on, closing up on each other as they approached the head of the ramp. When they reached it, Niarva brought his leading troops to a halt. He had already ordered scavengers to find and make a supply of torches. Again he faced the army. He held out his hand and a torch was placed in it. A fire was kindled and the torch blazed. Niarva held it high above his head. He said nothing. He simply turned, and started down the slope. In that moment, Niarva was suddenly aware that he had just ensured himself a place in the scripture that would surely be written when all this was over. More torches were kindled. The army came down after him. By the light of the flames, the Gywannish went down into the tunnel.

It was a haunted place. A vision of where a lost soul might finally be confined, seemingly endless, high vaulted and knee deep in black oil-slick water. Heavy sluggish mist lay on the water's surface and long spindly stalactites hung like spears from the roof. As Niarva led the way, moving slowly through the water, he left a long roiling V behind him that was broken into pieces by the ranks that followed. The torches' blaze was reflected off the water and the tunnel walls. In the darkness beyond the edge of the light, unseen things splashed and scuttled while the wampyrs chased and ducked and dived. The Gywannish advanced without thought. They were numb. They were in hell. There was no point in imagining the next terror until it actually came.

The further they got into the tunnel, the further their spirits sank. The Gywannish were an army of automatons, putting one painful foot in front of the other without question or thought. There was no will but the Master's. There was also still no sign of an end to the tunnel. Even Niarva halted and stood staring forward without focus. No matter how many signs and portents, no matter how lofty their mission, human beings could do only so much. They couldn't even look forward to the end. At the end of their journey, they would have to fight a battle. All they could do was to listen to the splash of each step echo back off the stalactites and the dripping walls. In the moment when it all seemed so mountainously impossible, the voice started.

'Don't fear the strangers.'

It was pure and melodic and it cut across all the slap and splash of the army.

'Don't fear the strangers.'

Whoever it was had put a melody to what had once just been a chant. A second voice picked up the refrain. Some said it was Gywann who started the singing but later there would be debate about that.

'Don't fear the strangers.'

More voices came in. The stalactites began to vibrate. The singing gathered strength.

'Don't fear the strangers.'

The Gywannish were tapping down to some hidden reserve. The voices were swelling.

'Don't fear the strangers.'

Weapons were brandished.

'Don't fear the strangers!'

A group of women came in with a descant.

'Fe-ar! Fe-ar!'

Basses joined in. A wampyr howled.
'Fear, fear, fear, fear.'
'Don't fear!'
'Fear, fear, fear, fear.'
'Don't fear!'
'Fe-ar! Fe-ar!'
'Don't fear the strangers!'
It ran back from the walls and roof.
'Don't fear the strangers!'
Even though they felt dragged down by the oily waters, their pace quickened. Singing, they marched on down the tunnel; singing, they finally saw the light at the end. Singing, they emerged into a red sunset across which the thunder rolled. In front of them they saw the line of Killer defences. For a moment the singing faded. A Killer wardrum sounded. Then another and another. A terrible cry went up from the Gywannish and they started forwards at a run.

Twenty

HORFON WAS pressed flat with his face in the dirt. Each time the ground vibrated, he tried to press down harder as though he believed that he could will himself into the earth. His eyes were tightly shut and he was terrified. Behind him the minefield was exploding. The first assault of the Gywannish weapons had created total confusion. An entire company of airborne Killers had dropped in among the mines and started a chain reaction. A side effect that the explosions created was thermals which could throw a man in a flying-belt completely out of control and even upset a carriage. Debris thudded into Horfon's back. He tried to crawl forwards but more mines went off. There were more of the flashing explosions produced by the terrible Gywannish weapons. They seemed capable of taking out whole sections of ground. The Gywannish were everywhere, painted like savages, black and green, screaming and howling with their black flags and banners. A boy, scarcely more than his own age, appeared out of the swirling dust and smoke. His hair was matted down and his eyes looked crazy. His only garment was a ragged pair of baggy black pants. He was bleeding copiously from a cut over his left eye but he determinedly clutched a homemade bapgun. Horfon remained absolutely still and pretended he was dead. Even from his limited viewpoint, it was more than clear that the city's defenders were being separated into small groups and mopped up one at a time. The boy looked around twice and then ran off in another direction. A small squad of Iron Fists was attempting a last stand with their backs to the wall.

The worst thing was the noise. The awful, earbursting booms and the shouting and screaming that went between. Horfon had always imagined that when battle came he would know what to do: someone would tell him what to do. Nothing had prepared him for the absolute confusion and the overwhelming, gut-wrenching fear that all too easily imagined a hundred possibilities for immediate death. All he could do was hug the ground. There was no doubt that it was the end and all he could pray for was how. He was silently begging providence that his end would be fast and painless when someone started to kick him hard in the ribs.

'Get up, damn you! Get up and move or I'll pulse you where you lie.'

The voice of authority triggered a reflex in Horfon that over-rode his fear. There *was* someone to tell him what to do. He dodged another kick and scrambled to a crouch. A heavily moustachioed Wingleader was glaring down at him.

'You snivelling little runt! You want to live forever? Move up! Move!'

The Wingleader landed a final kick on Horfon's backside. It sent him stumbling forward into the smoke. All around him were other doubled-over grey tunics, other Legates moving forward, crouched over with their pulsers held out in front of them. Their shoulders were hunched and their heads down close to their chests. It was as though they believed the packs on their backs would shelter them against blast and shrapnel. To Horfon, they scarcely looked human. Strange two-legged creatures that carried their own shells like snails or turtles. The worst part was that he was no different. He was simply another terrified beast creeping forward, living through this nightmare. Something black and green moved in the smoke over on his right. Horfon blindly fired his pulser. The others were doing much the same thing. Horfon wondered where they were supposed to be going. Were they advancing or retreating? For an instant the sky cleared. It was still going crazy with unearthly colours and patterns. The smoke closed in again. The explosions didn't stop. Suddenly there were more figures. Everyone opened fire. The Wingleader was screaming.

'Hold your damn fire until you know what you're shooting at! You'll be killing each other if you panic!'

A heat bomb burst beside them. Horfon was blown off his feet. His exposed skin felt scorched. He tried to get up but the blast from a Gywannish weapon seared him a second time. He was face down again with his ears ringing and his vision a mass of disorganised flashes. He felt himself lifted up bodily.

'Don't lie there pissing yourself, boy! Run! Run!'

The Wingleader propelled him roughly forward. The two Legates in front of him were running towards a blast crater.

Dead Killers were scattered all around it. He stumbled over the bodies and dived into the pit. There was an explosion behind him. He looked back and the Wingleader was no longer there. One of the other Legates in the crater was in bad shape. He was bleeding from both a head and a leg wound. He was screaming.

'Oh my Lord! I'm gonna die! Oh shit! Oh shit! I'm going to die! Oh my Lord! I'm going to die!' Then he stiffened and slumped. The second Legate turned and looked at Horfon. 'I think he was right!'

'Androx!'

She wiped her face. 'Horfon?'

'That's right.'

There was another nearby explosion. They both threw themselves flat. A Killer rolled into the crater. His helmet was gone and half of his hair was scorched away.

'It's a fucking slaughter. We can't do anything against those weapons. Those fucking savages are walking all over us. Did you see the whole fucking company go into the fucking minefield? Did you see it? Shit!'

Horfon nodded. The Killer seemed to be talking to keep himself from falling apart.

'I was over the wall. Five of them pointed those fucking weapons at one of the loaders. It just fucking vanished. It fucking melted!' He started to shiver. 'Shit!'

A Killer officer appeared on the edge of the crater. He started ranting at the three of them. 'Get the fuck out of there or I'll kill you where you lie! Move, you shits! What do you think this is, a whore's picnic?'

He was waving his pulser. Horfon and Androx were half prepared to go back into the battle. The Killer simply snatched up his pulser.

'We lost, fuck you! We lost!' He shot down the officer who convulsed and sprawled, half in and half out of the crater. The Killer stood up. He started laughing. He flapped his arms. 'We're safe here. Lightning never strikes the same place twice.'

There was a small explosion and his head vanished. His body flopped down, twitching, right across the crouching forms of Horfon and Androx. Blood poured all over them, but they both remained absolutely still. There was shouting and yelling all around them. A third Killer body flopped into the crater, more streamed past on either side, clearly in full retreat. Some turned and fired their pulsers in a final, heroic pretence at an ordered withdrawal but the majority simply fled. Androx clapped Horfon on the shoulder. 'Time we moved up too.'

'We'll be killed for sure.'

'I don't fancy waiting here until the final ranks come slitting throats to make sure the dead are really dead.'

There was now a solid wave of fleeing Killers and the main body of the Gywannish was close behind. For a few seconds, Horfon and Androx crouched, hesitating on the rim of the crater, and then they ran, taking advantage of the most dense press of fleeing Killers. Heat bombs burst on either side of them but they just kept on running. Horfon regularly glanced around to see that Androx was still beside him. His uniform was suddenly splattered with blood. It didn't seem to be his and he had no curiosity about whose it might be. He just went on blindly.

Up ahead, there was a commotion. A bunch of thirty or forty Iron Fists were attempting to rally behind the cover of a wrecked aircar. A senior officer in a ripped and bloody tunic was in among them. He was screaming hysterically at those who continued to fall back. His eyes had the glaze of the insane and he shrieked about how death was the final duty. After a few minutes of making little progress, he actually climbed up onto the top of a downed machine and stood brandishing a ceremonial dagger. Almost immediately, he was shot down.

Now the Gywannish were in among them. The Killer rally was terminated by a pair of heat bombs. Horfon noticed that the noise of the strange silver tubes had moved away a little, as though they had been directed to another section of the wall. The Gywannish that were all around seemed armed only with pulsers and a few bapguns. A few just had clubs, although they were quickly arming themselves with the weapons of the dead. Hand-to-hand combat was breaking out all around. Some of the Killers refused to go without a fight. They kicked and clawed and slashed with their daggers; only numbers finally dragged them down.

Horfon couldn't see Androx. Hands smeared with green dye grabbed for him. It was unthinking, cornered instinct that fired his pulser. The arms windmilled back. Suddenly, he was fighting. He was part of the battle. He spotted Androx. She was also fighting back, grappling with a wiry Gywannish woman who was trying to crush her skull with an iron bar. Androx managed to get a hand twisted in the woman's hair. She swung her around and as she swung, Horfon fired. Androx staggered towards him. They almost touched but then a heat bomb exploded. The blast threw them against the side of the crashed aircar. For a few moments, both were out cold. It couldn't have been too long, however, because when Horfon came to, smoke and dust were still swirling around. A jagged hole in the side of the hull led to the aircar's interior. Dragging Androx behind him, he crawled inside. The dead steersman was still strapped into his seat. Horfon ignored the body. He looked back. Nobody seemed to have seen them. An ovoid Wasp aircraft flew slowly across the battlefield. Explosions blossomed around it. The Gywannish were prepared to fire on the Wasps even if they seemed incapable of actually hitting them.

Androx opened her eyes. 'We've lost, haven't we?'

Horfon wiped the sweat from his eyes. 'For the moment, we're still alive.'

The battle seemed to be passing them by. The noise of fighting had moved on. The worst of it now seemed to be coming from well inside the shattered defences. The Gywannish advancing past their hiding place were mainly old people and children. Gangs of kids were moving among the dead, clubbing and hacking at any who still showed signs of life, laughing and squealing as though slaughter was a kind of wonderful game. Worse than the children, however, were the wampyrs who finally brought up the rear. During the peak of the fighting there'd been no sign of them. They'd hidden back in the darkness of the Poldar Tunnel, seemingly terrified by the noise and flame of the battle. Once, however, the conflict had moved on, they emerged cautiously from its mouth like stooped, flightless birds of prey; their filthy black rags hung from their shoulders like dead wings and their heads swivelled watchfully as if they might panic at any moment. Despite their clear trepidation, though, they relentlessly sniffed and snuffled their way towards the wreckage of bodies.

The wampyrs moved from corpse to corpse in short, nervous rushes. Some let out little howls of glee as if they couldn't believe their good fortune. Horfon and Androx watched from their hiding place in silent horror. Right in front of them, one particular creature with an impossibly long, pale face, black hair like rotting seaweed and a peculiarly deformed spine was crouched over a fallen Killer. It glanced around as though expecting some kind of threat, baring its teeth and hissing for good measure. At one point, it had looked directly at the two Legates, but its sunken, slitted eyes were unable to see into the shadows under the aircar's broken hull. Apparently satisfied that it wasn't about to be attacked by one of its fellows, it hunkered down and searched for a suitable rock. After discarding two or three, it hefted what seemed to be the correct one. It held it poised over the dead Killer's head and then brought it down hard. It was a precise, practised blow which split the skull like a walnut. It prised the two halves apart, dipped its scooped fingers into the exposed cavity and then raised them to its mouth.

Androx began to shiver. She was as white as a sheet and looked as though she might throw up at any moment.

'We have to get away from here.'

'Sssh.'

'We can't just lie here waiting for those things to find us.'

'There's nowhere to go, and besides, if you don't keep quiet, they'll hear you.'

The sky strobed and there were series of rolling booms from the upper atmosphere. The wampyrs took off as if they'd been shot. Most of them fled for the safety of the tunnel. A few remained, staring up as though waiting to see what would happen next. Horfon could feel his nerves starting to go. He reached for Androx's hand and gripped it tightly. She tried to stifle a small gasping sob.

'I don't want to die. I want my life. I want my fair share.' Suddenly her voice was angry. 'They've got no right to expect me to die.'

Horfon remembered all the dozens of ways he had hoped and wished and imagined Androx coming to him for comfort. None of his daydreams had been anything like this.

'Perhaps later, after dark, we could take off these uniforms and try and go into the city.'

Androx looked up at the violent flashing sky and shook her head. 'I don't think it's going to get dark. I think there's something terribly wrong. The storms, the colours in the sky, the two suns and now this . . .'

A final hysteria was edging into her voice. Her fingers were digging into his arm. He noticed that she had gone into battle with a fresh manicure.

'It . . . wasn't . . . supposed . . . to . . . be . . . like this way. We were safe. The Wasps kept us safe.'

'They say the Wasps are leaving us.'

Androx's eyes were wide and desperate. 'But why? What did we do? We always did what we were told. We were good.'

'We'll probably never know why they went.'

Androx's shoulders sagged. Her voice was suddenly soft. 'Horfon.'

'What?'

'Will you put your arms around me?'

'I . . . of course.'

He awkwardly clasped her to him. He was stiff and tentative.

'Hold me tight. I think I'm going to start shaking.'

He increased the pressure of his arms but he was still selfconscious and awkward. Androx was suddenly angry. Some of her previous spirit had reappeared.

'I said hold me, dammit. I'm a woman, not a sack of flour.'

He jerked in confusion. She fell against his chest. Abruptly she was sobbing. Automatically he stroked her hair. She cuddled against him. For a long time they just lay, not even thinking, taking comfort from each other's warmth. Then she started to move against him. Something other than fear and depression moved somewhere inside him. Her lips were on his neck and he could feel her breath. Their lips met. Was this it? Was it actually going to happen to him in the middle of a battlefield with the dead all around? He couldn't believe it. When it came to it, were they nothing more than animals? He closed his mind as tightly as he could to everything but physical sensation.

Twenty-One

THE GYWANNISH streamed through the breach in
Heizen's line. Two loaders lay on their sides, two more
were no more than heaps of fused metal. The attackers
swarmed over these freshly created slagheaps, ignoring the
burns that came from bits that were still too hot to touch. A
fountain of dust and smoke erupted on the inside of the
wall. The Killers were in headlong retreat, fully aware that
there was little that they could do against the Gywannish
weapons.

Gywann himself didn't follow his people through the
wall. He had indicated that the black banner should be
planted on a small knot on the outer edge of what had been
the minefield. He would wait there until he felt that enough
of the city had been secured. Sulanda and a small escort
waited with him. Gywann, after the effort of selecting this
vantage point from which to watch the storming of the city,
had relapsed into stonefaced immobility. Sulanda was a lot
more animated and even led the escort in a ragged cheer
when the smoke of a second explosion billowed up behind
the wall. In fact, they were so intent on watching and
applauding the battle that, at first, they failed to notice the
approach of the aircar.

It came from the direction of the Blackwater, low and
very fast. It was running at something close to top speed
and little more than a hand's-breadth above the ground.
Sulanda was the first to spot it out of the corner of her eye as
she glanced at Gywann.

'Incoming aircraft!'

She grabbed Gywann and tried to pull him down to the
ground. They were an obvious target beneath the tall
banner. The craft was of the same design as those used by
the Killers and there were at least half-a-dozen figures on
the open deck. The escort had their weapons out and
trained on the flying machine. It kept on coming.

'Take no chances. Bring it down!'

'Wait!'

The figures on the deck were waving. The aircraft started to slow. Its occupants went on waving. The aircar executed a slow half-turn and came to rest some thirty or forty paces from the knoll. It was possible to see the warpaint on the bodies of those on board. They continued to wave and shout. The escort relaxed slightly. As soon as the craft touched ground, almost everyone on the deck jumped down and started running towards the knoll. It was possible now to hear what they were shouting.

'Have you heard the news? Have you heard the news?'

Sulanda turned to the nearest of the escort. 'Have you seen any of these people before?'

He scanned the approaching faces and shook his head. 'Come to think of it, no.'

Sulanda raised a warning hand, but it was too late. The rest of the escort was moving to greet the new arrivals.

'What news? What's happened? Has the city fallen?'

The newcomers and the escort reached each other. The leaders on each side embraced. Suddenly the newcomer produced a hidden knife. With the smooth speed of an expert he stabbed the escort in the stomach. He twisted, ripped and pulled it out.

'The news is that you're dead, sucker.'

The escort dropped to his knees, holding in his stomach, with a look of total disbelief on his face. More of the newcomers pulled out knives and cut down their welcomers. There was blood and confusion. Before the remainder of the escort could react, the newcomers had snatched up the weapons dropped by their victims and, without hesitation, burned down those who were left. Only Gywann and Sulanda were spared. She ran towards him screaming.

'They're Killers! Run! They're Killers!'

One of the Killers, a woman, laughed and held up her dagger.

'Did you recognise it, honey? You know a Killer knife when you see one?'

She deftly threw it. It took Sulanda neatly between the shoulder blades. She sprawled in the dirt almost at Gywann's feet. Now Gywann was alone. The Killers slowly advanced on him, grinning wolfishly. They were clearly enjoying themselves. Gywann's eyes cleared.

'So you've come for me, have you?'

'That's right, prophet, we've come for you.'

He didn't resist. While two of the Killers gathered up the

other fallen weapons, the rest manhandled Gywann to the aircar. The last man to climb on board hesitated.

'What about the banner?'

'Burn it.'

The last man took careful aim. The black banner vanished in a blossom of flame. The dust of the battlefield swirled up as the aircar lifted. On the deck, they manacled Gywann and then began to wipe off the black and green warpaint. On this return journey they headed straight for the city. They went for safety in height. The battle still raged down on the lower levels. The Gywannish with their hellspawned weapons were walking over all resistance, but they still had more to do than take pot-shots at a high-flying aircar. As the Killers cleaned themselves off they shot bitter, hate-filled looks at Gywann.

'Yeah, prophet, what deal did you do? How did your slime get those fucking weapons?'

A second Killer looked around at his mates. 'What I want to know is, if those fucking weapons existed on this earth, how come we don't have them? Our boys are being massacred down there!'

A third couldn't believe that their marshal could let them down. 'They must be from the oldtimes. The suckers must have found them, must have dug them up someplace, the fucking bunch of rat vomit.'

He pulled on his boots, stamping down hard on the deck to get the heel just so. He stood up and walked to where Gywann lay chained. 'What's the story, pigfuck? Where did you get those weapons?'

Gywann didn't reply. He was blank. He didn't appear to even hear the Killer. The Killer nudged him with his toe. 'I'm talking to you, pigfuck.'

Gywann stared straight across the deck. The Killer aimed a kick at him. The squad leader was on his feet.

'Cut that out! Damn it, you know there's to be none of that. He's wanted in one piece. Unblemished, boy.'

'He's got it coming.'

'You know what unblemished means, Iron Fist?'

The Killer stiffened. 'Yes sir, I know what unblemished means, sir!'

They were interrupted by the shout of the lookout.

'Something just peeled out of the shadow of this tower and it looks like it's an intercept.'

'What kind of something?'

'Looks like one of ours.'

'That don't mean nothing these days. Belts and helmets! Take those new Gywannish weapons, but nobody open fire!'

The deck was a sudden scramble of activity.

'It's still closing. Still looks like one of ours.'

The Iron Fists were in position. They waited. The other craft was much like their own. It carried Killer insignia. Unlike theirs, though, there were only two figures on the deck.

'It's signalling it wants us to pull over.'

The squad leader yelled to the steersman.

'Slow down but hold course.'

The other craft came around and ran parallel with them. The two figures on the deck were in full uniforms and helmets. One was much larger than the other. The big one wore a gold helmet. The smaller one spoke into a hailer.

'Have you succeeded in your mission?'

'I don't know what you're talking about.'

The larger one took the hailer. 'I know you have your orders but I don't have time to fool around. Do you have the man Gywann or not?'

'I don't know what you're talking about. I can only report to Marshal Heizen. I'm under his direct orders.'

'Marshal Heizen is dead.'

There was a gasp from the Iron Fists. The squad leader came to spinesnapping attention. 'Sir, permission to speak, sir?'

'Speak.'

'Sir, how did the Marshal die, sir?'

'He died on the barricade, leading his men.'

'Sir, at least that's a blessing.'

'Indeed.'

The officer allowed a full half-minute of silence and then he went on.

'Marshal Heizen is dead. The codewords died with him. There has been need for considerable changes in plan. I don't have time to wrangle with you. Will you co-operate with me, Iron Fist?'

The squad leader was in a quandary. He had been told to report to the Marshal and no one else, but if the Marshal was dead what was his duty? The voice of authority won out.

'Yes, sir. I will co-operate with you, sir. What do you want me to do?'

'You have the man Gywann?'

'Yes, sir!'

'Have you obtained any of the new weapons?'

'Yes, sir!'

'You will first transfer the man Gywann to our craft.'

'Sir, I thought he was to go directly to the Tower.'

'Are you listening to me, Iron Fist? I just told you that our Marshal is dead. We are in an extreme emergency situation.'

'Yes, sir, I understand, sir!'

'Well, good, perhaps you can now start to transfer the man and the weapons.'

'Yes, sir!'

The two craft pulled alongside each other and both slowed to a stop. They swayed slightly in mid-air as the Iron Fists secured them together. Half the Iron Fist crew belt-lifted over to the second vessel. Gywann was handed across and, with considerably more reluctance, the Gywannish weapons were stacked on its deck. For a few moments they stood around as if waiting for instructions. Somewhat impatiently, the big officer in the gold helmet indicated that they should return to their own craft and cast off. The squad leader was still less than happy.

'We have no orders, sir. Everything has been changed. What are we supposed to do next?'

'Return to the Tower, get some food and then report to me. I'll return there in an hour or so.'

The squad leader snapped off a stylish salute. The two craft separated and moved apart. The officer in the gold helmet raised his hand, the aircar executed a sharp turn and accelerated away. The Iron Fists immediately gathered around their leader.

'What the fuck was that all about?'

'Is the Marshal really dead?'

'You heard the officer.'

'Shit, I don't believe it.'

'We're going to have to.'

'What I want to know is what're we going to do next?'

The squad leader rounded angrily on the speaker. 'You know what you're going to do next. You're going to do exactly what the fuck you're told to do. That's what you're going to do next.'

'We should never have handed over those weapons. With a few of those we might have stood a chance.'

'We might stand a chance if we got rid of these uniforms and hid out among the civilians until all this was over. We're beat and we might as well face it.'

Just to emphasise the man's point, the sky began to strobe worse than before. The squad leader snarled at him. 'I'll hear none of that kind of talk.'

'It's true enough.'

'You want to go off this fucking deck?'

'No, but . . .'

'Then put a cover on the talk. That goes for all of you.'

'So what do we do next?'

'We obey orders. We go back to the Tower and report to that officer in an hour or so.'

'What was the name of that officer?'

Something in the pit of the squad leader's stomach sank very rapidly.

'I don't know.'

'You're in a lot of trouble, squad leader. They'll probably have your cluster for this.'

'Shit.'

The Killers' Tower was now in sight. The rest of the flight was conducted in silence with the squad leader wondering what would happen to him if he couldn't locate the big officer in the gold helmet. The rest of the squad looked on with the covert smugness of subordinates who have watched an immediate superior royally fuck up. As far as the squad leader was concerned, it wasn't a moment too soon when the steersman swung the craft into the landing stage and the docking crew started to haul it in. It was the landing stage from which they'd started out, the one that was reserved for Iron Fist special assignments. They felt perfectly justified in jumping down from the craft like weary heroes, even though the ground crew did look at them a little strangely.

The squad leader nodded to the chief of the docking crew.

'You can leave it out. We may need it again quite soon. We're just going in to eat and get new orders.'

The chief of the crew looked at him as if he was insane. 'What the fuck are you talking about?'

The squad leader frowned. 'What?'

The chief pointed. 'He's been fretting for you suckers to get back for an hour or more.'

The squad leader turned and looked. The bottom fell out of his world. Unconsciously, his left hand encircled his right forearm and squeezed as hard as it could. In front of a large entourage, Marshal Heizen had emerged from the shadows of the interior and was walking directly towards him. A last brief flutter of hope died. A senior officer in a gold helmet was marching beside the Marshal, but he was far too small to be the one to whom he'd given Gywann.

'You have the man, Iron Fist?'

The squad leader snapped to the most rigid attention. 'Marshal, sir, it's a blessing to see you alive, sir.'

'That's a maybe, but do you have the man Gywann?'

'Marshal, sir, no sir!'

'Your mission failed?'

'Marshal, sir, no sir!'

'Explain yourself.'

'Sir, we disguised ourselves as Gywannish as instructed. The man Gywann was, as predicted, isolated from his forces. We killed the escort and took him into custody.'

'So where is he?'

'Marshal, sir, I handed him over to the officer.'

'What officer?'

'Sir, as we came into the city we were intercepted by one of our own aircraft.'

'That could mean anything, the way things are at the moment.'

'That's what I said, Marshal, sir.'

'There was an officer on this craft?'

'Sir, in a gold helmet, sir, a big man. He told me that you were dead, sir, and that I should hand over the prisoner because all plans were changed.'

'And you did?'

'Marshal, sir, yes sir. I was simply following orders. I also handed over the Gywannish weapons.'

'What weapons?'

'We took the escorts' weapons after we killed them, sir.'

'How did you kill the escort, Iron Fist?'

'Sir, with our knives, sir.'

'I don't suppose this officer gave his name, did he?'

'Marshal, sir, no sir!'

Heizen turned to his entourage. 'Trenhyass has him. I'll have to go to him and start shouting.' He glared at the squad leader. 'I demand a suicide from your squad. There's thinking here that's a lot less than straight.'

A silence fell over the entire landing stage. The docking crew broke off from their work. The squad leader looked around at his men. Their faces were hard. There would be no compromise. The squad leader's face became like stone. He stripped off his flying-belt and let it fall to the ground. He turned and marched smartly across the landing stage. He didn't falter. At the edge, he never missed a beat. He walked straight out into space and vanished. One man in the squad relaxed ever so imperceptibly but Heizen didn't miss it. He gave the slightest of nods. 'You too, Iron Fist.'

The second example also didn't falter. Heizen looked at each of the squad in turn. 'I think I want the rest of you.'

They dropped their belts, they turned, they marched straight for the edge. Just one remained. She faced Heizen. She pulled off her helmet. On her face was a look of pure contempt.

'My thinking's straight, Marshal Heizen, I'm going over the edge because we fucked up, but what about you, Marshal Heizen? How's your thinking? Are you with the programme? You've lost the city, Marshal, sir, and you won't admit it.'

She turned and started towards the edge. Heizen's voice cut like a whip. 'Freeze it right there, Iron Fist!'

She didn't resist. Her captors halted her in front of Heizen. The Marshal looked her up and down. 'Take her to the Gallery and examine this thinking that she considers so straight.'

They marched the Iron Fist away. Heizen made a dismissive gesture to his entourage but somehow it didn't quite work. They all started back inside the Tower and, for the first time in many years, he wondered about the expressions behind the helmets that were all around him.

Twenty-Two

SHAFIK KRAYMON dropped the gold helmet to the deck. The aircar tilted slightly and it rolled until it came to rest in a scupper. The Poet also removed his helmet. He set it down so it wouldn't roll. It was too much like a head.

'How do you breathe in those things? I thought I was going to sweat to death.'

Kraymon chuckled. 'I always knew it about Killers. If you yell at them loud enough they'll do whatever you want. They're like overtrained dogs. You can't keep anything in a cage and feed it on raw meat and still expect it to think for itself.'

The Halls were in sight and the Legate steersman, who was also in Killer uniform, turned the craft towards them. He continued to climb. He was on a course for the highest point in all the city. The Heaven Hand was a giant stone hand with its palm turned upwards to the sky and the fingers slightly curled. It was some four hundred metres from fingertip to wrist and truly majestic in its lavish folly. It had originally been built five centuries earlier by one of the most excessive tyrants in all human history. The construction had taken more than a decade and close to four thousand workers had died in the effort. In the palm of the hand there was a clear, freshwater pool with falls and fountains. The heel of the hand was big enough for banquets, performances or orgies. The fingers provided mooring points for aircars and carriages. The Heaven Hand had proved to be the tyrant's final monumental extravagance. Only a few weeks after its completion he had been thrown off the edge of his creation by a mob of vengeful subjects. The actual design of the Hand had been the final straw that had triggered the uprising. From the lower levels it looked as though it was making a timelessly obscene gesture. It was the posthumous revenge of an architect who knew he was going to be executed once his plans were complete. Kraymon and the Poet once again noted the unfortunate set of the giant fingers as they leaned on the rail and watched the large and somewhat ludicrous structure come closer. The Poet, however, had something more on his mind than the events of five hundred years past.

'The one thing I don't understand is how you and the Protector knew that they were going to try and capture Gywann.'

Again Kraymon chuckled. 'We didn't. It was a lucky guess. The Protector and I had been talking earlier about how Heizen might try something of the kind when the battle for the city began to go against him. When the Killer ship was spotted, we decided to go after it.'

'But why go yourself? A squad of Legates could have done what we did.'

'I like to mess with the Killers. There's so much in their attitude that offends me.'

'So why did I come with you?'

Kraymon laughed and clapped him on the shoulder. 'Because you're my pal, Jeen Vayim.'

The aircar nosed its way between the index and middle fingers. The Heaven Hand was no longer the site of libertine fun. For the last few days Trenhyass had adopted it as his headquarters. It was the one place that could give him a full panoramic view of the city and the sky. A Legate mooring crew grabbed the ropes that were thrown them and hauled the craft in. The Protector had already been warned of the aircar's approach and was standing waiting on the index-finger dock.

'Do you have him, Shafik Kraymon?'

Kraymon nodded to the shackled figure lying on the deck. 'I have him; it was exactly as we thought. He's not, however, very communicative.'

Legates helped Gywann onto the dock and removed the Gywannish weapons. Kraymon and the Poet jumped down from the craft. The Poet glanced around with a fair degree of wonder. He had never been at a place even similar to the Heaven Hand. He felt a little dizzy. The sky was so huge and the ground was so far away. The sun was starting to set in a sky that had stopped strobing and was comparatively normal. The Legates set Gywann on his feet. The Protector walked slowly around him. Gywann stared straight ahead, not even acknowledging that any of his captors existed. Kraymon cleared his throat.

'I . . . er . . . think we can strike those chains from him.'

Trenhyass raised an eyebrow. 'You do? He must think he's in the inner circle of hell, surrounded by devils.'

'Maybe, but if you want to talk to him, you're going to have to wake up something inside him. You're going to have to get in touch with the human parts of him.'

'You think there's a non-human part?'

Kraymon nodded. 'Yes, I do. I think it's probably keeping him mute right now. It might also help if we put hot food and drink in front of him. He's been living off polyps and dirty water for over a month. The sight and smell of food ought to rouse something.'

Trenhyass pursed his lips. 'I'll take your advice.'

The Poet interposed himself into the conversation. 'Would you take a piece of advice from me?'

'The way things are going, I'll take advice from anyone.'

'Remove that gold thing.'

'The medallion and collar?'

'Yeah, that thing.'

The Protector indicated to the Legates who were removing Gywann's manacles that they should also remove the ornament. A Legate pulled it over Gywann's head. He was going to hand it to Trenhyass, but Vayim held out his hand. 'If I may.'

Trenhyass fixed him with a stare. 'Loot, Poet?'

'A small experiment, my lord.'

He slipped the collar over his head. For a few moments he examined the medallion and then let it rest on his chest. He spoke very quietly.

'If you could all please pay attention to me.'

Everyone within two hundred feet glanced quickly in his direction. They stood staring for a couple of seconds and then turned away as though they couldn't remember why they'd looked that way in the first place.

Jeen Vayim let out a whoop of glee. 'I knew it!'

A number of the people nearest to him turned and smiled mechanically.

'Of course you did.'

The Protector had been watching the exchange. 'Would you like to explain?'

Jeen Vayim took off the gold collar. 'It's some kind of enhancer. It seems to amplify people's responses and levels of acceptance of what the wearer might say. The first time I saw Gywann speak to a crowd, I suspected he must be using something of the sort. He was talking such nonsense and

223

yet he was going over so big. I knew people were stupid but I didn't think they were that stupid.' He turned the collar and medallion over in his hands. 'I suppose this must come from the same place that the silver weapons came from.'

'Wherever the hell that is.'

He tossed the collar and medallion to Kraymon. 'Here, you take the thing. It's too damn tempting for me to hold. I'd start trying to make myself God.'

Kraymon laughed. 'Maybe I'll give it back to you when this is over. You could be the best damn poet on the whole planet.'

Word came that hot food was ready for Gywann. The Protector indicated that everyone should follow him. The whole group around the captive prophet skirted the pool. The dark, crystal-clear water reflected a darkening sky that flashed with bolts of red, yellow and orange. The Protector scowled. 'I shudder to think how much radiation we're absorbing from all this.'

The heel of the Hand had been designated a temporary mess area. Gywann's meal had been set at an isolated table and the rest of the area had been cleared. The Legates seated him but he took absolutely no notice of the food. He just continued to stare straight ahead.

'Maybe he's burned out. Maybe there's nothing more left to him.'

'I don't think so. I have a feeling he has more to do yet.'

After waiting for half an hour, Kraymon grew impatient and went to the mess counter and loudly demanded beer. As he walked back, having finally bullied himself a brimming mug, a formation of five red spheres flashed across the sky. Kraymon took a drink. 'So what do you make of them?'

'Those were the same as the ones you saw out in the swamps?'

'As far as I could tell.'

Two Wasp ovoids went past, low over the city. Another five of the red spheres were in hot pursuit. A Legate came running.

'My lord! All the lights in the Wasp compound have gone out!'

Trenhyass nodded. 'I expected it. I think the days of the Wasps on this planet are close to an end.'

'They are at an end. The mopping-up is going on right now.'

Everyone turned. Gywann had spoken. His eyes were focused. He loaded his fork with food and put it in his mouth. The Protector waited politely for him to finish chewing. 'And will our new masters be here soon?'

Gywann took a swallow of beer. He seemed absolutely normal and human. 'Soon.'

Kraymon grunted. 'Don't eat too much. You're likely to make yourself ill.'

'I can't remember when I was ever so hungry.'

A sun appeared in the dark sky where no sun should be. For almost a minute it blazed as bright as day and then faded to nothing. Trenhyass looked hard at the still-eating Gywann. There was something eerie and unnatural about the way that he had so abruptly been switched on.

'How soon will they be here?'

Gywann shrugged. 'I can't say for sure. Since the weapons came, they don't tell me very much. A lot of what they do tell me, I don't understand. At least, this part doesn't understand. There are so many parts of me, it becomes confusing.'

'What do you mean, parts of you?'

Gywann made an impatient gesture as though he considered it obvious. 'Parts, I mean parts.'

'You mean you're not always the same person?'

'I'm always the same person, but sometimes I'm other people as well. Things, too; other things.'

'Can you explain?'

'No. All I know is that it hurts a lot of the time.'

An all-enveloping sound came down from the sky; it was short and deep with frequencies well below the range of the human ear. It was as though God had coughed. Gywann glanced up. 'The fight is beyond the atmosphere. When it's over, they'll come.'

'And you will lead humanity?'

Gywann put down his fork. He shook his head. 'I don't think I'll lead anything. I believe I was only designed to pave the way. As far as I can tell I was supposed to die some great spectacular death, but something went wrong.'

Gywann looked a little rueful. The Protector's voice was almost sympathetic. 'Do you want to die?'

Gywann shook his head violently. For the first time since he'd spoken he made a move that wasn't quite natural. 'Oh, no. No, I don't want to die. I'm afraid of the pain and the fear, but I don't have any control. They don't care about my pain. I don't think they understand about human pain at all. If they did, they would never have taken me.'

'So they did take you?'

'Oh, yes, they took me. They took all the parts of me.'

'Huh?'

'There was more than one taken. I am the combination of all.'

'Where did they take you? How? When?'

Gywann picked up his fork and tried to start eating again. His hand was shaking so much that he couldn't get the food to his mouth without dropping it. He threw down the fork. 'I don't know. I don't know what was real and what was a dream.'

'When the Killers had you in custody – you talked about the blue friends and the tiny dancers.'

'The blue friends?'

'That's right.'

Gywann looked wistful. 'The tiny dancers?'

'Right.'

'I know the blue friends.'

'So what are they?'

'I don't know. I'm not the part that remembers these things.'

Kraymon took over the questioning. 'How many parts are there?'

Gywann shuddered. His shoulders slumped. 'I don't know. One part doesn't see all the others. There's the part that hears and leads. There's the part that preaches. There's the part that loves and the part that receives the messages, the part that knows. And then there are all the little parts that can do nothing, that can never get to the surface but are frightened all the time.'

Gywann placed his hands flat on the table on either side of his plate. His head dropped and his face was hidden by his hair. Kraymon didn't seem convinced. 'And are you one of the frightened ones?'

Gywann lifted his head. His face had changed. Weakness and confusion had been replaced by strength and confidence. 'Of course not.'

He was the prophet again. He took a drink and started on his food. Kraymon shrugged and turned to the Protector. 'I don't know what to do with him.'

Trenhyass massaged his injured shoulder. 'I think, before too long, he may be deciding what to do with us.'

Gywann regarded him with clear, unblinking eyes. 'You are an intelligent man, Protector Trenhyass.'

Trenhyass bowed. 'I do my best.'

'It hasn't gone unnoticed.'

Another Legate came running. 'There is an aircar with Killer markings approaching, my lord.'

'That'll be Heizen.'

Gywann put down his fork. 'I hope you can keep him away from me. He always wants to torture me.'

'You've pretty well wiped out his army.'

'He brought it on himself.'

'The Killer aircar is coming in to dock, my lord.'

Gywann looked up at the Protector. 'What is my status here? Am I your guest or your prisoner?'

The Protector half smiled. 'Let's leave it that you're my prisoner for the moment. It'll make it easier for me to deal with Heizen. Who knows? In a few hours, I may be your prisoner.'

The two men looked directly into each other's eyes. Neither moved until a Legate interrupted them. 'The Killer vessel is about to dock, my lord.'

'Issue the Gywannish weapons. This may become a little tense.'

Heizen came across the Hand with his usual gang of Iron Fists. The Protector noted that three of them carried the silver Gywannish tubes. His expression didn't change. At least his firepower was twice that of the Marshal. His own bodyguard had six tubes between them.

'You can afford the time to leave the battle for the city, Marshal Heizan?'

'You saw fit to interrupt a major strategy. You even saw fit to have your men disguise themselves as my officers.'

'I was only trying to stop you making a damn fool of yourself, Heizen. What were you going to do, offer Gywann to his followers provided they laid down their arms and went back to the swamps? Or were you going to execute him in front of them and hope that they'd be totally demoralised?'

Heizen halted. The Iron Fists half raised their weapons.

'So, it's all going to come out into the open, is it?'

'You're a spent force, Heizen. My only orders for you are to disengage your men and negotiate surrender. After that, you had better look to your own salvation.'

'Have you taken leave of your senses, Trenhyass?'

227

The Iron Fists' weapons were imperceptibly coming up. The Poet edged closer to Kraymon. 'Give me Gywann's collar. If they start a firefight up here, we'll all be dead.'

Kraymon handed over the collar and medallion. Jeen Vayim slipped it over his head. The Protector was completely calm. He replied to Heizen so everyone could hear.

'Quite the opposite, Heizen. I am recognising the reality in which we live. The Wasps have all but left. In a matter of hours we shall be dealing with an entirely new and equally superior species.'

As if to emphasise his point, a Wasp ovoid came barrelling from across the Blackwater with three red spheres on its tail. They flashed over the city and vanished beyond the far horizon. Almost immediately there was a brief orange flash from the direction in which they'd gone. Heizen watched it fade and then faced Trenhyass. 'You don't really believe the Wasps are leaving, do you?'

'What other explanation is there for what's going on?'

'It's some trick.'

Trenhyass laughed out loud. 'Why in the world would the Wasps want to trick us? We never understood them in the first place!'

Heizen took a pace forwards. 'And I suppose the man Gywann agrees with you?'

'I do.'

'You've lost it, Trenhyass. Maybe it was your injury or maybe your mind has started to go. Whatever the reason, you're no longer fit to rule.'

'And you intend to step into the breach?'

'Someone has to restore order before the Wasps do it themselves.'

'I knew that you were obsessive, Heizen, but I never realised that you were stupid.'

Heizen ignored him. He addressed himself to the assembled Legates.

'I know you people have a great loyalty to your Protector but the time has come for you to put that loyalty aside and concentrate on the greater good. There is insurrection in the city and all that Lord Trenhyass can do is to consort with the criminal madman who started all this bloodshed. Put down your weapons and let my men take him and the man Gywann into custody.'

Trenhyass said nothing. Some of the Legates looked at

each other but they made no other move. A tall Wingleader stepped forward. He held one of the Gywannish weapons. 'You're a madman, Marshal Heizen. If anyone started the bloodshed, it was you and your Killers. I, for one, have no intention of putting down my weapons or letting your butchers lay a hand on the Protector.'

It was showdown time. Jeen Vayim knew that the explosion would come any second. Heizen half turned as if he were about to give an order to his men. It was time to do something. Jeen Vayim made his voice as firm and authoritative as he could.

'Let's all relax, shall we? Why don't we all relax and stay right where we are. Let's lower the weapons so nobody gets hurt.'

The Poet could actually feel the tension ease. The sense of power was intoxicating. Some lowered their weapons, some didn't. Even so, the feeling was immense. He could understand how that alone could have made Gywann crazy. He spoke again.

'Why don't we all back off and lower our weapons? Everybody lower their weapons.'

One Iron Fist still had his weapon pointed at the Protector. Unfortunately it was one of the silver tubes.

'Let's all stay real still, shall we, while I go and talk to this guy.'

Jeen Vayim approached the Iron Fist who held the weapon as if he were dealing with a dangerously skittish animal. He remembered what Kraymon had said: *If you yell at them loud enough, they'll do whatever you want.* When he was right in front of the Killer, he let go with the loudest parade-ground bellow that he could muster.

'Do you hear me, Iron Fist?'

'Sir, yes sir, I hear you.'

'Then put down that fucking weapon! All of you! *Put down your weapons!*'

Instinctively the Iron Fists obeyed, grounding their pulsers and taking one pace back in strict drill-squad order. Kraymon was instantly there gathering up the weapons. He grinned at the Poet. 'You're doing pretty good.'

'Ain't I just.'

At that moment, Heizen whipped around. 'What the hell do you think you're . . .'

Kraymon punched Heizen in the face as hard as he could. There was a lot of long-term frustration in the punch. The

Marshal went sprawling. He came up with a hand pressed to his face.

'You've broken my damned nose!'

'I'll blow off your damned head if you make a move!'

Kraymon had the big, four-barrelled pistol in his hand. He glanced at the Iron Fists who were starting to go for their grounded weapons. 'You all hold it too! Put those weapons back on the ground or Marshal Heizen loses his head!' He signalled to the Legates. 'Disarm them.'

One Iron Fist resisted. He pulled out his dagger but he was quickly overpowered by half a dozen Legates. He and his companions were led away. Heizen got slowly to his feet, blood pouring from his nose. Jeen Vayim took off the gold collar. As he did so, he caught Gywann staring intently at him. It made the Poet uneasy. It was as though there was some kind of bond between them. It was a bond that he didn't particularly want. Another Legate messenger hurried up to Trenhyass.

'My lord, word has come over the talkie. The last major force of the Killers has surrendered. There are now only scattered pockets of resistance. They are being quickly mopped up. The Gywannish have yet to enter the middle levels, but if they do they'll encounter nothing to stop them.'

Trenhyass slowly nodded. He turned to face Gywann. 'It would seem that the city is yours. Perhaps I am now your prisoner.'

Heizen lurched into the picture. 'Don't be ridiculous. Kill him now. Without a leader, the Gywannish are nothing. You have your Legates. You could crush them. Kill him, Trenhyass. Kill him!'

'You can't adjust, can you, Heizen? You can't accept that your power has gone, your Killers are dead or have surrendered. You are nothing. You are stripped of your rank. You can go if you want to, provided you give me an assurance that you will do nothing in the immediate future but take care of your own life.'

Heizen's face was sharp with bitter anger. 'I'll give you no such assurance. Someone has to rule humanity.'

'But it will not be you!'

'And you intend to stop me?'

'Indeed I do. In fact, I am going to do it right now.'

The Protector put his hand inside his tunic. It came out holding a gun. It was small and nickel-plated, an incredibly valuable antique. It fired small lead projectiles. He pointed it at Heizen. The Marshal took a step backwards. 'You aren't serious.'

'I'm very serious.'

Trenhyass fired. The gun made a sharp, loud crack. Heizen spun around. He stood for a moment, then his legs buckled and he fell.

Trenhyass lowered the smoking gun. He regarded the still-twitching body with an expression of distaste. 'Somebody remove this thing.'

The stunned Legates sprang into action, relieved to have something to do. Gywann stood up for the first time. 'It is possible that our saviours will be able to make use of your experience in leadership and diplomacy.'

'Surely you will lead humanity. It's your history.'

Gywann smiled sadly and shook his head. 'I won't lead anything for much longer. I'm really just a communication device.'

Twenty-Three

THEY STAGGERED out, charred and blackened, with their shoulders bowed and their hands raised in the old, old gesture of surrender. Bloodshot eyes stared dully out of sweating faces that couldn't believe any of it. Defeat was something that didn't happen to the Killers. Tunics were still smouldering and trailing smoke. Some had to be supported by their comrades. Others stumbled forwards, still walking but so badly burned that they screamed if anyone touched them. The last holdout had given up the fight and the survivors were coming out from behind the shattered defences. The victorious attackers looked on, silent and awed at the carnage they'd created. The Tower of the Killers had been designed to look like a place of death and now it had become one.

The Killers, although hopelessly outclassed by the weapons of the Gywannish, had fought with a ferocity that bordered on the insane. Inside the Tower they had retreated and retreated. Each floor and each corridor had to be won individually. The cost to the Gywannish had been appalling. As they fell back, the Killers had left suicide squads and booby traps. The attackers had been forced to cut through walls and floors in order to flush them out. The Killers' stubborn resistance only broke when their numbers had been whittled down to a mere few hundred.

When he was assured that the last of the Killers had indeed given up the fight, Niarva was gripped with an overpowering need to get out of the place, out into the air. The rooms and corridors stank of death and destruction. He knew that he'd reached his limit. He couldn't take any more. At the start he had thought of the battle as something noble, as a cleansing act that would rid the city of tyrants and devils. The reality had been something else entirely. Sure, there had been an exhilaration to the fight, but there had also been the horror, the deaths and the mutilations, the stench of flash-burned flesh and the ghastly screams of the injured and dying. As he retraced his steps towards the nearest landing stage he tried not to think about how, on the way in, every yard had been bought with the lives of his friends and his companions. Each intersection bore the marks of a fierce firefight. The red walls were scarred and blasted and bodies littered the floor. A few of the Gywannish rearguard were trying to give help to the wounded. There was little they could do. No medical supplies had come with the sacred weapons. The Gywannish had been prepared to die in their holy war. Nobody had thought about the chance of being maimed or mutilated.

At a major corridor intersection, two weary-looking Gywannish fighters waved. 'Hold up there, Niarva.'

Niarva halted. 'Is there a problem?'

'Some of us broke through into the Gallery of Questions.'

'And?'

They shook their heads as though they didn't want to remember what they'd seen. 'It's a place of devils, a bad place.'

Niarva looked around at the red and black stonework and the broken statues. 'I can imagine.'

'There are fifty or so prisoners up there. What do we do with them?'

'Let them go. What else can we do? The Adjustment applies to all of us.'

'Some of them are not . . . normal. Too much has happened to them.'

Niarva closed his eyes and gently shook his head. He was only a man, what did they want from him? He couldn't solve all the problems of this place. He couldn't cure the sickness.

'All you can do is . . . do what you can for them. There are going to be a million problems. We've planned nothing and now we've got the city. It's insane. We're going to have to make it up as we go along. Until now we've thought of nothing but this damned battle. Maybe we never really expected to win it.'

They seemed to want to detain him further, but he pushed past them and walked on. With an overwhelming sense of relief he emerged into the night air. Fires were burning in the lowers and the distant sound of shouting and singing floated up. Far below, they had started to celebrate victory and liberation. Up on the Tower, halfway to the clouds, he wasn't ready quite yet to either rejoice or even get drunk and forget it all for a while. Presently he would go down and join them, but for the moment he wanted to be on his own.

He felt as though he'd been carrying a great weight for a very long time. Strangely, it proved terribly hard to put down. He wasn't even able to enjoy his solitude for very long. After what seemed like only minutes, Bobvo hurried up. He looked extremely troubled. 'News has come from the ruins.'

'What news?'

Bobvo was having great difficulty coming out with the words. Niarva frowned. 'What is it? What's wrong?'

'The Master has been taken.'

'What?'

'His escort was killed. Their bodies were all there but there was no sign of the Master, alive or dead.'

'How were they killed?'

'Some were burned as by our own weapons, but others had been stabbed; it looked like the work of the Killers.'

'But if the Killers had taken him, we'd have found him here. He'd have been imprisoned in the Gallery of Questions.'

'Perhaps they took him away to some quiet spot and murdered him.'

Niarva shook his head, he didn't want to believe. 'It's not like Heizen. If he had captured the Master, he'd have made much more of it. He wouldn't have had him spirited away and killed in a ditch somewhere. Heizen would parade the Master through the city, he'd stage a huge public execution, he'd want everyone to see him die. Heizen would use him as a weapon. I think we have to assume that the Master is alive and being held somewhere.'

'Where?'

'There's only one other man who could have the Master.'

'The Protector!'

'Right.'

Both men were silent for a few moments but Niarva's mind was racing. 'We must do our best to stop this news spreading through the army. Let them do their celebrating tonight. In the morning we storm the Halls. The Legates shouldn't cause too much trouble. Get some crews together. Tell them to find all the flying-belts they can.'

Bobvo nodded. 'Is there anything else?'

Niarva shook his head. 'No. Hurry along and try to hold yourself together.'

Bovbo started away. Niarva called after him. 'What of Sulanda?'

'She's dead. She was stabbed in the back. Even the great banner was burned.'

'This is a bad business.'

'Very bad.'

For a long time Niarva stood staring out across the city. Bitterness and an empty hungry feeling had swamped the satisfaction of victory. Too much had been lost and many friends were gone. Even as he watched, the fires below him were destroying the familiar landmarks. The old world had gone for good and he was too tired to imagine the new one. In the last few gruelling weeks, though, he had developed the instincts of a fighter. Even in the depths of anguish he still remained watchful. When the riding-lights of a carriage swung into sight, and appeared to be heading directly towards the Tower, he immediately beckoned to a number of Gywannish who were working on the other side of the landing stage.

'Are all the lights out of action?'

'No, there's a few still working.'

'See if you can focus something on that aircraft. You see it?'

'Yeah, we see it.'

A spotlight flared into life. It sliced sections in the sky until it picked up the craft. It was a fairly ornate carriage and, as Niarva had assumed, it was coming in the direction of the tower.

'It's putting out flags.'

'There's a flag of truce on the port spike . . . a black flag on the other.'

'What the hell is that supposed to mean?'

'Maybe we should take no chances and blow it out of the air.'

'Hold your fire, damn it. We respect a flag of truce.'

'There's the insignia of the Protector on the side.'

'Perhaps he's come to surrender.'

There was hard laughter. Niarva didn't join in.

'Maybe he has at that.'

The carriage was coming in very slowly. It was as though whoever commanded it was taking great pains to demonstrate his peaceful intent. It made a wide turn, followed all the way by the spotlight. Two figures stood side by side on the deck. One wore a white robe, the other a dark uniform.

'I don't like this.'

'Just hold your tongue and stay alert.'

The carriage starting edging towards the dock.

'Kill the spotlight. We don't want to confuse the steers-man.'

The spotlight went out. The carriage bumped against the fenders at the edge of the stage.

'Get some lights up.'

About a third of the sun-guns around the edge of the stage came on. The rest remained dark.

'Moor it.'

Limpet clamps were slapped onto the carriage's mooring plates. It was secured. The two on the deck remained motionless. No one else emerged from concealment and no armed men sprung a trap. Niarva allowed himself to relax a little. He walked forwards to see who these individuals were, and what they wanted. The two stepped carefully down. They came into range of the lights. Niarva stopped dead. He couldn't believe what he was seeing. He took a step back. Everyone else on the landing stage stood frozen.

'What trick is this?'

'Don't be afraid.'

Gywann and the Protector were coming towards him, walking side by side. His Master was walking with the devil. Why would his Master walk willingly beside Trenhyass? The man was a fiend, he was the servant of the dark strangers and all that was bad. An idea presented itself to his reeling mind. Could it be a double, someone who just looked like the Master? Whoever it was, he raised a cautious calming hand. Niarva took no chances and tugged his weapon from his belt. His voice was cracking. 'Stop where you are. Don't come any closer.'

The two halted. Gywann, or the man who looked like him, smiled sadly. 'You don't recognise me?'

'Don't move!'

'Do you want to harm me, Niarva?'

'I don't know who you are. How can you be my Master and be with *him*?'

'Much has changed.'

'The devil has become a friend?'

'We move to the future, we can't sit growling in the past.'

'But *him*?'

'He has surrendered the city to me.'

Niarva lowered his weapon.

'I don't understand. What about the bodies of your

236

escort? What about Sulanda? We thought that you'd been taken by Killers.'

'I was taken by the Killers. I was also rescued by Shafik Kraymon.'

'The betrayer?'

'The time has come for us to revise our judgements.'

'We should forgive devils and betrayers?'

'We have to.'

'What has changed everything? None of this makes any sense.'

'The Wasps have gone.'

Niarva tried desperately to adjust his thoughts. Only a matter of minutes earlier, he had been attempting to deal with the disappearance of his Master. Now his Master was standing in front of him, telling him that everything he knew had been turned upside down.

'The Wasps have gone?'

The Protector took up the explanation. 'While you've been fighting for the city, the Wasps have been fighting in space. You saw the lights and the explosions and the new suns. It was a conflict we couldn't even imagine and the Wasps were defeated. They have either been destroyed or they have fled. Very soon, the victors in this fight will land and take control of our planet. Those are the same ones who gave you your weapons.'

'Our Saviours?'

Trenhyass' mouth twisted wryly. 'That's what your Master calls them.'

'The Protector prefers to view them as just another set of aliens.'

Niarva was still having trouble accepting what he was being told. His Master had completely changed. He seemed human, fallible even. Niarva's expression was one of total incredulity. 'The two of you have made a deal?'

'It's time for us all to grow.'

Incredulity turned to revulsion. The other Gywannish gathered around in an uncertain circle. All the pain and tension of the day rushed out of Niarva in a single scream.

'What's going on here? I fought for the Adjustment. We all fought for the Adjustment. We bled and died for our Master. We didn't fight for *deals*!'

'You didn't die and you don't know what you fought for.'

Things were exploding in Niarva's head. '*This is blasphemy*.'

Gywann put his hand inside his robe. When he removed it, the gold collar was looped around his fingers.

'There is no time for this.' He held up the medallion. 'This is the core of your faith.'

'NO!'

The Protector suddenly became angry and impatient.

'Will you put a cover on that? I will not listen to you shrieking like a whore at a funeral. We have a few hours to organise our responses to a fresh invasion from space. Your religious delusions are a luxury we can't afford. You have to know the real situation. You command the remaining armed forces of the whole damned planet.'

Ideas were coming at Niarva like hammer-blows.

'You're still the Protector, aren't you? You didn't surrender anything.'

'Of course I'm still the Protector. I've been representing humanity to conquering aliens for twenty-three hard years and I don't intend to stop until somebody *really* removes me. Nobody has my experience, and I'm not about to turn the job over to an amateur. You have to be very careful with aliens. If they don't like you, they are quite liable to wipe you out, all of you, the whole damned species.'

Niarva looked like a man who wanted to flee. What he was hearing was worse than the horrors of battle. 'Why are you telling this to me? I don't have any part in all this. I don't know anything about aliens. I only saw a Wasp once in my life. Before I followed the Master, I was a hustler on the Oldmarket.'

'Then maybe you'll have at least some basic street sense.' The Protector's eyes were hard, they allowed Niarva no escape. 'You'll need everything you've got. You're in the middle of this whether you like it or not. You have taken the city, you Gywannish have to run things now. Your people have taken the place of the Killers and they'll have to do their job. Your people have to take on their responsibilities and restore some semblance of order, damned fast. If you like, you have to become Marshal Heizen.'

The Protector smiled grimly as Niarva looked sick.

'Maybe you're not Marshal Heizen, exactly. The Wasps liked us in a crude, military, feudal system. This new bunch has gone to some trouble to create a religion for us. Bearing this in mind, I expect you'll end up with some title like Hammer of the Faith. Even a Hammer of the Faith should start out knowing the truth. We have to perform for the aliens. I represent humanity while you do your best to keep it quiet, and well behaved.'

Niarva clung to the last shreds of stubbornness. 'It was the Master's victory. He should represent humanity.'

'I can't represent humanity.'

The sky was shot by pulsing veins of violet.

'Why not?'

It was Trenhyass who answered. 'Your master is not altogether human.'

Niarva looked at Gywann in horror. 'That's impossible.'

'It's true.'

'It can't be.'

Gywann put a hand on Niarva's shoulder. 'As far as we can piece it together, I was taken from the earth a long time ago. The aliens, our Saviours, worked on me. They implanted things of their own. The job they did was far from perfect. My personality is fragmented and there are long periods when I go into a trance state and scarcely function. All we are sure of is that they can control me and that they can send messages through me.' He handed the collar and the medallion to Niarva. 'You will have to lead the faithful.'

Niarva was speechless. He mutely took the gold ornament. Finally he found his voice. 'But you, what will you do?'

'I will help you for as long as I can. Right now it seems as if *my* masters want me aware, truthful and lucid. I don't know what will happen to me when they release their grip. I suspect that some of their implants are malfunctioning. I may not live very much longer.'

First one, then another of the Gywannish, who had been standing listening in a frozen circle, fell to their knees.

'Master, say it isn't so.'

The rest followed suit. 'Master, say it isn't so.'

'If you are to die, we'll die with you. We're not afraid.'

Trenhyass glanced quickly at Gywann. 'I'd nip that in the bud if I were you. It could spread to the whole damned army.'

Gywann faced Niarva. 'Put on the collar.'

Niarva did as he was told.

'Now tell them what I tell you. Stand up.'

Niarva was a dutiful echo. 'Stand up.'

'You have no cause for sorrow.'

'You have no cause for sorrow.'

The handful of Gywannish got to their feet. There was no

missing the relief that was sweeping over them. The voice of authority was telling them what to do.

'You will go now and prepare for the coming of our Saviours.'

'You will go now and prepare for the coming of our Saviours.'

'It will be a time of rejoicing.'

'It will be a time of rejoicing.'

'When the Saviours appear in the sky, you will lead the people out to greet them.'

'When the Saviours appear in the sky, you will lead the people out to greet them.'

'And you will forget all that you heard here tonight.'

Niarva hesitated. Both Gywann and the Protector stared at him. Wearily, he repeated the phrase.

'And you will forget all that you heard here tonight.'

The Gywannish left the landing stage. They all had the distant, blissful look of fanatics whose faith has been restored. Once they were gone, Trenhyass permitted himself a second thin smile. 'Now you, too, are part of the deal.'

Niarva scowled. 'I don't think I'm the one you want. I can't do this sort of thing.'

'You should have thought of that before you started your uprising.'

Niarva gave the Protector a long hard look. It was as though the last of his innocence had fallen away.

'But maybe I'll learn; perhaps one day things will be different between us, my Lord Protector.'

Trenhyass sighed inwardly. Beneath the religion and the insecurity and the ignorance, Niarva was another one who would have to be constantly watched.

Twenty-Four

THEY CAME down with the magnificence of Gods. Even Shafik Kraymon was forced to blink and shake his head. The Poet muttered under his breath.

'And the Angel of the Lord came upon them and the glory of the Lord shone round about them and they were sore afraid.'

'Huh?'

'Old stuff.'

'Oh.'

There was a long silence as both men stared open-mouthed at the radiant sky. Finally Kraymon gathered his wits sufficiently to grunt. 'They're going to make us ignorant. They're going to replace knowledge and intelligence with awe.'

The Poet went on staring. 'Hasn't that always been man's big beef? That he was too smart for his own good? Adam and Eve? Prometheus? Wignod? They were all a nuisance. Under all the struggling, hasn't there always been a covert hankering for blissful ignorance.'

'More old stuff?'

'I'm a poet.'

'Stick around, you may be needed.'

It was the Poet's turn to grunt.

The sky prepared the way for their coming, heralding their arrival with a display of atmospheric disturbance surpassing anything that had gone before. Mountainous thunderheads circled in a giant, majestic vortex. From the same central point, sheets of coloured lightning following an approximate spectrum, red, orange, yellow, green, all the way towards violet, radiated out like ripples on an enormous pond. Jagged white bolts jittered between the tallest towers of the city and strange metallic winds curled through the lowers. Beneath it all, dull thunder rolled and boomed without a break.

As the morning wore on, the spectacle became increasingly violent and frenetic. The coloured flashes paled to almost nothing as crackling sheets of white static took over the sky. The thunderheads folded in on themselves like curling rings of dense smoke. A small dark shape appeared at the focus of all this exploding energy. A fearful hush fell over the waiting crowd. Were they really coming? The dark shape grew big. It was round, either a disc or a globe, it was hard to tell, silhouetted against the sheets of white fire. Compared with the sky, it was less than impressive. The big crystalline starships of the Wasps had been much greater objects of wonder.

The globe continued to descend. As far as anyone on the ground could see, it was just a big featureless ball, a reddish colour. If anything, it was drab. A certain disappointment was edging its way through the massed humans when, without warning, the sphere disintegrated. At first, it was almost as though it were on fire. Parts of it boiled off like smoke. A gasp ran through the crowd and then suddenly the sky was full of the red spheres. They seemed to be everywhere. They dropped on the city, they dropped on the Blackwater and they dropped on the swamps and ruins in between. They zipped among the towers, ran low over the water and hovered above the crowds of humans who were moving out to all the available open spaces. The globe hadn't been a solid object at all. It had simply been a collection of hundreds upon hundreds upon hundreds of spheres somehow glued together. When the first wave of them rained down, there was a moment of panic on the ground. People glanced around for a place to run. There was nowhere. The crowds went on for as far as the eye could see. Then suddenly everyone seemed to know that the red spheres meant them no harm. They were emitting a high harmonic tone that had an instantly calming effect. Ragged cheering broke out. The spheres were only a side-show. The main event was still to come.

Maybe it was the same process or maybe it was something different but everyone also seemed to know where to go. From above, it looked as if the whole population of the city was making its way to the edge of the swamp. The Lassus Fields were the focus of all the movement.

Humanity came on foot, noble and common alike. One of the Wasps' final acts had been to shut off the power that was beamed out to all the flying machines. Through the night, some had continued to run on residual energy, but by dawn all aircraft were grounded and useless. Among the crowds on the ground, the mixtures ran into a patchwork of confusion. Gywannish, reeking from battle and bleary from a night of drunken revelry, trudged beside a Proprietor and his family who had never set foot on the ground before, and gangs of disbanded Legates with the insignia torn from their uniforms shared wine with dullfaced middle clerks. For people who were about to face an absolute unknown, the crowds were almost lighthearted. Fear of what was to come had been sublimated and replaced by a serene, and even here and there a carnival, atmosphere.

Kraymon and the Poet had been among those who'd started out in a carriage, but as soon as the controls went haywire they had brought it down on the roof of the small squat tower of a minor Proprietor. It was situated close to the edge of the inhabited city and afforded them an almost uninterrupted view all the way to the Blackwater and out across the Great River. It also afforded them a considerable quantity of gratuitous food and drink. The Proprietor had clearly arranged a small party so he and his guests could watch the events of the day from the roof. Somewhere along the line, the urge to go out to the open spaces had apparently become so strong that they had left the refreshments where they lay and set off to join the hordes who were trekking out of the city. A pair of disgruntled guards initially challenged Kraymon's and the Poet's right to drop uninvited from the sky and start helping themselves to the finest wines and the rarest delicacies. A good look at Kraymon and a brief conversation, however, was enough to convince them that had their master been there in person he would have immediately extended his hospitality to these two close associates of the Protector.

Jeen Vayim refilled his glass and decided he could get used to this kind of life. He glanced at Kraymon, who was carving a thick slice off a haunch of maron. 'You don't feel an urge to go down there and mingle with the crowds, then?'

Kraymon answered with his mouth full. 'I feel a beckoning, but I can ignore it. I've been around enough humanity lately to last me a very long time. What about you?'

The Poet shrugged. 'I can feel it but it's not that strong. All along, I've seemed to be immune to this kind of thing. I never really understood exactly what it was with Gywann. I'm content to watch from here.' He raised his glass. 'Maybe that's why I'm a poet.'

'Because you're insensitive?'

Jeen Vayim shrugged. 'Who the hell knows.'

'One thing I do know is that one mutha of a job's being done on us. The air's full of all kinds of suggestion.' Kraymon tore off a large hunk of bread and slapped the meat on top of it. 'I'm having the devil of a time resisting it.'

A red sphere had stationed itself in midair just off the roof. The Poet walked over to take a look at it. He couldn't quite shake the feeling that it was looking back at him. Kraymon turned away. 'This bunch is going to go to a lot of trouble to get us to like them.'

'You figure they're insecure?'

Kraymon looked at the flashing sky. 'No.'

Again they watched in silence. The Poet went back and helped himself to more wine. 'What are you going to do when all this is over?'

Kraymon went on munching. Then: 'I'd like all this to be over before I start making plans. The Wasps brought plague with them. We can only wait and see what these suckers will bring. If we come through okay I'll probably head for the outlands. I feel the need to be alone again.'

There were four starships. At least, it looked like four starships. Immediately before their appearance the sky went insane. The clouds swirled and fragmented and then fled away from the storm centre. The colours were swamped by a single sheet of pulsing white energy. At the centre it was too bright for the naked eye. Among the humans the feeling of carnival subsided. A great silence fell over the crowd. The throb of the thunder grew louder and louder. Sub-bass frequencies, almost below the range of human hearing, vibrated out of the ground. At the other end of the scale, high harmonics cut through the thunder like a distant extraterrestrial choir. Sections of the crowd fell to their knees. Even Kraymon and the Poet stared at the sky, at a total loss for words.

The storm centre grew unendurable, and then in the centre of the brightness, they appeared. For long minutes they hung in the brilliant, throbbing sky. Nobody on the ground could look directly at them. They were just indistinct shapes against the intolerable glare. Then the thunder subsided and the sheets of energy began to fade. Soon there was nothing left but a clear blue sky, the four alien ships and a pleasant drone of mid-range harmonics. Humanity had its first look at the vessels of its new ruler.

Each of the starships was not, as had been first assumed, a single solid object. Each was a collection of a dozen or more independent parts. Long, irregular triangles radiated out from a semi-disc at each ship's centre, almost like the petals of some giant flower. They just floated together in perfect formation, held in place by forces that the people on the ground could neither see nor even guess at. Each part was covered with tiny lights like a crusting of jewels. Some changed colour, others flashed on and off with differing rhythms.

The centre disc of the lowest ship became separated from the rest of its parts. It began to descend gradually; people started to get an idea of just how big the alien ships really were and how high they had stationed themselves. The disc alone was huge, perhaps three hundred metres across its diameter. From this it was easy to calculate that the complete cluster that made up one of the alien starships was well over a mile long. As it came down it was also possible to see that it wasn't the smooth, even disc that it had appeared from a distance. Its exterior was covered with all manner of strange shapes and protuberances. The lights that had seemed so tiny when the disc was high in the sky turned out to be huge glowing ports. These in turn were surrounded by much smaller lights that also flashed and changed colour. The underside of the ship was covered with domes of various sizes. Some of the domes also glowed with their own translucent life. Between the domes, clusters of long, filament-like antennae trailed downwards, giving the disc something of the look of a creature from the ocean depths.

It came down over the Blackwater. When it was only a few hundred feet above the water it shot out two bright beams of violet light. They went straight down. Where they touched the surface of the water, it thrashed and boiled. The crowds watched, spellbound. Was this the way the Wasps had arrived? Had they provided a show of shows? Few in the crowd would have cared. The descent of the disc had brought a wave of serene euphoria to the humans. Most smiled. Some cried.

'Isn't that the most beautiful thing that you ever saw in your life? Isn't it the most beautiful thing?'

Shafik Kraymon had growled in his throat and started on the Proprietor's brandy. 'There's a selling job being done on us and no mistake.'

The disc came to a halt. It was possibly a hundred and fifty feet above the Blackwater. The violet beams abruptly vanished and the turbulence on the river vanished with them. The disc remained in the air with no visible means of support except that the surface of the water directly below it was depressed into a concave bowl that exactly matched the shape of its underside. For almost an hour it sat and waited. The crowds stayed equally silent and motionless. The euphoria had passed. Now they were blank, locked onto the ailen craft. As they waited the casualties started. Many fainted, a few went into convulsions. Now the sky had cleared, the sun was hot and remorseless. Particularly for some of the Gywannish, it was the last straw. The battle for the lowers may have been brief but, coming straight after the terrible march from the swamps, it had pushed them to the limits of their endurance.

'If they don't do something soon, they're going to lose half the audience.'

A loud metallic cough echoed across the water and back from the towers. One of the largest of the domes on the underside detached itself from the body of the disc. A large sphere, maybe ten metres across, freed itself from a cuplike, hemispherical mount. As it broke contact with the parent ship, its colour changed to a pale turquoise. It dropped almost to the water and then, just a few feet from the surface, it started towards where the humans were waiting. Nervousness spread through the crowd. It was no longer possible to pretend that not only a terrible moment of truth was at hand but that that moment would start a new and unknown epoch in the history of man.

The turquoise sphere came on across the water, across the swamps and across the dry ruins. Formations of red spheres fell in both above and beside it. Now the newcomers had reduced themselves to more human proportions, fear was starting to replace awe. The spheres seemed to be moving in the direction of the Lassus Fields. They were in among the crowds and people were actually fleeing in front of them. The blue-green sphere was suddenly the symbol of unstoppable alien power, and in rushes of sudden panic the humans were becoming aware of their own powerlessness.

Gywann and Trenhyass waited alone by the dry pool in the centre of the Lassus Fields. Moments earlier there had been a crowd around them but as the sphere came closer they had backed away. The turquoise sphere was now going exceedingly slowly, at scarcely more than a walking pace. The small spheres skipped around it and ran circles, as if they too found the slowness agonising. There was absolutely no doubt that the group of alien machines was homing in on Gywann. It was coming towards him with the sun behind it. Trenhyass wanted to put a hand up to shade his eyes, but he resisted the temptation. The sun was gone. The big sphere was shutting it out. Trenhyass blinked. Were they deliberately being placed in shadow?

The sphere stopped.

'At least they came to us.'

Trenhyass found that his fingernails were digging into his palms. Up until that moment he had believed that he was perfectly calm. He wanted to see a door start to open. He wanted to see them. He suddenly and very urgently wanted to get that first moment over. There was, however, no sign of a door, or port, or anything. It was a featureless blue-green ball. Then a faint gold shimmer spread over a small triangular section near the ground. When the shimmer faded, the section of the sphere's outer wall faded with it, leaving a three-sided aperture so small that a man would have to stoop to get through. It was too small to afford any clear view of the machine's interior. The Protector muttered under his breath. 'At least they're smaller than us. It will make a change from looking up at the Wasps.' He felt good that he was able to defy his own fear.

A slender gold ramp emerged from the aperture and slowly extended to the ground. The end of the ramp spread sideways to create a small platform. It started to resemble a squared-off, flattened spoon. The metal from which it was constructed seemed to be coated with a strange clear substance. It was as though a thick liquid was running down the ramp, except that instead of spilling onto the ground when it reached the bottom, it seemed to curl around onto the underside and vanish from sight.

They emerged.

Two entirely different creatures came down the ramp. To be precise, one came down the ramp and the other simply floated. Trenhyass couldn't imagine how they could even come from the same species. Allies or symbiotic? Part of his mind was working like one of the lost computers, clicking down the possibilities. The alien that floated was nothing more than a puffball. Feathery tendrils radiated from a central point to form a perfect, fluttering sphere.

(Maybe that was why they were so fond of spheres.)

The one that was actually on the ramp was dark blue and looked like fungus. It was a short, squat, almost conical mushroom. The edges of what Trenhyass could only think of as the mushroom cap fringed into articulated fronds that waved like expressive tentacles. Trenhyass was experiencing a certain difficulty in coming to terms with the fact that these aliens were virtually comical. He had to get a grip on himself and remember that the humour was strictly his subjective viewpoint. He reminded himself that these were the beings who had put the hundred-times-more-sinister Wasps to flight.

(What would these creatures be called by the humans?)

The blue fungus had a metal band secured around the middle of its thick body/stalk. The body/stalk ended in the single undulating foot. Trenhyass wondered if the strange substance that seemed to flow down the ramp somehow aided the foot's movement, like a slug moving on its trail of slime. They reached the platform at the bottom of the ramp and stopped. Trenhyass could feel people closing in behind him. When there was no sign of immediate danger, curiosity had taken over. Trenhyass could also feel how they were very near the point of turning into a mob of dumbstruck primitives.

(Whatever happens, let us maintain some kind of dignity.)

Something spoke inside his mind. It was far too loud to be intelligible. It was like a psychic shock. He could see those around him cringe away as if they had felt it too. Another blast shrieked through his head but this time, towards the end, the intensity noticeably diminished. Whichever of the two was doing it, fine adjustments were being made; at last whichever it was got it right. There was a nonverbal whispering, smooth and seductive. It wanted to make him feel warm and safe and tranquil. It wanted him to like and to be liked. A faint rosy aura had formed around both the aliens. They were good. They were kind. A pastoral scene crawled from somewhere in Trenhyass's memory. In a lush green meadow, sheep grazed in untroubled peace. Equally secure white rabbits frisked around them. Trenhyass had never seen anything remotely resembling this. It was from a dream.

(Stereotyped mass symbolism? Telepathy? Mind control? Whatever it was, it was a good deal more complex than the Wasps' imprecise translators and threats of extermination.)

Trenhyass felt warm, there was the taste of sugar on his tongue, his Mommy was coming for him, he was going home. It was going to be wonderful. A dark-blue puppy was looking at him with big, moist eyes, a silver fairy was offering him three wishes, he was so happy he felt on the verge of tears.

(What were they doing to him? What did they want? Was this happening to everyone in the crowd or was this just for his benefit?)

Up on the roof of the tower, Kraymon watched through a spyglass. 'Can you feel all the stuff flying about in the air?'

The Poet had started on the brandy. He looked profoundly uncomfortable. 'I can feel it but I don't like it. I know it's supposed to be appealing but it just doesn't work on me. I wish they'd get all this over and let us get down to whatever's going to pass for business as usual.'

Kraymon handed him the spyglass. 'Just so long as we don't have to look like them.'

'Huh?'

'Didn't everyone try to look like the Wasps? You never saw so much black. The Killers wore black, the Gywannish wear black. Even you wear black most of the time. Trenhyass is still doing it. You'd think he would have changed his trim for his new masters.'

Jeen Vayim peered through the spyglass. He was surprised how powerful it was.

'He doesn't seem to be doing much of anything right now. He and Gywann are just standing and staring at the new aliens.'

'Then it's probably the best thing to do. You can trust Trenhyass. He's indestructible.'

Trenhyass was a lot less certain of his indestructibility. He felt himself being swamped. Reality was starting to fade. Everything was lacking substance, washed over by thick syrupy colours and an infantile need for comfort and warmth. It took considerable effort to turn his eyes away from the newcomers and wrench his head around to look at the people nearest him. They were crying. They were already in love with the newcomers. He felt like the chief of some primitive tribe that has come face to face with the invaders. Don't worry, confused little savages, we will take care of you. We will turn you into children. We will smother you with candy and mommy love.

(Are they pulling this stuff out of Gywann's head or are they getting it from all of us?)

Again Trenhyass wrestled his attention away from the bombard of alien affection and looked at Gywann. He was immobile. He had relapsed into the statue state. Perhaps they were using him again. They seemed to be trying to form more focused images.

(They're sending pictures.)

It was all tranquillity. Sunrise over a lake that was as still as a mirror. Smoke from a hearth curling up through clear, frosty air; a summer orchard heavy with fruit; poppy fields in the hot afternoon sun; neat orderly streets; children walking in ordered columns. More kittens. Peace. Plenty. Order. Houses clustered in a mountain valley. Chestnuts roasting on an open fire. The sheep were back. This time a friendly shepherd was driving them.

(Okay, you bastards, I'm starting to understand the deal.)

An idea was coming. It started with an image of Wasp culture strung out across the galaxy, old and cold and arithmetical, always moving and spreading in their infinite progressions until, after a million or more years, they finally came into contact with the blue-and-white goodness, the blue friends and the tiny dancers. Two great and alien empires touched. There could be no co-operation. It was a trial of strength. One empire would have to absorb the other. There was a moving, diagramatic image of the blue-and-white goodness flowing into the Wasp empire along its lines of occupation.

(It's all too well prepared. They've done this before.)

The few planets in the Wasp empire that had evolved civilisations welcomed the blue-and-white goodness as a liberator. Peace. Plenty. Order. The blue friends and the tiny dancers came as messengers from the beyond. They brought the news that the universe wasn't only a place of evil. They brought the three true gifts. Peace. Plenty. Order.

(So what do you want of us?)

The answer was immediate. It was all laid out at his feet. A simple agrarian civilisation. White roads and neat little houses. No war, no strife, no dissent. A readymade religion to arbitrate behaviour. Peace. Plenty. Order. And, of course, discipline. This was what the blue friends and the tiny dancers brought to any civilised planet.

(And, no doubt, they removed thought and progress, and didn't have to fear a challenge for another million years.)

The picture was one of a vast galaxy that sang a single harmony. The stars were offering their friendship even to a sorry species like humanity. Human beings could, for the first time in their history, feel that they were partners in the brotherhood of the cosmos. The beauty of the stars shone out across the immeasurable blackness. Through the blue goodness, man could be a part of it all. There was a murmuring in the crowd. 'Yes.' 'Oh yes.' 'Let's us be a part of it all.' Peace. Plenty. Order. Discipline. Belonging to it would all be so good.

(How do we know that toxins and micro-organisms aren't flooding out of your craft, aren't killing us already? How do we know that we haven't all been made sterile by the radiation from your space battles or whatever it was?)

The saccharine flooded back. Blue was good. Blue reassured. Blue would cause no harm. Blue was love. Peace. Plenty. Order. Discipline. Tranquillity. Love. Blue was love. Relax.

(Okay, suckers. Get to the threat.)

Trenhyass wished that he hadn't asked. A corner was lifted and he saw. The pictures inside it were too alien, too real and too graphic. A species of threadlike air-dwellers was wiped out as the surface of their planet was scorched and levelled by a terrible fire from the sky. A moon was split into fragments by the power of the cluster starships. White energy and red flame lashed out. Then the glimpse was shut off. The message was short but clear. Peace. Plenty. Order. Discipline. Tranquillity. Love. Without question.

Some sections of the crowd had started to sing. Many still wept. Some cried out loud. They loved the blue friends. They welcomed the blue friends. They wanted to belong. They wanted to live in a world of peace and plenty. They wanted a life that was ordered. Somewhere a woman was beating on the ground and howling. Others were pushing forwards to try and reach the sphere. They wanted to touch it, to actually feel its miraculous power. The Gywannish were linking arms to hold them back. Worship was moving towards hysteria. Although by far the majority of the huge crowd could see nothing of the aliens except fleeting glimpses of the sphere, the feeling quickly spread. The singing grew and grew. The crowd started to surge dangerously.

(Did these things really know what they were doing? Did they really believe they could create a pastoral paradise with people who'd been locked up in an impossible city for two hundred years?)

There was another surge very near Trenhyass. An enormously fat man who seemed to want to throw himself on the sphere was struggling with the Gywannish. Others became involved. The scuffle slipped sideways. A few people panicked and stampeded out of the way. Trenhyass was sent sprawling. He fell towards the aliens but crashed into some kind of invisible barrier. The aliens were protecting themselves. The humans nearest them were hosed down with waves of blue affection. It didn't work. For a few moments Trenhyass thought that he was going to be crushed, then the Gywannish were around him, helping him to his feet.

Gywann's eyes opened. He took a pace forward, towards the barrier. Trenhyass put out a hand, but he brushed it aside. He stepped through with no apparent effort. He walked across the space that separated the men and the aliens and stepped up onto the platform. Trenhyass was convinced that he'd be killed but all that happened was that he too was surrounded by the rosy glow. It was a picture from an icon. The noble human with the equally noble aliens. The prophet with his gods. The ultimate illusion.

(Maybe that's it. Maybe he'll lead us into the wilderness, like Moses.)

The ramp lifted. Not retracting, just lifting the three figures over the heads of the crowd. The sphere gave out a high musical hum. It lifted and moved forwards. The aliens were going to show themselves to the whole crowd. It was an unashamed piece of show business. Before it got out of range, Trenhyass projected one single image. It was of a small, angry monkey shaking its fist.